AMBITION

Immodesty
Blaize

EBURY
PRESS

1 3 5 7 9 10 8 6 4 2

First published in 2010 by Ebury Press, an imprint of Ebury Publishing
A Random House Group Company
This Edition 2010

The Random House Group Limited Reg. No. 954009

Addresses for companies within the Random House Group can be found at
www.randomhouse.co.uk

A CIP catalogue record for this book is available from the British Library

The Random House Group Limited supports The Forest Stewardship
Council (FSC), the leading international forest certification organisation. All
our titles that are printed on Greenpeace approved FSC certified paper carry
the FSC logo. Our paper procurement policy can be found at
www.rbooks.co.uk/environment

Typeset in Adobe Caslon by Palimpsest Book Production Ltd,
Falkirk, Stirlingshire

Printed in the UK by CPI Cox & Wyman, Reading, RG1 8EX

ISBN 9780091930073

To buy books by your favourite authors and register for offers visit
www.rbooks.co.uk

With Special Thanks:

Thank you to Kalani, Jeffrey and Andrew, also Ellen Taylor, David Simon, Clare Conville and particularly Gillian Green at Ebury. Finally, thank you to Las Vegas, Nevada for always showing me the good side of your face.

For Kalani

Chapter 1

Sienna Starr released her firm, zeppelin-like breasts from her bra, smiling to herself in the knowledge that she looked incredible, dressed in nothing but diamonds and a spotlight. Turning to face her audience, cheers and wolf whistles filled the air as she elegantly draped herself over the enormous five-foot-high, deep-cut diamond, twinkling and blinking in the light beside her. She languidly stretched into the perfect pin-up pose, her lethally long legs glistening with a sprinkle of gold dust.

Mounting the prop with cat-like grace, she perched there dramatically on the slowly rotating diamond, silky black hair cascading down her back, curls bouncing softly on the smooth caramel skin of her shoulders. The music ended with a shudder. Sienna grimaced. This was the second time this week Murray had screwed up her track midway through her crescendo. She hauled herself off the diamond and took her bow on the tiny stage, smiling through gritted teeth. The crowd hadn't noticed the blunder as they whooped and clapped at the picture of perfect Amazonian beauty before them, only for the vision to be snatched away by blood-red curtains swooping in front of Sienna, their velvety whisper drowned out in the catcalls of the audience but their distinctive aroma of stale smoke and sweat all-pervading.

'He left me out there in silence like a lemon again!' wailed Sienna as she clattered from the stage through the wings and straight into the cramped dressing room. 'I mean, how hard is it to play a song right to the end, for chrissake! Give me strength!' There were murmurs and grunts of support from the cast of girls from behind their mascara wands and blusher brushes as they busied themselves getting ready for their own acts. 'If I've made it through that audition, there's more than a few things I won't miss about this place,' grumbled Sienna as she flopped into the chair at her station and crossly yanked off her glossy wig to reveal her own chestnut locks crammed beneath a wig cap. She popped the cascading raven hair onto one of the mannequin heads on her dresser before reaching for a sharp, fiery red bob.

'Oh, come on, Sienna, don't act all innocent. I bet you already had that part before you even set foot in the audition,' piped up Britney from behind her hand mirror as she sat tweezing her eyebrows at the next dresser.

'I'm sorry?' Sienna laughed uneasily as she roughly pulled on her wig.

'You heard.'

'Sure I heard, but I'm not sure I understood?'

'Well, put it this way,' Britney sighed, lowering her mirror to look Sienna in the eye, 'you'd only been dancing for, like, ten seconds and you were featuring here, then ten minutes later you were headlining. I don't suppose your name had anything to do with that?'

'Britney Ferry, how could you say that!' shrieked Honey from across the room, pitching her afro comb through the air, and missing its target by an inch. 'Sienna got here fair and square, by working her butt off and being a damn fine dancer. And it doesn't take a rocket scientist to figure out that she inherited that talent but she's got here with her own hard work. Jeez, girl, there's enough bitches making the world unpleasant without having one of them here in this veal crate of a dressing room. Now get back to your moustache!' There was a collective gasp and Britney retreated behind her hand mirror. An awkward silence descended on the room, punctuated only by the sounds of Candy crunching loudly on her carrot sticks as the strains of a boisterous audience filtered through from the club.

Sienna hastily teased her wig into place as she willed her blushing cheeks and the prickling sensation behind her eyes to subside. She was more than capable of defending herself but, even so, she was grateful to her friend Honey for speaking up on her behalf. The last thing she wanted was a catfight with Britney backstage. Neither did she want to prolong her embarrassment at Britney's cruel dig by looking upset. Being known as the daughter of Tiger Starr was a mixed blessing as far as Sienna was concerned. As much as she was driven to follow in her famous mother's footsteps, Sienna also wanted to make Tiger proud by doing it on her own genuine merits. Theirs had been a terrible, poignant, bittersweet roller coaster of a love story, and Tiger had forfeited so much for her daughter throughout her life that now it was Sienna's turn to give something back.

Sienna's naked ambition had once been her downfall and it also had brought her own mother's reputation crashing down beside her in spectacular fashion only a few years earlier. Sienna had always believed Tiger Starr was her glamorous big sister. Growing up in the intimidating wintry shadow of an aloof, untouchable famous icon, Sienna's jealous insecurity had led her to a desperate act. But, with fate favouring sweet irony as so often it does, it was Sienna who naively orchestrated the investigative press story that would reveal to the world that Tiger was her mother. She had unwittingly lifted the lid off the terrible truth of how she came into the world. At the tender age of fourteen, her mother had had her own childhood brutally ripped away from her. Raped by her teacher, Tiger had been forced to relinquish her baby daughter to the care of her staunch Catholic parents before being virtually banished from her home. Tiger – then known as Poppy Adams – had reinvented herself with a new identity. But she had endured the torture of many years of painful silence for her child's sake – watching the daughter she loved grow up to become a resentful 'sibling'. Once Sienna had unwittingly shone the spotlight on the truth, it mercilessly unpicked every memory, every conversation, everything she thought to be real, and shone a whole new light on a whole different life.

Of course Tiger had made it clear that she had never given up hope of them being able to rebuild their lives together, and after twenty-three years the two women had been able to forge their rightful bond as mother and daughter. Sienna had grown up a lot in the last couple of years. When she thought back to the bitchy, arrogant little cow she'd once been – thinking the world owed her something; spoilt rotten and cosseted by her surrogate parents, taking her famous 'sister' for everything she could get out of her, and spreading her ill-will like some jealous, covetous brat – she felt thoroughly ashamed of herself, and of course sticking half of Colombia up her nose had really been the icing on the cake. But life had forced its lessons upon her in the cruellest way – what child ever deserved to live with the knowledge that she had been born out of such cruelty and abuse upon her mother? But like Tiger, Sienna was a survivor. Adversity had carved her into the figure of a dignified young woman albeit, like her mother, with a shadow behind her eyes that betrayed the sadness and scars of her past. But now that Sienna possessed a freshly chastened humility, she also found herself without the security of her former tough shell, nor the bald confidence her coke habit had once given her. Britney's spiteful words had stung her back there. Whilst past events might offer her some kind of defence, Sienna had learned her lesson about airing her dirty laundry in public. Britney's outburst wasn't the first of its kind to come from bitter and jealous showgirls and it certainly wouldn't be the last either. That would be Sienna's cross to bear for the time being at least. Fortunately, something had already caught her eye in the mirror to distract her from her rapidly descending miserable cloud of frustration.

'What the hell's that?' Sienna asked, turning to point at the huge shadowy mass eclipsing the doorway to the props closet.

'We're not really sure,' chimed Candy and Shandy, looking up in unison from their leg stretches.

'It arrived in the second half,' explained the exotic-looking new co-feature, Paige, as she wrestled her gown over her shapely hips. 'Damn that last slab of cheesecake,' she cursed.

'Well, whatever it is, it looks like a giant poop,' declared Candy.

'Yeah, and it's like . . . as big as my car!' gasped Sienna, wide-eyed.

'And it keeps catching on my costume every time I walk past,' moaned Shandy. 'This room is small enough as it is. If that snags on my lace and crystals there'll be hell to pay.'

'But what is it?' asked Sienna again, sidling up to the

unidentified mass of painted brown paper mâché, examining it for clues. 'Wheels?' she murmured to herself, poking at little castors with her painted toes.

'It's for the new speciality act,' revealed Honey with a dramatic whisper. 'She debuts tonight. She's here for a month apparently. Fanny la Mouche. She's out on the fire escape warming up.'

'Oh, the glamour,' sighed Sienna.

'What does la Mouche mean?' lisped Candy, hair pins now poking out from between her plump red lips as she worked away at securing her headdress.

'Who knows,' shrugged Honey, 'but Ma and Pepper have been booking some rather avant garde acts these last few months, dontcha think?'

'Ma's been a bit avant garde herself lately, I reckon,' replied Candy. 'Maybe dementia's finally setting in. That or chronic gin-induced euphoria. Mother's ruin indeed,' she sighed, eliciting grunts of agreement from Shandy.

'Well, I'd like to know what made her think that big ol' poop might be sexy,' said Paige, inching her dress zipper carefully up her back.

'It's not a poop!' giggled Honey. 'It can't be. That's a whole other show! Ma and Pepper wouldn't be catering for those types yet, not 'til things get real quiet out there at any rate!'

'How can it possibly get quieter than this?' questioned Candy, raising her eyebrows incredulously and gesturing in the direction of the stage. 'You see bigger crowds at the all-you-can-eat buffets across the Strip!'

'Ladies and gentlemen!' came the muffled boom of the compère, filtering through to the dressing room on a wave of cheers. 'Without further ado, it's time for double trouble with our resident twin temptresses; try and contain yourselves, fellas! Please welcome to the stage Candy Labra and Shandy Leeeeeear!'

'Oh jeez, we're up,' squeaked Candy, securing the last pin in her huge candelabra headdress and cracking her knuckles before following Shandy swiftly through to the stage, their thousands of dangling crystals clanking and tinkling as they went.

'You know what, girls?' announced Sienna, brandishing a lipstick in the air as she addressed the room, 'if we do get into the Follies' new show, maybe I *will* miss this decaying old dump. Where else would you get a poop on wheels on the same bill as identical twins on chandelier trapezes? God bless the Monte Cristo.'

'It's not a poop!' chorused the girls loudly by way of reply.

Sienna had been at the Monte Cristo for two years now. When she had first set foot in the place it had a reputation for having the best, in fact the *only*, genuine burlesque in town. Its eccentric proprietors had an equally formidable reputation. Now in the dusk of her eighties, Pepper was an elegant yet feisty choreographer who had spent her best years building her own legendary status as a burlesque star alongside the vintage greats: Lili St Cyr, Blaze Starr, April March and Sienna's own grandmother, Coco Schnell. Ma 'Toots' Barker had also been a burlesque legend in her lifetime, but Ma had readily given up the hot lights for a life of luxury as the moll of a notorious Baltimore mobster.

The Monte Cristo had been one of Pinkie Di Carlo's nightclubs in the fifties in addition to outfits he had in Atlantic City, Baltimore and Cuba. Pinkie was omnipresent, running those joints with a rod of iron with the vixen-like Ma at his side. During the fifties the Monte Cristo had been a magnet for politicians, big player movie stars and every fellow heavyweight in the Mob, from Bugsy Siegel to Meyer Lansky, and Pinkie was the charismatic 'goodfella' in the epicentre. The FBI were all over his businesses like a rash, and Pinkie brazenly flirted with them in his own inimitable style, thriving off the drama, ultimately knowing he was always one step ahead. He never took life too seriously like that. Pinkie knew the name of his über glamorous club would conjure associations with the Cuban cigar, which is why the logo on his matchbooks was of the identically named French fried ham sandwich instead; that was just his mischievous humour all over. He was also known as being able to charm his way out of anything. Despite oft-whispered tales of violence and bloodshed, Pinkie's charm made it all strangely unbelievable somehow. In fact there was speculation over the full reach of his crime syndicate; rumours abounded that his rackets were merely gambling based and the Monte Cristo was simply a laundering operation; spending his days despatching bullet-riddled corpses in the Nevada desert just didn't seem Pinkie's style. Yet there was no doubt 'the Monte' was the social hub; the ultimate backroom that brought all the major players together from every walk of life. Pinkie led the high life: perilous, thrilling, lavish. Life was good. Until one day back in 1976, Pinkie disappeared. Just like that.

Ma took over the club in impassive silence, stepping into the lion's den and taking over her man's affairs unquestioningly. Word had it that Pinkie's 'numbers' racket, a lottery extortion of sorts, was his unglamorous undoing, and after the FBI swooped, he jumped bail and headed for Acapulco before the floodgates of questioning turned on his other 'ventures'; but Pinkie didn't leave before signing his property portfolio over to his mistress. One by one Ma offloaded his clubs but kept his favourite going: the Monte Cristo. It seemed it was her one enduring link to the past, to Pinkie; her one great love.

Ma cleaned out the gambling but kept the burlesque and nude revues going, right throughout burlesque's wilderness years, battling the new and more popular American trends of the 1980s for table dancing, go-go and neon Lycra. She watched her crowds diminish and the revenue fall away, but she held things together with savings stashed away from years of creative living with Pinkie; she resolved to weather the storm and keep his club alive in the spirit he would have wanted. Sure enough, when burlesque started to make its comeback in the late 1990s, she saw the return of the glamour crowd. Only gone were the politicians, mobsters and Hollywood bombshells, now replaced by celebrities and sporting heroes' wives. The FBI still kept their wiretaps going on the Monte Cristo, holding out for that one key to Pinkie's whereabouts. Mob connections ran deep and Ma knew she was being watched and looked after from afar, and even to this day both she and Vegas stayed tight-lipped about what happened back in '76.

Pepper joined forces with Ma Barker when, after thinking about setting up her own burlesque club in Vegas a few years back, she quickly realised she wanted Ma as an ally, not a competitor. Pepper was received with open arms; true legends were supportive of each other, and the showgirl 'family' always took care of their own, much like the Mob. Sienna had been beside herself when she made it through the auditions for the Monte, especially after her mother had regaled her with outrageous stories of Pepper and Ma's heyday. Even when Pepper had retired from the limelight she had choreographed many a show for Tiger over the years.

Sienna still remembered her first night at the Monte like it was yesterday – she still recalled those butterflies she felt as she tentatively stepped out in front of her audience for the first time – and she still cringed at the memory of her ill-fitting wigs and her clumsy costume malfunctions as she shook her tail feathers for dear life up there on that glamorous little catwalk. But her gusto, not to mention the combination of an incredible pair of tits and never-ending legs, ensured Sienna Starr was a big hit from the start. Huge. All the dancers praised her with knowing nods for having Tiger Starr's 'heat' and 'fire', which in truth made Sienna a little bashful, to have that kind of connection with her own mother. She was quickly promoted to headline regularly, and sure enough, that intoxicating feeling of being the high-voltage glamorous starlet had stayed with Sienna every single time she performed since. She finally understood what had held her mother in its grip for all these years.

But it seemed that the more polished Sienna became as a performer, the shittier the club became. There was no denying Pepper was simply running out of energy, and Ma's drinking was getting the better of her. The carpets stank of sour champagne and disinfectant, rotting with sugary spillages, cigarette ash and the dirt of life, the flock had all but rubbed from the wallpaper which was now ripped and peeling, the stage was littered with pock marks and splinters, and all except a handful of lights in the lighting rig had checked out long ago, which often resulted in a less than flattering shading on any performer not stretched wind-tunnel-tight with facelifts.

Pepper and Ma hadn't been uncovering the hot new acts for months now, and the once A-list crowd of actresses, supermodels, celebs and rock stars had rapidly given way to the raincoat brigade who didn't want the hustle of a clip joint and who could make a warm beer last the whole night. All the best acts who performed to the once-incredible audiences now bypassed the Monte in favour of the sleek casinos. Ma and Pepper couldn't even afford those girls now anyway. Those who were still hanging on in there were performing out of loyalty to Ma and Pepper, and a desperate yen to recapture the Monte Cristo's glory years, although deep down everyone knew they had seen the last of those halcyon days.

'What're these big-ass panties doing on *my* rail?' demanded Britney in the dressing room. 'Where's the name tag . . . *ugh*! These have clitty litter in them! *Ugh!*'

'Wooh, someone's been getting excited in their gusset out there!' howled Shandy, breathless from her performance.

'Yeast infection more like! Ugh, these must be riff-raff chorus-girl panties. Get them away from my beautiful gowns!' wailed Britney, flinging the offending sequinned knickers at the fire escape.

'Calm it, Brit, we don't have a house mum on wardrobe any more,' snapped Candy. 'Anyway, who's nicked my bloody Elnett? That was a full jumbo can!'

'Here, I've got mousse,' said Shandy.

'It's not the same! I need my Elnett back, now!'

As the rabble of the hot cramped dressing room continued about her, Sienna hurriedly pulled on her extravagantly rhinestoned red ringmaster jacket and reached for her beloved leather bullwhip, mounted in a neat coil on the wall above her dresser. One last check in the mirror revealed an exquisite sight – six feet of pure leggy loveliness, clad in hundreds of thousands of crystals. Her bejewelled G-string settled between her pert peachy buttocks as her intricately rhinestoned bustier peeped from beneath her sparkling ruby tailcoat edged in gold braid and epaulettes; even her stocking tops twinkled with Swarovski as they clung snugly to the smooth curve of her sleek thighs. One thing her mother had taught her was never to underestimate the power of the rhinestone. Finishing off Sienna's ensemble were jet-black feathered plumes radiating from her headdress, freshly steamed and fluffed up, and bobbing perkily as she now strode out of the dressing room and into the wings.

'Have a good one, babe,' she heard Honey shouting after her as she settled in the wings, kneading the leather of her trusty whip in her gloved hands and contemplating her big entrance. She needed to regain her ground after the last undignified exit from her diamond act. Taking a deep breath, she closed her eyes, and desperately tried to muster a few butterflies in her stomach in preparation for the straggly yet rowdy crowd. Oh, for a two thousand-seater theatre with audiences sipping champagne, dreamed Sienna. A sharp tap on her shoulder brought Sienna's head whipping round to look beside her. There stood Amanda from the chorus line grinning gormlessly, her scrawny frame barely filling the tiger-striped body suit she was zipped into. She looked more like a neutered malnourished house cat in blue eye shadow than a ferocious, exotic wild animal needing to be tamed.

'Amanda, what a surprise. Where's my usual girl?'

'Chastity? Um . . . she had an unfortunate date with the Ritalin, she peaked a bit too early . . . she's out the back talking to the wall again,' ventured Amanda feebly.

'Christ,' sighed Sienna, tapping her stiletto irritably as she looked to the heavens and bit her tongue, making a mental note to ask Ma to allocate her a more competent assistant for tomorrow.

'So you've been taught the routine?' she asked.

'Sure have. Be gentle!' giggled Amanda.

'Gentle? Amanda, I'm a lion tamer out there. Have you actually seen my act? I need you to be—' Sienna regarded Amanda breaking into a goofy smirk as she nervously fiddled with her quilted tiger ears. 'It doesn't matter,' Sienna sighed kindly. 'Just – try and be cat-like at least. Slink.'

'Slink – like a snake?'

'No, that's slithering,' explained Sienna patiently. 'Just be elegant, okay, and for God's sake keep moving when I aim for you with the whip.'

'Yes ma'am,' said Amanda, breaking into another wide-eyed grin.

'And none of that stupid smiling!' whispered Sienna as

she heard Griselda the tranny compère winding up their introduction.

'But we're told to smile—' started Amanda.

'Just smoulder!' hissed Sienna. 'Or at least look like you're angry!'

'Oh, I never get angry, ma'am.'

Sienna rolled her eyes as she braced herself for her entrance. 'Lions led by donkeys,' she muttered.

'Oh, is there a donkey coming on stage too?'

Blue cheered and wolf whistled from his vantage point in the audience as Sienna brought her routine to a roaring climax, cracking her whip like a warrior before snaking it around her curves as her long legs straddled her glittering circus podium centre stage. He smiled to himself, seeing shades of that familiar Tiger Starr fire up there even on the modest stage, and enjoyed a tiny shiver of excitement at the news he was about to tell Sienna. He caught her eye as she struck her final pose and signalled for her to join him after her act.

Five minutes later she appeared at his side in her ever-glamorous civvies, panting for breath. She flung her arms round Blue's hulking bulk and tweaked his little pencil moustache playfully.

'How's my favourite fairy?' sighed Sienna, giving him a squeeze.

'I'm fabulous, devotion. And look at you! Looking divine, darling, loving the lounge suit, very Liz,' gushed Blue, 'but who the fuck was that bit of candyfloss in the catsuit on stage with you? I've seen more talented inbreeds.'

'Blue!' scolded Sienna. 'God, I can tell you've been working with Brandy Alexander.'

'Hmm, yes, darling, Brandy's reputation precedes her. Sharp as Ajax and bitter as lemon, that one. Stunning though. She must have a painting in the attic,' said Blue, rattling his champagne glass in view of the bartender. 'Two more over here, Jeffrey! In fact make it a bottle!'

'Oh no, sweetheart, I only want a glass—' started Sienna.

'You're kidding!' said Blue. 'We have something to celebrate, young lady!'

Sienna regarded him thoughtfully through narrowed eyes, wondering if he was bluffing her. 'Blue, don't get my hopes up. Have you actually got news on the casting?'

'Let's just put it this way, you're one step closer to being the next – um – Tiger Starr!'

'No way . . . did I get in?'

Blue gave a little nod and a teensy tear of happiness squeezed itself onto his cheek. 'Not just a chorus-line dancer, darling. With your knockout figure you're going to be one of the "Venus in Furs" showgirls.'

Sienna squealed like a banshee, turning heads away from the stage as she jumped up and down at the bar, her thick chestnut hair tumbling about her shoulders as she span herself round in excitement. Abruptly she stopped. 'But sweetheart – Pepper – what will I say to her?' she gasped, her full lips quivering.

'Oh, give me a break,' laughed Blue. 'You can't flutter an eyelash in this town without everyone knowing. She knew before me! She's always known it was only a matter of time before she'd lose you to a bigger show, darling.'

'You're kidding! Oh God, so who else—'

'Well, I'm sure they'll find out soon enough . . . but you mustn't say anything until it's announced by the casino. Honey Lou and Paige Turner got through too. Congratulations, darling,' said Blue, reaching his bulging arms round Sienna for a bear hug.

'Oh wow!' gasped Sienna. 'Paige! The gorgeous new girl! Maybe I should invite her to move in with me and Honey. It would be perfect with all three of us working on the same show! Oh Blue, this is just the best news – ever! Wait 'til I ring Mum!' And with that Sienna ripped herself from the embrace and dashed off to the dressing room, all legs and hair. Blue turned his face to the stage, still grinning with pride at Sienna's achievement. She had deserved this break, and she had worked hard for it. Blue also knew she had given a false name in her audition; that girl sure as hell wanted to prove she could do it on her own.

As Brandy Alexander's personal dresser in the show, Blue got to hear everything, from chorus-line chatter to the casino bosses' plans before they had even made them. More than any leading lady, Blue was the real reigning queen of the Follies Hotel Casino. And he couldn't be more thrilled that Sienna would be working on its biggest show yet – 'Venus in Furs'. Blue had been Tiger Starr's best friend and confidante for many years, and, charged with the role of fairy godmother to Sienna, Blue was immensely proud of her progress, and even more pleased that he'd get to keep an even closer watch on her, now they were both working on the same show. He had seen the naïve Sienna of yore being ruthlessly taken advantage of in the past, and since she was blossoming into quite the starlet, the last thing she needed was to let the seductive and highly addictive charms of Vegas distract her from the glittering prize she deserved.

Blue swigged his champagne and surveyed the ragtag audience before him. Spotting a couple of the well-known local lounge lizards at the bar, he raised his glass to them with a cheeky nod and a wink. Imagining Sienna having to bite her tongue not to tell the girls the amazing news backstage, Blue couldn't help wondering if she wouldn't be sad to move on from the Monte, but he had a gut feeling Sienna would always be there for Pepper whether she was dancing at the club or not. Pepper was virtually family, and birds of a feather stick together. Blue turned to the stage as Griselda introduced Fanny la Mouche. As the velvet curtains parted to the thudding grind of The Cramps' 'Human Fly', Blue's jaw dropped as an angular string bean of a girl unfolded herself from the sunroof of a large brown paper mâché dump on stage and posed there, clad in shimmering bottle-green spandex and a shiny black helmet sporting huge red rhinestoned fly eyes.

'Fanny the Fly?' murmured Blue, nearly dropping his

champagne flute in horror. 'Oh Jesus and Mary, she'd better not be getting any chocolate mousse out . . . '

'Cheers, baby, and congratulations! Here's to my beautiful woman,' murmured Max, holding aloft his Scotch. 'With you on a winning streak like this, I think you're going to bring me luck tonight.' He leaned in close to Sienna, his breath warm and heavy. She tilted her face up to his, letting him plant a deep kiss on her soft lips as his free hand wrapped around her tiny waist, pulling her in close. For a moment she forgot there was anyone else in the room as she drank in the musk of his skin and clung to his taut, broad chest. She wondered if life could get any better as she finally pulled away to look into his beautiful hazel eyes. Max planted a tender kiss upon her nose, sending butterflies fluttering feverishly through Sienna's stomach. Her moment of reverie was curtailed by the croupier clearing his throat gently.

'Mr Power, are you in or out?'

'I want to change dealers,' answered Max curtly, pulling away from Sienna abruptly, a flash of irritation in his eyes as his casino host appeared from the ether by his side.

'Mr Power, may I escort you to another table,' whispered the host.

'No, just change the damn dealer.'

'Of course, sir.' Before Sienna could blink, Max had three new hands of blackjack in place under a new croupier. Knowing she had lost Max's attention again, Sienna settled into her seat, a tiny sigh squeaking its way from her lips as her eyes lustfully grazed over her boyfriend's striking profile. Sometimes she had to pinch herself to remind herself that she was Max Power's girlfriend. After her last ass-hat of a boyfriend had got her hooked on cocaine, slept around and, well, tried to kill her mother, Sienna was certainly due a Prince Charming, and it looked as though Max Power fitted the job description perfectly. At thirty-two years of age, he was a beautiful six foot three inch-tall strapping package of dark brooding looks with an overseas telephone number as a bank balance. The only son of Kerry Power, the infamous self-made Irish tycoon, Maximilian Power had made his own mark on the world as the genius entrepreneur behind Silver Slipper Airlines – a luxury airline that specialised in recreating the vintage glamour travel of yore. Passengers had exclusive VIP lounges sheltered from the riff-raff of the airport, and upon boarding ate caviar and foie gras to the strains of Frank Sinatra, with 1950s-style pin-up perfect hostesses pouting their Marilyn lips whilst serving up gimlets and dry martinis with their prim white lace-gloved hands. Lavish in-flight entertainment ranged from manicures and beauty treatments to vintage film classics, from *Casablanca* to *Scarface*. A well-appointed cocktail lounge on every aeroplane maintained the vintage bachelor-pad chic.

Max was a risk taker, there was no doubt. He had set up Silver Slipper Airlines in the wake of 9/11 to cries of alarm and outrage from those around him who merely saw a lunatic attempt at radical business to try to compete with his father's legendary meteoric rise. Most wondered why Max didn't just quietly live off his father's billions and keep his head down. Why be greedy and foolishly meddle in business he clearly knew nothing about? What they didn't know was that Kerry Power had every intention of making his son learn the hard way – as he had. There would be no free rides for family. Kerry's sadistic streak was well concealed; few knew he exerted the iron grip of his power to create obstacles for poor Max as sport, in life as well as business; his son always had to be ten steps ahead. Max developed a head for business early in life out of necessity. Kerry didn't believe in things like pocket money – instead, he set 'tasks' for his son. For Max's thirteenth birthday there were no remote control cars or computer games; instead Kerry bought him a shitty street in Belfast. The birthday card read 'What the Luftwaffe and terrorism couldn't manage, the Planning Service have. I've generously given you a few years to plan how to develop your new street into something pretty you'd want the Powers to live in. You'll thank me.'

It was no wonder that by fourteen Max was unofficially 'selling' his first business in shoe polishing for the prefects at Eton, or that by sixteen he was expelled for running a book for organised dormitory bare-knuckle fights. By the time he was twenty-one, Max had turned his street into a little goldmine, not by following his father's misleading clue of a luxury development, but by installing low-overhead, high-revenue high-rise flats, laundrettes and betting shops. If Max saw an opportunity for making money, he had learnt to go after it, and as the years rolled on his appetite for risk grew. So at the age of twenty-three, in the wake of one of the world's most pivotal events in history, counter-intuitiveness told him he could temper the public's unease at the prospect of a bleak and frightening future by offering them refuge in the safety of the past. For the few hours they were travelling they could take shelter in the cocoon of a fantasy world.

It was his first big business gamble and everyone was watching, waiting for him to fall. Support and investment was a problem; it became apparent to Max that the fickle finger of fate had ensured his family connections would go against him; few seemed to want to do business with any relative of the fearsome and rapacious Kerry Power. Max persisted against all odds, and he was duly rewarded; Silver Slipper Airlines became his first big business triumph. He had floated the company after just five years and share prices continued to rocket. Needless to say his father publicly shrugged off his son's success as beginners' luck; and he certainly never mentioned to a soul that he had actually warned all major investors not to back the venture. He had enjoyed testing just how resourceful and determined his Maximilian could be; after all, who wanted a sappy little coward for a son? What didn't kill him would only make him stronger, in Kerry Power's eyes.

By the time Max set eyes on Sienna Starr at the Monte Cristo he was easily the most eligible bachelor on either side of the Atlantic. And like many men before him, it wasn't long before he was a regular 'John' at the club, in amongst the ever-increasing raincoats, and always in his corner seat; entranced by Sienna's exquisite performances . . . not to mention her killer legs. Of course, all the girls knew exactly who Max Power was, and he had a regular stream of burlesque beauties shimmying up to his table of an evening, vying for his attention – and always swatted away accordingly by Ma Barker, who was determined her customers should enjoy the shows undisturbed.

The one woman Max would have wanted to entertain at his table was Sienna, but she never came. It only served to water the tendrils of intrigue; of course Sienna's mother had equipped her with the golden rule of keeping herself unattainable to her male admirers. 'When you step off the stage, watch you don't step off the pedestal,' Tiger used to warn her. Sure enough, that picture of the perfect alluring goddess under the spotlight that Sienna portrayed, oozing sexual confidence, commanding every pair of eyes in the room, had Max hooked. It had taken him two months before he could secure a conversation with Sienna, by which time he would have swum through shark-infested oceans to get her. They had been together for six months now, a world record by all accounts for Max Power, since he had certainly been known to take advantage of having his pick of the ladies. But now in the echelons of the glitterati, Max Power and Sienna Starr were as enviable a couple as they were successful and beautiful.

Sienna whipped her head round as a buzz of activity went up in Max's entourage stationed at the doorway to the private gambling salon. The casino host slid from out of nowhere into place at Max's side.

'Mr Power, Ms Brandy Alexander is here for you,' he murmured discreetly as the dealer smoothly scooped Max's latest pile of lost chips from the green felt.

'Is she now,' replied Max evenly. 'Always wanted to meet her. My baby's going to be in her show, you know,' he grinned, planting his hand firmly on Sienna's thigh.

'Oh, I'm only a showgirl,' mumbled Sienna modestly into her drink, waving her hand dismissively. 'It's nothing, I—'

'Bring Ms Alexander in,' interrupted Max. 'My girl should meet her in person.'

Sienna gasped as the security ushered the new guest into the salon. Brandy cut a breathtaking presence in a long, slim cream gown, folds of smooth satin clinging to her breasts like thick cream over peaches and skimming over straight, snake-like hips. A mane of sun-kissed hair was swept back as though held in the grip of a strong breeze, the natural glossy waves offsetting her razor-sharp cheekbones and strong jaw. Brandy's stride forwards was slow, for dramatic effect, as her green eyes locked on to Max.

'Good evening, Mr Power, I was told you were here at the Follies,' purred Brandy. 'I couldn't let you visit without extending a . . . personal welcome.'

'Pleasure to meet you, Brandy,' said Max, extending a hand. 'I've heard so much about you – I can't believe our paths haven't crossed before.'

'Indeed,' Brandy replied coolly, flicking her gaze over to Sienna, who was respectfully standing to attention.

'I'm sure you must know my girlfriend, Sienna?' asked Max, putting his arm about Sienna's shoulders. 'She's going to be in your show. That's why we're here celebrating.'

Brandy paused to look Sienna up and down.

'Celebrating? How romantic of you.' She spoke slowly. 'You know, I have the final say on all my dancers,' she continued, 'and I never forget a face – or a name, Miss . . . ?'

'Starr,' answered Max, 'daughter of—'

'Tiger Starr. Yes, I know of her, of course,' smiled Brandy enigmatically. 'Intriguing, Sienna, I swear I had you down on my files as Brigette Bordeaux. How . . . curious.'

Max sniggered into his hand and Sienna blushed beetroot.

'Yes, what a ridiculous name indeed, Mr Power, I must reprimand my assistant for that little mix-up. Anyway, Sienna did an excellent audition, you know,' Brandy said, turning back to Max with her smile on professional full beam, the flush on Sienna's cheeks finally subsiding.

'Hear that, babe? Brandy thinks you're excellent. Like mother like daughter, eh?' Sienna cringed as Max squeezed her proudly.

'Well, I shall leave you both to your celebration. What a pleasure to meet you both and, er, see you in rehearsals . . . Sienna.' Brandy winked, turned on her Jimmy Choos and swept from the room.

'Max, I think it's time for me to head home,' said Sienna, concealing the tremble of embarrassment from her voice.

'What? We just got started! I'm about to hit a winning streak!'

'Oh. Do you mind if I leave you to it? I have been working tonight, remember. You can come back to mine when you're finished?'

'Sure. You okay, baby? You were quiet back there. Don't tell me you were starstruck?'

'Er, yeah, I guess I must have been a little,' replied Sienna with a grimace, knowing now was not the time to explain that Brandy had a terrifying reputation and simply frightened the crap out of her. It seemed as if she'd already got off on the wrong foot by being caught out lying about her name in auditions. Brandy wasn't the kind of woman to sympathise with a girl who was trying to make it on talent or hard graft. Everyone knew, and conveniently forgot, that Brandy had masterminded her own career over the years in genius stepping stones from escorting, to clever casting-couch manoeuvres on everyone from celebrities to directors and every piece of frantic, determined social networking in between. And if she was as insecure about her own performance talents as Blue had witnessed as her dresser, there was also no way Brandy would want any relative of Tiger Starr within a hundred miles of her show. But Max would never understand all that, decided Sienna. Best to change the subject.

'How about I warm the bed up for you?' she suggested with a coquettish smile.

'That's more like it. Take the limo home, I won't be too late. If Lady Luck smiles on me in the next couple of hours I'm bringing home something black and quilted from Chanel for my lady, okay?' Max swept Sienna's hair away from her shoulder and kissed her softly on the neck. 'I want you in Manolos and stockings later, nothing else,' he whispered into her ear.

'In that case, don't expect any sleep, darling,' Sienna said as she reached for Max's upper thigh and squeezed lightly.

'Thank you, sir, enjoy the rest of your evening,' said the casino host, smiling as he handed over a large white gift bag emblazoned with the Chanel double 'C' logo. 'Security will escort you straight to your limousine.' Max hummed as he strode through the casino, trailed by his allotted goons, swinging his gift for Sienna in one hand. He hadn't actually won at all tonight, but as with all 'whales' like Max, the casinos liked to take care of their every whim to lure them and their millions back to their tables; limos, jets, personal shopping – a complimentary Chanel purse was a drop in the ocean against the big money Max had just disposed of back there on the green felt. At least Sienna would interpret the gift as meaning he had a lucky night; he definitely didn't want her thinking he was just some loser. He'd make his money back the following night anyway.

'Mr Power, we must stop bumping into each other like this,' came a familiar voice behind him. Max swung round, coming face to face with Brandy Alexander, a voluminous silver fox fur slung over her shoulder, its paws dangling forlornly at her breast, and a diamante heart-shaped clutch swinging off her manicured little finger.

'Hello again,' smiled Max warmly, 'and please, call me Max.'

'You partying, Max?'

'No, I'm off home.'

'Alone?' Max sensed the casino security breathing heavily behind him. He turned and nodded for them to leave.

'I need to grab a few hours' sleep – no rest for the wicked,' he explained.

'You didn't answer my question,' said Brandy crisply, turning away and sashaying towards the car valet. Max hesitated for a moment before rushing to her side obediently. 'I mean, really, the night is young, Max,' she continued. 'I heard you're quite the party boy.'

'You heard right.' He was quiet for a few seconds. 'Actually . . . I'm just about to go party.'

'Oh? Things are looking up.'

'At my girlfriend's. Party of two.' Max couldn't keep the smirk off his face. Brandy wobbled on her heels and came to a standstill.

'I see. Can I at least offer you a ride?' She spun round to look at him enquiringly as a silver Bentley screeched up beside her. The car hop jumped out to hold the door open for her, only to be waved away with a flick of bright red talons, leaving the pair alone.

'Thanks for the offer but I have a ride,' said Max firmly.

'Hmmm. I'll bet I go faster than your ride. I'm known for unparalleled performance,' replied Brandy, turning the atmosphere cold with a faint sneer.

'Well, my ride doesn't have as many miles on the clock,' retorted Max sharply. Brandy's eyes flashed with fury before she grabbed at his neck and clamped her lips to his. Max pulled back immediately, dropping the Chanel bag in his haste.

'What the – I don't wanna do this.'

'Chanel? For me?' gasped Brandy, looking down at the bag, her hand leaping for her breastbone dramatically. 'Why thank you, you shouldn't have. But you really didn't have to throw it at me, darling.'

'I said no. I'm not doing this.'

'Oh, you're not, huh?' scoffed Brandy. 'Oh, lighten up, for God's sake, it's just a bit of fun. I don't believe you don't want to anyway. I think the truth is you can't.'

'Excuse me?'

'I know you want me, everyone wants a piece of Brandy. You're just scared. Big boy like you? Can't handle me?' Max narrowed his eyes at the beautiful woman before him as he felt the prickle of red mist descend upon him. Just who did this arrogant, hard, puffed-up bitch think she was talking to? No-one ridiculed Max Power. He took in her flawless, lightly tanned skin, her sharp nose with a smattering of honey freckles, full soft lips, golden highlights amongst soft chestnut hair, a smooth Botoxed brow, and green eyes glazed with a blend of sex and spite. Max grabbed for Brandy's wrist, making her yelp in surprise. He wanted to shake her, slap that mocking sneer from her face. Yet he found himself mesmerised as she held his gaze, slowly licking her lips before letting a hint of a smile curl its way across the corners of her mouth. Max turned her away from him and pushed her slowly up against her car, leaning his weight into her back.

'No, babe, you can't handle *me*,' he whispered in Brandy's ear as he grasped roughly at the satin of her gown, pulling it up about her slim boyish hips to expose firm bare cheeks. Max pushed his hand between her legs, his fingers sliding into her as she spread herself, purring like a cat. He groaned softly and held his hand up there in the moistness, faltering as he buried his face deep in the thick, soft fox fur at her shoulders, feeling a wave of sickly nausea as he breathed in her heavy, cloying perfume. Slowly he began to slip his fingers in and out, his other hand reaching to unzip his fly. Brandy cried out in pleasure as he finally grabbed her waist and slammed his huge cock into her.

A solitary drip of champagne plopped into Sienna's champagne flute on the bedside dresser, and as she popped the empty bottle back into its now-tepid ice bucket she chastised herself inwardly for managing to drink the whole lot on her own. She had drawn a hot bubble bath once she got home, before dressing in her finest silk stockings and highest heels ready for her gorgeous Max. Knowing he would be a little while, she had indulged in the guilty pleasure of a generous slice of chocolate cake in bed whilst savouring her *National Enquirer* from cover to cover. She knew that indulgences like carbs and partying would be out of the question once she was in the Follies. With their weekly weigh-ins looming, Sienna had a final few days to cram in some last enjoyment of her remaining bad habits before her new life of lettuce, water and vitamin pills beckoned.

Now, with the champagne gone and the birds starting to sing outside, Sienna slipped her heels off and snuggled beneath the covers with a little sigh. Max was obviously on a good roll at the casino. At least that would mean incredible morning sex when he eventually got home. A shiver ran up her thighs at the thought. She nuzzled into the sheets, wondering if life could get any better. Finally her world was taking shape – nothing but calm seas ahead after all her traumas of the past. She had a focus, she had landed her first part in a big Vegas show, she had friends, she was having a fabulous time living in her mum's plush pad in Vegas with her best friend Honey, her fairy godmother Blue was nearby to watch over her, she was on track to making her mum proud as punch of her, and finally she'd found her beautiful Mr Right who loved and respected her and was about to come home to her arms. For the first time ever, life is truly wonderful, thought Sienna as a blissful wave of sleep rolled over her.

Chapter 2

Paolo Mendes turned the key in the lock and gave the stubborn door a kick. A mildewy waft of stale air made a bid for freedom from within. Paolo glanced over his shoulder and waved a goodbye to the shuddering rusty truck now hauling itself noisily from the parking lot out onto the freeway, before stepping over the threshold into his motel room. At his feet was a folded note; he took an educated guess the proprietor was taking a polite approach to chasing his late rent payment. Paolo sighed and popped the note onto the Formica cabinet next to the door, resigning himself to the fact that if he got as badly paid every day as today, he would have no choice but to bunk with the Mexicans in one of their cramped rentals. He'd only had a rockery to dig today. Four hours waiting by the roadside next to the DIY store with Eduardo and Tiny, and all they'd been picked up for was a lousy garden. Paolo was no stranger to bad living conditions; his life so far hadn't exactly been one luxury holiday after another, but he always at least tried to move forwards in life. Things could always be improved with a bit of old-fashioned hard graft, he'd always found. But right now, the thought of top and tailing it four to a bed while he found his feet in Vegas was going to be a hard pill to swallow.

Paolo surveyed his room and tried to appreciate its luxury in light of what he might be coming home to this time next week. The carpet tiles on the walls weren't so bad, they muffled the sex noises from the neighbouring room, and at least the carpet was a neutral colour. And even though he just had a single bed, it meant there was space to walk around in, and he had a rail to hang a few clothes. There was even a small refrigerator in one corner of the room which, once Paolo had bleached away the rotting, unidentified sticky leaks, was now good enough to store a few nights' worth of sandwich fillings and a beer or two. Cleanliness was next to godliness in Paolo's eyes. When the world outside is turning to slurry, if your home is clean you can come out fighting, he'd always said. Even when Mami had hit rock bottom, and Paolo was working every hour to support her and keep her off the streets, he still managed to find time to keep their home spotless. Mami may have finally given up, but there was no way Paolo was going to give into the squalor her life had become. At least Paolo's father would have had a smug smile on his face if he could look down and see him now; he'd always said his son would never amount to anything. Of course, sending his son to a mental institute when he was no more than a boy had been a great first step in fulfilling that prophecy. There had been nothing wrong with Paolo's sanity, but when his father wrongly concluded that his young son was gay, the nuthouse was seen as the only way to 'cure' him of his apparent affliction.

Paolo stripped off and showered. As he stood under the steaming water he breathed deeply and held on to the tiled wall, wishing he could wash away his grief as he let the comforting wetness envelop him. Soaping away the dirt and grime from his body, he relented and let tears run down his face, merging with the rivulets of water; his loud choking sobs swallowed up by the cranking of the boiler. His father would have said that real men don't cry, of course, but as his mind replayed that last day at home in the Bronx, Paolo would have defied any son not to shed a tear.

The smell had hit him the second he stepped through the door. The ancient old record turntable was loudly scratching its way over and over in its last groove. A trail of black vomit led to his mother's body, now cold, her olive skin a deathly shade of pale save for the bruises from the last truck driver she'd serviced. It was all still too fresh in Paolo's mind. It was still hard to believe that Mami was actually gone now; that vivacious beauty chipped and whittled away to nothing more than just another Puerto Rican hooker, spent before her years. Another statistic. Another death by addiction. Paolo knew he could not let life swallow him up as it had his mother – he had to take control. All that was left now was hard work. And a sister he needed to find.

Turning off the shower and wrapping a towel about his

hips, Paolo wiped an arc of steam from the bathroom mirror. Through the smudged moisture he studied his lithe slim body, toned from manual labour, lean from his years of dancing. A sneer curled at his mouth as he took in his slender dancer's thighs. No wonder he couldn't shift the ballast like the Mexicans could. Still, those arms may be slim, but they were pure wiry muscle. His skin had the colouring of creamy coffee, but even that couldn't disguise the dark circles beneath his beautiful almond eyes. God he looked tired. Paolo wearily dried himself and walked through to the tiny bed. Perched on the edge, he reached for the floor to retrieve his tatty jeans from the crumpled pile of work clothes. Just fifty bucks in the back pocket for the day's work. How far was a measly fifty bucks going to take him? There was no doubt Paolo had a lot to do now. He had changes to make. Mami's death was a constant reminder that life was too short; if Paolo wanted his luck to change he'd have to change it himself. It wasn't going to be an easy ride, but he wasn't daunted. The first step was to find his sister. That shouldn't prove too difficult, he thought, smiling fondly as he eyed up the sleek, glossy 'Venus in Furs' brochure from the Follies Casino sitting on his bedside table in pride of place, radiating colour like a precious jewel in a room full of shit-coloured carpet tiles.

Chapter 3

'Careful with that divan, it's vintage!' barked Paige, clanking her bracelets as she flailed her arms theatrically.

'What did your last slave die of?' muttered Blue in between puffs and pants, as he plonked the moth-eaten velvet chaise longue in the guest bedroom with a loud thud, the pink upholstery exhaling its own musty puff of dust. Blue stood straight and surveyed the towers of boxes piled up around him, as Paige fussed with the bubble wrap on a large framed print of herself. He was beginning to regret his magnanimous offer of help to Sienna's new lodger – not that he was entirely sure he'd offered in the first place.

'How did all this lot come out of that tiny room you were sharing?' asked Blue, wide eyed and fanning sweat from his brow, wondering more pertinently how in hell this girl from nowhere had persuaded him to hump boxes on his day off.

'I had to keep my furniture pieces in the other girls' rooms,' said Paige, nonchalantly, 'and I persuaded them to give up some of their wardrobe space. They'd have been squeezed out eventually,' she declared matter-of-factly, absorbed in admiring her self-portrait. Blue jerked his head round at the comment.

'Well, you certainly lucked out with this room,' he said firmly, dusting off his hands and heading for the door. 'I can assure you it's a rare thing for girls on dancers' wages to live in a home like this.'

'Oh, I know I'm a very lucky girl, lil' ol' me in a big show, new friends, and now a big room all to myself, it's perfect,' said Paige, her voice suddenly thick with syrupy sweetness. Blue flicked an eyebrow at the gorgeous bosomy creature standing among all her worldly possessions, smiling sunnily. God, she's stunning, thought Blue, suddenly struck by the loveliness of her thick dark hair piled up in a casual messy tangle of bouncy curls, the look of classic vintage Hollywood twinkling in her big, baby-doe eyes, and a figure men would weep for, poured into a pair of tight Capri pants with a little cotton shirt knotted at her tiny waist, which only served to accentuate the full curve of her hips even more. Blue was shocked to feel a tiny twinge in his gingham slacks and decided there must be a camp air about this new girl he couldn't quite pinpoint. Something of a brunette Jayne Mansfield, perhaps.

'Lord, if I was straight,' he muttered. Paige cocked her head slightly and blinked her big brown eyes blankly. Any slight suspicion Blue might have had back there for her manipulative streak was allayed by the conclusion he had probably credited her with too many brains for that kind of scheming.

'So where's that lovely drawl from?' he inquired. 'It's a little – East Texas?'

'Hell no!' stormed Paige. 'Why I'm from ... Chin-quapin,' she continued, tightly.

'Chinqua ... Chin ... sounds kind of familiar but I can't think where it is?'

'It's a lil' town in Louisiana,' said Paige hesitantly.

'Oh, cool!' remarked Blue. 'I love New Orleans. All that vibrancy, all the incredible music.'

'Yeah,' gushed Paige, relaxing again. 'That's why the performing is in my blood!'

'Indeed,' smiled Blue, entranced. 'So does that mean your family were in the biz too?'

'Oh, shoot!' exclaimed Paige abruptly. 'Would you just look at the time? I need to put a lil' something in my grumbling tummy, got to keep the metabolism nice and fast or these hips will start looing me jobs!'

'Come join us for lunch, darling,' laughed Blue. 'In fact, Sienna's already laying out a special welcome spread down-stairs. You won't be left wanting for anything now you're here, I can tell you. Sienna certainly likes to look after her girlfriends. And if she's anything like her mum it'll be champagne followed by champagne, with a little cham-pagne for dessert. Welcome to Chez Starr, lucky lady,' and with that he swept from the bedroom in a waft of glad-ioli scent.

'Yes, darling, lucky indeed,' murmured Paige behind him with a grin. 'I always manage to make my own luck, don't you worry.'

Sienna set about uncaging the champagne cork

downstairs as Honey Lou laid out platters of fresh smoked salmon and garnish.

'Balanced meal, girls?' said Blue as he breezed into the kitchen.

'Sure thing, baby. We have to eat well, now we're watching our waistlines. Protein rich gravadlax, vitamins in the lemon wedges, carbs in the Veuve,' chirped Sienna, popping the cork and giggling as the champagne ejaculated over her hand with an irreverent fizz.

'Blimey, you're in good spirits,' remarked Blue. 'Have you already been at the aperitifs?'

'No, I'm just excited. We start on the show this week, and now Paige has moved in we're a proper girlie household. It's not just me and Honey rattling around with Mum's antiques.'

'By antiques you mean me? You know I'm only visiting!'

'No, the furniture, silly. Not that I'm complaining!'

Sienna hadn't always lived in the luxury she now enjoyed at her mother's Seven Hills mansion. She had been way too cool to lodge with her mum when she first relocated to Vegas, and had shared what could only be described as a 'humble' apartment with her pals Honey and Blanche, located off Sierra Vista on the corner of what Sienna fondly referred to as South Crack Boulevard and East Shit Street; namely a dodgy part of town that housed mostly illegals and drug dealers in cheap rentals. Sienna's mother, Tiger, used to go crazy that she was waking up to humming birds and palm trees outside her window while her daughter was waking up on the other side of town to cockroaches and the local rent boys fucking in her alleyway. Tiger had even sent her husband Lewis over to try and rescue her daughter on more than one occasion, but Sienna had insisted she wouldn't take handouts, and would pay her way and work up to her own luxury pad one day. Besides it wasn't like she was hanging out with the locals; her life centred around her new dancing job and sleeping, with long stretches of costume-making squeezed in between. More to the point, Sienna wasn't keen on her mum cramping her style as far as house parties or vetting any potential love interests she might want to bring home. Not that her crappy apartment would ever be a breathtaking setting for any romantic activity, but it was having the choice that counted.

Blanche soon jumped ship when she had a whirlwind affair with an out-of-town real estate developer on vacation, who proposed to her within four days and promptly installed her in his LA pad with five Chihuahuas and a fast little red coupé for when she wanted to alleviate any cabin fever with retail therapy. Even though Blanche's absence freed up more space in the apartment, the girls missed their buddy. And then a cockroach infestation moved in. It was tough being young, broke and living in a dump. Passing themselves off as the most glamorous, otherworldly creatures for work at the Monte Cristo felt almost dishonest when they were living in such abject modesty. Sienna was starting to feel the strain of clearing used needles from their yard every weekend and living off noodles, but she was petrified that if she told her mum, she'd lose her freedom if she was made to live under Tiger's watchful eye. Besides, she needed to show she could be independent; Sienna had developed a fear that if she didn't work hard for something, karma would snatch it all back from her somehow. This had happened with her life in England and she wasn't about to take things for granted ever again.

So when Tiger announced within the year that she would be moving to LA to pursue her fledgling movie career, she smartly asked Sienna and Honey if they would move in indefinitely, pretending to them that they'd be earning their keep by house-sitting. The girls practically left skid marks behind them in their scramble to install themselves in Seven Hills. Sienna could now grudgingly admit that it was a step up from their last apartment. After all, it did have a swimming pool, a tennis court, six enormous bedrooms and two sweeping gold staircases coming off a grand hallway paved in marble and big enough to accommodate a roller disco. Blanche also dropped in on the girls much more now, whenever she needed a weekend away to rant about her husband's latest affair, or to show off the new Bulgari bauble he had apologised with.

Despite the visits from friends, Sienna and Honey did feel a little swamped on their own in such a huge house; so inviting Paige Turner to lodge with them seemed a no-brainer, and helped Paige to at least enjoy life in Vegas on meagre dancers' wages. She seemed pleasant from Sienna's short experience of her at the Monte Cristo, and there was something reserved and self-contained about her that appealed to Sienna. She intensely disliked drama queens, with the exception of her fairy godmother Blue, and there was a little of the 'strong and silent' about Paige. Now, surveying the lovely lunch spread taking shape in the kitchen, Sienna felt butterflies in anticipation of the fun she would have with the girls as they embarked on a new chapter in their lives.

Paolo counted his cash onto the counter and nudged Tiny excitedly as the sales assistant wrapped the Italian suit with seasoned efficiency. Tiny had tried to persuade Paolo to go for something a little more 'money' like a white tux, even offering to lend him some of his gold jewellery to 'class' it up, but Paolo was focussed on channelling how the Italians would dress back in New York, and whilst he couldn't exactly afford Valentino, Paolo had found something sharp in charcoal grey that gave the same look. It may have been his burning ambition for all these years to take his dancing onto the big stage, but the thought of wearing white was just too John Travolta even for him. Paolo was sticking to a classic look for such an important meeting. With his slim frame and Latino colouring, his new purchase looked hot and he felt the part; certainly not like some loser about to move into Tiny's weekly rental with nine of his friends, who couldn't even afford a beer between them, let alone a night uptown in a casino.

'So when do we get to meet this sister of yours, buddy?' asked Tiny, bowling out of the shop with a swagger. He didn't usually get to frequent such upmarket joints as Italian Suit Connection.

'How about never?'

'Aw, c'mon, she's a dancer, right? Must be cute. And if she looks anything like our pretty boy Paolo here . . . '

'Ha ha.' Paolo was used to teasing about his boyish good looks and lithe dancer's frame. At least he knew with Tiny that it was done out of affection. 'Well, the law of genetics says she looks like me. But I don't think she's the type of girl you'd like, Tiny. I haven't seen her for nearly twenty years but even as a girl she was . . . well, high maintenance, you could say.'

'Jeez. Shame. Only just got shot of Juanita. She spent all my money on nails an' hair an' shit, only for some other gringo to be getting all the benefits. *Puta*.'

Paolo felt suddenly nervous. At least he would look the part when he met his sister after all this time. He wondered if she really was the same person, or maybe she had mellowed . . . He could hope, although a nagging feeling deep down told him that leopards never change their spots.

Paige gasped as she opened the door to the master bedroom. The huge gold tiger's head of a doorknob had given her a clue that this was likely to be Tiger Starr's old bedroom, and her curiosity had got the better of her. Now as Paige stood there in the doorway, a cream and gold 'Hall of Mirrors' fantasy greeted her eyes, with ornate Baccarat crystal furniture twinkling everywhere and two walls of mirrors that made the room look as big as a palace. Paige caught sight of her own silhouette reflected into infinity and cursed the fullness of her hips. Darn, she needed to get back in the gym: her recent slacking off the regime was showing. Sighing, she ripped her eyes away to survey the rest of the room. The bed was raised on a platform with some kind of cream llama counterpane and a tufted silk chaise on either side with gold baroque panels rearing up behind. On one of the crystal dressers between all the candelabra, Paige could make out a delicate filigree frame housing a photograph of Sienna dressed for some kind of evening occasion. Next to it was a large framed picture of Tiger Starr in her wedding dress being lifted up by her husband; Tiger caught unawares in the shot, laughing her head off. Paige immediately recognised the famous image from the pages of *Vogue* and all the gossip columns, back when Tiger had married her manager, Lewis Bond, a couple of years ago. So this was the grande dame's headquarters, obviously being preserved for when the queen swooped into town, thought Paige admiringly, indulging herself with delicious thoughts of how much easier her own life would be if only she had a famous parent too. Not feeling bold enough to wander inside the room on her first day, she pulled the door softly closed and padded furtively across the hallway. The girls were sure to be at the gym for at least an hour or two, so she may as well grab the chance to explore since she hadn't had the official tour yet.

Paige opened another door and let her jaw fall open. This was by far the most ridiculous bathroom she'd ever happened upon. Huge marble columns reared up around a carved circular bath, with an elaborate chandelier hanging directly over the tub. A trompe l'oeil of clouds covered the ceiling. Paige laughed out loud – this was exactly the kind of thing her own mother would have sneered at. Anything fancy or high and mighty was frowned upon in the Turner household; if a trailer could pass for a household, that is, which only served to drive Paige even further towards her dreams of superstardom. Forget the Miss Krispy Syrup Queen pageant crown that she had narrowly lost to that trashy bitch Velveeta Weinstein in her tarty majorette boots, Paige was above all that now. She was heading for the big league and nothing less from now on. She found herself walking through into the master bathroom and perching on the edge of the tub. Goldfish-shaped taps no less. She turned them on just for the pleasure of seeing water pouring from their wide guppy mouths. Oh what the heck. The girls wouldn't be back for some time and Paige wasn't going to pass up the opportunity to take a bath in this crazy tub. She thought her new en suite was the height of luxury, but this was off the hook! She was going to enjoy every second of staying in this house. Paige was stripped and pouring bubble bath into the steaming water within seconds.

Max roared up next to Sienna's convertible before cutting the growling engine of his Porsche. He reached out for the beautifully wrapped gift next to him. Damn that Brandy for swiping the Chanel purse he'd carefully chosen for Sienna. He'd had to nip into Hermès and use up the last of his credit at the Encore to snap up a neat purse and matching scarf. Max knew it would appeal to her European tastes – only Sienna could make a headscarf look chic in the Vegas sun. He tried to push his guilt to the back of his mind as he strode up the driveway, knowing at least he was coming good and giving Sienna a nice surprise now. The first dalliance in his relationship had caught him unawares and he had no intention of repeating it. He may well have had his pick of every beautiful model, actress and heiress put together, but he knew in his heart that Sienna loved him for him, not for his money. Plus she was sexy as hell. She was a keeper. And if she ever found out that he'd cheated on her, he suspected he wouldn't see her for dust. Max rang the doorbell and waited. A breeze rustled the palm trees and no-one came. Maybe the girls were having evening cocktails by the pool. Max smoothed his linen suit down and waited patiently.

'Oh!' exclaimed Paige loudly as she swung the door open, furtively clutching a tiny fluffy towel about her; her chest heaving, making it quite obvious that she had scrambled for the door from across the other side of the house.

'Hi, Sienna in? I'm Max.'

'Hi! Yes, er – no! Actually I thought you were her. She's at the gym with Honey,' Paige panted, looking relieved. 'I was in the bath. I thought she'd come back for something.'

'Damn.' Max felt a genuine stab of disappointment. 'Knew I should have called her. I was going to take her out.'

'Oh . . . ' Paige trailed off as though suddenly transfixed by the mirage of the disgustingly handsome Max Power before her.

'And you are?' asked Max, evidently concerned as to the identity of the stranger apparently making herself at home.

'I'm Paige, I just moved in. I've seen you at the club a few times actually,' she said, pulling herself together immediately and holding her hand out.

'Right,' said Max, shaking hands cordially. 'I remember Sienna saying something about a new housemate, come to think of it. So you work at the Monte?'

'I did. You haven't seen my act?' Paige concealed any disappointment seamlessly. 'I'm the one who twirls four tassels.'

Max looked at her blankly.

'You know, one on each ta-ta and one on each cheek?' Paige continued hopefully, surreptitiously smoothing out her hair and leaning into the doorframe elegantly.

'No, must have missed you. Can I come in?' Max was feeling irritable that Sienna wasn't available. Now he wanted to see her more than anything. Why wasn't she home? Did she know somehow about Brandy? Gossip travelled fast in Vegas. He didn't dare to wonder.

'Sure, come in,' said Paige, stepping aside. 'I'm in the "Venus in Furs" show with Sienna now, you know,' she continued, trailing behind Max as he headed straight for the gilded staircase.

'You're cool with me leaving this gift upstairs for Sienna?' he asked, glancing over his shoulder.

'Of course!' Paige hurried up the stairs behind him. 'Wow, what is it?'

'When did she say she'd be back?' asked Max, ignoring the question as he strode into Sienna's bedroom.

'Oh, not for hours,' lied Paige.

'Shit!' Max was really pissed now. He just desperately wanted to see her, be sure she knew nothing about Brandy, and make love to her, make her his all over again. He needed to feel her close. What was so interesting about the gym anyway? It wasn't as though she even needed it. 'Oh well,' he sighed, 'I won't drag her away.'

Paige fiddled with her towel, awkwardly rearranging it to fill the silence. Max crossed to Sienna's bed and carefully tucked his gift for her just under the black fur counterpane, up near her pillow.

'Just so she sees it just as she pulls the covers back for bed,' he murmured, patting the blanket smooth. Paige stood at the door and watched transfixed as Max gently lifted a black satin blouse Sienna had discarded on the floor. He held it for a second before carefully laying it on the bed. He turned towards the door.

'Thanks, Paula.'

'Paige,' she said, startled he had obviously forgotten her name already.

'Yeah, thanks for letting me come in,' he said, approaching the door. Paige was rooted to the spot.

'Can I get by?' laughed Max politely.

'Ooh!' Paige squealed unconvincingly as her towel magically dropped from her hands to reveal her naked moist body, planted between Max and the stairs. Max bent down and picked up the towel, holding it out for Paige.

'Here, you dropped this,' he said flatly, not batting an eyelid. Paige took the towel, defeatedly sinking back against the doorframe as Max trotted past and back down the staircase.

'Tell Sienna I'll be at the Wynn if she wants to come and see me later,' he shouted into the wind as he left the house, not even looking behind him. Paige stood bemused at the top of the stairs, clutching her towel and waiting for the front door to click shut. Turning on her heel she headed back into Sienna's bedroom and went straight for the blouse Max had laid on the bed. Slowly she sank onto the soft mattress, and ran her fingers along the soft creases of the dark satin. She held it up to her nose and inhaled deeply. Chanel No 5, a little hairspray, and ... Sienna. Paige sat there for a minute or two, lightly caressing the fabric before taking the blouse back to her bedroom and laying it carefully in her drawer amongst her own newly unpacked clothes.

Chapter 4

Rows upon rows of make-up stations created long narrow corridors, which opened out into an equally regimented costume area, its rails and racks climbing up the walls with every fabric texture and colour catalogued and crammed into their labelled allotted spaces. Endless identical pairs of shoes were pigeon holed; a closer inspection revealed the height of the heels to vary between pairs to compensate for any height difference there may be from dancer to dancer, the official height requirement allowing for an inch of leeway. The show producer was notoriously exacting about the conditions placed on the dancers in all his shows, and 'Venus in Furs' was no exception. The entire cast now formed an orderly line behind a pair of scales, as Basil the company 'mum' weighed each girl and measured her waist, hips and bust. An excited hum sprinkled the atmosphere in the room.

'Next!' ordered Basil, sticking his pencil behind his ear. Sienna crossed her fingers behind her back as she stepped up onto the scales and willed herself not to look down. She quivered her way through the ensuing pregnant silence before Basil asked her to step off to be measured. Not daring to breathe out as he wrapped his tape around her trim waist, Sienna began to feel lightheaded. Just a few more seconds and I can let it all hang out, she told herself, turning pale.

'Sienna Starr.'

'Yes, sir,' she puffed, letting her chest heave as she snatched a gulp of air.

'These breasts. Can you do anything with them?' asked Basil in his soft but precisely measured British accent.

'Er – like what? Tricks? Nipple tassels?' A loud snigger travelled from the back of the queue. Basil rolled his eyes.

'They're just too big, dear. They the real thing?'

Sienna blinked and nodded, terrified.

'Hmm. You'll have to take some weight off then, see if you can get them down at all, dear. At least a cup size . . .'

'Oh, but – am I too heavy?'

'No, your weight's fine, but these assets are going to, er, stand out, shall we say. This may be a topless revue but it ain't a strip joint; neat and petite is what we need to aim for. See what you can do, dear. Might help if you try not to fling them around on stage. For God's sake don't stick them out. They'll be under the spotlight before the rest of you gets there.' Sienna's face reddened as Basil scribbled in his jotter.

'Don't worry,' he continued without looking up from his notes, 'just cut yourself down to 800 calories a day and you'll be there in no time. Oh, and you may as well cut your hair short, dear, lovely though it is; it'll be ruined from all the wigs and bucrum caps. Much easier all round when it's short. Next!'

Sienna bit her lip and sloped off, suddenly riddled with self-consciousness. She looked furtively at Paige and Honey in the queue and mouthed a 'good luck' at them, before finding her make-up station and slotting herself into her chair. Staring forlornly into the mirror, she scraped her luscious hair back from her face, trying to imagine it cropped, like she had as a gangly, coltish teenager. She sucked her cheekbones in and pouted a little, but it was hopeless. Whichever angle she looked at herself she now hated the picture staring back. And those C cups just kept leaping into the frame and catching her eye now. She slumped into her dresser and willed herself to disappear in amongst the furniture. This wasn't her idea of a great first day. She hadn't even danced a step yet.

Casting her mind back, Sienna remembered the directors talking about some 'fine tuning' the girls would have to do if they got in to the cast, but starving herself into a B cup was going to be a tough call. She put her head in her hands and tried to snap herself out of her gloom. No wonder all the gyms are open twenty-four hours, she realised miserably, thinking of all the dancers in there working out at three in the morning after their shows were finished. When the directors had addressed the cast that morning they had forbidden the girls to be seen out partying – and God forbid drunk – as they were representing

'Venus in Furs' now. They needn't have wasted their breath
as it was evident there would be no chance to even flirt
with the idea of socialising, what with rehearsing,
performing, working out, tanning, manicuring and meas-
uring micro-calories. Sienna couldn't see how she was ever
going to see any blue sky between the theatre, wholefoods,
the gym, and her pillow. So much for 'the glamour of the
showgirl'. Still, this was the dream she had set her heart
on, so she was going to have to get used to it. Although
she couldn't have felt more like a Crufts reject right now
if she tried.

A thick, nauseating smell of musk suddenly assaulted
Sienna's palate and brought her head whipping round, just
in time to catch Brandy billowing past, making her
entrance in some kind of voluminous chiffon blouse
arrangement over tight cigarette pants, a large quilted
Chanel purse covered in strings of pearls and gold double
Cs slung over her shoulder. She looked eye wateringly
expensive and that handbag was to die for, she thought,
guiltily wishing Max had bought her a Chanel instead of
Hermès, gorgeous though it was. Sienna resisted the
sudden urge to light an incense stick to purge her nasal
passages of Brandy's perfume, deciding it was so pungent
it had probably turned the air flammable anyway. She
simply sighed loudly and set about arranging her make-
up caddy. She had packed a small teddy bear within. Well,
if Sienna was going to be here a while she reckoned she
may as well give her station a personal touch; make it her

space. She scoured amongst her make-up for some eyelash glue to stick the photo of her mum in place on her mirror. Within seconds the peace was shattered as Brandy's cut-glass voice screeched out.

'I don't care, it's too big. You could stand a pint glass on those cheeks. A lifetime of lipo couldn't salvage that ass. Christ.' Sienna sat at her mirror and cringed at the cruel jibe, feeling instantly sorry for the poor recipient.

'But I think she'll lose any excess with a diet, dear,' countered Basil's unflappable tones, 'and besides the shape's great, just look at the muscle tone; it's pert and rock solid.'

'Exactly, and it's way out of proportion. That's the cruelty of genetics, I'm afraid, it ain't gonna budge. I've seen enough to tell – the best she could hope for is a job as J-Lo's stunt ass.' Sienna winced as she listened. Brandy was a cow alright; in her dreams she could have an ass like la Lopez, thought Sienna.

'Stop prodding me like I'm cattle! And I'm not a *she*, I do have a name, you know!' shrieked a familiar voice. Sienna gasped and ran to the group of girls clustered around Brandy. Sure enough there stood Honey in a face-off with the bitch.

'Good,' snapped Brandy, raising her manicured finger to poke it in Honey's face, 'because you can take your name and make it along with all the other hoochie mamas shakin' it over at the Velvet Taco. Believe me, that's the only kind of "dancing" you should be doing with that back-side. Don't worry, there are plenty of men there who'd pay good money to have their faces up close with that weapon of mass destruction.' A gasp swept round the room. Honey lunged forward at Brandy but Basil already had her arms restrained firmly in his hands. Some of the onlooking girls now had their nails nervously up at their mouths, their eyes wide. Brandy simply stood there and smiled calmly as Honey struggled in vain against Basil's grip.

'You're so fired,' said Brandy evenly.

Blue hummed as he minced through the parking lot towards the stage door, armed with posies for the new girls, along with a stack of blank cards for Brandy to sign by way of congratulations for the new cast who were refreshing the hit show. Of course, Brandy would never think of such a sweet gesture herself, but Blue was happy for his good thoughts to be passed off as hers. After all, a happy dressing room made for a happy production, which made for a happier Brandy, and that made Blue's life immeasurably more pleasant. Not that anyone was really fooled into thinking Brandy would ever initiate such an act of kindness from the heart; her reputation for being utterly objectionable was widespread, not to mention thoroughly well deserved.

Blue had stayed on in Vegas after his muse, namely Tiger Starr, had moved on to pastures new in Hollywood. There was really only one thing that could separate Blue from his best friend, and that was a handsome man; although his latest relationship with a seriously cute classical boy band member was definitely entering its twilight after a reasonably fruitful couple of years. Plus, Blue knew three was a crowd, and he wanted to give Tiger and her new husband Lewis time alone in the blissful honeymoon period of their new life together. It had taken them long enough to finally get it on as a couple and they had plenty of making up for lost time to do. Besides, Blue now had his hands too full with the albatross that was Brandy Alexander. Blue had been headhunted to work as her personal costumier and dresser for the last year and whilst the pay was fantastic, it was a thankless task. He had been flattered to be groomed for the job at first, when they could have had the legendary Bob Mackie for the same money instead, but less than three hours into the job Blue realised exactly why the pay cheque had to be so high. Brandy wasn't Cher in the superstar stakes by a long chalk, but she could have elicited a slap from Mother Teresa with some – in fact, most – of her behaviour. Blue was happy to admit he was thoroughly prostituting himself working for Brandy; he certainly wasn't doing the job for pleasure. Now, as he signed in at the backstage reception desk, he braced himself and prayed the wind had been blowing in the right direction that morning when Brandy had got out of hopefully the right side of her bed.

'You can't just fire her like that!' interjected Sienna bravely as Honey fled from the dressing room, red-faced and keeping her eyes to the ground.

'Oh? Someone here has an opinion suddenly,' said Brandy, turning slowly to face Sienna. 'Oh, Ms Starr, you of all people. I'd have thought better of you. You know how the industry works.' Her eyes glistened with malice as she looked Sienna slowly up and down. It made her shiver visibly.

'We know we all have to polish our bodies that extra inch before opening night,' ventured Sienna nervously, 'and we all accept it's part of the job, but Honey dances like magic, it's why she got through, right? You didn't have a problem with her figure then. She has an amazing body.'

'Yes, to a certain kind of . . . not-so-gentle-man, perhaps. Honestly, I have no idea how she got through. I would have sifted her out straightaway, personally. Perhaps her press shots were a few years old.'

'That isn't nice! She works damn hard on her figure and you know she looks amazing!'

'Sweetness, this is showbiz and showbiz ain't nice.'

'Yes. I can see how you've done so well, now,' muttered Sienna under her breath.

The onlooking chorus line drew back in fear, and those who caught Sienna's response now turned away and busied themselves checking their faces in the mirrors.

'What did you say to me?' asked Brandy through gritted teeth in a dangerously measured tone, crossing her arms dramatically.

'Nothing, my – stomach grumbled,' trembled Sienna.

'Are you determined to join your friend? Or are you going to tell me what you just said?' demanded Brandy, grinding the sole of her stiletto slowly into the floor for effect.

'Coo-eee!' came Blue's voice as he wafted into the dressing room. 'Ooh what's this, a mothers' meeting? Or hasn't the whale weighing finished?'

No-one dared to laugh.

'Huh,' Brandy snorted. 'Looks like the queen in shining armour just saved your ass, Ms Starr,' she sneered.

'Brandy, what are you doing out of your palace? Mixing with the proles backstage? Most unlike you.' Brandy shot Blue one of her nuclear death-ray glances that told him his joking was as welcome as a pork chop in a synagogue.

'I think we're done here,' said Brandy, turning on her heel in a gust of fury and locking herself noisily into her private dressing room, following up with an ear-splitting blast of Led Zeppelin vibrating through the walls. From the look on Sienna's face Blue knew he had yet another day of pure, unadulterated, Brandy Alexander-shaped purgatory ahead of him.

'I'm coming home with you,' insisted Sienna, tears running down her cheeks as she clutched at Honey out on the fire escape.

'No! You go back in there, you hear me? If I made it into this show, I'll make it into another one,' said Honey firmly. 'And stop that crying. That bitch ain't worth so much as a snivel. I know there's nothing wrong with my butt, I'm a size four! I'm too angry to even – why I'd – ugh!' Honey put her hands to her head in exasperation.

'Oh babe, I'm going to have you reinstated. Let me see if I can talk to her again.'

'No!'

'Yes! Well, how about I talk to Blue and—'

'Sienna, don't you understand? I can't go back in there – the embarrassment! They were talking about me like I wasn't even in the room. And what'll I tell my folks now? "I'm sorry but your daughter failed because of her big fat ass"? How's that for a headline! Dad thought I was getting high and mighty coming to Vegas in the first place. I'll bet he's just waiting for me to go back to London with my tail between my legs.' Honey's voice cracked.

'Well, that won't happen, because you're staying put in Vegas,' reassured Sienna, 'and you can get your old job back at the Monte for a start.'

'Oh great, they'll probably all laugh at me there too. Britney Ferry will be dining out on it for weeks, especially when she hears it was my slab of a backside that got me fired. God, I'm such a failure!'

'You are not! Besides, Brandy obviously has a hang-up the size of Puerto Rico and her stuck-on tits combined. She's probably eaten up with jealousy because you have the perfect peach most girls would die for. Let's face it, I don't see Beyoncé crying into her pot of millions about *her* amazing curves. Honey Lou, you're gonna be in another show before you know it. You'll see,' Sienna continued steadfastly.

'Listen, I need to go home, babe, have a cry and get it

out of my system. And you need to go back in there and be brilliant.'

'How can I? It's not fair,' snuffled Sienna, feeling her own eyes welling up.

'No, it's not fair, but like Brandy said, it's showbiz, and you know how it works. We're not real people, we're just objects in one big pantomime. I tell you what you do, you make sure you dance for your life in the understudy auditions this afternoon, and you get cast as Brandy's understudy. Then you sneak double cream into all her coffees every day until her damn ass is too fat, and you get to be the star . . . ' Honey broke off with a hollow laugh.

'Seriously, babe,' she continued, 'I can't say as I envy you, working for her. But you gotta stay in this show for both of us. You're gonna be huge one day.'

'We're both gonna get there, darling,' whispered Sienna. 'Just one thing . . . '

'Yeah?'

'The big butt thing . . . please, not a word to anyone. I'm mortified,' pleaded Honey in a hoarse whisper.

'As if!' muttered Sienna, embracing her in a bear hug and depositing sloppy tears all over her cardigan. 'And you know it's not true. You're gorgeous. Anyway, spare a thought for me. When every other girl in town is getting hair extensions and having herself pumped up I have to make my breasts disappear and cut my hair off.'

'But you'll still be the sexiest boy in the show . . . '

squeaked Honey hopefully. The girls managed a giggle as they shared a tight hug.

Sienna took a deep breath in the wings as she counted herself in, waiting for the current dancer to finish the last steps of her showpiece before presenting the next girl. On the next bar of eight Sienna switched on her smile and took to the enormous stage, gliding in long elegant strides to the swelling strings of the dramatic music. She knew if Brandy was watching she'd never make the understudy post after her display of rebellion earlier, but Sienna could see the director and production staff sitting out there with their notepads, and since the understudy got a slightly bigger pay cheque – and a chance at headlining – Sienna was giving it her all, not to mention in honour of her dear friend Honey. She stretched her endless legs that extra inch with her high kicks, she jumped a cat's whisker even higher, she arched her back into position until her spine tingled and she smiled until her cheeks ached. She knew in her heart she was flawless and it felt great. Finishing with her parades to the directors she felt energised. Finally, this was what she had wanted on her first day, to dance on this amazing stage, feel the heat of the lights, look out at five thousand velvet seats eager to be filled. As the music wound to its climax, Sienna ended her audition piece, leaving the stage as Paige came on.

Twenty rows back, Blue sat with Brandy as she huddled in with the director, vetting each performance. On the beautiful set in front of them, Paige Turner stumbled for the third time and struggled to regain her poise. Blue rolled his eyes, fully expecting Brandy to storm off any minute.

'That's our girl,' said Brandy triumphantly. Blue nearly swallowed his gum.

'Beautiful, but not as beautiful as Brandy Alexander,' she said, referring to herself, as she often did, in the third person, 'and not such a good dancer as to outshine Brandy when she takes her little break shortly. Perfect.' Blue opened his mouth incredulously but nothing came out. He knew Brandy was insecure but she'd really topped herself this time – making sure her understudy wouldn't show up her shortcomings in the talent stakes.

'I'm tellin' ya, buddy, just get it down you. I can't believe you never said nothin'. You can't blame us for all thinking you were moody. We're feeling guilty now.' Tiny lined up the beers and a row of tequila shots in front of Paolo. Eduardo, Raoul and Jesús rotated the salt and lemon.

'Seriously, I can't even buy a round of drinks right now, guys,' said Paolo, hanging his head a little.

'No worries, buddy, you've had enough on your plate with your mama and all that,' chipped in Jesús. 'These are on us. Enjoy and forget everything for a night.'

The four men knocked back their shots and screwed up their eyes as they sucked on their lemon wedges. Paolo was grateful the Mexicans had taken him under their wing. In many ways he felt bad for muscling in on their work supply since he came to town a few weeks back, but since his Sheriff's Card showed up his convictions, he knew he'd have no chance of a regular casino job with those felonies against his name. Work was tough to get in this town as it was, and Paolo was pretty sure the casino bosses wouldn't buy some tired old sob story of him being driven to his crimes. But Paolo could hardly feel sorry for himself. He was half Puerto Rican, half American, so he could at least get a bona fide Sheriff's Card, unlike Tiny and the gang who were illegals and stood no chance. That was why when the tourists would drive anywhere off the strip, chances were they'd see groups of Mexicans hanging out by every garden supply or home improvements store, hoping to be collected for cash-in-hand labour at a private residence. But Paolo had spent many years feeling like a second-class citizen in New York, and so he knew what it was like for the Mexicans on the West Coast. He didn't mind hanging out with them in their separate bars and discos. It was a pretty happy family on the whole. And the Mexican girls were kinda cute too.

'Hey, pretty boy,' said Jesús, nudging Paolo in the ribs, 'that pocket rocket from earlier is coming back over. Look, guys, she's with a friend! Check. It. Out.' The Mexicans sucked their teeth as a very short, pretty young girl who was somewhat spilling out of her white Lycra dress came sashaying over, her slightly nervous-looking friend trailing behind her.

'Hey ladieeees,' drawled Tiny, placing his five-foot-tall

and five-foot-wide frame between them and the boys. 'You want some tequila?'

'That's a kind offer, er—'

'Tiny.' He held his hand out.

'Hi Tiny. I'm Sharon. And this is my friend Rosa.' Tiny shook their hands before heading straight for the bar for another round. Sharon smiled tentatively at the group and sidled over to Paolo. He thought she'd been making eyes all evening but hadn't liked to assume anything. Giving her the quick once-over, he liked what he saw. Henna'd hair against olive skin, kind eyes and plump, blow-job lips. He reckoned if she could shave thirty pounds off she'd look like a young Salma Hayek. And ditching the tacky revealing Lycra would be a good move too. But those wide hips were sexy as hell, thought Paolo. He bet she could dance a mean samba.

'So, Sharon, huh? That's kind of an unusual name for a Latina . . . ?' Paolo began.

'Yeah, before you ask, Mama had a thing about Sharon Stone,' she laughed, pre-empting the question. Paolo laughed with her and let himself relax a little for the first time in weeks. Maybe he could actually start to think about a girl after all. He hadn't been able to bring himself to even consider such a thing since he'd skipped New York. Looking at Sharon's pretty face as she chattered away he felt a stirring that he hadn't felt for some time.

Chapter 5

The lovemaking was incredible. But it was as much by way of apology as it was a spontaneous deep yearning. Max knew he had hurt Sienna by refusing to allow her to meet his father, but just couldn't bring himself to tell her the truth. Kerry Power had arrived in town that morning unannounced, and Max had been summoned for an evening appointment. Kerry did this occasionally, usually to spring a nasty surprise on Max, but unusually for this trip Kerry had skipped his private jet in favour of one of his son's Silver Slipper aeroplanes. It was therefore to be assumed that Kerry was snooping. For what purpose Max really had no idea but it was a sure bet it wouldn't be to offer him a new business opportunity. Whatever it was he was sure would be revealed this evening over one of their 'bonding' stints on the poker tables, a game he'd been introduced to by Kerry as soon as he was old enough to shuffle a deck of cards. He just hoped Kerry wouldn't be accompanied by one or more of his 'girlfriends'. Max always found it such a ridiculous charade, and his dad's choice of pro-hos were always such bland company; beautiful on first impact, but on closer inspection waxen, pulled tight and generally mute. Max wondered if it was simply because his father was such a tyrant he preferred his escorts not to speak unless spoken to.

Not that Max had anything against professionals – he just didn't choose to socialise with them. Kerry had bought his son his first hooker for his fifteenth birthday – what a nightmare that had been. By the time Max had figured out who she was and what the deal was, he'd become so terrified she would report back to his father on his perform-ance that he'd finished the job before the boat had even pulled into the harbour, and from that point onwards he stood no chance of even getting the sail up. Max never liked to think that one's formative experiences had to neces-sarily set the tone for everything that followed, but he'd found as he'd grown up that he had come to appreciate the honesty of paying for sex. All the regular women he dated just wanted his money anyway – so he'd rather hire an escort, get the cash on the table right away, and not be ripped off. Plus prostitutes were honest. Truthful. Much more honest than the scheming gold diggers out there; at least hookers didn't pretend to be servicing him for any other reason than the money. None of all that insincere fawning over his 'charisma', or his 'chivalry'. Those were the kind of women who'd be racking up his credit card bill with beluga caviar and Cristal and whispering sweet nothings, whilst looking over his shoulder in case someone richer might be walking into the room, or checking out if there was a movie director he could introduce them to.

So Max saw nothing wrong with having one or two preferred broads on the Power payroll since his regular relationships had been generally disastrous. Besides, beautiful women could be so boring; as though they'd always attracted the men and so never felt the need to work on their personality.

Max had known Sienna was different right away. She'd ignored him for a start. Whether tactical or not, it made him more determined to win her attention. Of course everyone rushed to tell him who her famous mother was, which made him rise to the bait even more. Tiger Starr was bound to have schooled her daughter in the dangerous art of the tease, and when it came to games, Max never could pass up a challenge. He was irked to find himself tongue tied from their very first conversation; women had always tried to impress Max, but Sienna hadn't done this. Sometimes she would just lean back, watch and listen. Max hated to admit to himself that he turned shy in her presence. One of the problems was that Max only usually bedded women he didn't really care about. Deep down he was scared to be himself in front of this amazing creature. What if she rejected him?

A worry had flitted across Max's mind before their first 'date' that Sienna might have some combative maneater-ish act in person, so he was secretly relieved to find her rather demure offstage. Not boring in the least, just a touch of class. Amazingly she could actually hold lengthy conversations about subjects other than herself or the calorie content of a cocktail onion, and she could crack a joke with the best of them – but she was such a lady with it. And what had happened to women being ladies these days? Max recalled faint early memories of his dearly loved mum before she had passed away, the way she had such elegance and dignity. Her style and class was natural somehow, despite being born into poverty. Max remembered how people were immediately drawn to his mother in a room yet she never had to grasp for attention; she was magnetic. Perhaps because she had seen everything on the road from rags to riches alongside her husband. Dora Power could somehow relate to anyone and find common ground, be they a beggar on the street or a hardened cynical businessman. Her stellar social networking had a big hand in the growth of Kerry Power's business empire from modest beginnings breeding race greyhounds – his rise certainly wasn't aided by his own limited social charms. Dora was definitely a fine example of the old adage, 'Behind every great man is an even greater woman.'

Though Max couldn't face the fact that a truly great woman would never have stood by a man like Kerry Power. Neither would she have starved herself to death, an anorexic wisp of a wreck by the end; surrounded by riches and luxury but desperately trying to control her life in the only way she felt she could. Max squared it with himself that Dora Power simply wanted the best for her family, and was determined never to return to the squalor that she had shared with Kerry when they married at sweet sixteen. If that meant standing behind her husband and turning a blind eye to bad behaviour, so be it. Family came first.

There was no way now that Max was going to introduce Sienna to his father. He didn't want his old man leching all over his gorgeous girlfriend, and he certainly didn't want Sienna sitting there having to make conversation with one of his dad's vacuous nipped and tucked morons of an escort. Besides, it was a little too close for comfort. Sienna was smart, she'd figure out the deal. Imagine if she started to suspect the same of Max? He may share one or two of his father's vices, but they were under control. He was no chip off the old block, and never would be. As for Kerry, he was a nasty piece of work plain and simple, and Max didn't want his father befriending Sienna as an opportunity for manipulating his son, especially as it was obvious Max was serious about her. Kerry must have seen them in all the gossip columns; he never missed a trick. It was certainly the longest Max had been pictured with the same woman in living memory.

So when Sienna had eagerly offered to accompany Max that evening, excited at the thought of being introduced to his family, it had been tough for Max to explain why he was forbidding her to accompany him. Sienna had gone through every possibility, getting more fraught and hysterical with each – was he ashamed of her? Was her job an issue? Was there someone else? What was he hiding?

Max had eventually pacified Sienna with sweet talk,

and that great leveller, an unbelievable session of love-making under a red sunset in the swimming pool. Sex with Sienna took his breath away. Apart from being horny as hell, she had some positions in her range that gave Max palpitations. Now, as he stood waist deep in the warm water with Sienna sated and perched languorously on the edge of the pool, her long legs wrapped tightly around his muscled torso, he stared deep into her beautiful eyes, still slightly streaked with mascara from her earlier tears. Max felt weak with love and lust. He leaned in for an urgent kiss before pulling her back into the pool, eliciting a tiny squeal from Sienna. His father could damn well wait. Max was already rock hard and ready to go again.

The fuck had been more of an emotional release than a mark of any real earth-shattering desire. And whilst Sharon bore the least possible resemblance to her namesake, Paolo definitely thought she was cute. He'd never been one of these sleazy guys who could just nail anything that offered sex on a plate. He was old-fashioned like that; he had to like the woman, respect her. Having to witness from afar what his father did to Mami all those years back, coldly cutting her off and sending her back to New York like he was sending back an unwanted Christmas present, he had always sworn he would never treat a woman with anything other than respect.

In any other circumstance Paolo would have probably been more attentive to Sharon's needs. It was just unfortunate that this was the first time he'd even been able to think about getting laid for the last couple of months since Mami had checked out. He probably wouldn't even have accepted her indecent proposal if Tiny, Eduardo and Jesús hadn't been answering on his behalf. Paolo hadn't even been sure he'd be able to perform, he'd been so numb inside after Mami's death. And that wasn't exactly something he could bring up, standing there in the club with his pals.

Of course, Sharon couldn't believe her luck snagging such a gorgeous guy and had brought out all her best tricks. She clearly thought she'd been a big hit, but how could Paolo tell her the reason he'd actually burst into tears after he'd orgasmed was that all he could smell on her neck was the thick cloying smell of Dior Poison which his mother used to get as a special sweetener from her dealer when she shifted an extra kilo of smack to the other hookers? Poor Sharon had thought she'd really brought Paolo to his knees when she'd seen tears. She'd even valiantly taken carpet burns on her ass from the wall tiles.

But when she had tried to give him a saucy wake-up call this morning, Paolo had made an excuse about being late for work and managed to get her dressed and out of the motel room within ten minutes. He'd had no intention of going to work today though, which made him feel guilty. Not half as guilty as he'd felt when Sharon had bashfully said she was pleased he didn't seem like the 'fuck 'em and never call again' kinda guy, as he gently guided her out of the door. Paolo didn't even know if he'd ever be able to get it up again under the circumstances, let alone how he felt about getting back on the dating train. Right now, he had something far too important to concentrate on, and that was finding his sister tonight. Taking the day off work meant he didn't look craggy or tired after a day of gruelling cheap manual labour. He knew he only had one chance to make a first impression with her.

As he now looked into the mirror he checked himself out in his new suit and knew he cut a good dash. He felt ready for his big moment. He'd already checked with local contacts in the know the venues his sister went in the evenings, and there were a couple of regular haunts for him to try. There was no reason for the introduction not to go smoothly, and he would just be himself. The only wild card would be if she recognised him or not – he had no idea how much she had blocked out her past; he certainly couldn't imagine she'd been proud of what she'd done. That would be the interesting part.

Paige Turner breezed into the Monte Cristo and claimed a spot at the bar. She found it strangely pleasant to come to the club as a punter rather than for work, and she found herself feeling both smug and a tiny bit sorry for the girls who were still stuck here. The Monte certainly had more charm from this angle, she thought, looking around. Whilst it still looked run down, the audience clearly didn't see the crapness and shoddiness that *really* went on backstage. She could now see how the peeling paint and worn away wallpaper could, to a romantic, add to the myth of 'old Vegas' and tap into the idea of 'vintage charm'. Within minutes Pepper had appeared by her side with a cocktail menu.

'Hey stranger, nice to have you,' said Pepper warmly. 'Is Sienna joining us?'

'She sent me a message to say she'd meet me here,' said Paige, opening her drinks menu and running her eyes down the long list of dubiously named cocktails. What the hell was a 'Meaty Martini', she wondered to herself, nearly heaving when she read the words 'vodka' and 'cube of Spam' in the ingredients. With fare like that on the menu, no wonder their audiences were a bunch of baying wolves some nights – they probably came into the joint perfectly normal until they had their meat-based cocktail with Whisky Fanta chasers poured down their necks.

'So, you've started rehearsing the new show now!' said Pepper excitedly. 'How's it going? And don't leave out any gossip!' she warned. Paige kept her eyes dutifully on the Meaty Martini, as she didn't want to be the one to say that Honey had been fired, or that she'd made the understudy position over Sienna, who everyone knew full well was the better dancer.

'Oh here she is!' announced Pepper enthusiastically.

Paige was relieved to see Sienna strolling through towards them, beaming. Good, thought Paige, she can break the news. And in the meantime she was going to order a glass of champagne, nice and simple, impossible to mess up. Sienna greeted the ladies with post-coital radiance and big hugs before setting her new Hermès purse on the bar and settling elegantly onto her stool.

'Hi darling,' gushed Pepper, 'and wow, you look – glowing! New face cream or something?'

'No . . . just love,' sighed Sienna dreamily. 'Hmm, I love being in love,' she murmured. Paige fidgeted on her perch, barely able to stop herself making puke fingers into her mouth. She sensed neither Pepper nor Sienna would find it funny, and since she'd only just moved in with Sienna she should probably be on her best behaviour for a little while at least.

'And it started right here in the Monte!' said Pepper. 'That's worth celebrating in itself. Shall I get you ladies a cocktail?'

'Champagne,' blurted Paige.

'Great idea, one for me too,' added Sienna. 'In fact we should make it a bottle. Paige made it as Brandy's first understudy this week so we have to celebrate,' she announced graciously.

'Really?' Pepper paused for a second too long. 'Oh, right, yes, congratulations, Paige!' she said, nodding towards Jeffrey behind the bar who snapped to attention.

'Heyyyyyyy ladies! Have the prodigals returned?' came

a brash voice from behind, accompanied by its even brasher owner.

'Griselda!' greeted the girls in unison, turning and eyeing up their favourite drag queen, his garish sequinned gown flapping as he ploughed inelegantly through the tables, sending one or two drinks flying in his wake, but beaming a wide, snaggle-toothed smile all the way.

'Wow,' said Paige, 'that's some interesting hair you got going on tonight, sweetie.'

'Why, thank you, honey,' said Griselda, proudly patting the huge white-blonde mass of what resembled an eighteenth-century cotton wool pompadour, teased to within an inch of its life.

'You look like a burst sofa,' sniggered Paige.

'Ooh, hecklers already?' replied Griselda, struggling to raise his eyebrows any higher than they were already pencilled.

'Have you missed us yet, darling?' asked Sienna warmly.

'Of course, my child, it just isn't the same without you. Although now Chastity and Mercedes are doing feature acts in your place, it at least gives me more comedy material to work with.' Griselda cackled, hoisting up his fake breasts within a dress that looked like it was a size too small and then taken in some. Sienna and Paige suddenly looked at each other in silence and grimaced conspicuously. Pepper put her hand to her nose dramatically.

'Oh God, excuse him, ladies, he hasn't stopped farting

since he's been taking the new hormones. It travels off the stage, you know, I swear it's driving customers away. I reckon it's why Ma's been poorly the last few days.'

'Better out than in,' said Griselda defensively, 'and a miserable Griselda makes for a miserable show for everyone.'

'You're not kidding there.' Pepper grimaced at the girls. 'He still makes everyone's life hell whichever direction the wind's blowing, never mind his own. Remember what he used to be like on a day when he didn't feel pretty enough?' groaned Pepper.

'Huh,' snorted Griselda. 'You mock, darlings. I may have a face like an unmade bed but I'm an elegant little creature and I deserve some respect, even if it is through a cloud of fart!' he huffed.

'On that note, save your funny lines for the stage, lady, second half starts any minute and there's at least fifty people in the audience tonight,' said Pepper, wafting the air about her.

'Well, lovely of you girls to come back and visit Aunty Griselda, think of me slaving it out in this little maggoty sweatshop while you're glamming it up in the Follies ... lucky bitches. Now, where are my grapes? Someone peel me a grape. And I'll need a minute on my Pilates mat before I can go on and beguile my adoring audience! Any celebs in the house tonight?' And with that Griselda lumbered off like a shimmering hod carrier towards the stage.

'Did I just hear correctly back there, Pepper, that Ma isn't well?' asked Sienna.

'Afraid so, darling. She just isn't right. I'm certain it's a relapse and that she feels it too; she keeps talking about wanting to just enjoy herself on her way out. She's upstairs in bed. I've made her take a few days off. If I didn't force her to lie down she'd be behind this darn bar with the punters until she dropped down in front of them.' Pepper lowered her voice to a whisper. 'She's forbidden me to call the medics just yet; she doesn't want word getting out or the vultures will be circling. You know who I mean . . . that's why I'm pretty sure she knows this is her last hour in the sun.' Pepper look furtively from left to right. Sienna realised the old lady was shaken despite her bravado. She reached out to give Pepper's hand a squeeze, and shot her an apologetic look, knowing it was a conversation for another time when they had some privacy.

'So has Honey been in to see you at all?' asked Sienna, changing the subject. She'd thoughtfully given Honey some space the last few days; her friend was a sensitive thing and so Sienna hadn't wanted to rub it in her face that she was trotting off to her rehearsals every day until Honey had got on her feet again. Sienna hadn't actually seen her much apart from crossing paths in the kitchen over a skimpy plate of lettuce and protein, times at which Honey had seemed chirpy enough, if a little distracted. Sienna had optimistically assumed her buddy had been back to the Monte to get her old job back.

'No. I haven't seen her, darling. How's she getting on in the show?' asked Pepper. Sienna's heart sank at the news. What had Honey been doing all week? she wondered.

'Oh, I'm sure she'll be in,' said Sienna, uneasily. Jeffrey clattered a champagne bucket onto the bar.

'You'll have to excuse me, girls,' said Pepper. 'Just seen a regular I should say hi to.' Sienna immediately turned to Paige anxiously.

'Honey's hardly been around since she got fired, you know. I hope she's okay; I'd hate to think of her licking her wounds all on her own somewhere. She should have friends around her,' Sienna said, looking at Paige earnestly.

'Stop worrying, she'll have been auditioning. I've heard her zipping in and out of the house. And I know she's been using up my damn Frizz Ease on her mane so she must be going to appointments.'

'I do hope she's okay,' sighed Sienna. 'Auditions can be so soul destroying . . . '

'Sorry to interrupt, ladies,' said Jeffrey discreetly from behind the bar. Sienna span round.

'I know you already ordered champagne yourselves – but the gentleman over to your left would like to pay for it as a gift from him.'

Paige and Sienna immediately eyeballed the row of men beside them. All were engrossed in what was unfolding as Griselda parped his way onto the stage in a colourful fanfare of flatulence, with the exception of one man. He looked cool in a sharp dark suit over a slim athletic frame, standing out from the old regulars at the bar who all sported their usual untucked shirts and unshaven jaw lines. He stared intently at the girls before breaking into an enigmatic smile, slowly lifting his tumbler and cocking it at them. Paige span her stool to face Sienna. 'Shall we accept?' she proffered.

'I don't know. He's definitely a new lounge lizard . . . ' Sienna paused as she considered. 'He's probably passing through town for a conference . . . ' she hissed through the side of her mouth. 'Either way he looks like he wants some "therapy".'

'He looks . . . ' Paige took a furtive peep and span round dramatically again. 'Yeah . . . I guess he's got that look of a tourist on a mission. But how do you know he's a John? Maybe he just wants some conversation?'

'Who knows,' sighed Sienna, 'but half the clientele here think anything with breasts is available for extras. Even Grizzly Griselda . . . who only has man boobs on offer underneath the padding. Although I think he's been known to oblige for the blind drunk. Yeesh.' Sienna shuddered at the thought.

'You know – I'm sure I've seen this mystery guy before,' murmured Paige. 'His face seems . . . familiar somehow. Has he been here before? Maybe he's important. Or an actor?'

'God no,' laughed Sienna. 'If he was even remotely famous, he wouldn't be sending us drinks, babe, he'd be expecting us to roll the red carpet out for him instead. I'm telling you, he just wants to buy some company and he's trying to charm us because we're two pairs of legs and tits perched conveniently right in front of him.'

'Oh? But Max made a massive play for you, remember, even when he could have the most beautiful women in the world literally falling at his feet.' Sienna blinked at the sting of the backhanded compliment. Paige continued blithely. 'I'm intrigued now. Let's just take the champagne.'

'No thanks, I can buy my own. Trust me, he's a trick, and I really haven't the energy for getting rid of him once he thinks he's in with a chance,' countered Sienna quietly, still smarting from the earlier comment.

'Oh, lighten up, darling, it's a drink, not a life sentence. Why pay for it ourselves? If this guy wants to splash the cash then that's fine with me. It doesn't make *me* a tart.' Paige swung her stool back round to face Mystery Guy, nodded and mouthed a 'thank you', before motioning to Jeffrey to serve the champagne. Sienna took a good look at the man with a discreet sideways glance. Chances were he was probably just a harmless tourist, but there was something about him that made her feel uneasy. She just couldn't quite put her finger on it.

'And now, ladies and germs,' came the voice of Griselda, cutting through Sienna's concentration like a rusty hacksaw, 'please give a special, warm and fuzzy Monte Cristo welcome to our next star with her in-famous magic hand-kerchiefs ... where will she hide them tonight? Brace yourselves ... put your hands and napkins together for Mercedes Bends!!!' The crowd cheered as the girls sat coolly at the bar, Paige swilling back her champagne and fantasising about the possibilities of Mystery Guy.

Brandy rolled her eyes and cursed under her breath as she watched Gem Green stumbling conspicuously into the huge floor-to-ceiling mirror. She sprang up from the table and put her arm about his shoulders.

'The door's on this side, sweetie,' she hissed, turning him in the right direction and looking about her to see how many of the other diners were watching.

'No, this is the door, I just can't find the handle,' snapped Gem irritably, his gnarled hands padding across the mirror in his quest, depositing smeared fingerprints.

'Of course,' said Brandy through gritted teeth whilst shoving Gem firmly towards the heavy glass door next to the mirror. 'Oh look!' she exclaimed in faux surprise. 'Why, here's the handle, sweetie!'

'See, I told you,' said Gem, finally locating the door and opening it with a flourish, flashing her a smug look before barrelling off to the restroom.

Brandy slipped back to her table and composed herself with a hit of vintage Rémy. Just how much longer could she bear to service the salty old dog? she wondered to herself. She was wasted on him, she thought, eyeing up the talent in the restaurant. Gem may own half of Vegas but he could barely even see these days; how could he ever appreciate Brandy's beauty and all the effort she made any more? All it meant was that he wanted to feel his way around her much more, which was starting to make even Brandy's strong constitution curdle. Why he kept up the charade when everyone knew he was practically blind as a bat now was beyond her. Why, he was probably merrily pissing into the wash basin right now. All those billions he'd made, but there were still things he couldn't buy, she mused. That didn't include Brandy, of course. No, she was very happy for him to supplement her income with a mansion, a fleet of cars and unlimited credit at his Follies Hotel, not to mention a legitimate job in 'Venus in Furs' to keep her public profile nice and prominent.

Brandy usually dined alone at the Follies' Michelin star restaurant, before either attending some showbiz party or raking in some sneaky gifts on her back if another of her business connections happened to be in town. But Gem took priority this evening; his wife had discovered a couple of his latest love children and had just cut all the crotches out of his entire *couture* suit collection, so the presence of Brandy's warm bosom was required while Gem cried into his lobster bisque for a few minutes. More importantly, she knew he'd hit the poker tables across town later. That meant a new wardrobe would be on the cards, since the casino hosts usually tried to dispatch the girlfriends on expenses-paid shopping trips so they wouldn't be there whispering in the gambler's ear and distracting them from losing piles of cash. Since Brandy was about to take a few months off on a chartered yacht to recover from her total cosmetic overhaul, a new cruise collection would be timely, especially if it could be obtained without having to dip into her own ever-swelling bank account.

The 'trip' was well timed; forget recovering in an LA retreat, far too close to home and far too likely she'd bump into other celebs. No, a break from the party circuit and a newly nipped, tucked and enhanced face and body meant she would make a big impact back on the scene after a few months of laying low after her recent drama. Brandy's last 'official' engagement to a B-list movie star had just ended very publicly. She'd cannily released a few stories of his 'loose fists' onto the grapevine and turned up to a couple of functions with a rather convincing purple eye-shadow 'bruise' smudged into her eye; truth was she had been through her fiancé's cash within two years and he was now asking her to actually contribute to their lifestyle together. The cheek! She'd dispatched him before he could say 'ho'. He'd definitely outlived his usefulness anyway and Brandy was ready for the next rung on the ladder; Hollywood was so yesterday anyway. She needed a new gimmick now, an exotic Arabian prince or something. The Americans certainly got impressed by a title, after all. Although quite who the aristocracy thought they were had always amused Brandy. Why, they're just lucky sperm, she thought. What did they ever do to earn their title except be born? At least if Brandy Alexander clawed her way in there as an ersatz princess she would have fucked her way to her honour good and proper, clinging on for dear life with every manicured false nail on the way. Hard work well rewarded!

One thing was certain, aristocrats certainly knew how to live in luxury, not the trashy flashy showbiz way where you could look the part in a hired Lamborghini whilst living in a dump in Hollywood, but the opulent, stinking money way – unlimited fur, gold, diamonds, yachts, caviar and most of all, proper high-society moving and shaking; most suitable for Brandy. She could imagine it already: the prince and the showgirl indeed! Maybe she could even give up the shows and turn her hand to designing fine jewellery instead or something equally fabulous; or at least anything she could put her name to and pay someone else to do the clever stuff. So long as it opened doors for more status, more money, more fame, more diamonds. Brandy had it all perfectly mapped out in her head alright; she had a plan for every possible pathway and there was nothing that would get in her way. Success could only ever be measured in fame and column inches, after all; nothing else counted. Hell, she'd have her own darn theme park before long. Forget Dollywood, imagine roller-coasting over the curves of a giant Princess Alexander? The ultimate trip.

Brandy reached in her Chanel purse for her compact. Lipstick could be reapplied in public in the afternoon, so Gem always told her, but never in the evening, as it was vulgar. Pah! What the hell could the king of Vegas possibly know about the limits of vulgarity! Brandy chuckled at the absurdness of it all before admiring herself in her compact, dreaming of tiaras and ballgowns.

'Brandy?'

That was bloody quick, thought Brandy, wondering if Gem had even made it to the restroom. She took her time, carefully finishing a final slick of lipstick, knowing how much it irritated the hell out of Gem when she reapplied at the dinner table. She snapped her compact with a flourish and looked up, clearing her throat to pitch her 'cutesy' voice just right. She stared and blinked, unable to quite believe her eyes at what stood before her. She stared for what seemed like hours. Her pulse raced in shock and she opened her mouth but all that came out was a strangulated squeak. If she didn't know better she would have thought she was looking into a mirror in some crazy parallel universe. Those same green eyes looking back at her, cheekbones you could open an oyster with, smooth skin the colour of cappuccino, thick dusty blond-coloured hair.

'Hey sis,' said Paolo, nervously holding his clammy palm out to Brandy.

Mercedes triumphantly pulled a pretty polka-dot silk scarf from her pussy and the crowd cheered.

'Get offffffff!' shouted a heckler.

'Ooh, we have critics in the audience tonight, boys and girls,' said Griselda through the mike as he rushed onto the stage with the wind behind him and ushered Mercedes into the wings, leaving her lone silk scarf stranded on the stage.

'It's a tired old punchline,' complained the heckler. 'When's she gonna pull it out of her arse?!' Boos and hisses rang out in the crowd.

'Well, I never,' said Griselda, fixing a malicious glare on the heckler. 'You know where the Velvet Taco is for that sort of thing, darling. Our girls here are pure class,' he said, puffing up his hair with one hand. 'And to prove it,' he continued, bending to pick up the scarf from the stage, letting out a huge fart as he came back up, 'one hundred per cent polyester, it says here on the label.' The audience chuckled. 'Do you know how many polys were killed to make this fine scarf? Ooh and it smells of – er – roses too,' he said, wafting it gingerly under his large pelican beak of a nose. 'Hmm, I wondered where they'd been keeping all the bouquets backstage today.' The crowd roared with laughter.

'Another classy night at the Monte,' sighed Sienna, shaking her head. Ma and Pepper must be in another world. Schtick was one thing but where was the glamour these days? Sienna fretted about how ill Ma was. She'd certainly have to be at death's door to be anywhere other than in the club, ruling her beloved Pinkie's legacy with an iron rod.

'Oh my goodness, the champagne guy just upped and left, and not a peep,' said Paige, nudging Sienna and motioning over at the empty space at the bar. 'Didn't even hafta talk to him. So he *was* just a nice admirer after all.'

'Hmm. Maybe. Can't tell any more,' said Sienna absent-mindedly.

'Hey, there's a *really* cute guy at that table,' said Paige, her eyes already darting elsewhere, 'and I swear he keeps looking at us.' She giggled tipsily.

'Yeah. Whatever,' said Sienna, her thoughts turning to Max and realising she was missing him already after their amazing early evening lovemaking. He was like a drug. The more time she was with him, the more she needed. They'd felt so close tonight, like neither had wanted to let go, but she was paying the price with the biggest come-down now he was gone from her side. She wondered how he was faring with his father tonight. She had gleaned that Max had a troubled relationship with him, but she wished he'd just drop the 'tough man' act and open up about it – that would be a real mark of strength. The irony wasn't lost on Sienna that she could be more under-standing than Max could ever imagine, given her own past.

'For real, Sienna! Check the cute guy out,' urged Paige, jostling her housemate playfully.

'Babe, c'mon. Are you on heat tonight?'

'Aw spoilsport,' whined Paige. 'You found your Prince Charming in the Monte. Why shouldn't I cast my net here too?' Sienna found herself unable to argue with that. And after all, Max was the catch of the century.

'Okay. You got me. Let's window shop for any "perfect tens", and then it's home – we have an early start in the morning,' relented Sienna, comforting herself with thoughts of sweet dreams of Max.

'You're my only family now both our parents are gone,' pleaded Paolo. It wasn't going very well. Once Brandy had stopped goldfishing back at the dining table, she had ushered Paolo over to the far end of the restaurant bar to afford them some privacy. Paolo had obviously been hopeful for a display of affection but Brandy had fended him off with a drinks menu waved dramatically under his nose. Why on earth did people think it was a mistake they'd lost touch with someone? Brandy had thought sourly. There was usually a darn good reason for someone to avoid contact for eighteen years, and Brandy still felt no prick in her conscience about orchestrating her brother's demise. In fact she thought he'd have got the hint after Daddy had him sent off to the institution when they were children. And yet here he was, all these years later, wanting a reconciliation? Well, there was no accounting for stupidity; he'd obviously inherited their mother's brains.

Brandy had now been yawning her way through their small talk for a full ten minutes, the conversation having as much emotional warmth as her weekly interaction with her dry cleaner. That is, until Paolo broke the news about their Mami's death. Brandy had immediately perked up at that point, even ordering another glass of champagne for them both, much to Paolo's ill-concealed distress. But it was true that Brandy had felt a wave of relief at the news, for now there was no chance of some low-down Puerto Rican streetwalker mother appearing to embarrass the hell out of Brandy as she made her way up the fame ladder. Her biography had been carefully crafted to hint at a touch of exotic Latin spice in her background without once revealing exactly who – or what – her mother had been. No, the only person Brandy had ever cried real tears over was dear Daddy. The way he had stared lifelessly up at her after his heart gave out. She knew she probably shouldn't have been fucking his business partner when she was fifteen, but Daddy simply had to understand that he wasn't giving his daughter enough attention. Sure, he gave her dance classes, acting classes, couture, credit cards, ponies, a Malibu pad for parties, and had even got rid of Paolo and Mami at her behest, but Brandy always needed more. Even in the womb her greed had meant she had come out three times the size of her poor younger twin, meaning Paolo had been in incubation for a nail-biting few weeks. Brandy was obviously destined to be a winner from day one, and it was a dog-eat-dog world out there anyway. She'd already refused to answer to her 'drab' birth name, Luisa, by the age of ten, choosing for herself instead a name far more fitting for a princess. There was always someone more pretty, more popular, or more wealthy who Brandy needed to catch up with as she grew up, and Mr Topley-Bush was giving her some well-deserved rewards that Daddy couldn't. It was no wonder Daddy had checked out when the shock of his little princess screwing his middle-aged business partner proved too much.

Brandy hadn't been sure if it was the principle of the affair or the actual vision of Daddy's innocent little sugar in a strappy leather harness knelt on the solid oak office bureau delivering the mother of all blowjobs to Mr Topley-Bush whilst having the NASA desk paperweight slid up her pussy rhythmically that had finally killed her father. Brandy had cried buckets as she cradled him, waiting for the ambulance. She had only been showing initiative, after all; she just hadn't expected Daddy to be walking into his office on a Sunday like that.

'So I just want to say – look, I don't hold anything against you, Brandy. We were just kids when I was sent away. I'm sure you didn't mean for it all to escalate like it did. Twelve is so young. Things get out of hand in life sometimes, I know that. But you're my only family now.' Paolo looked pleadingly into his sister's eyes, looking for a flicker of warmth. 'I just want us to – maybe get to know each other now. It's not too late. We are twins; that bond doesn't just die.'

'What do you want, Paolo, is it money?' asked Brandy directly. 'You know, with Mami not being around any more to support you with her hooking and all that.'

Paolo sat back in his chair and let his mouth drop.

'No, Brandy, you don't understand, *I* was supporting *her* once I finally got released from the mental home. She didn't have any money. All her cash from the men went on booze.'

'And smack.'

'Yeah,' sighed Paolo, his eyes downcast. 'That's why I've been doing cash-in-hand jobs since I came into town. My felonies show up on my Sheriff's Card. I stole a couple of times, you know . . . food and stuff . . . I got caught stealing meds for Mami from a hospital. Doesn't sound good, I know, and I'm not proud of it. But what could I do? I needed to get stuff for Mami. She was in a real bad way, Brandy, and . . . I couldn't support both of us and her habit on my wages teaching salsa and doing bar work. Forget getting the stage work I always dreamed of, I had to graft every spare second of the day just to keep Mami going. The cops came down hard on me because they knew Mami, they thought she was trash, and assumed I was going the same way too. And so now? Well, I've no hope of getting any job in the casinos. But the Bronx has too many bad memories for me to want to go back there.'

'Console yourself for a start that you'd never have made it on to the stage like me. You never got to the level I did before Daddy sent you on your extended vacation. He did you a favour really. So let's get the story straight,

Mami bows out, you're seeing me in all the magazines and you decide to tap your dear sister for some cash. Am I right?'

'No!' insisted Paolo. 'God, no, I can always find ways to earn cash somehow, always have done. Brandy, you're all I have left now. I don't know, I thought – I thought we could be friends. It's not like we grew up together after what ... '

'After what I did? You can say it ... '

'No, it's okay, I haven't come for retribution. I just want to move on in my life, I just want us be friends. That's all.'

'How gallant.'

'I'm trying to reach out here, sis. Although there's just one thing I wanted to know. Did you ever tell our father the truth after he sent me away?'

Brandy tapped her foot impatiently and left the question unanswered as she cast her eyes about the restaurant. She could see Gem Green motioning for the cheque. He'd be off to the poker tables soon. Brandy was losing interest in this whole drama rapidly.

'I can help you get a job on the show,' she said suddenly. Paolo's face lit up.

'What? For real? You don't mean ... '

'Yeah, I can get you in as a cleaner or something,' Brandy sneered cruelly, waiting for a reaction.

'Oh cool, I mean, yeah great,' smiled Paolo, genuinely grateful. 'Anything, sis. Wow, I really appreciate that. Jeez, that would be great to even be near other dancers. Who cares what I'm doing. Just the smell of the theatre, the hairspray, the greasepaint. Beats digging rockeries, that's for sure! Wow, thanks!'

'Okay. Let me find my guys and I'll get them to have a word with you. Why don't you meet me outside in . . . ' Brandy checked her Rolex. 'Say fifteen minutes and I'll see what I can do?'

'Great!'

'In fact, meet me in the parking lot. I may as well give you a ride home too.'

'Oh, that's so cool! Thank you!' beamed Paolo, standing up and brushing down his new suit proudly. 'I'll head down there right away and wait. Thanks again, you don't know how much it means.'

'Indeed,' said Brandy, leaning back gingerly and grimacing as Paolo attempted to kiss her on the cheek.

Fifteen minutes to the second and Brandy was in the parking lot with two of her goons, looking on as they beat the crap out of Paolo. She stood well back so as not to get any blood spattered on her gown. Her guys were doing a fine job. Paolo was now curled up in a ball, groaning with each blow.

'Get his face, boys,' Brandy barked, examining her nail polish closely for chips. If Paolo thought he could waltz in to her life looking fine and fit with better skin than her, he was tripping, thought Brandy. Let alone with a thinly veiled attempt to tap her for money with a guilt

trip; if he thought he was getting one single bean off
Brandy Alexander's plate, he obviously knew nothing about
her. Evidently, since he'd fallen for her offer of a job – and
a ride home! As if! Brandy had been rather pleased Mami
was gone – it meant any nasty little skeletons or surprises
could be ruled out – and now she was wiping out Paolo
from that equation too – if not for good then at least for
another twenty years. She could get thoroughly comfortable with that. Brandy called off the boys as Paolo's wailing
for help was finally irritating her. She went over to survey
the damage. Paolo was covered in blood, shaking and
sobbing.

'Nice work, darlings. Radio through and let them know
they can put the security cameras back on in five minutes,'
she purred over at the heavies.

'Now, dearest brother,' said Brandy, getting as close to
Paolo as she dare, 'you're going back to where you came
from, okay? Take your cheap suit and your big, pretty-boy
green eyes back to New York. I've done you a big favour
like I did all those years ago. Now, I'm going on a nice
vacation this week, and when I return my life will carry
on as normal, without you in it. Got that?' Paolo groaned
by way of reply as he clutched his stomach.

'Oooh, what's that?' asked Brandy, crouching and
stretching her hand out to Paolo's neck as she spied something glinting underneath all the blood. 'Something shiny?
I like shiny things.'

'Mami . . . It's . . . Mami's,' cried Paolo softly.

'A crucifix?' said Brandy, holding the pendant between her thumb and forefinger as she knelt down beside him. 'Oh Paolo,' she laughed softly, 'my dear, dear brother. Jesus won't save you now, darling. He couldn't save Mami and he can't save you. It's every man for himself, you should know that.' And with that she ripped the cross from her brother's neck and popped it in her purse with a flourish, before standing and turning on her heel, leaving Paolo on the floor behind her, bleeding.

Chapter 6

The sliver of raw steak sat uninvitingly on its plate on the dresser. Despite its alleged properties as a cure for a black eye, Blue couldn't imagine how this little slice of topside was really going to do anything for the bruise blossoming over his right eye. How unladylike, he thought to himself, wrestling the slippery chilled meat into place before shivering at the metallic smell of cold raw flesh so close to his nostrils. Blue had switched to a waistline-trimming macrobiotic diet the second he'd bagged his gorgeous sweetheart Julian two years ago, so now the only meat he usually allowed to pass his lips wasn't fit for conversation at the queen's tea party.

Blue gave a little snort at the thought of Julian and their rapidly declining relationship. It just seemed to be one long squabble these days. Needless to say it was yet another of their public fracas that had landed Blue with a smart left hook last night in Pure nightclub. Blue had always allowed for the fact that someone in the music industry as beautiful as Julian might just play the field, but Blue certainly hadn't expected him to be playing footsie with a girl in front of him, let alone a girl with a mean left hook. They trained so darn hard these days, you couldn't tell if you were dealing with Arthur or Martha half the time, Blue mused.

Unable to stand the smell of raw steak any longer, Blue decided to bathe his bruise in chilled champagne instead; a much more likely source of healing properties than a cow's backside. Making his way into his kitchen, he wondered how he would conceal the swelling at work, and decided a nice rhinestoned eye patch would do the trick. He was sure he had one somewhere in his dressing-up box from the time when a supermodel had conjunctivitis on a shoot a few years back; he just needed to have a little rummage around. It didn't matter if he was a few minutes late for work now, since Brandy had left yesterday and wouldn't be clocking him in for a few blissful months. Blue could hardly contain his joy at the prospect of all that time without the vicious old bag breathing fire in his direction every other second. Today would be practically like a vacation with just the hapless yet gorgeous Paige to worry about. Blue found himself breaking into a cheerful whistle.

Paolo checked himself in the rear-view mirror of Tiny's truck, which he had borrowed for the morning, and which was now parked up at one of the Follies Casino tradesman's entrances. The reflection staring back was the result of a few hours' careful dressing and strategic grooming that morning. A baseball cap pulled down low to hide a steri-stripped gash above his eyebrow, aviator shades to hide a black eye, a hoodie pulled tight around the neck by the drawstring hid bruises where the goons had gripped Paolo's throat, and a thick, even covering of Sharon's foundation over his angular cheekbones hid the friction burn of a boot-sole. Paolo's lips were still a little swollen but there wasn't much he could do about that. Some women paid good money for the effect, he thought to himself, a hollow chuckle escaping.

Paolo's get-up certainly made him look dramatic, but he didn't want his cuts or bruises making him look like some thug from downtown, or some vagrant that security would have whisked off the premises in a gnat's breath. No, all he wanted to do was search Brandy's dressing room for his crucifix. It was a slim chance he'd find it. If his sister had realised how much it meant to him she might well have already disposed of it, especially considering she was positively glowing last week at the news of Mami's death. But Paolo was desperate to retrieve his one remaining reminder of his mother. Even if his mission was fruitless and he didn't find the crucifix, he wasn't going to skip town at Brandy's command without knowing he'd at least tried.

Paolo reached for Sharon's compact from the glove box and gave one last dust of powder to his cheekbones. His bruises were in full bloom after a week but they'd fade soon enough, and they were faring well under make-up. Thank God no bones had been broken. It had taken a while to be able to walk properly after the beating though, so Paolo was happy to have to wait a week to approach Brandy's workplace – he had to be sure she was away on the vacation she'd mentioned or else there was no question she'd have him ejected immediately if she thought for a minute he was back on her patch. Paolo wasn't quite sure yet how he would sweet talk his way past the stage door but he could be pretty silver tongued when needed – after all, he'd been in enough scrapes with the cops to have learned how to bargain with even the most unreasonable jobsworth. Paolo was annoyed at all this trouble just to try to get his crucifix back, but it was all he had left of his Mami. Brandy had only taken it to spite him; it wasn't even worth much except for sentimental value, which clearly wasn't something she gave a crap about. At least Paolo knew now that his sister hadn't changed one bit. If anything she'd curdled even more over the years, if that was possible. But at least now he'd be able to get on with his life knowing he'd at least tried to make an effort to mend bridges.

Paolo suddenly felt a pang for Sharon as he snapped her compact shut and placed it carefully back in the glove box. He'd told her he had an important interview and couldn't turn up looking like a hood. She'd been more than happy to help him cover up his cuts and bruises. Sharon would be upset when he went back to the Bronx. She had been like Florence Nightingale the past week, feeding Paolo chilli-chicken soup and dosing him up with arnica and vitamin E to help him recover. He hadn't meant for her to even see him in such a state, she'd just turned up at his motel room unannounced, hoping to ask him out for a beer. Paolo had only answered thinking it would be his landlord wanting his week's rent. Sharon had burst into hysterical tears when she first saw Paolo's face; he told her he'd been set upon by a gang of drunk British tourists in Union Jack T-shirts. It was the only thing he could think of on the spot, and he was too ashamed to tell the truth; Sharon had seemed fairly convinced. Before he could bat an eyelid, she had installed herself in his bedsit, switching to nurse mode. Overwhelmed that someone even cared, Paolo had offered to pay her for her time, but Sharon got upset at that and threw his only china plate at the wall. Paolo realised it had been taken completely the wrong way, but he was unused to anyone doing something nice for him; he'd never had that before. He only wanted to attempt to show his gratitude. He didn't have much money but didn't know what else he could possibly offer.

As a few days passed Paolo fretted that this nurse-patient arrangement would forge a closeness in Sharon's mind that wasn't there for Paolo. She was a sweet thing, but he hadn't felt a big chemistry when they had fucked. Neither could he tell her about his Mami now; she'd probably be hurt he hadn't mentioned it before. The last thing Paolo wanted to do was hurt Sharon; she was a genuinely lovely girl. Maybe he'd make out he was leaving because he couldn't pay his way in Vegas. He hated lying, but the truth of being run out of town by his own sister was pathetic. Besides, what would Sharon really want with a total failure like him? On paper he was no more than a convicted, penniless son of an overdosed hooker. If anything, he was saving her from ending up with a loser.

A few cars were now pulling up around him in the parking lot and Paolo knew he needed to get his mission over with before too many of the 'Venus in Furs' cast poured in for rehearsals and spotted him in Brandy's dressing room. He focused on the task in hand and swung down from the seat of Tiny's truck. He strolled slowly and confidently – though not *over*confidently – towards the stage door. He wanted to keep his manner the right side of approachable and unthreatening to ensure a successful blag onto the premises. A couple of pretty dancers with kit bags slung over their shoulders approached from the other direction. They gave Paolo a horrified look before nodding a hello and hurrying on ahead towards the stage door. This immediately worried him – perhaps he really did look like a tramp – or his attempts to hide his battered face had been less successful than he'd hoped. He tried to ignore the tendrils of self-consciousness creeping over him. He'd be in and out in all of ten minutes with any luck. He nearly walked straight into another dancer. Her loud gasp registered in Paolo's ears, and he immediately bowed his head, hiding his face from her.

'Oh my God, sorry, I'm not late really, I've been here

ten minutes already, I was just stretching outside,' garbled the girl at Paolo before scooting ahead of him and through the stage door without so much as a backward glance. Mildly puzzled by her outburst, Paolo looked about him but couldn't see anyone else she might have been talking to. He shrugged and leaned in for the double doors. He had no idea what kind of security would be at reception, but he kept his fingers crossed that they'd be easy to charm. The receptionist looked up and gasped dramatically. Paolo had a sinking feeling that his bruises must be coming through already. Dammit, he should have checked his foundation one last time. He held his hands up in a mercy gesture and gave a wry smile, ready to switch on the charm.

'Brandy! What are you – you're back! How – when . . . ?' started the girl on reception before springing up from her seat, wringing her hands. Paolo was silenced; his smile froze. That certainly wasn't a greeting he had expected.

'I'm sorry, I had no idea you were staying on in Vegas,' blustered the receptionist. 'I thought you were flying last night – your vacation – only – well, no-one informed me your plans had changed. Oh wow, you're already in your dance gear and ready to go. I don't think the crew are all here yet,' she continued without breathing. 'You just get to your dressing room, Miss Alexander, and we'll take care of everything.' She motioned for Paolo to move on down the corridor. Paolo stayed rooted to the spot in astonishment, wondering if he'd just entered some kind of parallel universe. Was this a wind-up? This madwoman surely couldn't think he was his own twin sister? Why, he was clearly . . . wearing make-up . . . shades . . . oh yeah, and unisex sports apparel . . .

'Er, Brandy, you okay?' asked the receptionist. Paolo paused, not knowing what was the right thing to do or say. This was surreal. He did the first thing, the only thing, that came into his head.

'I'm fine,' he squeaked, clearing his throat and flashing a plaintive wobble of a smile. 'Just a bit off-colour,' he purred softly and wandered slowly down the corridor, unable to believe his luck. Ten minutes, and he could grab his necklace, be out of there and packing his bag before Brandy came back from her vacation to find him and send him back to the East Coast herself in a coffin. Now where in hell was he going in this place? As he drifted away, he couldn't fail to hear the receptionist shrieking down her telephone.

'Blue, you better get your fairy ass down here now. The bitch is back and she's looking like a bag of shit in a track-suit. Sound the four-minute warning!'

Blue puffed his way down the corridor, adjusting his rhine-stoned eye patch hastily. Just what the hell was Brandy back for? She had decided the cast change was the perfect strategic opportunity to nip off and take a few months' break to 'rest' herself. Then she'd come back with a bang looking ten years younger to a wave of fresh publicity, once the new cast was settled in and her understudy had made a thoroughly average impression. So why was she still hanging around? Blue chastised himself for relaxing too soon. It was bad enough she was returning to her reign of terror, but Melody on reception had reported that she was so bombed out she'd hardly been able to speak and was even in her sweats in public. Well, it wasn't exactly the first time Blue had seen Brandy rolling up to work high if she'd been out partying; although she still usually managed to keep the polish on the surface, thinking nothing of coming to the theatre in a pristine Versace cocktail dress and 'red-carpet hair' from the night before. Blue could only imagine she'd got so wasted last night she'd forgotten she had a plane to catch. Brandy had been known to forget what day it was, leading the kind of life that was one eternal party. Occasionally Blue would have to confiscate the arsenal of exotic prescription drugs from her bottomless purse if she'd been going for a few nights in a row. He rolled his eyes, knowing that her moods usually went through the gears of game show host, to unbearably stroppy, to downright aggressive, to passing out. She'd get so bad sometimes she could have a row in her dressing room with herself.

Blue braced himself and burst through into the show-girls' dressing area to be confronted by the sight of a small group of the chorus girls huddled nervously whispering to each other as Paolo drifted quietly from one station to the next, apparently looking for something. Blue sighed. Yep, Brandy's wasted, he thought. Shapeless tracksuit, cap and shades? Come-down apparel. Dead giveaway.

'Brandy, dearest,' said Blue, wafting towards Paolo to take his arm. Paolo flinched fearfully.

'Darling, wow, you're still in Vegas? Come into your palace, devotion,' urged Blue, wanting to get his boss into the safety of her dressing room – for everyone *else*'s safety, that is. Plopping Paolo onto Brandy's velvet throne, Blue closed the door of the dressing room and shut out the escalating hum of gossiping whispers from the gathering chorus line.

'You want some vitamin C to sober up, sweetie pops?' asked Blue in his baby voice usually reserved for, well, babies or drunk diva adults, as he checked Brandy's mini-bar for some orange juice. His offer was greeted with silence.

'Okaaaay,' he pressed on, pouring sweet sticky juice into a champagne flute, 'now tell Aunty Blue why you didn't make your flight? You okay, devotion? I thought you were all psyched up for your surgery?' Blue looked up from his juice pouring to see Brandy hanging her head as she fidgeted in the throne, sitting awkwardly on her hands.

'Brandy?' asked Blue, knowing in his gut something was very wrong. She would have picked a row with him by now, surely, Blue thought to himself. And what was with the incognito disguise in her dressing room? Blue decided to take a calculated risk while the queen bee was in such an anaesthetised state. He reached over and pulled off the hat and shades.

★   ★   ★

Sienna and Paige looked at each other with raised eyebrows as a piercing squeal rang out from Brandy's locked dressing room.

'Thank God. Hopefully he's put the bitch out of her misery,' said Tashonya as she pulled on her dance tights. The whole company was now assembled in their large dressing room, preparing for a fresh day of rehearsals.

'Yeah, Brandy was off her face, wasn't she!' laughed Alexia. 'Did you see that hoodie she was wearing! And what was she doing checking out all our make-up stations like that?'

'She was on the warpath for something, for sure,' grumbled Tashonya.

'Yeah, I knew it was too much to hope that we'd be free of her for a few months,' said Alexia. 'Oh goodness, Paige!' she shrieked suddenly.

'Oh God, yes! Paige, you won't get to take her role now! Oh babe, that's a bummer, are you okay?' asked Tashonya, rushing over to Paige's station.

'Yeah, I guess,' sighed Paige. 'You know, I really thought that understudy part was gonna be my lucky break.' In fact, Paige had wanted to throw something when she heard the news of Brandy's return as she'd walked in. She'd been a feather frond away from stardom, and now it was cruelly snatched back. Just like when that horse-faced Velveeta Weinstein had stolen the beauty pageant crown that Paige had been assured was all hers after administering a private flash of her perfect naked breasts at the ageing director of the Krispy Syrup Co. Evidently Velveeta had been prepared to go the extra inch with him – or the extra seven inches to be precise, the tramp. Obviously she wasn't fussy about what kind of Krispy Syrup she put in *her* strudel-hole.

Now, as Paige looked about her at the beautiful chorus girls titivating themselves at their mirrors, she knew in her heart that four months as the star of the show had been a jammy move, especially after being so terrible in her audition. If something seemed too good to be true, it usually was. But that didn't ease the frustration one bit. Paige was annoyed that Sienna hadn't exactly come to her emotional rescue either; she was far too preoccupied with some crap to do with loverboy Max. Paige kept a glimmer of hope that Brandy had just missed her flight or something silly. God forbid she'd had a change of heart and would be staying in Vegas. If that was the case Paige might well have to resort to some old-fashioned tried and tested desperate measures for sabotage to get her chance in the spotlight.

'Brandy, what the hell have you done with your extensions? Ripped them out or something? And what's with the eye? You gotta tell me what happened! You've been seeing that bastard John again, haven't you?'

Paolo stared at Blue and blinked.

'I thought you'd moved on from him! Has he done this to you, Brandy? Your hair! All your luscious locks gone!

You gotta get one of your wigs on, Christ! And your face . . . I thought you'd exaggerated all that domestic violence stuff for the press.' Blue caught himself before he said any more, realising he'd have to tread carefully or risk another black eye himself. He fingered his own eye patch protectively, conscious that Brandy hadn't even mentioned his own appearance yet. Paolo hung his head and cleared his throat to say something. Nothing came out.

'At least that's what you told me, Brandy, remember?' blurted Blue, trying to regain ground. 'I even thought I saw you drawing all those bruises on your face when you wanted to get rid of him.' A wave of guilt washed over Blue as he remembered the times he'd laughed about Brandy's cartoon black eyes. They'd looked so phoney! But perhaps they had been real after all? His guilt was assuaged within seconds, however, by memories of how many things Brandy had thrown at *him* in the dressing room when he pulled a corset too tight. Well, she still wasn't saying anything as she sat before him now. Maybe she was in shock? Blue wondered. Or maybe she'd simply got a taste of her own medicine for a change? Scratched, beaten, her hair butchered off; Blue would never wish violence on any human being. But then Brandy Alexander was barely human. Why, she'd practically scalped Viva, her last understudy, when she got a little too much attention for Brandy's liking. Although as she sat before him in the dressing room now, Blue could almost for a second, through the bruises, see something – softer – in Brandy's face. He looked carefully. Those cheekbones were as sharp as ever, that jaw as chiselled, the eyes still sparkling green but there was something . . . maybe one or two wrinkles he'd never noticed at the eyes – or at least the one that wasn't swollen under all the make-up . . . He just couldn't put his finger on it.

'Devotion, you don't need to say a thing. You wanna go home? I'll escort you back to your house right now,' offered Blue magnanimously.

'No, I—' Paolo blurted, his eyes laced with panic as they darted around the dressing room.

'Oh, you wanna work, darling? Take your mind off things? That's a good idea. The cruise can wait. You can always reschedule when you're feeling up to it. You sound husky, by the way. You're not back on the weed too, are you?'

'Sore throat,' whispered Paolo softly.

'Here, drink the OJ,' soothed Blue, mentally building a juicy picture of a dramatic screaming match between Brandy and John, laced with narcotics, champagne, fists and a large pair of scissors. A pleasurable little shiver ran up his back at the sheer *Dynasty*-ness of it all.

'I just – fell down some stairs,' ventured Paolo.

'Sure you did, devotion,' said Blue cooperatively, knowing it was never a good idea to press Brandy for information. 'Well, whatever happened, on the bright side you were gonna have a facelift, new cheeks and chin and a new nose anyway,' he reassured. 'They'll be able to fix you up better than ever. And don't worry, your secret's safe with Aunty Blue.'

Paolo stared back, a look of pure bewilderment on his face.

'C'mon then. Let's get you into your leotard,' said Blue. Paolo's expression turned to one of horror.

Sienna really couldn't deal with Paige's childish temper right now. Her stomach was eating itself as she starved her way through her first week of rehearsals, and she'd just had to miss a call from Max while Blue addressed the cast in the dressing room to announce that Brandy was staying on in 'Venus in Furs' until further notice. Sienna had been trying to pin Max down for days, and missing his call in order to listen to bad news made her want to hurl one of her dumb calorie-controlled, gluten-free breakfast bars at Brandy's Botoxed forehead for causing such a shitty start to her day. Sienna felt so depressed, and surviving on little more than lettuce wasn't helping her mood. Max had suddenly bailed out of their last arrangement for a date, saying he had to go away on urgent business. It wasn't something Sienna would have ordinarily minded, but they'd been so close that evening in the pool, so in love. The sex had been unbelievable. But like a light turning off, Max had been so distant since his meeting with his father last week. It made Sienna insecure as hell.

'I mean, she doesn't even need the work,' fumed Paige, angrily yanking a brush through her wild brunette mane.

'Why can't she just piss off on her extended vacation and leave a door open for someone else? Sienna, you're best mates with Blue, can you get him to talk to her and—'

'Paige, please!' begged Sienna, desperately trying to listen to her voicemail in peace. 'You'll get your turn, sweetie. Brandy'll call in with a hangover soon enough and you'll get your moment in the spotlight, you'll see.'

'But four months of glory, Sienna! Down the drain! I was gonna be up there in lights for four whole months!' Paige took a sideways glance at Sienna's hair, before tying her locks into an identical neat high bun, giving herself a nice natural facelift. 'I bet Brandy did this deliberately! The cow!'

'Paige!' snapped Sienna crossly, her head pounding with calorie withdrawal symptoms. 'This isn't about you, darling. Brandy's a law unto herself. Put yourself in poor Honey's shoes, she got fired. You're still here, okay? And you still have the understudy part. So you wait a while to solo, big deal, at least you're next in line in the wings, babe.'

Paige blinked in surprise at the outburst.

'Oh, I'm sorry, darling,' Sienna said immediately. 'It's just my thumping headache – and Max, I can't get hold of him. Damn you, Max Power!' she cursed at her phone, shaking it crossly. As if on cue, it vibrated.

'Max!' Sienna gasped as she answered the call within a heartbeat. 'Where are you? No, didn't you get my messages? Atlanta? Well, at least there's no gambling there, I s'pose . . . don't snap at me like that, Max, I'm not having a good day, I just . . . what's wrong with you? Why are you talking to me like this? Yes, of course I know you have clients but . . . okay. I miss you . . . ' Sienna trailed off and put her phone back on her dresser quietly, her long-awaited conversation clearly at an end. She picked up her make-up brush and silently powdered her blushing cheeks.

'Trouble in paradise?' murmured Paige under her breath as she kept her eyes on her own reflection at her make-up station, barely able to keep a smirk from creeping onto the corners of her perfect rosebud lips.

Paolo had locked himself into Brandy's bathroom at the first available opportunity. How in hell had this all snowballed so quickly? Paolo could hardly wrap his head around it; sure, he and Brandy had been identical as beautiful children – he'd always had such a pretty face. But he hadn't thought for a second he would pass for a chick at thirty. He didn't know whether to laugh or cry. One thing was clear, Paolo was already agape at the revelations about his sister that had been pouring from Blue's unsuspecting mouth. It was like being a fly on the wall. Now Paolo had a much better understanding of why everyone had recoiled in fear everywhere he walked. His bitch of a sister was clearly a one-woman walking apocalypse.

Paolo stared in the mirror, deeply aware of the five o'clock shadow emerging at his jaw line. He wondered what path to take. Climb out of the bathroom window now and run for his life? Where to? There was no way on God's earth he was going back to the East Coast if Brandy wasn't here to drag him back by force with her goons. It was so incredibly tempting to try and stick it out for a day at least. He was still too injured to be much use at manual labour and hanging out with showgirls at a luxury casino sure beat moping around his grim apartment for the day. And who knew what secrets he could discover about Brandy by walking in her Manolos for a day? But could he really get away with it? What would happen if he got found out? Paolo's mind reeled with a world of possibilities and a strong sense of mischief. It was simply too good an opportunity to pass up – and if he got the chance to wreak a little havoc in Brandy's life in the next few hours, well, then he figured he was more than due a little payback.

It was now or never – he had to get into character and fast. Brandy's huge dressing room was an eye-opener in itself. A tacky velvet upholstered throne, tasteless marble and gold-effect console, and two vast walls of floor-to-ceiling mirror, smattered with lipstick kisses and groaning with pasted-up news cuttings of herself. Paolo imagined Brandy making love to herself in the mirror like the narcissistic bitch she'd always been and let out a snort. The room was over-spilling with a cornucopia of bouquets, feathers, wigs and jewellery, but the icing on the cake had been when Paolo had spotted the 'Press for Champagne' button installed into the wall next to the light switch. He'd almost cracked a bruised rib trying to keep himself from roaring with laughter at that one. He was pretty sure even Mariah Carey didn't have her own Cristal hotline when the champagne urge called. He was pretty sure he had just enough ammunition so far to get inside her head for the day at least. But how to get through it without anyone noticing Brandy now had hairy hands, an Adam's apple and a cock?

'No spitting on the walls,' said Butter, the club's dumpy hostess, as she ushered Honey from the dressing rooms into the main lounge. 'We may not all be ladies here at the Velvet Taco but we leave that behaviour to the punters.'

'Uh huh,' grunted Honey, trying to muster some enthusiasm.

'And no chucking champagne on the floor, it rots our carpets. Pour it into the ice bucket when they're not looking. It's a ten per cent commission on champagne, twenty-five per cent on liquor bottles.'

'Right.' Honey nodded.

'Now, etiquette,' continued Butter, pulling out a chair for Honey to sit on at the back of the lounge. The room was huge, some kind of twenty-four-hour strippers' hypermarket, thought Honey. No peeling wallpaper or red curtains here. The Velvet Taco had a vast pink neon walkway extending out from a huge pink velvet vaginal stage entrance, leading off to various podiums, two of which were currently occupied by dancers, grinding wearily.

'No kissing, no touching, blah blah you know the

licensing rules,' rattled off Butter, illustrating her points with the requisite two-inch-long, squared-off French manicured nails, 'but the golden rule is, *never* mess with another girl's money. Got it?' Honey looked back at her blankly.

'I mean, if she's working a guy, you don't disturb her or go to her table without being invited. You never call her by her name in front of people, you don't know what name she's using that night. And if you see her outside the club, that's doubly important, especially if she's with a guy. A nod will suffice.'

'Got it,' said Honey obediently.

'And it helps to share your tips with the waiting staff and security here. They'll look after you, seat you with the high rollers and bachelor parties.'

'Of course.'

'Now, let me take you to the overspill room,' said Butter, motioning with a talon. Honey looked up anxiously. 'Not that kind of overspill,' the hostess sighed. 'It's for busy nights or if we have male strip troupes in town.'

'It's okay, I've got the idea,' said Honey. 'I need to get working. When can I start?' Butter broke into a broad smile.

'Great, we'll just go through your papers in the office now. You have everything?' Honey nodded her reply.

'Great, so we'll give you some shifts this week. Welcome to the Velvet Taco.' Butter shook Honey's hand firmly. Honey manufactured a polite smile.

★   ★   ★

Blue rapped on the door.

'Devotion, you close to being ready? The girls are waiting.'

'Just a sec,' came Paolo's muffled voice. The dressing-room door swung open dramatically and Paolo presented himself, still sporting his tracksuit, any new stubble at his jaw covered in a mint green face pack, and his short hair wrapped up in a turban of a towel.

'Darling,' he purred gently, getting into his stride as the room snapped to attention, 'I'm feeling a little fragile. Do you think I could just watch the cast rehearsing? I'm sure the understudy can mark my parts for today, no?' He flounced his newly gloved hand onto his hip and posed in the doorway, bevelling his ankle in a ladylike manner. He hoped he wasn't overdoing it. He didn't want to come across too obviously like the trannies his Mami used to invite back to the house.

'Sure,' beamed Blue. 'Paige will be fine with that, I'm sure. Paige?' he bellowed.

'Yes, ma'am!' Paige was at Blue's side within seconds, beaming at Paolo. He smiled back at her gorgeous face.

'You can mark Brandy's part, can't you, darling?' asked Blue.

'Sure can. Thanks, Brandy, I won't let you down!' gushed Paige, all traces of her earlier temper now gone.

'Okay, get out there, girls, the director's out front waiting, leave me to my sewing machine,' barked Blue, clapping his hands theatrically.

Paolo beamed smiles at the girls as they traipsed past in line, and quickly realised his sunny disposition was garnering more than a few shell-shocked stares. He immediately traded the smile for a scowl, reminding himself that Brandy had been a bullying, bitching block of ice. It wasn't a role Paolo was slipping into effortlessly, but he'd have to learn, and fast. Although he did wonder how feasible it would be to give these poor girls the gift of seeing what Brandy Alexander might be like if she was normal – without totally giving the game away. He tried not to stare too obviously as the last of the chorus line tripped past.

A lone, deep sigh escaped from the far corner of the now-quiet room. Paolo turned his head to be confronted with the sight of possibly the most exquisite woman he'd ever seen, unfolding herself from her chair and slinking her way towards the stage entrance on her long elegant legs, a despondent swing in her shapely hips. Paolo's eyes darted all over her, unable to take enough of her in. The girl's beautiful eyes were red as though she had been crying, and she snuffled into the sleeve of her sweatshirt as she walked. Paolo tried to suppress an untimely tickle in his throat. The girl looked round and glared. Paolo found himself crossing his legs. God, she was stunning. Paolo's heart pounded as he stared at her from behind his ridiculous face mask. Was it possible to fall in love with someone within seconds? The girl's eyes clouded over with loathing.

'You really have no idea, do you?' she snapped in a strong English accent.

'Huh?' said Paolo, still mesmerised.

'You have no idea how you screw with other people's lives. Or if you do, you sure as hell don't give a damn. And you know what? I don't give a damn any more either,' the girl turned square on to Paolo, folding her arms over her ample bosom. God, this creature was magnificent.

'I mean it, I don't care any more, Brandy. If you want to fire me like you did Honey, you go for it. Because this kind of atmosphere you create isn't worth coming into work every day, I can tell you. I'd rather go back to the Monte. Do what you like. This entire week's been sheer misery, and if this is what work is gonna be like every day in this show, you can keep it.' Wow. Brandy really had been a plague, Paolo thought.

'Well?' The girl's lip was wobbling. Oh no, please don't cry, thought Paolo. He couldn't bear watching girls getting upset. He reached out to put an arm about her shoulder.

'Don't you dare lay a finger on me,' hissed the girl.

'Oh I wasn't – I was – only . . . '

'If you're gonna fire me let's get it over with,' she repeated.

'No! Not at all,' said Paolo softly, wondering how to soothe her without giving his game up. 'Sorry, I've had . . . PMS,' he blurted, knowing the second it came out of his mouth it was a pathetic cliché.

'Permanently?'

'Yeah, something like that,' said Paolo cautiously, attempting a weak laugh. 'You just get on stage with the girls – darling,' – Did Brandy ever call people *darling?* Paolo wondered, trying to remember his only recent conversation with her last week.

'And I hope your day gets better.' Jeez, that was corny but Paolo had no idea what to say. The girl stared blankly at Paolo, the wind visibly taken out of her sails. Paolo's heart was still pounding in her presence.

'Oh, okay. Blimey. Thank you, Brandy. I appreciate that.' She gave a long, puzzled look at Paolo before turning for the stage, and walking away. No, please don't go, thought Paolo, frantically trying to think of an excuse for them to talk for longer.

'Wait,' Paolo called out. She turned to face him. 'I was just compiling a list of girls to er – book in for a facial – my treat – er, how do you spell your name?'

'What do you want?' said the girl slowly.

'Oh, I know, embarrassing, spelling's not my strong point.'

'I mean, why the niceties? A facial? You actually expect me to be convinced by that? What do you want from me?'

'Nothing. Just thought it would boost morale.'

'Morale? What morale? You make it your policy not to mix with us lowly chorus girls anyway.'

'Exactly. I can see there's obviously some ground to make up.'

'S. I. E. N. N. A. And two "r"s in Starr,' enunciated the girl slowly after a long, suspicious pause. She looked straight at Paolo with her beautiful almandine eyes. 'You know what, Brandy, I think you should go home and get some rest. You just don't seem yourself at all. You can afford to take today off, you're the star of the show. Why don't you get some sleep and come back fresh tomorrow.'

'Hmm. You know what, I may just do that. Thanks . . . Sienna,' smiled Paolo, figuring he just about had the courage to bluff that ride from Blue straight to Brandy's house. All he needed to do was pretend he'd lost the door key – he was sure Blue would have a spare. Paolo hoped to God he was doing the right thing. But his encounter with Sienna, let alone uncovering more about his sister, was far too spellbinding for him to turn his back on life at the Follies just yet. Maybe he could stick it out for a few more days – weeks even. If Brandy was safely in an operating theatre before going on her cruise to recuperate – and he'd found the glossy yacht brochure in her dressing room that promised absolute isolation from the outside world – then why shouldn't he walk a few yards in her shoes and enjoy the view? She'd practically sabotaged *his* life without too much of a conscience, after all. He realised that once he took this step into Brandy's life there was no going back, he'd have to follow through all the way. And if his mask slipped and he got found out, he knew the real Brandy would be back in Vegas and filling her brother with bullets quicker than he could say jockstrap.

Chapter 7

Max swilled back the last of his whisky in one gulp, and motioned at the bottle-blonde air stewardess to bring him yet another refill. Stretching his legs out, he flicked his eyes over the film menu card absentmindedly. It had been a disastrous week and he needed to unwind, but he couldn't seem to loosen up. The half bottle of whisky was at least helping some. Maybe *Debbie Does Dallas* would have really got him in the right headspace, but the Silver Slipper private jets tended to be furnished with more tasteful fare.

Max tried to push the meeting with his father to the back of his head but Kerry Power's warning was hanging over him like a shadow. Max had assured his father over their Kobe beef and vintage Chianti last week that he was on top of things with Silver Slipper Airlines. Of course, Max should have known that if any of his stockholders were having worries about their investment they'd be straight on the phone to Kerry Power. The awkward fact was Max hadn't been entirely straight with his bondholders, but then what successful businessman ever was? He could only imagine the shady deals his father must have orchestrated over the years. All Max had done was to advance himself a little cash. After all, work was stressful, and stress relief came at a high price. A little gambling, the expensive women before Sienna . . . his leisure overheads were high. His personal casino debts had certainly escalated wildly in the last couple of years.

Max's business headquarters were based in Dallas. His clientele were affluent and Silver Slipper flights mainly reflected that, with the most popular routes being to Florida, Macau, Monaco, the Caribbean and Saudi. But business had taken a bad turn since the recession had hit. Even the very wealthy were feeling the pinch and less willing to pay over the odds for luxury flights than they once had been. In addition to which, when Max had floated the company his taste for gambling was already well developed, thanks to the sterling example his father had set for him in his formative years. Max knew he'd need just a little cash injection to tide him over and clear a few little gambling debts, so he had sold a minority shareholding in Silver Slipper, whereupon he issued some new stocks and shares to raise more capital. This was of course meant to finance the company, but he cleverly managed to 'intercept' a good chunk of it to donate to his personal leisure fund. The problem was Max had already managed to offload most of it at the blackjack tables in a very short time. Now one of his bondholders was getting fidgety at Max's evasiveness over company figures, claiming the public accounts weren't adding up. Kerry Power had been called upon to step in.

Max had been confronted by his father at their meeting. He didn't want his ridiculous son embarrassing him in the industry, he had said, before demanding Max replace the shortfall in funds immediately. If he didn't come up with the goods, Kerry would have to fund the gap himself to save face and avoid riling his industry cohorts. Kerry would then personally see to it that his debt was paid by whatever means necessary. Max was terrified. Stories of defectors sent to their concrete graves in the foundations of his father's latest high rise development weren't myths, he knew that for sure. The fact Max was his own flesh and blood made no difference; in fact, it made things worse. It had been Kerry's favourite pastime to torment and bully his son from the start. The old bastard had always accused him of being a mummy's boy, and would claim he was 'toughening him up' for his own good.

Max was now returning from a fruitless trip to Atlanta, where he had been attempting to raise enough cash to solve his spiralling situation. He had initially gone to the banks in Dallas to raise more capital straight after his father issued his ultimatum, but the banks couldn't understand why Max needed more money so quickly after financing Silver Slipper. All they could offer was a substantial cash flow loan, so long as he could prove the money was there and the loan was capable of being paid back.

Of course, with all the cash spent this was going to be impossible. Instead Max had come up with what he thought was a genius strategy to raise investment for a new plane-leasing venture. He would lease aeroplanes to other airlines as well as his own, giving himself the chance to skim a good portion off the top to straighten himself out. But he was now flying back from his meetings empty-handed. The investors had practically laughed him out of the boardroom.

'We can't understand it, Max, you only raised capital two years ago,' they had said. 'You say business is booming. Yet we're hearing from our contacts in Dallas that you're not making your aviation fuel payments. How so? And now you want to set up a *leasing* company? We're not sure you can pay the leases on your *own* fleet, Max . . . '

There was no doubt, Max realised, he was screwed. Sienna was already suspicious at his behaviour this week too. That was all he needed, for work to fuck with his relationship too; he wanted a proper future with the only decent woman he'd ever had. He was coming to the conclusion he'd have to secure more credit from one of the casinos and gamble his way out of this mess. It was what had got him here in the first place, after all. He could do it . . . he'd have to. It was the only option; being in debt to his father was worse than jail. At least he'd come out of a cell alive. The air hostess placed a fresh tumbler of whisky in front of Max and gave a flirtatious smile, flashing bright white teeth. 'Marilyn' was her name, embroidered onto her lapel in a florid swirl of gold stitching, although it took Max a few seconds to decipher through his alcoholically blurred vision.

'Anything else, Mr Power?' Marilyn asked. Max chugged back his whisky in one go, pulling a face for a second as the heat hit the back of his throat.

'Don't suppose you have any Jenna Jameson for me to watch, do you?' he enquired hopefully.

'Oh, I'm sorry, we don't have any of those sorts of movies,' Marilyn said with a little giggle. 'Is there anything else on the menu you'd like, Mr Power?'

'Which menu?' he asked idly, letting out a dissatisfied huff.

'Here's the movie menu,' she said, handing him the card he'd glanced over earlier. 'Or . . . ' An awkward pause.

'Or what?'

'Well, it depends what exactly you require, but I may be able to help if you wanted some . . . light entertainment? Charisse is preparing your evening meal. I think she may be another ten minutes.' Max liked this air hostess. She was speaking his language. He was used to women throwing themselves at him, and he had to admit it was useful sometimes, especially when everything was turning to shit. Like now. He made a mental note to see to it that Marilyn got a raise.

'Okay, you're on, I'll take the tasting menu, please.'

'With pleasure, Mr Power,' said Marilyn with a smile, deftly removing a crisp white lace glove as she knelt down beside him. She opened Max's fly and let his already hardening cock escape. She lightly trailed her glove over it. Max moaned and settled back in his seat, getting comfortable. Once her other glove was off, she massaged Max expertly until he could wait no longer and pushed her mouth down onto his cock. He let out a satisfied groan as she took his whole length deep down her throat. Now this was how to relax.

Hearing a polite cough from above, Max looked up. There stood the other air hostess, standing obediently with a tray of food. She looked discreetly in the other direction, awaiting orders.

'Ah, Charisse,' greeted Max, holding Marilyn by her platinum hair as she pumped away. 'Get your skirt up. Wanna join in the aperitifs?'

'Mr Power! That is not in my job description!'

'Aw, c'mon, baby. I'll give you a bonus.'

'I can't be bought,' she said angrily, shooting a disgusted look down at her colleague.

'Oh, don't give me that. You're an air hostess, it's what you all do. What else are you gonna do to pass the time apart from waitressing?'

'How dare you!' Charisse shrieked.

'Okay, I'll fire your ass then!'

'I'll sue your ass then!' she spat back at him.

'Try me!' he yelled at her as she stalked away furiously.

'Frigid bitch,' he slurred under his breath, settling back in to let Marilyn finish what she'd started. Why didn't he just stick to the professionals for jobs like this? he wondered, feeling his boner wilting. Great. A flaccid cock and a lawsuit from an uptight trolley dolly. A winning end to a week from hell.

Chapter 8

Paolo admired his artwork in Brandy's dressing-room mirror. Perfectly plucked and pencilled eyebrows, beautifully contoured cheeks, smooth liquid eyeliner and expertly applied false eyelashes. It had been fairly easy. While Brandy had been blossoming in her teens as the picture-perfect, spoilt Valley Girl in sunny LA with Daddy and all his money and real estate, Paolo was spending his weekends in South Bronx sobering up his Mami's Puerto Rican lady-boy friends with coffee at their cockroach-ridden rental. Mami's friends could be fun company sometimes; they weren't all as bombed out as her and at least they looked out for her when they were working the streets. The most beautiful one, Ramone, was studying to be a beauty therapist but was doing extras to pay for his final cock-to-frock operation.

Ramone liked to look after Paolo on some of the nights Mami was out. He said he didn't like the thought of a nice young boy being on his own so much, especially in South Bronx: he could easily get bored and end up falling in with a bad crowd. Truth was, Ramone loathed his side-line and would take any excuse not to have to go out and turn tricks. Paolo never thought that the lost evenings they shared messing around with face packs and hot wax and trying out different make-up for Ramone's beauty school assignments would ever come in handy later in life.

Ramone had also used the time to teach his charge a killer left hook; something he occasionally employed himself if his Johns objected when they discovered that they weren't being serviced by a lady. He thought every teenage boy in South Bronx should be able to take care of business. Paolo was grateful for this when his salsa teaching jobs were scarce and he wound up with another short spell in jail for stealing meds for his mother. In return Paolo had repaid Ramone with dance lessons; well, if he was going to become a proper lady then he'd need to be a little lighter on his feet. Ramone had sadly died not long after his foray into salsa and merengue. It seemed he blew the wrong truck driver and took a beating he couldn't recover from. They hadn't been the best of days by most people's standards but for Paolo being part of some kind of family, however abnormal, was better than being alone in the misery of the sanatorium.

All these years later Paolo thought he might be a bit rusty with a make-up brush, but no, it had come flooding back to him quite naturally. 'Blend is your friend,' Ramone always used to tell him when he'd practise new looks on Paolo's pretty face. Looking in the mirror now, Paolo was pleased with his handiwork. He had plenty of reference for Brandy's make-up look from the news cuttings pinned

all over the dressing room. He was a dead ringer, even if
he did say so himself. Well, he would be, he thought,
letting out a chuckle. He selected a spice-coloured lip liner
and carefully lined the swollen pout he'd been given cour-
tesy of his sister last week, before filling the lip colour
with a creamy Sophia Loren nude-coloured lipstick. Paolo
checked Brandy's photographs again. Ah, beauty spot.
Paolo drew the perfect black beauty mark on his right
cheek to complete the Brandy Alexander face. Brandy with
a well-concealed black eye, that is.

Paolo carefully lowered one of Brandy's stage wigs over
his own hair and set it with a spritz of Elnett. The picture
was complete, at least from the neck up. Paolo was feeling
more confident about his second day at the theatre. As he
fluffed up the wig gently with a paddle brush he reminded
himself he had to be alert at all times and pick up the
ropes bloody quickly. At least he could always blame his
apparent absent-mindedness on the effects of his 'bad fall'.
He would have to make damn sure he wasn't rumbled.
This was too good an opportunity to screw up and he had
too much to lose by being sloppy.

Now for his ensemble. He'd spent the rest of yesterday
in Brandy's palatial walk-in wardrobe, once Blue had let
him in to the house with his spare key and helpfully written
down the security code for the alarm. Apparently it wasn't
unusual for Brandy to forget it and set off her own alarm
in her bombed-out state after long partying sessions. Paolo
had barely looked around the rest of the mansion, deciding

priority had to be given over to carefully sifting through and testing out outfits. His whole motel room would have fit into her wardrobe twice. It had been a job to know where to start. Since anything crutch conscious was out of the question, Paolo had shortlisted a rehearsal wardrobe of harem pants and a nice range of high-necked tops under which he could wear a stuffed bra. He just kept Ramone in his mind as his muse. As he pulled the harem pants on, Paolo took a moment to notice his smooth, shapely ankles in the mirror. After putting together his first batch of outfits at Brandy's, he'd plundered her bathroom cabinets for beauty products before crossing town back to his motel room, whereupon he'd stayed up late into the night waxing all over, even his hands. He couldn't risk doing all that at Brandy's place; she was bound to have staff checking up on the place. If one of Brandy's housekeepers saw evidence of major hair removal or found incriminating detritus in the trash cans she'd be bound to smell a rat. Although with no cash coming in from casual labour he wouldn't be able to keep the rental going much longer, as nervous as he was about actually being right in Brandy's lair. He knew the time would come when he'd have to send her staff on a vacation so he could take up residence on her couch temporarily without scrutiny.

There was so much to remember already but Paolo just thought of it as playing Barbie in a movie. He figured once he'd got the initial mammoth task of de-fuzzing out of the way it would be manageable to maintain. Thank

God he'd excused himself from any dancing duties; all this lot was enough of a performance as it was. He'd told Marty the director that the 'fall' had left him too sore to dance. After a few minutes of fumbling Paolo had one of Brandy's bras on, heavily stuffed, and neatly concealed beneath a cute sequinned dance top.

In the remaining few hours before dawn, Paolo had barely slept thinking about what he had got himself into, but he felt right about his decision to stay on in Vegas. Or rather, the prospect of returning to the East Coast filled him with so much dread in the pit of his stomach to the point of nausea that nothing would make him go back there. Why would he want to go back to the Bronx with its memories of Mami and his own horrific past? He'd rather be a vagrant than ever go back to that. It seemed only fitting, and curiously poetic, that his sister should accidentally proffer this opportunity in Vegas in the most unexpected way, after the lifetime she had stolen from him and their Mami all those years ago.

Paolo had adeptly blocked out the misery while he had to live through it. But finally breaking free of the Bronx after Mami died left him looking at the horrifying scene from afar. Perversely it was somehow easier to cope when he was a brushstroke in the painting, but now, standing back, the picture was one grotesque masterpiece of misery, abuse and addiction. Paolo couldn't look at it, let alone ever put his head right back in that space by returning to the East Coast. He had no idea what would happen in four months when Brandy returned to claim her life back. Or indeed if he could keep up the pretence for that long. He'd just have to cross that bridge when – or if – he came to it. Paolo shuddered, and now set about inspecting himself from every angle in Brandy's dressing-room mirror. He couldn't risk a single whisker giving the game away. He was so absorbed in the task of transformation that he didn't realise it was the first time in twenty-four hours he hadn't been obsessing about Sienna Starr, with her beautiful soft skin, dreamy English accent, endless legs and striking face. She had blown his mind yesterday. But there was no time to devote to that fantasy right now, when he needed all his concentration focussed on the job in hand. Finally satisfied that the figure looking back at him was pure Brandy, Paolo made his way to sit with Marty and engage in a morning watching the girls rehearsing. At least he'd get to steal some quality glimpses of Sienna's knockout body without suspicion.

Blue sighed as a trio of squealing teenage blondes in skinny hipster jeans came scampering over.

'Oh, please,' huffed Blue, wandering off to look in a shop window while Julian pandered to his fans. Photos were taken, autographs given, and one of the girls had insisted on having her T-shirt signed across her breasts.

'You really enjoy all this shit, don't you?' moaned Blue as they finally moved on and made their way towards the Ferrari dealership.

'What's the problem? I'm cute,' shrugged Julian.

'And gay,' reminded Blue.

'Oh stop it, you're turning into a nag.'

'You're turning into a spoilt brat.'

'Pot? Meet kettle, we'll get along just fine.'

'I'm just saying, stars with class don't need to perform when they're off stage. Can you just switch off for five minutes while we have stuff to do, or are you gonna break into "Nessun Dorma" for the whole mall in a minute? God, you're so needy.'

'God, you're so jealous,' snapped Julian, waving and grinning at another passerby who had their camera phone out.

'No, I just think that a true star doesn't need to try desperate measures to grasp for attention every second. If you weren't so busy with that ludicrous display with that *girl* the other night in the club I wouldn't have this freakin' black eye! You're just addicted to attention and you don't care where it comes from! Girls I ask you! Don't you have actual work to get on with?'

'Yeah and my work is about looking good, okay? My fans love it so get over yourself, grumps.'

'Yeah, alright, pretty boy, and that's all you're gonna have left cos your last album didn't do so well, did it?'

'You don't know what you're talking about – we've just done thirty tour dates!'

'Yeah, as the support act. For "Sealion" Dion at that. I don't exactly call that a star billing. And why are you taking your top off in every bit of press you do now? What's that all about? You're just a singing six-pack now, are you?'

'Well, at least I can take my top off in public – unlike you.'

'I can't believe we're even having this conversation, when I'm taking you to choose *your* birthday present.'

'You started it!'

'How old are you? It's like being back in the playground talking to you sometimes!'

'At least I'm on the right side of the age gap . . . '

Blue felt a red mist descending. He had tried at first to bite his tongue but there was something about Julian that seemed to unleash his inner bitchy queen lately. It was now almost a frequent daily occurrence for him and Julian to be bickering, but Blue wondered why they couldn't even manage to zip it while they were on their way to choose a fancy car for his birthday.

'I can just call Ferrari right now and cancel our appointment,' said Blue flatly, 'and the party I've been planning.'

'Party?'

'Oh, yes, that's right, I didn't mention it, did I, darling? All the hints you've been dropping – well, I've been organising something.'

'Oh? You invite Paris Hilton?'

'Oh, God, you're so D-list, I give up!' snapped Blue, exasperated.

'Megan Fox?'

'Oh, you'd love that, wouldn't you!' Blue felt his pocket vibrating and took out his phone. Brandy.

'You know, this may actually be the first time in living history anyone's ever been pleased that Brandy Alexander is calling,' he muttered to himself.

'Fire Paige Turner from the understudy position,' said Paolo as their cocktails arrived. Blue groaned loudly and put his head in his hands in despair. He'd just dispatched one child in his hotel suite after buying him a toy car, and was now clearly dealing with another.

'It doesn't work like that, Brandy. I'm just your dresser,' explained Blue. 'You have to talk to Marty about it, you know that!'

'You talk to Marty for me,' pleaded Paolo, taking a swig of his Cosmopolitan. He was desperate for a whisky mac, but he had to stick with something girlie. Detail was everything. Why do people ruin good liquor with fruit? he wondered idly.

'Why can't you talk to Marty yourself?' asked Blue. 'You're in his pockets all the time.'

'I'd feel bad asking him to demote Paige.'

'You feel *bad* about it?'

'Sure.'

'Brandy, are you okay? Since when did firing anyone ever make you feel *bad*? I thought it was what you did when you needed cheering up?'

'I . . .'

'And why do you want me to do your dirty work anyway?' asked Blue. 'You usually do your own, and everyone else's too.' He looked down his nose suspiciously. Paolo grimaced and reminded himself to get in character more.

'Look, Paige obviously really wants that part but she stinks!' Paolo snapped, swishing his hair dramatically for emphasis.

'I know, and *you* put her there, devotion!' retorted Blue.

'I – I did? Yes, that's right I did . . .'

'Because she's not as pretty . . . or as good as you . . . *remember?*'

Paolo strained to stop himself from laughing. That was Brandy all over. She'd never been the greatest dancer. It was what she'd found so frustrating when they were children. She'd drag Paolo to every class going – ignoring their father's objections that no son of his should ever be seen in ballet tights – as she hated to go anywhere alone, much less strain her wrist carrying her own kit bag, and then she'd get hysterical if he brought out some jaw-dropping Gene Kelly move and bring the house down. It was more than a sore point that Paolo had to keep his dancing basic in front of Brandy if he was to have a quiet life.

'Well, Paige does move like a frozen leg of lamb,' started Paolo carefully, getting into Brandy's psychology, 'and . . . she has this fixed face when she's concentrating . . . like her G-string is up her backside . . . I think that she makes everyone else look much better than they really are so maybe my logic wasn't quite right.'

'Right . . .'

'So put Sienna Starr in as Venus and stick Paige back into the showgirls. She'll blend in.'

'You want me to take this to Marty with your blessing?'

'Would you?'

'I'd say I don't have much choice. Can I get it in writing?'

'Just tell Marty I'll only be happy with Sienna!' Paolo insisted with a final hair swish.

'You got it,' sighed Blue.

Paolo smiled inwardly as he gulped back his horrible sticky Cosmopolitan. Maybe he really could put some of Brandy's wrongs to right without blowing his cover. Well, this was just a start but when he'd been watching morning rehearsals with the director, Sienna Starr had mesmerised him with her stage presence. Leaving aside her obvious beauty, she had shone like a true headliner. It seemed ridiculous, not to mention unfair, that the most talented dancer in the whole production was wasted in the showgirl line. Her heart was sure to belong to someone already, realised Paolo. Women like her don't come along too often. Whoever he is, he's one lucky man, thought Paolo miserably.

Julian's hotel suite was kitted out in seventies cocaine-baron-style. Black satin panels covered the walls with inset speakers, floor-to-ceiling windows gave a magnificent view of the Strip, and neon-lit stairs led up from the fur-draped circular bed to a hot tub in front of the vast picture window, with tall palms arranged artistically and an assortment of Arabian-style cushions scattered on the floor. A golden pole glistened in the middle of the room. This would have been on the record company ordinarily but since they'd dropped the band after completing their last tour dates, expenses were on Julian. He hadn't wanted to mention it to Blue; he needed to keep up the air of success. *Takes money to make money*, Julian reminded himself. He wasn't overly concerned; he'd find another deal. Anyone as good-looking as him and with his deep silky baritone was gold dust. He could always ditch the other boys and go solo. Unlike them, he didn't mind which way he had to swing. He knew he'd find himself in the right A&R man's bed; and his baritone wasn't the only thing that was finely tuned.

Julian adoringly checked out his washboard abs in the mirror. His eyes travelled upwards to take in his thick tawny hair with a sexy short wave, piercing blue eyes and a devastatingly pretty face. A smattering of freckles at his nose gave him a boyish appeal that, along with a toned muscular body, was an irresistible combination. He'd been in town for a week seeing Blue, and whilst he seemed to be turning into a queenie drag of late, Julian had to keep him sweet as not only was he a more than generous boyfriend, he still had myriad useful contacts to be used. Julian never liked to leave a fruit unsqueezed of its juice. So far Blue had got him well in there with the gay mafia, and everyone knew they ran the business of show, not to mention the even more glamorous world of fashion. Thanks to Blue, Julian was well on his way to having his fingers in both those pies. He could just see himself as the face of Armani.

And of course, without Blue he'd never have had an inroad to the living legend in her own leopard-skin bed sheets that was Brandy Alexander. Man, she had a voracious appetite for the young men. Not only had she been the one to convert Julian in the first place but she'd completely worn him out in the first stages of their hot fling. Thankfully she could be sated with designer shoes as much as a good hard workout, which suited Julian perfectly; they'd had quite a little 'arrangement' going on that he suspected not too many of his partners would identify with. He knew she'd keep the fling confidential too; they both had too much to lose by blowing the proverbial whistle on each other. Julian relied on Blue's contacts and couldn't risk his wrath if he found out, and Brandy had made it clear her celebrity stock would go right down if the gossip rags found out she was fraternising with a 'lowly' boy-band member. She'd be sorry for making that point so vociferously once he became the next big fashion muse, but for the moment, it was in everyone's interests for Julian to keep his penchant for the ladies under wraps. His only little slip up in front of Blue at the club last week had been fairly easy to explain away as a crazy fan who took it too far.

'I'm all yours!' squealed one of the tall skinny blondes from earlier as she skipped out from the bathroom towards the bed in nothing but a pair of six-inch Versace heels and a ton of eye make-up.

'Get on the bed, baby, and get those heels in the air. I bet you have really cute tanned feet.' Julian smiled, feeling an immediate hard-on.

'Uh, like, whatever,' giggled the blonde, jumping on the fur counterpane and rolling around playfully, arching her back and mussing up her hair. Julian joined her on the bed and grabbed her ankles.

'Fuck me, baby,' gasped the blonde, grabbing at her tiny little titties with both hands. She pushed her groin up towards him expectantly, her scrawny hip bones jutting out like icicle shards.

'Not yet,' panted Julian, rubbing his cheek feverishly over the delicate arch of her foot.

'What's the matter? Don't you want me? I know I have to lose, like, ten pounds before bikini season,' she whined.

'Are you wearing a toe ring?' Julian murmured hotly.

'Uh, like, oh my God, they were so nineties,' sniggered the blonde.

'How about socks? Will you wear some socks?' asked Julian between heaving breaths.

'Uh, are you serious? Like, what-*ever*.'

Within five minutes Blue had walked into Julian's suite armed with a conciliatory bottle of Chateau Lafite to be confronted by the sight of his beautiful young boyfriend furiously beating one off over the bemused blonde's newly be-socked feet.

Chapter 9

Honey checked out her new weave as she settled in front of her mirror. Hoochie mama, she thought to herself with a sigh, fiddling with the big bouncy blonde curls which cascaded down to the small of her back. She wasn't too sure about this shade with her coffee-coloured skin. Butter had insisted she'd be the spitting image of Beyoncé this way, although with all these curls Honey could only think of Lil' Kim. Butter had also told her to ditch the red nail polish and get with the squared-off French manicure, better still with a few rhinestones inlaid. It was what the guys liked. Red nail polish confused them and made them think of their mothers, she had told Honey. 'None of this classy fifties shit,' she'd said. 'This is about giving them what they want. You want good tips, right?' Honey despaired. Her eight-inch high-brand new lucite stripper platforms were pinching already. If hoochie was what American men wanted she really should cut her losses and flee back to London in a shot. She'd never find a decent husband here!

Honey straightened out her gleaming white bikini and

figured it was time to get on with it. She'd been introduced to Destiny, Cobra and Sapphire who were her dressing-room buddies for tonight and they were already out there on the floor, sucking up all the tips. She'd get another part in a show soon, Honey reassured herself, trying to snap out of her mood. And as mortifying as this was, it was better than returning to the Monte with everyone knowing why she'd got kicked off a hit show. This wasn't going to be for long, and she may as well make some good hard cash while she was here. If she took Brandy at her cruel words then at least her ass was going to earn her a good income. With a heavy sigh Honey fluffed up her hair and strutted out on her stripper heels to make her big entrance through the velvet vagina.

'I just don't understand it,' said Sienna meekly, scooping green salad onto her plate. 'I'm really sorry, Paige, I feel a bit weird about the whole situation. I think Brandy's been acting kind of strange these last few days, sweetheart. You mustn't read anything into it.' Paige forced a smile as she chewed a mouthful of juicy steak, which she fully intended to throw up in ten minutes' time.

'Sounds like Brandy's like this all the time,' said Max dismissively, nodding in Sienna's direction. 'All that stuff with Honey too. You shouldn't take it personally, Paige, you'll get promoted to another big part soon enough,' he shrugged, stretching himself out in his chair and gazing up at the stars in the cloudless sky. Max liked eating al fresco. He liked a lot of things al fresco in fact. He popped a juicy olive into his mouth and shot a lusty look across the table at Sienna, who was awkwardly pushing green leaves around her plate. The afterburn of guilt always made Max more attentive, and he was totally appreciating Sienna's charms in full tonight. Particularly the low-cut little number she had on now. Her body drove him nuts every time. Why she was on rabbit food now was a mystery to him. Didn't she realise it was unattractive to be neurotic about food? Every man knew it was a dead cert that a woman who could enjoy a truffle or savour a spoon of buttery hollandaise would be much more likely to lap up every sensory pleasure in the sack. Besides, right now Sienna could put ten pounds on each ass cheek and still look hot. Max made a concerted effort to keep his mind off spreadsheets and his spiralling debt for ten minutes while he had Sienna in front of him. Who needed cheap air stewardesses for fun. They were just McDonald's to Sienna's chateaubriand.

'So you're taking the part then, Sienna?' asked Paige slowly, before gulping back her wine.

'Well . . . I don't know . . . not if this is going to be a big deal for you, darling. It sounds corny but I feel like we're kind of a sisterhood, you know . . . and I wouldn't . . . '

'Sienna, I can't believe you're even considering turning it down,' cut in Max protectively. 'Paige, you wouldn't let her do that, would you?' Max shot a look at Paige. 'You took the opportunity when you had it, right? So go on, tell her – she should take the part, right?'

Paige looked at Max, startled.

'I mean, you want the best for each other, huh?'

'Of course,' said Paige, choking on her wine a little. Inside she was boiling at the whole scenario. In fact if there were chips on her plate she'd be spitting them right now. Twice in a matter of weeks her big chance had been snatched away and she was now expected to be *big* about it?

'I guess if you don't take it, someone else will . . . ' Paige swallowed hard on the words.

'There, job done,' said Max hastily. 'Now let's move on and stop talking shop – there's only so much tit and feather talk a guy can take over dinner. I have a plan for the weekend.'

'Oh?' asked Sienna expectantly, Paige noticing a little blush spreading across her cheeks.

'Yeah. I thought we could see the big fight at Caesars.'

'The fight? Oh . . . but . . . ' Sienna tailed off, the sparkle disappearing from her eyes.

'No "buts", I checked with the Follies and you have the whole weekend free. So get yourselves new cocktail dresses, and I promise I can get us seated next to Jay-Z. I'm inviting Brandy, too.'

'What?! Brandy? On my – are you sure?' asked Sienna, with a touch of frost.

'Sure. The more the merrier. It'll be great fun,' said Max decisively.

Typical man, thought Paige irritably. How the hell do they do that compartmentalising thing? One second Max is driving a nail into the coffin of her career, the next he's talking about grown men kicking the crap out of each other and new cocktail dresses! Paige regarded him through narrowed eyes, both hating him and feeling herself getting moist at the sight of him at the same time. Why couldn't she find a man like Max Power? Disgustingly rich, insanely connected, tall, dark, fit and horny as hell. He even seemed to be faithful, damn him; he hadn't so much as blinked when she tried the charm on him the other week. She placed a bet with herself that Mr Perfect probably had the perfect penis too.

'Max, I thought we were – you know,' Sienna stuttered awkwardly out of the side of her mouth. Max looked back blankly. 'Can we talk about this?' asked Sienna, sounding disappointed.

'Don't get heavy, babe, it'll be fun. Just relax,' said Max. Sienna responded with an awkward smile from across the table as the evening breeze ruffled its way softly through her hair. 'If you say so,' she sighed. 'I'm sure it'll be great. I guess Honey would love to come. I'll ask her when I see her. Paige, sweetheart, it wouldn't be a night out without you. Are you in?'

'Yeah, count me in,' Paige drawled, pushing her plate away and turning her attention to the key lime pie sat tantalisingly on Max's side of the dining table. She shov-elled a generous slice onto a fresh plate. It was all coming up again in a minute, so what the hell, she may as well indulge properly.

'Perfect,' said Max. 'And I'll look forward to the most beautiful broads in the room being on *my* arm,' he added with a grin. Paige melted a little, wondering if she detected a hint of flirtation. Maybe she could tease the bad boy out of Max if she really tried. Why should Sienna have absolutely everything, after all? Paige wasn't to know, of course, that Max had apparently forgotten it was Sienna's birthday the following weekend. All she saw was a whiff of petulance from her ungrateful housemate. Seizing the opportunity to show how appreciative she could be by comparison, Paige slipped off her mule and gently extended her leg under the table, resting her foot softly in Max's lap. She waited for him to pull back. Nothing. She gently wriggled her foot into his crotch. Max's hand was at her ankle within moments.

'Sienna, I have to go off for this meeting now, baby,' he said, winking as he held Paige's ankle.

'Er – yeah, sure,' said Sienna lightly. 'That's why I fed you up with good solid food – keep your strength up for the big boys.'

'So maybe I'll come back here tonight if it doesn't go on too long?' Max was now caressing Paige's ankle and staring deep into Sienna's eyes. Damn him, thought Paige, realising too late that he thought it was Sienna playing footsie. She snatched her foot back abruptly. Max looked startled.

'Trust me, baby, I'll be back,' he said.

'Sure, of course I trust you,' replied Sienna, giving him a puzzled look.

'Good . . . or you can come over to mine later if you prefer?'

'I have an early start so I should sleep at home tonight. And I have to put in a good session at the gym later too. I have weigh-ins to make these days, remember. It's no sweat whatever you decide to do,' she replied evasively.

'Okay, I'll call. I guess that means I should get on with work now,' Max sighed, standing up from the table. 'Bye, Paige. If I don't bump into you before, then see you for the boxing next weekend.'

'Can't wait,' smiled Paige warmly, watching as he turned to leave. 'I do love a good fight,' she murmured under her breath, plunging her spoon deep into her slice of gooey green tart.

Pepper had known he was FBI all along. Try as they might to be inconspicuous, they just had an air about them. Over sixty years of bumping and grinding had passed since her first strip at Skinny D'Amato's 500 club and her senses were finely tuned for sniffing out the Feds. Pepper slid a beer across the bar at him. The guy in the next seat looked up and smiled. Pepper recognised him as the new regular who'd sent champagne over to Paige the other week. She nodded and winked in acknowledgement.

'So c'mon then, out with it,' she grinned, turning her

gaze back to the Fed. 'We don't need to keep the pretence up. You've been coming here for the last few weeks, and I'll bet you're not turning up for the ugly tranny. I'm Pepper by the way. But you probably already know that.'

'Jack Weldon.' He proffered a hand which Pepper shook firmly. Not bad, she thought, giving him the once-over. Dark curly hair, coal-black eyes, a shadow of stubble, slightly crinkled at the eyes. Broad shoulders, chewed nails, no wedding ring. Pepper smoothed down her own neat white ponytail, wanting to make a good impression before the inevitable questions.

'You might have to wait a while to talk to Ma,' she announced.

'S'okay. I just wanted to come and soak up the atmosphere here,' smiled Weldon. 'Pinkie musta had some crazy times here, you can just feel it in the walls.' Pepper's face fossilised before him and she busied herself drying some glasses. Minutes passed.

'Said the wrong name, huh,' chuckled Weldon eventually. Pepper stayed silent. Weldon sucked his beer back. 'Okay, no games,' he said, holding his palms up. 'We know Ma's gonna die. And you know she's our last link to Pinkie.' Pepper said nothing. 'Detective Schwebel,' continued Weldon. 'Killed 1 March 1976. Pinkie's prints were all over the murder weapon.' Pepper didn't flinch.

'I'm not here to question you, ma'am. I will need to talk to Ma though.'

'She answered all your questions over thirty years ago,'

Pepper said finally, with a sigh. 'What more could you want? Just leave her to die in peace. Give an old woman some dignity.'

'Hey, I don't make the law,' said Weldon.

'This is all history,' said Pepper. 'Nothing's changed. Nothing new.'

'People don't just disappear.'

'This is Vegas. People disappear all the time,' laughed Pepper.

'You're an intelligent woman . . . '

'I know nothing about Pinkie, neither does Ma. This conversation is going nowhere.'

Weldon swigged his beer and studied the beer mat for a minute. 'Pinkie loved Ma,' he said quietly.

'No shit,' snapped Pepper.

'They had a bond.'

'That people like you wouldn't understand.'

'Sooo,' Weldon paused.

'Ah. You think he's gonna turn up to her funeral?' Pepper propped herself against the bar and raised an eyebrow.

'How do you know he's still alive?'

'What?'

'Well, an old man in his eighties, how do you know he's still alive?' probed Weldon, a hint of a smile curling at his lips.

'I don't.'

'But you just mentioned the possibility of him turning up to the funeral,' countered Weldon immediately.

'It's your job to know if people are dead or alive, sir. I don't know what you're getting at,' said Pepper looking Weldon straight in the face. She was too long in the tooth to feel intimidated by a cynical Fed.

'Just sounded like you might know, that's all.' Weldon smiled and finished his beer.

'Another one?' asked Pepper.

'Yes, ma'am. Thank you.' Weldon swept his gaze around the club. 'Nice. You've kept it old-school. So who are the girls?' he asked, nodding at the photographs mounted on the walls behind the bar.

'These are our alumni,' said Pepper proudly, sliding a fresh beer over the counter. 'All the legends who have worked here over the years. Look, here's Tana Louise the Society Stripper before she went back to Florida for good,' she beamed, pointing at a worn old picture of a stunning curvy brunette with severe eyebrows, perched on a chair and wearing a transparent nightgown, 'and this here is April March the First Lady of Burlesque, and, ah, here's the exquisite Lili St Cyr.' Pepper sensed all the men at the bar listening in on her tour of famous faces who had graced the Monte Cristo stage.

'And who's the girl in that one?' asked Weldon.

'Oh, her? That's Tiger Starr. Don't you recognise her?'

'Oh wow. Hot. She looks so different in that big movie she did. More – grown up. Hollywood does that, I guess.'

'Well, that's the difference ten years and a pink wig

makes, darling,' smiled Pepper, 'and this shot here . . . this is her daughter. Sienna Starr.'

'You're kidding! She dances too? Holy crap, she's gorgeous!'

'Yes, but she's not working here any more, I'm afraid. She moved on recently. They all do eventually,' sighed Pepper. 'She'll do well. Like mother like daughter.'

'I'll say,' came a deep voice.

'Oh, Mr Champagne over here has perked up. Can I get you a refill, sir?' laughed Pepper, clocking the guy in the next seat with his eyes lit up at the photographs.

'Just call me Ed,' he said coyly.

'Well, well, first names – you know that makes you a proper regular now,' said Pepper, reaching for the Bollinger, realising now was not the time to swap the good champagne for cheap Prosecco in front of Agent Jack Weldon.

Paige cursed as she clipped the kerb with Sienna's Ferrari. She'd despatched Sienna at the Athletic Club, saying she couldn't be her gym buddy this time as she needed some late-night retail therapy to take the edge off her day of disappointment; needless to say Sienna had fallen over herself to offer her downcast housemate the use of last year's high-performance birthday present. Spoilt bitch. She probably knew deep down that she'd only been given the part because Brandy finally figured out she could curry favour with Sienna's famous mum. Well, if Sienna's second-hand money and fame was going to secure her that part at Paige's expense, Paige bloody well deserved some of those perks in payment for what she'd lost. Now that she had Sienna's car to herself, all thoughts of strolling round the Venetian's *faux* daylight cobbled streets and bagging a few pairs of cute shoes had dissipated. Shoes were for pussies. Paige intended to drown her sorrows in a few bottles of good champagne. The wine over dinner had worked some magic already, but as she pulled into the parking lot of the Monte her mouth was watering at the anticipation of an ice-cold hit of bubbly. A few of those and she'd be pain proof, Paige told herself as she loosely parked the car. She knew she should be steering clear of drunk driving, having had a DUI and a heavy fine under her belt recently, but since this was Sienna's car who cared? If she got pulled she'd just pretend to be Miss Starr, easy. Now wouldn't that be something to wipe the smile off the princess's face, thought Paige with a cackle.

Paige was used to heads turning when she walked into a room; she'd made it her objective when graduating from a pigtailed tomboy clad in her half-brother's hand-me-down dungarees who made mud pies with all the boys in the trailer park into a glorious swan with curves in all the right places that she would never again be one of the boys, and tonight was no exception as she swept through the doors of the Monte Cristo. She expertly diverted attention from the hint of a stagger in her walk with a few dramatic hair swishes. Sliding up to the bar she waved over at Jeffrey, and took her coat off to reveal the blouse she had taken from Sienna's room a few weeks back. Well, she was having a bad day and thought perhaps she'd give herself some of the lucky bitch's *je ne sais quoi* if she wore it. It fit rather nicely, in fact. But then being Gucci, she supposed it would. Paige watched as Pepper said goodbye to a cute guy across the bar with dark curly hair. She craned her neck for a better look as she struggled to get onto a stool; and whether it was the fault of the claret at dinner or the five-inch Prada stilettos Sienna had 'lent' her, Paige lost her footing and fell to the ground with a lady-like squeal.

'Christ,' she muttered, wrinkling her nose at the foul smell of stale alcohol ingrained in the carpet, quickly pulling away and trying to haul herself up. Her stiletto had other ideas as it snagged in the hem of her skirt and brought her crashing to the ground again when she tried to stand. Paige yelped in pain this time. A dirty ripple of sniggers travelled round the club as the patrons saw just another girl who couldn't handle her liquor. Paige felt her face flush with embarrassment and pain.

'Let me help you,' came a voice from above. Paige clocked a pair of men's brogues at her eye level.

'I'm fine. Go. Away.' She forced the words out between gritted teeth, keeping her eyes down to avoid the embarrassment of meeting the stranger's gaze. Within seconds she let out another shriek at the pain now shooting through her ankle like a stabbing hot poker.

'I'm a physiotherapist. Here, let me check you haven't

broken anything,' came the voice again, closer. Paige looked up through eyes watering up with pain. She gasped at the man kneeling before her.

'It's you! Oh God, oh I feel so – so embarrassed,' she stuttered, as she realised it was the champagne guy from the other night.

'Ed. My name's Ed. Good job I'm here, huh? Don't be embarrassed, just let me check your ankle.' And with that Ed set to work inspecting the damage.

Max took a gulp of whisky and rotated the tumbler slowly in his palm, reminding himself that coming to the Artisan, one of the few hotels in Vegas without a casino, was for his own good. A couple of pretty brunettes had recognised him and were eyeballing him from the bar. He nodded politely before shifting in his chair to block them from view. He wasn't in the mood for silly little girls. He had been close tonight, close to losing the last million he had left in credit at the Golden Nugget. Then his luck had turned. He walked out of there five million up, and straight over to the Bellissimo to clear one of his markers before he had a finger removed by one of their 'associates'. Business investors could always be flannelled for yet another week but his digits could not be replaced. Of course, Max knew how much casinos hated to see their money leave the premises. Because when you 'borrowed' it from them and lost it on the tables, it wasn't real money that had been lost, nothing had left the building – but when you *won* it and then walked away with hard cash to put it straight in the coffers of another casino? That really hurt. Tough, Max had markers all over town to be settled and he intended to have all limbs, kneecaps and appendages intact for a long time yet. Another chug of whisky. Max tried to think ahead to his next move. After today's terminally long conference calls to the UK, he was no closer to raising that finance to start a leasing company. It was becoming obvious – with word on the grapevine that something was amiss with Silver Slipper – that the sharks were smelling blood. He could forget about getting a good price for offloading more of his shareholding. At least tonight Lady Luck had given him a sticking plaster for his spiralling debts. But really, he knew he was just running to stand still.

Max swirled the last ice cube in his glass and knocked back the last of the whisky. One of the girls from the bar sashayed past on her way to the bathroom, tossing a smouldering glance in his direction. It was wasted, for the only thing on Max's mind was what the hell he would tell his darling Sienna. Sorry, sweetheart, you're going out with a bankrupt; lost the businesses, the home, everything – mind if I move in and sponge off your mother's money for a while? Oh and make sure you aren't seen on my arm, or none of the stars'll want to be near you – they all think poverty's contagious, you know. Oh and can you lend me a buck for the slots while you're at it? Yeah, he could just imagine it now. Back to being the little guy. Max recalled the time he had invited his first proper girlfriend for a Power Christmas – not the cheap call girl his father had arranged for the previous birthday – no, Daisy was the wide-eyed daughter of a local publican, much to the chagrin of Kerry Power and his social aspirations. Max still remembered walking into the drawing room after the turkey lunch to find his father groping Daisy with one hand as he clamped his palm firmly over her mouth. Max would never forget the fear he saw in his girlfriend's eyes. Kerry had simply roared with laughter when Max ran up, trying to pull him off her, and a good smack across the head had sent him flying to the ground. Kerry's words rang out, as young Max had fled from the room, hot on the footsteps of his petrified girlfriend: 'Well, someone had to do the job properly.' Some Christmas that had been. Max had never been able to live with the guilt that he hadn't been able to protect his girl. Kerry had paid the family off to keep quiet. Max never saw Daisy again.

Looking at his empty glass, Max motioned for the bill. He couldn't stomach another whisky; he just needed to be near Sienna. But how could he ever tell any of this to her? She'd never understand what it was like to have a father who made you sick to the stomach. She didn't even have one as far as he was aware. What would she know? How could she ever understand the pressure Max felt? That hamster wheel his father had got him onto. One where there was always someone richer to buy out. Always someone more successful to usurp. How would anyone ever want to be with him if he lost everything? Max pinched the bridge of his nose. He could never be the loser again, that was one thing he'd have to make sure of, whatever it took. He threw a crisp fifty onto the table with one hand and reached in his pocket for his phone with the other. Well, if he was calling it a night on the poker tables, he'd have to get a hit some other way. And he wasn't about to take his mood to Sienna. Besides, a girlfriend required effort and care while Cinnamon could be in and out of his house, and have the job done to his specifications, within twenty minutes tops. He had her on speed dial under 'Room Service'. Max pressed 'dial' without a second's hesitation.

'Make it rain, baby, make it rain!' squealed Cobra from her podium as Honey writhed on her knees on the catwalk to ZZ Top's 'Sharp Dressed Man', a shower of dollar bills flying through the air and fluttering down onto her firm glowing skin as she arched her back and flung her blonde curls rhythmically. She crawled towards the whooping and baying men like a prowling panther as the guitar solo crescendoed, and scooped up her cash, stuffing notes into her G-string with winks and flirtatious smiles.

'Man, you're a natural!' congratulated Cobra breathlessly as both girls exited through the velvet vagina back to their dressing rooms.

'You reckon?' asked Honey, all traces of her earlier stage smile completely vanished, a despondent grimace in its place.

'Oh sure, I mean, all new girls are a novelty at first but you killed it back there!'

'Oh. Thanks. It's not really the kind of performance I'm used to.'

'Well, you coulda fooled me,' said Cobra with a friendly pat on Honey's back. 'You grind it like a pro.' Honey wasn't sure if that was a good thing. She looked on as Cobra counted out her cash and secreted it safely away in her locker, leaving a few fifties hooked strategically in her G-string. Honey took her cue and set about doing the same.

'The feature will be on soon. Wanna go out and watch?' asked Cobra, smoothing out her waist-length blue-black hair.

'Feature?'

'Yeah, this week's actually has a decent act.'

'What do you mean? They have acts here?' Honey asked, hopefully.

'Sure – you know how features work, right? We usually get the porn stars – we even had Tera Patrick once. They come to sell their merch and do a turn on stage. Thing is, sometimes the features have terrible acts. They should just stick to the fucking.'

'Right . . . ' Honey couldn't stop herself from heaving a sigh. This wasn't exactly the description of the glamorous and revered 'features' they used to have in the burlesque clubs in the fifties.

'You okay, doll?' asked Cobra, cracking her gum noisily

and looking up at Honey through her four pairs of false eyelashes.

'Yeah,' said Honey quietly, trying to muster a smile. 'I guess . . . I guess this wasn't where I saw myself when I came to Vegas.' Cobra raised her eyebrows. 'No offence!' said Honey hurriedly.

'None taken,' laughed Cobra. 'You're not the first to say that, and I doubt you'll be the last. But if it was that easy to do this job, everyone would be doing it. It's hard graft. It's a hustle. And the good features on the circuit? Man, they're like superbreed dancers. Vanna Lace who was here last week? Body like Miss Universe. You know how hard it is to get a body that perfect? It's a full-time job in every sense. And it's what you gotta do if you want to make this pay. Cos we don't do this for the cultural stimulation, I can tell you now. But you know, you'll settle in. All the girls get hooked so it can't be that bad.' Honey looked alarmed. 'Sure,' continued Cobra, 'we have loads of dancers from the shows here, they come after work. They can't afford not to strip, the wages on the shows are so crazy bad. Why do you think I ended up here? I'm five foot seven, too short to be a showgirl, could only ever be a chorus-line dancer. Hard work, crap money, being here was a no-brainer. And then there's the pro hos who still come back.'

'Pro hos?'

'You believe it. You met Cinnamon out there earlier?'

'Sure, she's gorgeous.'

'Yeah, in the *dark*. You don't wanna be too close when the sun comes up, I'm tellin' ya. Anyway, Cinnamon operates in ways you can't believe: princes, sheikhs, you name it, she rakes it in, cars, apartments, cash . . . We're talking serious levels of wealth.'

'And she still works here too?'

'Exactly. Money. It's like a drug. It's like – how much more can I make? That's all they're thinking. Mind you, Cinnamon would step over a dying man for a quarter,' added Cobra, giving herself a liberal spray of deodorant. Honey wilted into her chair, not knowing whether to laugh or cry

'Hey,' snapped Cobra. Honey looked up at her and bit her lip. 'Just be cool, you'll be fine. Nice girl like you, just get out there, scoop up the tips, don't think about what else goes on. It's just business. Wanna go out and watch the feature?' Honey looked back blankly. 'C'mon, she's really funny,' reassured Cobra. 'Did a show last night as a hot dominatrix bitch. She got these two Japanese guys up on stage and tied them to the poles; they love that kinda shit. Then she put leather hoods on each. She was doing a scorching steamy strip, got the whole club laughing that the guys up there couldn't see the spectacle. Then – wait for this – she put big bunny ears on them, and took their wallets and went through them up on stage, took a few dollars out . . . then she had this velvet purse thing and took out a Polaroid camera. She took snaps of herself in her G-string and her huge bejewelled tatas with the guys tied up in hoods and bunny ears and put the Polaroids back in their wallets. The whole place was in hysterics!' cackled Cobra. Honey found herself giggling and relaxing a little. 'Oh, and one more thing . . .' added Cobra, making for the door.

'Uh huh?'

'Your stripper name. Gilda Lillie. Not very – sexy, is it? Gilda?'

'It's a classic old—'

'No, no, no, we gotta get with the times. You can do better than that. I see you as more of a "Candy".'

'Er . . .'

'With a "K"! Brilliant!' whooped Cobra. 'It's so good you don't need a surname. Damn I'm good,' sighed Cobra, snapping her fingers for effect. 'Come on Kandy with a "K", let's go and make some dollars, girl!' Honey followed behind Cobra, trying to think of the money and reminding herself she'd be back in a big show soon.

'So Ed . . . ' slurred Paige. 'Shall we go to another bar?'

'Blimey. You're a wild one,' laughed Ed.

'Yeah, baby, bad to the bone,' she said with a hiccup. The pain of her ankle had worn off now, anaesthetised by a bottle of champagne, three brandies and a couple of tequila shots, although she was feeling a little queasy, it had to be said. She'd been relieved when Ed had informed her she just had a sprain, nothing that a bit of rest and a good support bandage couldn't cure. Ed was older than she would normally go for – mid to late forties she reckoned – but he'd seemed so masterful, the way he'd tended to her sprain, she quite fancied him. There was no doubt he was fit, for an older guy. Tall, athletic frame, muscular arms and big hands, sandy hair in thick waves, a great tan and warm eyes. She reckoned he must have been drop-dead gorgeous in his twenties. Plus he had the cutest twang. Paige was convinced it was Australian although he insisted it was an English accent. He said he was in town looking for physio work, that he'd been touring with an English rugby team but wanted three months out for a change of scenery. Paige figured anyone vaguely medical must earn packets, and he'd paid for her evening so far, so she was sticking to him like steristrips tonight.

'So you were saying you used to work here,' asked Ed, sliding another brandy into Paige's hand.

'For my sins. Why?'

'I was just looking at all the photos on the wall. I spotted yours. Who's that next to you?'

'Sienna.'

'You worked with her too, then?'

'Work with her? I live with the bitch.' Paige hiccupped again.

'Oh?' Ed sat up a little. 'She's not nice?'

'She's great! Beautiful. Rich. Boyfriend. Nice. Pretty. Thin. Tits. Boyfriend. Gorgeous. Nice. Yeah she's great! She's got it all! Including my j-j-job . . . bitch.'

'Oh?'

'She pinched the part I wanted. Or rather, her mom did. There's no way she coulda got that on her own. People with special bloody privileges keep getting in my way, Ed! It would have made me, you know. It should have been me. I was this close!' Paige slumped down into her chair. 'You know Tiger Starr?'

'I've – heard of her,' said Ed.

'That's Sienna's mother. I'm telling you, she bought that part for Sienna. I don't believe she was actually any good in auditions or she woulda got it first time round. And she didn't. I did.'

'You know that for sure? That she paid her way in?'

'Well, it doesn't matter now anyway,' snapped Paige. 'I'm washed up, good for nothing, my ankle and everything . . . '

'Steady, Miss Drama Queen, it'll heal – you can put weight on it in a couple of days. Just go easy on the rehearsing for a few days. Maybe just learn your steps from the sidelines this week. It won't stop you dancing, don't worry,' Ed laughed softly.

'I hope you're right.'

'I see injuries like this all the time. Don't worry, it's not serious.'

'Ed?'

'Yeah?'

'I can help you.'

'Oh?' smiled Ed, looking amused.

'Yeah. Well, all us girls need massage and we get injuries

on the shows. We have recommended physios but it doesn't stop us going elsewhere. Shall I spread the word? You wanna be our new mascot?' Paige slapped his thigh firmly with her hand.

'Hey, that sounds amazing,' said Ed, breaking out into a huge smile. 'Thanks, Paige.' He placed her hand back on the bar and looked at her warmly. 'What would make me really happy is if I could escort you home safely, you know. I have my car – you direct me to your house.'

'No, it's fine,' protested Paige.

'Really, I'll take you right to your door. What part of town do you live in?'

'I said it's fine! The Ferrari's outside.' A pause. 'Oh God! I didn't pick Sienna up from the gym! Oh Ed!' Paige burst into peals of laughter, imagining Sienna still on the running track four hours later. 'I gotta pick her up!'

'You can't drive in this state!' protested Ed. 'Wait, did you just say Ferrari?'

'Sienna's,' groaned Paige, rolling her eyes to the ceiling. 'Oh Sienna,' she mumbled, 'why can't we all be like you ... what am I saying ... course I can ... done it before. And with one last grunt Paige bent over and vomited between her legs onto the Monte Cristo carpet.

Chapter 10

Crisp sunshine beat down from a cloudless blue sky pierced only by palm trees and casino towers. The tranquil scene in the Follies parking lot was the perfect vision of an urban Toulouse-Lautrec as styled by American Apparel: showgirls basked in the sun, squeezing the last few minutes and valuable cigarette puffs out of their mid-morning break. Fluffy pink legwarmers contrasted against toned fishnetted legs, neon leotards clung snugly to tight butt cheeks, and bosomy curves swelled gently beneath pastel ballet wraparounds. Cigarettes were waved dramatically for effect and elegant displays of stretches and splits mingled with the perky bobbing of topknots interjecting gossipy conversation. Paige limped outside with a clatter through the double doors, sheepishly fanning her green complexion.

'You feeling any better?' asked Tashonya.

'A little bit. It comes and goes in waves. I'm positive it was the steak Sienna cooked me last night,' said Paige, manoeuvring her tightly bandaged ankle carefully as she perched on an ornamental flowerbed. Sienna wasn't there to face her allegation as she was working through her break with Brandy, a fact that was clearly adding insult to Paige's injury.

'Eww, who'd have thought,' said Svetlana with a catty glint in her eye, 'poisoned by Brandy's new successor! Still, on the bright side at least you know you'll make tomorrow's weigh-in no problem.' A groan swept through the group of girls like a yawn at the prospect of the weekly check-in. Meanwhile Paige clutched at her throbbing head and swore to herself she'd never drink alcohol again. Details from last night were still sketchy in her mind. It had taken a good couple of hours that morning for her to piece together how on earth she had managed to get Sienna's Ferrari home in one piece, until it had filtered back into her memory that her new friend Ed had insisted on driving her and depositing her safely. He had been so obliging, and she hadn't even had to give him anything more than a kiss after he'd paid their whole bar tab – not that it would have been a hardship to have his big manly hands all over her body. He wasn't exactly Max Power, but at least Paige's faith was temporarily restored that gentlemen existed after all . . . although she had a fleeting suspicion he may have just wanted to try out the Ferrari. A wave of nausea hit her again and she turned and buried her head in the flowers, throwing up to cries and squeals of disgust from the girls.

'And hold, two, three, four, and blackout!'

Sienna held her arms aloft in her final pose at Marty's command before sinking to her knees on the huge stage to catch her breath. Talk about baptism by fire, Sienna had a mountain of choreography and cues to catch up on since the latest cast swap. Sienna wondered if Brandy's caprice reared its head so dramatically every week. She just couldn't find it in herself to trust that Brandy wouldn't dispose of her just as suddenly as she had Paige. The thought nagged in the back of her mind, and trying to soak up her first day of routines like a sponge whilst keeping her armour plating in place in front of Brandy was mentally exhausting already. Sienna was almost thankful that Marty and Glitter had been working her so hard that the grande dame had barely been given a spare second for a catty remark all morning.

'Well, that nailed it,' said Marty from the front row, looking over at Glitter, the choreographer, who nodded encouragingly as he patted his brow and adjusted his crotch in his tight gold dance pants.

'She's picking up fast, we'll be fine,' said Glitter in his thick Italian accent. 'Brandy? Whaddya think, *princepesa*?'

'Yeah she's – great,' said Paolo quietly, looking thoughtfully at the stage.

'So. We move on?' asked Glitter. A long pause ensued. 'Brandy?' pressed Glitter.

'No. This isn't right,' said Paolo, shaking his head.

'Okay, Brandy, what's the problem now?' asked Marty quietly, rolling his eyes at Glitter to issue a subtle storm warning.

'There's no problem as such. I mean, it all looks okay.'

Paolo paused. 'Actually, that's the thing. It's okay, not "oh wow"!'

'Well, these are just your parts, you're not seeing the rest of the production—'

'It's just a bit . . . *basic*, don't you think?' cut in Paolo. 'I mean, Sienna's eating this for breakfast. Can't we add some faster choreography in places?' Paolo jangled the bangles which snaked up his arm for emphasis. 'This is a tit 'n' feather *dance* production, not a strip show, Marty. Sienna may have been rolling around on a grand piano spending hours getting a bra strap off in her last job but she can really dance!'

'I'm aware of that, but . . . Brandy, these are your parts, you can't keep up with anything faster,' said Marty quietly through clenched teeth. 'Glitter designed this to work to your – er – strengths, remember? Your beauty. That sort of thing. Your costumes do all the work anyway, and—'

'No, I think we could try harder,' purred Paolo petulantly, enjoying the perks of Brandy's legacy of autonomy.

'Remember why you got rid of Viva, your last understudy? People started wanting to see her, not you,' hissed Marty insistently. A smile escaped onto Paolo's lips at the revelation. 'Besides,' Marty continued, 'we don't have time to fuck around with new steps. Glitter has his work cut out teaching your parts in a few weeks as it is. Now step off the pedal, and let's not complicate things.'

'I may not be up to scratch for the new showgirls' first night,' reminded Paolo. 'I had quite a fall. Sienna may have to do this herself. Besides I'd originally planned to be away on my little break, remember? You're lucky it went wrong and I'm still here.' Paolo rose from his seat. 'I say we try harder.' He hoisted himself up onto the stage, before discreetly checking his wig felt secure.

'Sienna, I want to create some better steps for you,' announced Paolo. Sienna regarded him suspiciously. 'You know, something to make you shine more,' he insisted. 'You've gotta radiate as the star if you're playing Venus. That means a few more special moves. Let me try a couple of things for you, watch.'

Sienna raised her eyebrows at the unexpected burst of creativity and generosity from her boss, before quickly clearing her throat, nodding briskly and obediently getting into position.

'Cue music!' screeched Paolo in that voice Brandy used to use when she was ordering him around in the play-ground. Sound filled the theatre, booming out through the monitors. Counting himself in, Paolo walked through Brandy's part. Sienna wasn't the only one who could pick up quickly; Paolo breezed through it. 'Keep it running!' he ordered. As the music rolled on he added in a few lightning-quick steps. Paolo felt his heart pumping with adrenalin. God, it was amazing to be on this stage, he thought to himself. Absorbed in the moment, he added kicks and jumps, before spinning his way expertly to the front of the apron for a final pose.

'Something like that?' shouted Paolo over the music,

smiling at Glitter and Marty. They couldn't say anything while their mouths were open. Remembering himself, Paolo added a clumsy kick and a purposeful stumble, topped off with a goofy giggle.

'Brandy, you've been rehearsing hard,' remarked Sienna. 'You're more than fit enough to do your own parts in a few weeks.'

'Oh, thank you – oops!' squealed Paolo, quickly feigning another trip for dramatic effect. 'Oh, did you see that? My knee, it's still just so – so sore,' he said, wincing a little. 'Let's assume you'll be covering for me, darling. That way no-one's disappointed if I don't heal in time.' Paolo barely dared to hope he would still be in Vegas by then. It all hung on whether he could keep everyone convinced, and how long he could string out not performing before it blew his cover wide open. The likelihood of him ever being able to come up with a solution for how to do Brandy's topless acts or be seen in a G-string was zero. But returning to the Bronx was not an option; it was a question of hanging in by his false nails, or falling to the dogs snarling, foaming and gnashing their teeth below.

'*Mamma mia*, okay, Brandy, if that makes you happy then take Sienna through your steps,' said Glitter, looking shell-shocked. 'I'll record the new sequence,' he added, reaching for his digital camera. '*Cavolo!* Who's she been fucking this weekend?' asked Glitter under his breath. 'Michael bloody Flatley?' Marty shook his head and snorted.

Up on stage, Paolo got into position in front of Sienna and started to talk her through the steps. Sienna followed obediently.

'Wait,' she said timidly, her earlier prickles dissipated. 'I'm really sorry, I can't get the second bar of eight. What foot am I leading off?'

'Here,' said Paolo, turning to face her and putting his hand lightly on her hip. He could smell her perfume, and a faint waft of freshly shampooed hair. He tried to ignore the butterflies in his stomach from standing so close to her. 'Ready? And step, step, kick turn.' Paolo span her round gently. 'And hips, and hips, and turn.'

Paolo smiled as Sienna came to rest, facing him. 'Good. Now do those hip moves with a straighter back so they aren't so grindy, like this . . . ' Paolo reached his arm gently around Sienna, putting his hand on her back to guide her. 'And hips, and hips . . . and hips, and hips . . . ' Paolo could feel Sienna's breath on his cheek. The music had stopped. Paolo pulled back as though stung by a wasp.

'Oh, was that okay?' said Sienna, startled.

'Yeah, perfect.' Paolo wasn't about to tell her that he had the beginnings of a raging boner. He turned to Marty and tried to think of Susan Boyle, anything to keep the erection at bay. 'Brandy's feeling pooped,' he announced, fanning himself with a limp wrist. He was sure his sister was just the type of diva to refer to herself in the third person. 'Shall we take five? Everyone else has had a break. I think we can take one too, no?'

'Sure,' acquiesced Marty. 'We'll get working on the chorus. You girls take a breather.'

Paolo sashayed his way through to the dressing rooms, with Sienna following closely.

'Brandy?' Paolo span round to face her. God, she looked stunning even with a face bare of make-up and with straggly wisps of chestnut hair escaping from her topknot, thought Paolo, finding it difficult to make eye contact while unclean thoughts were filling his mind. 'Just wondered, in case you won't be able to perform for the relaunch like you said, do you – do you think I'll get this right in time?' asked Sienna.

'Sure. You're a fast learner,' smiled Paolo.

'Oh and Brandy, I just wanted to say . . .' Sienna paused and bit her lip. 'Thanks for giving me a chance. You seem different now we're getting down to work. I obviously got you wrong and – I'm sorry I was so rude before. I was so upset about Honey. I was out of line. Well, anyway, I can see you're a great dancer, and I just don't want to let anyone down.'

'You'll be fine,' said Paolo, backing towards Brandy's dressing room, hoping to God Blue wasn't in there faffing around with hemlines so he could rip off the excruciating heels and rub his cramped feet in peace. 'There's a lot to cover but you can do it. I've seen enough dancers to know when they've got it.'

'Oh wow, thank you,' said Sienna, letting out a little laugh of relief. 'Just one thing . . . Honey?'

'Yes, sweetheart?' said Paolo hopefully.

'Why?'

'Honey . . . ' Paolo bluffed, realising he'd made a dumb mistake. 'Jeez I have a memory like a sieve. What was her full name? Remind me . . . '

'Honey Lou Parker. The one you fired for having a big butt, remember?' asked Sienna softly. A loud ringtone pierced the awkward silence. 'Oh, my phone,' she exclaimed, looking round at her make-up station. 'That'll be my boyfriend, I have to take it – do you mind?'

'No, no! Go ahead!' said Paolo, exhaling loudly as Sienna traipsed away. God, his sister was a piece of work. Every day – in fact every hour – seemed to proffer some new piece of shit that Brandy had stirred that he somehow had to neutralise. He turned towards her dressing room, to be greeted by Blue at the door proudly holding up the most minuscule fuchsia-coloured feathered G-string. Paolo gulped and immediately crossed his legs.

'This just arrived from Brazil, baby!' gushed Blue. 'Remember we ordered them ages ago in every colour! Is Brandy ready for a dose of coque feather?'

Honey woke to a shaft of warm sunbeam on her face, piercing through her eyelids. Gasping loudly, she sat bolt upright and checked her clock through her blinking.

'Noooooo!' she wailed out loud as she sank back into the soft pillows. 'Dammit!' she cursed. She yanked the duvet over her head to block out the daylight. Her show audition was taking place right now across town without her. She wondered if she had slept right through her alarm or if she had forgotten to even set the darn thing when she got home from the Velvet Taco this morning, she had been so tired. Gingerly she pulled the duvet from her face and looked down at the pile of cash on the rug next to the bed. With a heavy sigh she picked up the wad and sifted through, totting up her earnings. Not quite the week's wages Cobra had reckoned she would earn in one night, but pretty close. Honey was sure she could improve on it. She'd been observing Cobra carefully all night and that girl definitely had the sweet-talk routine down pat. It was like she instantly hypnotised men into reaching for their wallets. Honey wondered how someone got that gift – was it nature or nurture? Or maybe Honey just didn't get excited enough about money to let it do the talking. Either way, she hoped Cobra would give her some hints next time.

Honey suddenly wrinkled her nose at the pungent smell of cocaine wafting up from the notes in her hand, and tossed the cash back onto the floor in disgust. That said all she needed to know about the clientele. As she lay back and studied the sunbeams stretching their way across the ceiling, she kicked herself for missing today's audition, and wondered how she'd managed to get herself in this futile situation of trying to juggle working all night and then somehow making it to tryouts in the daytime; how in hell would she manage it without an amphetamine drip? Honey felt pangs of anxiety as she remembered her new stripper wardrobe had claimed the last of her cash and she had a tidy backlog of housekeeping to pay Sienna – she knew her best buddy wouldn't hassle her for it but Honey was living in this palace rent free. The least she could do was to pay for her food and bills. Honey sighed and curled herself into a ball. All roads pointed to money. She had to make it and fast. She had to get back on her feet. There would always be auditions, she reminded herself. She'd think of this as just a little detour and she'd get back on track in no time once she'd hoovered up some dollars and straightened herself out. If there was low-hanging fruit in her path, she may as well grab it en route to her dream.

'I'll take the steak, fried zucchini, pommes frites, a side salad . . . and extra blue cheese dressing,' said Paolo, looking up from his menu at the waiter and batting his eyelashes. 'And a side of stuffed mushrooms,' he added softly. He was ravenous; he could eat a horse. Week after week in his cheap rental, living off saltines with an occasional Budweiser for garnish was catching up with him. If the Follies petty cash was paying for this lunch, he was taking advantage.

'Brandy?' cut in Blue incredulously. 'Are you – pregnant, or something? With triplets? Christ, you usually live on champagne and plates of steam. It's all I can do to get you to suck on the lemon peel of your martini most of the time.' Sienna stifled a giggle.

'Oh!' exclaimed Paolo, fluffing his wig nervously, realising he had just entered dangerous cover-blowing territory. 'Oh, I was just testing to see if you were paying attention. What's wrong with a little giggle between friends! Ha haaa!' he laughed, forcing a smile. 'Umm, yes, I'll just take the, er, iceberg wedge, please. No dressing,' grimaced Paolo at the waiter. His sister hadn't shared his fast metabolism then, he realised miserably, as all kinds of delicious aromas from neighbouring tables began to taunt him. Maybe he could discreetly stuff a breadstick down when no-one was looking. He'd have to find out what new fad diet the chorus line were following and pray it was something Atkins-like so he could join in.

'Duck stuffed with foie gras,' ordered Blue, his own macrobiotic diet obviously well out of the window, along with Julian.

'Egg-white omelette with chives and a side of tomato salsa,' said Sienna cheerily.

'So, you girls seem to have bonded today,' remarked Blue triumphantly as the waiter whisked the menus away.

'Oh, you know,' responded Paolo, attempting to shrug it off nonchalantly. 'The sun's shining, we've got a pile of work to do, and Sienna – well, Sienna's almost certainly going to have to be Venus when the cast swap takes effect. Anyway, why does it surprise you that we get on? Like I'm supposed to be a bitch queen or something?' Paolo added provocatively. Sienna studied a bit of fluff on her jacket and Blue cast his eyes over the towering Botero statue in front of their table.

'So, Sienna, you seem to be bursting with sunshine all of a sudden,' said Blue, changing the subject unsubtly, 'especially after you've been moping the last couple of days.'

'Oh . . . yeah, I wasn't going to make a big deal,' she replied coyly, 'but it's my birthday soon and—'

'Ooh, we must celebrate in that case!' cut in Paolo, brightening at the thought of manufacturing some personal time with Sienna. 'A girls' night out?' he added hopefully.

'Wow, thank you for the thought, that's most kind but – actually when Max called earlier he sprung it on me that he was whisking me off to St Barth's tomorrow for a long weekend!' she declared, the slight edge of a squeal entering her voice.

'Ooh, get you,' crowed Blue. 'Jetsetter indeed!'

'I know, he played a trick on me saying he was taking me to the boxing with the boys, can you believe? He did it so I'd choose myself a new birthday outfit in advance without suspecting anything. He really had me going. I thought he'd forgotten. I feel like such a fool now; he must have thought I was being so ungrateful. I just wanted to spend time with him, that was all. I've barely seen him what with his workload and flying off all over the place for his meetings – and he's been so distant since our amazing time in the pool when he—'

'Oh stop,' interrupted Blue. 'I've swum in there, devotion, and I don't want to hear what goes on when no-one's looking, thanks. Anyway, Brandy, you go to St Barth's all the time, don't you?'

'I do, yes,' ventured Paolo, wondering where in hell it was. He'd never passed geography at school, and they hadn't taught him about luxury holiday resorts in the mental home. Italy maybe? Isn't that where all the saints were? Or France perhaps? Skiing maybe? Either way he was more bothered about purging his mind of ghastly thoughts of Sienna with another man. Lucky bastard.

'So maybe you can recommend some nice shops or restaurants to visit,' asked Sienna, turning to Paolo enthusiastically. 'I've never been and – oh my, I only have tonight to pack . . . I don't want to embarrass Max. Is it casual chic or more ostentatious?'

'Oh, you know, all those places just blend into one,' bluffed Paolo, hoping for a clue as to what hemisphere he needed to be in. 'You know me, it all rolls in to one big party sometimes . . .'

'Yes and the states I've seen you in I'd be surprised if you even knew what country you were in half the time,' laughed Blue. He'd discovered he could get away with being quite cheeky with the new improved Brandy.

'Oh, you don't know how right you are,' Paolo laughed weakly, desperate to move on.

'Hey, Blue, I thought Max would have let you in on the surprise! You're coming, right?' asked Sienna suddenly.

'Nooo, it's your special weekend!' protested Blue.

'Exactly. Max said it would be a party to remember.

Private jet, his pad, plus his Russian friends are having some kind of reception on their boat ... I know Max invited Honey and Paige already. Won't you consider it?' asked Sienna sweetly. There was an awkward pause and Sienna remembered with a sinking heart that Max had already mentioned something about inviting Brandy back when he was talking about the fight at Caesar's. Had that been a pretence too? Sienna realised as she gave a sideways glance at Brandy sitting silently across the table that she would have to confront the situation head on. 'Um, did Max invite you too, Brandy?'

'Yes ... ' bluffed Paolo, not knowing what the hell was going on but playing along as best he could. 'But – I won't be coming,' he continued, barely able to conceal his anxiety at the spiralling situation. 'We work together, I'd feel like I was intruding, I wouldn't—'

'Nonsense! If he invited you then you must come!' laughed Sienna as politely as she could manage in spite of her apprehension. 'It'll be fun.'

'Really, I couldn't, there'll be parties here this weekend to go to, I'm sure ... ' Paolo couldn't think of anything worse than being stuck somewhere watching Sienna and her boyfriend and having no escape route, let alone being exposed to all sorts of probing questions as Brandy that he'd never know the answer to. Plus he daren't even think about the wardrobe preparation he'd have to undertake. If it involved a boat that would mean bikinis and ... well, tucking – no, it was out of the question quite simply.

'I can't think of a single party in crazy Vegas that'll be even a fraction as hot as a weekend in the Caribbean,' said Sienna, graciously trying to smooth out the awkward atmosphere. 'Come on, the more the merrier,' she sighed. 'Blue? Mum will want you to keep an eye on me for a start. And Brandy, consider this an olive branch. I feel like we had fun today. I hate what you did to Honey, but well – she should be coming too so it's your big chance to make it up to her and be friends.'

'Well—'

'Let's just have fun and relax. We're going to have to be in pretty close quarters with all the rehearsals for "Venus in Furs" so it makes sense for us to get to know each other. And you've met Max already so . . . please, I'd love you to come.'

'Great,' said Paolo, choking slightly at the thought of how the hell he would get himself out of this mess. Caribbean? The closest he'd ever been was a packet of tropical dried fruit mix from the 7-Eleven. This was all catching up too fast and there seemed no way out. Blue and Sienna sat before him expectantly. 'I'd love to,' Paolo said, beaming back at the pair.

Back in the dressing room after hours, Paolo didn't know if it was the physical exertion of the rehearsals or being Brandy that was exhausting him so much. She was a vampire in the flesh, but even just playing the role Paolo felt every morsel of energy being drained, like he was somehow conjuring her. He sighed heavily as he absorbed his surroundings. Fake marble, the brash shine of gold veneer fittings, an arsenal of wigs and make-up and clothes everywhere. The only reflective surface not nailed to the wall was etched deep from years of racking out lines with a razor blade, and the stale ingrained stink of cigarettes mingled with the sickly sour scent of bouquets on the turn; the perfect reflection of his sister's life in a microcosm. Masks, smoke and mirrors, and a rotten core.

Paolo ripped open the wrapper on his third candy bar and idly pulled out one of the drawers in the dresser. A stack of pre-signed picture postcards of Brandy in all her feathered, nipped and tucked glory, two boxes of Trojans, some Valium and a sheaf of crinkled prescriptions for Ritalin and Demerol, nestling next to a pile of cards and fan mail. Paolo picked up one of the cards as he chewed. 'Wishing you all the best tonight. Try and keep some energy for later. Richard.' A whimsical postcard underneath: 'Dear Miss Alexander, Tonight is my eleventh time at the show! Your number one fan Stefan x.' Brandy certainly had her fans fooled, thought Paolo, reaching for one more card. 'Maybe the Mile High Club next time? Enjoy the flowers. Max.' What a coincidence. Sienna's boyfriend is called Max too, thought Paolo. Although by the looks of things Brandy had been steadily working her way through the *Bumper Book of Boys' Names* anyway, which kind of shortened the odds. Paolo on the other hand had never exactly been a womaniser. He'd been so absorbed with looking after Mami after he'd come of age, he'd only really had time for a few short-term girlfriends.

Paolo suddenly remembered Sharon. Shit! They were meeting tonight! Paolo still felt indebted after she'd nursed him and had arranged to take her for a piña colada as a small gesture. He suddenly realised he hadn't even started to scrape off his two inches of make-up, and Sharon would be on her way to his bedsit right now. Within a second he was scrambling for the door, praying he could make it home in time to restore himself to plain old Paolo before Sharon came knocking. He knew he needed to break it off with her as gently as he could. It was better that than her start asking questions about the curious changes in his appearance. His eyebrows were now sharper than hers and he was a whole lot less hairy too.

The huge bright red chilli stood gleaming on the stage, standing tall like an erect penis as a tiny sultry brunette weaved her way around it, winding her hips with smooth, snake-like stealth. Black hair bounced at her shoulders in thick bosomy curls and a dramatic white Mallen streak was swept back from her right temple. A vintage-style chalkboard framed in elaborate gold filigree displayed the name 'La Cholita' in an elegant swirl of white on black. Blue guffawed at the cultural pastiche, and sipped at his champagne, mesmerised by the pocket Venus as she worked her way around the stage, elegantly gliding then bumping and grinding, flicking the floor-length chiffon panels of her shimmy belt with her pelvis as her audience looked on, entranced.

'Tongolele,' he muttered, leaning back against the bar.

'Eh?'

Blue turned to find himself chest to face with a cute Latino.

'Tongolele. That's who the dancer looks like. You know, the Mexican burlesque dancer from the fifties?' The Latino looked back blankly before shrugging apologetically.

'I'm Pancho,' he said, offering his hand.

'I'm Blue.'

'Sorry to hear that,' replied Pancho, smiling, before wandering back to his table clutching a round of beers.

'Sense of humour. Cute!' murmured Blue under his breath, knowing instantly that he wasn't his type; too swarthy, especially after his clean-cut preppie-looking Julian, but able to appreciate his drop-dead handsome features all the same. Blue was unsure if he was missing Julian or not yet. Blue had ditched him immediately in the hotel suite after walking in on him. It was bad enough he suspected him of cheating on him with girls, but cheating on him with a pair of tennis socks? After he'd just bought him a Ferrari? Unforgiveable. Blue had already stopped off at Krave tonight and had one proposition from a cute blond dancer called Joey. Blue was a bit sick of showbiz kids after Julian, but Joey currently had a job as a centurion at Caesars and was cute as hell and up for some fun. After two years of being faithful, Blue was certainly tempted by the idea of seeing what was under Joey's toga. He'd given Blue a business card from a gay bathhouse across town and instructed Blue to meet him there for a warm-up. Blue now turned the card over and over in his hands, not sure if he was really up for action so soon after the humiliation of the sock incident. Blue didn't like to admit that Julian had really meant a lot to him. He was trying to handle it the best he could, but still needed convincing that Joey was the best remedy. Sighing, he popped the card in his inside pocket and looked back over at the stage to see La Cholita was now straddling the hot chilli.

'Ha, a novelty pole dancer!' chuckled Blue to himself as she began to execute a rather seamless selection of smooth manoeuvres on the chilli. Blue was ever so slightly impressed by her tricks. As she slid slowly down the length of the glinting chilli, she cheekily jutted her peachy butt over the edge of the stage and affectionately rubbed her cheeks on the head of the nearest John to a swell of applause and appreciative murmurings. Blue liked this girl. True vintage style, slightly slutty, and very funny. As La Cholita straightened and mounted the chilli once more, the John's chestnut-coloured toupee travelled with her, caught between her butt cheeks. A moment's silence while the toupee dangled there was followed by an almighty cheer erupting all over the room. Blue sprayed his champagne. The spotlight jerked up to the ceiling as the lighting guy fell to the floor in hysterics. The whooping and cheering got louder as La Cholita frantically grabbed the hairpiece from her butt, and tossed it back into the audience with an apologetic grin, only for it to be lobbed between tables, grown men now standing and joining in, circulating the glossy slice of hair, keeping it bobbing in the air back and forth. Griselda rushed onto the stage as the spotlight wobbled its way back into position.

'Give it up for La Cholitaaaa!' A red-faced besuited man came pelting past Blue, both hands up at his balding head, before slamming his way out of the club. Blue suspected he wouldn't be waving any dollars at La Cholita's hot *tamale* any time soon.

'Man, that's one hot chica.' Blue turned to see Pancho up at the bar again, having a round of tequilas poured by Jeffrey.

'Yeah, but she's not really my type,' replied Blue wryly.

'I'll say,' laughed Jeffrey, laying out a tray of salt and lemon.

'You guys know each other?' asked Pancho.

'He's part of the furniture,' explained Jeffrey, 'given he's so handy with a sewing machine.'

'Huh?' Pancho looked confused.

'See those costumes the girls wear up on stage?' asked Jeffrey.

'Sure. Hot!' replied Pancho.

'That's what Blue does. He's hard at it every day, sewing gussets and rhinestoning bras.'

'No shit!'

'Well, I wouldn't put it like that, Jeffrey, I don't just dress any old act,' retorted Blue.

'I'm selling our friend short,' laughed Jeffrey. 'Blue does the big shows. Not our modest little set-up here.' He grinned wryly.

'Well, not that thing up on stage at any rate,' tutted Blue, tossing a disapproving look at Griselda, who was looking distinctly flammable in his foot-high nylon wig and floor-length polyester gown.

'Wow, so you get to play around with bras and showgirls all day. Nice!' laughed Pancho. 'Hey, buddie, if you're standin' all on your own why not come and join us an' have a tequila?' Blue considered for a second before accepting. Within minutes he had been introduced to Pancho's pals and was admiring the friend called Tiny's blazer.

'It's just like Armani, only . . . pink,' said Blue.

'Let me let you into a little secret,' beamed Tiny, leaning in conspiratorially. 'It's . . . fake.'

'Noooo!' exclaimed Blue in mock surprise.

'Yeah, had a friend make it up from an original pattern.' Blue cast his eyes over Tiny's ensemble, the medallions, the crocodile shoes. He was rocking his own look, that was for sure. Blue admired that.

'You know, you remind me of someone I used to know in London,' said Blue. 'You kinda remind me of them, the shoes, the jewellery . . . very Dalston, very *i-D*.'

'Wow, didja hear that, Jesús ?' said Tiny, turning to his buddy. 'Our friend here says I look like I come from London.' Tiny puffed his chest out a little.

'Yeah yeah, now what's this freakin' thing up on stage? That a dude or one ugly-assed *chola*?' asked Jesús, pointing at Griselda. 'Bring on the real girls!' he shouted loudly up at the stage.

'Excuse my friends,' said Pancho apologetically.

Blue shrugged. 'I don't know what it is on stage either,' he said, 'but it sure could crack a mirror with that face.' The men clinked glasses and laughed loudly as Griselda introduced the house troupe, and a haphazard line of mismatched pasty blondes burst into view, their anaemic-looking dance captain Verucca Sock leading the charge like an over-enthusiastic girl scout.

'Christ, she's about as sexy as a tin of carrots,' complained Pancho. 'What's with those nasty greying girdles? My grandma wears those!'

'Where's the women!' Jesús could be heard exclaiming incredulously.

'I love this joint, Pancho, I really do,' sighed Blue. 'It has a . . . special kind of place in my heart. But if you ever want to see some glorious girls, come to the show I work on, it's the biggest on the Strip,' offered Blue, reaching for his inside pocket. 'In fact, here take my personal card and call me whenever you want tickets,' he said, passing it under the table. He didn't want everyone seeing it and asking for freebies.

'Hey, thanks, man!' Pancho beamed, pocketing the card immediately. 'Hey Tiny, Blue just gave me his details. We can get tickets to go see the show he works on!'

'Thanks!' said Tiny, appreciatively. 'So long as they got proper women I'm up for it! Now who needs a tequila? This is like watching the greasy-haired titless cheerleader rejects at summer camp.'

'I think I'm gonna make a move,' said Blue, deciding that maybe he would go to Pure nightclub in case Julian was there partying. Just one more look at his pretty face couldn't hurt, surely. Blue said his goodbyes and decided to make a pitstop via the restrooms, narrowly missing Griselda as he farted his way past.

'Oh look, it's the hecklers!' said Griselda with a glint in his eye as he came to rest at Tiny's table. 'The ones who were asking for real women.'

'Yeah that's right,' replied Tiny, rising to the bait fearlessly.

'Well, I can see by the pink suit it ain't women you're after, darling,' laughed Griselda.

'Who you talkin' to?' said Tiny, suddenly wrinkling up his nose. 'Ugh, what's that smell, dude, you been eating all those rotten tomatoes people been throwing atcha?'

'Ooh, a clever one!' screeched Griselda. 'But not clever enough for a bitchy gay boy.'

'Who you calling gay, mister?' said Pancho gruffly, wading in.

'Well, you were only sitting with the biggest pansy in town just then!'

'Blue? He never said he was gay! He just has good dress sense like me!' exclaimed Tiny.

'Darling, he'd make Liberace look like Warren Beatty. What's more, I saw him handing over his card.'

'He said we could call him for show tickets!' protested Pancho, turning red in the face, and reaching for the card. 'See? This is the show he works on.'

'Hmm, Triple X Bathhouse?' said Griselda, leaning down to read it. 'Sounds like one hell of a show, boys,' he cackled.

'Give me that!' growled Tiny, snatching the card from Pancho. He took one look. '*Hijo de puta!* He was grooming our Pancho!'

Griselda screeched with laughter before receiving a huge slosh of Tiny's beer straight in his face.

'That's the only thing you're gonna get in your mouth tonight, dude,' growled Tiny through gritted teeth.

Griselda immediately tossed his piña colada at Tiny.

'Argh! My new suit! *Puta!* Or whatever the hell you are!'

'Pink doesn't suit your skin tone anyway, dear,' retorted Griselda, turning to walk away. He didn't make the full circle before Jesús leapt on his back, with Pancho and Tiny springing for his legs to topple him. Blue minced out of the restroom within minutes, to be greeted with a mess of flying drinks and flailing limbs as the entire Monte Cristo joined in the fray.

'These troublemaking tourists,' muttered Blue, shaking his head and slipping out through the exit quietly.

'Catch you soon, huh?' said Paolo, standing at the door to his room.

'Oh, you're not going to ask me in for coffee?' asked Sharon, unable to conceal the disappointment from her voice.

'I'm bushed,' said Paolo quietly, casting his eyes downwards. He wasn't lying; he'd barely slept with the pressure of his new role on his mind. But the real reason he couldn't invite Sharon in was that he hadn't had time to clear the bathroom of all the make-up wipes, false lashes and detritus before she had arrived earlier.

'Okay. Well, thanks for drinks,' she said forlornly, leaning in for a kiss. Paolo awkwardly pecked her on the cheek, not wanting to give her any false ideas – or have her get too close. He'd got on well with her tonight, he really had, but how could he think about starting a new relationship when he had to spend so much time being a woman now? It was such high maintenance, he didn't know how they managed to even get out of the front door, what with everything he'd had to do in the last forty-eight hours. Not only that but he'd truly run out of cash now and he'd be giving up his rental this week. How would he explain his sudden graduation to the couch in Brandy Alexander's palace? It was all too messy by far.

'Why are you so distant?' asked Sharon, looking up at him with puppy-dog eyes. 'I thought we got to know each other better when I was taking care of you.'

'I know,' said Paolo, his heart melting a little. She looked so pretty. Maybe just one kiss. He leaned in. A loud squeal nearly pierced Paolo's eardrum.

'Oh my God, you have make-up smeared behind your ear!' shrieked Sharon. 'And your – your neck smells of perfume! So that's it! Another woman!'

'No!' said Paolo hurriedly, cursing himself for not taking all his make-up off properly. 'Well, not like that anyway!'

'I knew it!' sobbed Sharon as she backed away. 'And I bet you were with her yesterday. I came knocking yesterday evening and you weren't here.' Paolo groaned, casting his mind back to being in Brandy's pad choosing outfits and cosmetics, and thanking his stars Sharon hadn't been at the door when he returned home with armfuls of Brandy's clothes. Paolo's mind went blank. What the hell was he supposed to say? Where could he even start? There was no need for him to think. Sharon was already halfway across the parking lot, her choked sobs escaping into the sultry night air behind her. Paolo couldn't have felt more like a heel if he tried.

Chapter 11

Max's villa nestled in a lush outcrop that jutted into the clear azure Caribbean Sea. The view was breathtaking, the undulating swell of neighbouring islands meeting blue skies blemished only by an occasional white smudge of an aeroplane trail. Sienna dangled one long lean leg out of her hammock and rocked herself gently to the music wafting softly from the speakers concealed amongst the palm trees, melodic chords of jazz piano accompanying the soporific rhythm of waves rolling lazily onto the rocks below. The coarse, juicy grass that carpeted Max's huge terrace felt welcomingly cool between Sienna's toes, as a delicate breeze caressed her soft skin. Blue bobbed into view in the large infinity pool, stretched out on a lilo armchair, cocktail in hand. Sienna filled her lungs with fresh sea air and closed her eyes dreamily, soaking up the comforting heat of the sun. What an amazing setting for a birthday weekend – if only her girlfriends could have made it. Sienna felt terrible for poor Paige after a desperate top-to-toe search of her room failed to turn up her passport, and then Honey had unexpectedly bailed out too; Sienna had immediately panicked that it was to do with

Brandy coming and was all ready to uninvite her for Honey's sake. But Honey insisted she had an important audition that simply couldn't be missed.

Sienna was unhappy that she had seen so little of her best friend lately. They were like ships in the night, crossing paths on the stairs as Sienna left for work and Honey was coming home. Sienna wasn't exactly thrilled that Honey was having to waitress at one of the all-night snack bars. With the dismal wages they must be paying her Sienna would rather cover her share of the housekeeping herself and give Honey the chance to hit the daytime tryouts fresh and alert rather than exhausted from serving burgers all night for trashy tourists. Sienna subconsciously crossed her fingers as she now lay in her hammock that Honey would do a great audition today. Kind of weird to have one on a Saturday but hey, nothing about Vegas was normal.

'Mint julep?' asked Paolo, towering over Sienna's hammock with a platter of drinks.

'Perfect, thanks!' replied Sienna, eagerly liberating one of the cocktails from the tray. 'Max back yet?' she asked hopefully.

'No sign of him,' said Paolo tightly, clacking his way carefully across wooden decking to the pool to pass a drink to Blue, before retreating hurriedly back to the kitchen.

'Brandy okay?' asked Sienna. 'She seems upset. Her hands were shaking just then with that tray of drinks.'

'Hah!' scoffed Blue. 'That's just called one too many

martinis, darling. Either that or she's back on the Ritalin.'

'No!' gasped Sienna.

'Well, she used to pop 'em like M&Ms, although I thought she'd stopped all that recently. Anyway, more to the point, why isn't Max here enjoying the sun with us?'

'Business,' intoned Sienna. 'I wish he'd just learn to relax and stop working so hard. Just think, coming all this way and having this beautiful villa and then not even taking time to just sit back and enjoy it. Seems so pointless.' Sienna gulped back her mint julep and focused on a solitary fluffy cloud which had appeared up above.

'That's international playboys for you, devotion,' sighed Blue.

'He's no playboy,' giggled Sienna, unconvincingly. 'He just works too much.' Deep down Sienna had a sinking feeling that this whole trip may just be far more work than birthday orientated. Sure, it had started amazingly with a luxurious flight on one of the Silver Slipper private jets. Whilst she didn't take such opulent means of travel for granted, Sienna enjoyed every second of the extravagance; savouring the delicious fruit platters and cocktails on board and delighting in the kitsch Versace gold fittings and sumptuous soft furnishings. Her mum would have loved all that post-ironic-nineties chic. Sienna didn't think much to the air hostesses, on the other hand; they may have looked cute in their cheesecake fifties outfits but were definitely being frosty towards her. Sienna wondered if they were schooled in pretentiousness at Silver Slipper, or if it was just the usual envious bitchiness from girls who assumed she had an over-privileged life as Tiger Starr's daughter. Either way, she wasn't about to let a snippy waitress mar her birthday weekend. What bothered her more was her first inkling that Max would be down to business all the way seeing as he spent the entire flight with his nose glued to his laptop screen.

At least Blue and Brandy had been on good form, and by the time the foursome touched down in St Maarten spirits were high. The glamorous group were then transferred to a small private yacht and taken directly to the Russian billionaire Andrei Melnychanovich, who was waiting to receive them on his vast Philippe Starck-designed floating gin palace. Sienna's breath had been taken away as she saw the huge vessel looming up in the St Barth's harbour; a shining mass of polished whiteness glinting under the blazing sun. They enjoyed an immaculate lunchtime selection of canapés and cocktails and a live quartet. Blue was in seventh heaven in his surroundings, swapping high fashion and couture tips with his new audience whilst revelling in the fact that his white linen ensemble blended perfectly with the walls lined entirely with white stingray skins. Sienna, however, was a little awestruck by the spectacle, even feeling slightly self-conscious. She knew her mum went to such parties like this all the time, often even performing at them back in the day. But despite all the fabulous stories she'd come home with, she had been pretty protective about keeping

Sienna away from that scene, and not allowing her to get into the 'gilded cage' as she would call it. She always quoted one of her retired party-going friends who warned her against being inveigled by the 'exotic birds in the cage'. It was certainly an easy way to tap into one's insecurities, Sienna thought now, suddenly not feeling quite young, beautiful, leggy or moneyed enough as she looked at Max huddled with the host and his exquisite beauty queen wife. Even Brandy seemed strangely subdued for someone who had apparently been enjoying such luxury for years.

Max had then muttered something to Sienna about needing to discuss business before announcing he was staying on the superyacht for the afternoon and sending Sienna, Brandy and Blue ahead to his pad on St Barth's to make them comfortable and relax before the evening party he would be hosting. Whilst Sienna wouldn't ordinarily mind 'tagging along' on Max's business trip, in an ideal world she'd rather have known that was the deal from the start. Now she knew why Max had been keen on inviting her friends to keep her company. She felt slightly embarrassed that Blue and Brandy had probably worked that out by now too.

'I must say the perks of the lifestyle are good,' said Blue, paddling his lilo across the pool. 'I'd love that private jet we came in on for myself.'

'Actually, most of the stars timeshare them with each other. So you'll often get three or four actors or pop stars to a jet. It isn't all quite how it seems, as things rarely are,' said Sienna matter-of-factly, inwardly wishing she wasn't timesharing Max with his business ... much less his gambling.

'Ahhh. Thanks for taking the gloss off that dream for me, darling,' sighed Blue. 'Still, nice pink carpets and gold fittings though.'

Sienna turned her head lazily. 'D'you think I should call Mum?'

'Could do. I'm sure she'll call you tomorrow when you're officially twenty-three,' reassured Blue.

'S'pose,' squeaked Sienna forlornly. She was missing her mum. Tiger would know what to make of Max and their relationship if Sienna confided her worries; she was a woman to tell it exactly as it was. It was what Sienna needed right now, some good straight talking. Preferably with a cuddle, although a phone call would come in as a good second best. They'd enjoyed a couple of years in close company before Tiger had relocated to Los Angeles, although at the time Sienna had maybe not appreciated it as much as she did now in retrospect. It was true that Tiger did have a tendency to want to coddle her daughter which Sienna would interpret as interfering when she would rather figure things out for herself; but since they'd never had the chance to enjoy a normal relationship as Sienna grew up, she knew deep down her mum meant well and just wanted the best for her.

When they were alone they had some really fun times. Going out in public however was usually far too stressful because of all the press attention Tiger garnered. Sienna would find herself sharing her mum with the paparazzi, autograph hunters and new 'friends' who descended on them wherever they went. Sienna would smile and be serene but she could usually hear the soft hissing 'S's of people whispering her name and nudging each other, mostly with disgust as though she should feel guilty for being the daughter of someone famous; as though she had somehow begged for all this attention, as though she was desperate for that sign of belonging that the paparazzi flashes were supposed to give.

The burden of circumstance weighed upon Sienna as she knew she was either being written off as a talentless showbiz daughter who couldn't follow in her mother's footsteps if she kept her head down, or if she did well and made her mark, an over-privileged brat who had only achieved anything through her connections rather than any talent. *Damned if you do, damned if you don't.* Sienna burned to prove her critics wrong. She felt driven to make her name in her own right. As for the funny old fame game, Sienna didn't actually care for column inches, she didn't need adulation, she wasn't a natural exhibitionist and disliked the scrutiny that came with fame, but she hated the idea of being written off even more. Why should she be given the brush-off because ignorant, jealous people thought she had special privileges? If that meant that she had to prove her worth on her own terms, she would do it to make sure she could stand next to her mother as her equal . . . although it fed her paranoia to think that perhaps she could never truly know if she'd managed it in spite of her name.

Of course, had Sienna spent less time having her buttons pressed by resentful onlookers, she would have realised that deep down all she really wanted was the big 'A' grade on her report card, the big red tick for her hard work from her mum. Perhaps because she'd never had that growing up . . . because the truth was she'd never been allowed a real mother for all those years.

A smile curled its way into the corners of Sienna's lips as she remembered the recent peaceful times she had with her mum when they did normal things; like watching reruns of *Frasier* and eating takeout pizza, playing with Tiger's dog in the garden, splashing in the pool together, having a wardrobe swap session. Tiger had an amazing wardrobe, and although some of the gowns were a bit more serious than Sienna would ever choose to wear, she usually nabbed some cool designer outfits. Tiger wasn't always willing to hand things over, particularly if it was something she hadn't worn yet. Sienna ruefully remembered wanting to wear Tiger's short fuchsia-pink Versace Grecian-style dress for a party where there would be hot guys; yet Tiger had wanted to hang on to it for a dinner date with Lewis. Sienna had told her mother she should hand it over as she was too old for it anyway. It was a Pyrrhic victory: the look of mortification on poor Tiger's face had made Sienna want to eat her words immediately, and whilst her mum had wordlessly given up the dress, Sienna realised how much an edge even a light sarcastic comment had when it came to a showgirl and her appearance, especially for a woman about to enter her late thirties in Hollywood. Tiger may have been snagging her fantastic roles by working the kind of old-school glamour that the young starlets just couldn't emulate, but bucking the ageist trend was still no easy achievement, and Tiger was hypersensitive about how fine a line she was treading. Sienna had always thought it a cliché that looks were currency in showbiz, but it was only now that Sienna truly appreciated that they weren't just currency, they were make or break. Sienna felt a deep ache to pick up the phone and hear her mum's voice, and just tell her she loved her. But it was a sure bet Tiger Starr would be either on set or deep in meetings. Best to wait for her to call. Sienna untied her bikini straps and settled in for a few hours of sun.

Honey had discreetly stuffed two hundred bucks into the hand of the host as she stepped into the private Sky booth with Sapphire. There waiting for them were eight guys in town for a conference, already delving into the champagne that had been laid out on ice. All the Sky booths were furnished in black leather and chrome, huge plasma screens for when the sportsmen were in town, and floor-to-ceiling glass panels which allowed the patrons to look out over the whole of the Velvet Taco. Honey could make out Cobra down on the catwalk below, swishing her distinctive butt-length raven-black tresses. She had worked the Sky booth once already this week and come away with great money for doing very little. Those guys hadn't really wanted much in the way of dances, they just wanted to chat and hang out with beautiful girls and feel important by flashing their cash around a bit.

She'd much rather be in the Caribbean with Sienna, but she needed to be making money, not spending it. Not that Sienna would have let her put her hand in her pocket. But how could she hobnob with all those moneyed celebrities, socialites and moguls in St Barth's and tell them what she did for a living when they asked? She'd already had to lie to Sienna as she didn't want her visiting her at the club and seeing her getting hot and heavy with guys. Although it was a silly fib: flipping burgers was hardly more aspirational than what she was really doing. At least with the money she would make tonight she could take Sienna out for an expensive birthday lunch when she returned to Vegas. That would make her feel good, to do that for her friend. And then with whatever was left over, she would treat herself to some much-needed new clothes. She felt better already at the thought of retail therapy that didn't involve neon spandex or lucite heels.

'So what convention are you in town for?' asked Sapphire, getting straight down to business.

'World of Concrete,' replied one of the guys.

'So which one of you dirty bitches wants to dance for

me, huh?' asked his friend, eliciting a loud cheer and clinking glasses from the others. Honey knew in a second it was definitely not going to be a repeat of the other night, and braced herself with a smile of steel and a vision of fluttering dollar bills.

Paolo had only just managed to calm his nerves after his nightmare on the yacht. He knew this weekend would be tricky but so far it was a baptism by fire. It was bad enough that he'd not had his beauty sleep for days due to all the preparations: all the waxing, back, sack, crack, pedicure, manicure, exfoliating, buffing, no wonder it took women all year to get bikini ready. The private jet had lulled Paolo into a false sense of security that the weekend might actually be pretty fabulous. He silently thanked the heavens that he'd unearthed Brandy's second, Puerto Rican passport which meant he could make this amazing trip – hooray for duel nationality for a change. Max wasn't so bad after all and Paolo could grudgingly accept he seemed rather a catch for Sienna. Paolo had even started to really enjoy himself by the time they all boarded the mega yacht. Never in his life had he seen such luxury and opulence; he'd felt like he was on a film set. That soon turned into the set for a horror movie, however.

Paolo had gone for a trip up to the sundeck at Max's suggestion. He thought Max was being the perfect host in looking after his guests. But Max had immediately made a move, asking Paolo if he still thought about the hot,

filthy sex they'd shared against Brandy's car. Paolo's immediate reaction had been to want to splatter Max's handsome nose all over his handsome face with a good left
hook. Paolo had managed to rein himself in within a split
second however and unclench his fist. The irony wasn't
lost on him that Max would undoubtedly do the same if
he ever knew what was underneath the Gucci kaftan.

Paolo of course then clearly recalled reading a card in
Brandy's dressing-room drawer that had been from a 'Max'.
He boiled inside at yet more outpourings of vileness from
his sister. How could she do such a thing with the boyfriend
of one of her own showgirls? Brandy and Max were a good
match, of that there was no doubt. Once Paolo had been
able to compose himself he had hurriedly excused himself,
from the horrifying situation with some mumblings about
prickly heat under the sun. But he had barely managed to
conceal his shell-shock all afternoon. He had no idea what
he would say to Max when he eventually saw him again,
and he could barely look poor, lovely Sienna in the eye. He
just wanted to scream out to her to get rid of Max. What
Paolo would give to have such a stunning, smart girlfriend
for himself. But for now, he was stuck in this nightmare
and he'd just have to get through it the best he could.

'So how come Paige turned down this weekend?' asked
Paolo, trying to pick a benign subject for conversation as
he settled onto a lounger elegantly and swiftly arranged
his kaftan.

'Oh, you wouldn't believe it, she couldn't find her

passport, poor love,' said Sienna. 'The curse words coming from Paige's bedroom last night were probably being heard over the Hoover Dam, I reckon. Even worse, there was absolutely nothing I could do. I feel terrible.'

'Ha ha, I bet she can curse! I sense a spark in that girl!' laughed Paolo.

'Oh, I don't know,' countered Sienna. 'She's quite reserved and private. She doesn't get too "sparky" unless she's had a few flutes of champagne, then she can be a riot. That's when her drawl comes out too, have you noticed?'

'Yeah, I picked up on it a few times,' piped up Blue. 'Seems to be when she forgets herself, she comes over all . . . *y'all* . . . you know? It's dreamy,' he sighed.

'Where's she from?' asked Paolo.

'Chinquapin,' 'Maycomb,' said Blue and Sienna in unison. They looked across at each other.

'Maycomb?' laughed Blue. 'Have you been reading *To Kill a Mockingbird*, devotion?' he chuckled.

'Huh?'

'Oh, for God's sake, didn't you learn anything in that private school of yours, Sienna? Maycomb isn't real. It's a fictional town. You know the book? Scout? Atticus?'

'Thanks for embarrassing me! No, I hated English Lit at school. All that Shakespeare . . . *Withering Heights* . . . *Mrs Dalloway* . . . Okay so I must have heard Maycomb wrong, although I could have sworn that's what Paige said. So where is she from?'

'Chinquapin, Louisiana,' said Blue.

'Hmm. Sounds *kind of* familiar for some reason. Funny, now I think about it we always have so much to chat about but I've never heard her talk about her home life or her family.'

'Maybe she just doesn't see them much.'

'Yeah, I'm sure that's it. Poor love. Well, I'm glad she seems to be settling into the show okay.' Sienna turned to face Paolo. 'Mind you, I know she's pissed at you, Brandy, for hiring then firing her from the understudy position, so maybe it would be awkward for her being here after all,' said Sienna with a wry grin. 'Certainly made conversation stilted for *me* over the dinner table once or twice.'

'Oh, that,' said Paolo awkwardly, not wanting to be drawn into too much detail. 'I guess I've upset a lot of people,' he said thoughtfully, 'although – I thought I was saving Paige in the long run by swapping her. She was a little too inexperienced.'

'That's not what you said when you hired her,' reminded Blue provocatively from the side of the pool. Paolo thought for a second how best to handle Brandy's apparent switch from bitch to buddy.

'I think I may have been high,' said Paolo, expecting that part had probably been true. 'But you know, I've stopped all that now. Since the . . . er, fall. I feel different . . . '

'No shit, you've been waiting on us hand and foot all day. If I didn't know better I'd think an alien had taken over your body,' laughed Blue.

'I guess I have some bridges to mend,' said Paolo hurriedly. 'So, anyone for an iced coffee?' he blurted, changing the subject.

'Will you just stop fussing and sit,' said Sienna as Paolo rose and contemplated another stint in the kitchen.

'Yeah, Brandy, relax and get some sun.' Sun was the last thing Paolo needed: he was boiling under his wig, and he couldn't risk his make-up running. He had to stay cool as a cucumber, hence the reason for keeping mainly to the air-conditioned kitchen and venting his frustration about Max's appalling behaviour by chopping and pummelling lemons for all manner of lemonades and iced teas. Paolo just wanted to keep out of the way, away from the heat and away from awkward questions or any talk on the subject of Max Power. Plus to make matters worse, swimwear was strictly off limits, which in this heat was making things unbearable. Paolo was already wearing something as short as he dared go, in the form of one of Brandy's mono-chrome Gucci kaftans. He'd even bought some convincing 'chicken fillets' for Brandy's bras. He was exhausting her selection of cleavage-covering apparel; there wasn't that much of it in her wardrobe, needless to say. She clearly liked to display her wares; obviously something that had appealed to the likes of Max. Thank the Lord Paolo had great legs and shapely calves at least. This trip really was turning into a royal nightmare.

'Ooh, could you just rub some oil into my back while you're up,' asked Sienna, sitting up in her hammock and waving a bottle plaintively at Paolo. Oh, for chrissake, when did she take her bikini top off? thought Paolo as he crossed the grass, unable to take his eyes off her full, pert breasts, her dark nipples hardening visibly in the cool breeze which cut through the afternoon heat. This was going from bad to worse, he thought, tearing his eyes away and ignoring the twinge of an erection. He desperately visualised ice buckets and baseball, and quickly slapped some oil onto Sienna's back.

'There you go,' he said abruptly, handing the bottle straight back.

'Oh wait, is it rubbed in properly? You need to really rub it in evenly,' said Sienna apologetically. Paolo gritted his teeth and rubbed the oil slowly into Sienna's silky smooth, lightly tanned skin.

'Oh, that's nice,' she purred, arching her back. 'Wow, you have such strong hands, Brandy,' she remarked. That's it, enough already! thought Paolo, straightening immediately and flouncing towards the house. 'I can hear the phone,' he lied. 'Back in a minute!'

'Oh yeah, baby,' crowed one of the World of Concrete guys, as Honey placed a hand behind each of his shoulders and shoved her cleavage into his face for a few lingering seconds. 'Call me Bob . . . Mmm, you smell gooood,' he cooed.

'Really?' muttered Honey, feeling about as sexy as a fishmonger's block.

'So, Kandy, are you available and how much?'

'I'm right here, aren't I?' Honey replied.

'You know what I mean, are you – available?'

'Available for what . . . Bob?' asked Honey wearily, turning her back to him and grinding her backside near his crotch, rolling her eyes as she faced the glass panel.

'You're a smart girl . . . ' Honey suddenly yelped and sprang away from Bob's chair.

'Oh my God, call security!' she hissed, as Sapphire flew over to Honey's side.

'Oh gimme a break, you're gagging for it!' slurred Bob. Within seconds the club host was inside the booth and calling for backup.

'He put his fingers inside me,' said Honey, turning to Bob. 'You bastard!' she spat, before storming from the booth. Sapphire ran after her.

'Kandy, wait, it'll get sorted. He's just drunk – he'll get fined and ejected.' Honey kept walking. 'Oh, come back, Kandy! We'll finish the rest of them,' Sapphire persisted. 'There's no point leaving money on the table, babe.' Honey stopped in her tracks and turned to Sapphire.

'You really think I'm going back in there? He asked if I was available for sex!' Honey said incredulously.

'Yeah, happens all the time. Guys just think bikini plus money equals sex somehow. It's no biggie, he was only asking. Whaddya expect?'

'What do I expect? That there is such a thing as boundaries! That dancing here for twenty dollars a song should be treated no differently to dancing in a show for a twenty-dollar ticket!'

'Kandy, it doesn't work like that! We're practically naked, and the guys are dumb and frustrated. It's not like we're up on stage on a pedestal, it's all personal and one-on-one so it gets confused in the guys' heads. We lead 'em on and it goes nowhere. At least foreplay ends up with something; the Velvet Taco is all just one big dead end.'

'You can say that again!' said Honey furiously.

'Oh, come on, ignore it. They're all drunk anyway. Think who's walking away with all the money! Think who's got the power, babe!'

'Not me! Not when a dance in a bikini gives someone the right to stick their fingers up my vagina! I go to the pool – in a bikini – and I do *not* get guys sticking their fingers up me!' she yelled.

'I'm not defending it,' said Sapphire. 'Problem is we sell them the idea that – well, we look like we're in a permanent state of arousal, for chrissake! We stare up at them with our orgasm faces. We're right in their space. We grind our asses two inches from their crotch. We pretend we like them and we bat our eyelids like they're fascinating. We're like slot machines that get fed a dime, recite platitudes for a minute and wait for the next coin. These guys pay their twenty bucks to suspend belief for four minutes of an Aerosmith song, don't you get it? In their heads they think their twenty bucks just bought us.

214 • *Immodesty Blaize*

It's not right, I know that, but I'm just tellin' ya that's how they see it.'

Honey looked at Sapphire and shook her head. 'You're doing a great job of selling the "we've got the power" bit!'

'Look, you have to be strong enough to hold onto the truth,' continued Sapphire. 'You have to stand *above* their fantasy, because it only exists in their heads and their dollar bills. You don't need me to point out you're not actually a blow-up doll, for chrissake. Lemme tell you a secret. What I said back there? The "who's got the power" thing? It's just a crappy debate to sell books and college courses. I know because I did them all. They all contradict each other. You want the truth? There is no power. We all need each other. Who holds the guy's balls and their drunken fantasies and their insecurities between sharpened claws? I do, Kandy. And then who pays for me to do what I *really* want to do? They do. So they walk away broke and happy, thinking they've bought someone who doesn't actually exist, and I walk away happy knowing I can afford to keep dancing over the road in Jubilee, a proper show, for crap wages. It's no different to working in some office job you hate and being treated like a pea-brained servant so you can pay for the amateur surfing hobby that you really love or the Jimmy Choos that'll change your life. No-one writes books about the "politics" of that scenario! We all make choices. I just get paid for hard work plain and simple. Let's not overcomplicate it. You have to figure this out in your own head or you ain't cut out for the job, sweetheart. You're too young to take it so seriously; just enjoy earning good money here and spend it on something worthwhile. Hell, I train my ass off every day and take my dance classes to get this body fit and beautiful and I ain't givin' looks away for free for nobody whether it's here, or wearing fifty thousand bucks worth of rhinestones and feathers as a showgirl at Jubilee and showing off every last bit of classical ballet training I ever did. At least here I get paid well, so ask yourself – where am I worth more?' Sapphire gave a hollow laugh and looked squarely at Honey. 'Look at us, standing in a corridor in our bikinis as the sun's coming up. Let's just finish the job, get the cash and we'll talk some more tomorrow if you really want,' she sighed. 'It's too late for me to start comin' over all Susan Sontag, jeez!'

'You go back,' said Honey. 'I'm all done here.'

Sienna drew gasps of approval from Max, Blue and Brandy as she came down the stairs wearing a column of shimmering gold. She had liberated the Dior dress from Tiger's wardrobe an age ago, hoping she might one day have the occasion to wear it. The eve of her birthday seemed fitting. She felt incredible. As she crossed the large chic white lounge, Max sprung to Sienna's side, kissing her softly on the cheek and proffering his hand to lead her outside to the awaiting cocktail party he had arranged. Sienna didn't care that he'd had his head in business all day; she could barely stop her heart beating out of her chest at the sight of him looking so handsome in a crisp black Armani suit, his hair slicked back, eyes sparkling.

Sienna drew in her breath sharply as she stepped on to the terrace to gentle applause and welcoming murmurs from the guests. The garden looked incredible lit entirely with candles, and a jetty had been installed into the huge pool, providing a platform for a baby grand and its rather handsome pianist, who was playing softly accompanied by cicadas and the gentle rolling waves of the sea.

'Oh Max, how did you manage this in – what – three hours?' asked Sienna incredulously as she surveyed the idyllic scene.

'Thank my PA Jane,' he laughed, 'and Blue, who did a sterling job of finally getting you out of the sun and into the darn house so Jane could actually get the boys to work on decorating the place.'

'Ah, I wondered why I was getting all the skin cancer lectures from a certain person,' laughed Sienna.

'Don't think I was just doing it to get you inside. I was being serious, devotion. Besides, you're too young for your skin to start looking like your Hermès handbag,' laughed Blue before lunging for a cute cocktail waiter and dragging an uncomfortable-looking Brandy with him.

'Let's go and mingle with our guests,' said Max, taking Sienna's hand in his and guiding her from the terrace into the garden. Sienna felt every pair of eyes on her as she worked her way around the glamorous party. Andrei Melnychanovich and his family were there flying the flag for couture, a gaggle of excitable socialites had already descended on Brandy, and a few of Max's work associates were sharing canapés and island gossip with a selection of celebrity neighbours. Once everyone had been greeted and Max had attentively refreshed Sienna's champagne glass a couple of times, he led her out on to the jetty. The pianist took his cue to start playing 'When Did You Leave Heaven?' Max smiled at Sienna as a ripple of 'aahs' swept through the guests. Max took Sienna's hand and slipped his other arm about her waist to dance to the song.

'Oh Max, I can't thank you enough,' whispered Sienna, nuzzling in to his neck. 'This is just so perfect.' Sienna took in the delicious musky aroma of Max's skin and clung tightly to him, swaying gently to the wandering melody of the piano. Sienna closed her eyes, wanting to savour every second. A light evening breeze ruffled its way through her hair as the pianist made his way effortlessly through to the second verse. Suddenly Max was pulling away, furrowing his brow as he clutched at his chest.

'What's wrong?' whispered Sienna, her face contorting in concern as Max slumped to one knee. She crouched down in her beautiful gown, everything starting to move in slow motion in her head.

'Get up!' whispered Max, his hand at his breast.

'Are you okay, baby?' asked Sienna.

'I said just get up! Our guests are watching!'

Sienna reluctantly rose and looked awkwardly about her, as everyone looked on at the handsome couple in expectant silence. Sienna's heart started racing. Forget what the guests were thinking, what was wrong with Max? Should she call for help? As she looked back down at him, she gasped in shock, her hands flying up to her mouth, eyes wide.

Out by the Velvet Taco front door, Honey made a run for the flowerbed and hurled up.

'Hmm, so sexy,' said a guy sarcastically as he walked inside the club with his friends.

'Oh God!' whispered Honey to herself, unable to stop the tears rolling down her face as she walked into the parking lot and found a spot to sit on at the kerb. 'What the hell am I gonna do now?' she sobbed to herself, wishing she'd just gone to the Caribbean with Sienna.

'Bad night?' came a voice from behind. Honey's head span round.

'Josh,' said the guy, holding his hand out.

'Kandy,' said Honey, looking away again, 'With a "K".'

'Oh, I'm sure that's your real name,' he laughed, sitting down by Honey. She looked at him. Kinda cute in a nerdy way. Slim, glasses, shoulder-length dark hair.

'Need a ride?'

'No thanks,' she snivelled.

'Sorry, I just realised, strange man, huh? Doesn't sound good coming from a stranger.'

'What do you want?' asked Honey suddenly. 'It's just, I'm really not in the mood to be picked up, and just to be clear, I'm not available for sex, now or ever.'

'Whoa!' said Josh, with a laugh. 'I just thought you looked upset, but hey, I'll leave you alone. I was waiting for some friends. They haven't arrived so . . . '

'Sorry. I thought – never mind,' said Honey sullenly.

'You sure you don't want a coffee or something?' asked Josh.

'No. Thanks. I'm fine,' sighed Honey, wiping her nose on her sleeve. 'Another time maybe, just not tonight.'

'I gotcha,' said Josh. 'Listen, I'm gonna look for my buddies but if you ever want that coffee – here's my card.'

Honey extended a hand and took the business card.

'And by the way, you're very beautiful. Ever thought about modelling?'

Honey shook her head.

'You should. You could clean up with a face like yours. Tyra Banks eat your heart out.'

'You think?'

'Sure,' said Josh. 'You got my card. I can take you to a fashion party if you like, see the competition for yourself. Or I should say . . . you've got no competition.'

'Oh, I don't think—'

'Hey, no pressure. Think about it. It was good to meet you. I hope your night – day – gets better.' He smiled and started to walk away.

'Bye,' said Honey softly. Josh turned.

'If you change your mind about the party, there's a good one next week in LA. Call me.'

She nodded a thank you and watched as Josh made his way back to the club. She looked at the card.

'Joshua McInnes. Photographer.' Her mother always used to say 'everything happens for a reason'. As awful as it was, maybe that incident at the Velvet Taco had been put there by the universe to get her out of there, thought Honey. Maybe this modelling opportunity was where her luck started changing after all.

Paolo could barely keep his eyes on Sienna's face as her perfect full breasts heaved and wobbled dramatically beneath the sheerness of her black chiffon negligee.

He hadn't expected her to barge in to his room unannounced and certainly not dressed like this.

'I mean, I can't believe the diamond used to be his mother's,' gushed Sienna for the tenth time in as many minutes, 'and the design is so beautiful!' She waved her left hand under Paolo's nose again in case he hadn't seen the huge rock of an engagement ring the first time.

'Honestly, I swear I thought he was having a heart attack,' laughed Sienna, 'but he was fumbling for the ring in his inside pocket the whole time, how funny's that! I know he was hamming it up to get me going! Brandy, did you guys know? Were you in on it?'

'No, not us, we were just as shocked and thrilled as you, my dear . . . truly shocked,' said Paolo as enthusiastically as he could manage. Sienna didn't notice the awkward pause as she stared dreamily at her engagement ring.

'So – where is he now?' asked Paolo tentatively, unable to help himself from making the jibe. 'Only I noticed him disappearing with some of the guests?' Paolo checked his towel turban was still in place, and desperately scanned the room for any incriminating evidence. He had a couple of wigs in clear view in the bedroom but Sienna hadn't batted an eyelid at those. So many of the girls wore them in the shows, they didn't need to be a giveaway. The head-dresses really did wreck the girls' hair, and most of them were shorn short anyway. Paolo would have to be more mindful about unexpected visits like this. He forgot that female friends were so free and easy with each other, touching each other all the time, wandering around naked, borrowing each other's clothes, in and out of each other's rooms. He simply had to start thinking more like a girl if he was going to get through this.

'Max said he had a special poker game,' said Sienna casually. 'It's okay, he'll make it up to me later. I think he deserves a break for a couple of hours after he put so much effort into tonight,' she giggled.

'Yes, he certainly made some efforts this weekend,' mumbled Paolo with a hint of bitterness. 'But doesn't he want to let his hair down with *you* though? You're his new fiancée . . . sitting here so . . . sexy . . . like this.' Paolo struggled with the words and tried not to stare at Sienna's chest.

'Oh darling, we've got a lifetime together now.' Sienna gave a little sigh. 'And there was me worrying he was being all distant these last few weeks.'

'Hasn't he?' asked Paolo, biting his tongue as much as he could but unable to stop the digs from popping out of his mouth. He just wanted to scream out what a louse Max was, that he'd cheated on Sienna and that he showed no signs of stopping after today. But how could Paolo reveal the truth when Sienna thought she was sitting with the real Brandy, the very bitch who Max had been unfaithful with?

'I thought Max was hiding something from me, but I guess I misread it and was getting myself worked up over nothing. I think I underestimated how busy he's been at work.' Sienna paused for a few moments. 'Oh Brandy, I was so worried, I'll be honest. That day I had a go at you? Max had upset me. I guess it's been my fault for being such a paranoid bitchzilla. I'm guilty of having a short fuse occasionally, you see; it's the Italian in Mum's side of the family, makes us a bit sparky. Thing is, I do worry about Max's gambling, and he then gets annoyed because he thinks I'm nagging.' Sienna looked down at the floor. 'And I guess a small part of me always worries that I'm not good enough.'

'Stop right there!' snapped Paolo. 'I'm not having that. If I was – if I were a guy you'd be a catch. You're amazing.'

'I'm not so sure, Brandy. You see there's always this thing that people only want to be with me because of – Mum. You know, her money, her connections . . .'

Paolo was quiet. Poor cow. She really had no idea how much she had to offer as Sienna, as herself. Yet there was nothing Paolo could say to alleviate her hang-ups about Tiger. It was true he had heard a couple of the girls in the dressing room bitching in the past week that he must have done a U-turn about Sienna because of her mother. Paolo hadn't made the Starr connection at all at first, although now looking at Sienna he could see the likeness. Paolo had immediately understood why Brandy would have overlooked her for the understudy part, as it was bad enough that Sienna was a better dancer and more beautiful, but with a famous mother to boot? Not only that, but someone with a boyfriend she wouldn't have minded for herself. Brandy would have stuck needles in her eyeballs rather than let someone with those attributes have a chance to shine in the show, whether she was right for the part or not. Paolo also understood why Sienna was so eager and determined to prove she could work hard now. He in turn was even more determined she would have her chance when the show reopened to take centre stage. She'd earnt it.

'Oh, I can't believe I just told you all that. Dammit! I'm sorry I've made myself look stupid now – you don't even know me!'

'No, no,' said Paolo lightly, trying to keep his head calm. Here was a drop-dead beautiful girl sitting in front of him baring her soul while he was trying to sit on his hands to stop himself jumping on her and ripping that dumb nightie off her amazing body, whilst pretending to be a woman she could trust. Now he knew how Tootsie must have felt.

'I'm glad you feel you can talk to me. We have to work together, we may as well know that we have our cards on the table,' added Paolo sincerely, his own irony not lost on him.

'Brandy, I hope this doesn't come across as too personal,' started Sienna, 'but do you ever feel that circumstances you didn't create have meant that you've been tarred with the wrong brush?'

Paolo looked away. *If only you knew*, he thought, wishing he could just blurt everything out right now.

'I think we all have baggage when we start out,' said Paolo after a beat, 'but that's the thing we have to learn in life; we can't walk very far if we're carrying that heavy load with us. Gotta let it go, darling, if you want to get ahead,' he said softly, wishing he could ditch his own baggage fifty miles under the sea. Without a word, Sienna leaned forward and put her arms around Paolo in a bear hug. He froze rigid, hoping to God she didn't brush against his face and feel stubble.

'Oh, I'm sorry,' apologised Sienna, feeling Brandy's awkwardness and pulling away. 'I didn't mean to be over-familiar, it's just that I felt like you understood. So few people do. I don't think I do myself half the time,' she laughed uneasily.

'It's fine, darling,' said Paolo, 'I'm just a little stiff from the accident still. I wasn't pushing you away, really I wasn't.

Anyway, who needs all that heavy stuff, you're getting married! You have a nice big man to take care of you now, you don't need to worry,' said Paolo, the words almost sticking in his throat as he thought of what he wouldn't give for just one moment of intimacy with Sienna.

'Coo-ee! Can anyone join in?' came Blue's voice at the door.

'Come in!' said Paolo, his heart sinking even further. This was all he needed. He hoped to hell this wasn't going to turn into some kind of slumber party; he had stubble to shave and God knows what else on his checklist before tomorrow. He certainly couldn't afford to start dropping details now. But Blue was already settling in on the bed, Tia Maria in hand and ooh-ing an ah-ing over Sienna's ring again. Within seconds Blue had sloshed the sticky black liquid all over Paolo's bedspread.

'Oh heavens!' squealed Blue. 'I'm having a blonde moment. Let me clear it up.'

'It's fine!' insisted Paolo, rising for the bathroom.

'No, no,' replied Blue, 'I'm such a cack-handed fairy sometimes, let me grab some tissue.' He was in the bathroom within seconds, Paolo following closely.

'Blimey, Brandy, you've got enough hair-removal products here to prune a baby mammoth,' cracked Blue with a roaring laugh, as he stared at Paolo's soap bag overflowing with Gilettes, wax strips and depilatory creams. Paolo stood by all his make-up protectively as Blue began to unroll some toilet paper. Blue paused before looking up at Paolo quizzically. A flicker of doubt registered on his face before he minced back through to the bedroom. It was then that Paolo realised that Blue had seen the toilet seat left up.

Chapter 12

Monday morning. Freshly showered and shaved. Half an hour to kill. Ed hummed as he wandered past storefront after storefront in the Miracle Mile, feeling a little apprehensive about his first day of appointments. He wanted to make a good impression; his new friend Paige had rounded up several of her fellow dancers for deep tissue massage sessions. Easy money. What a fortuitous meeting that had been, when she'd literally stumbled into his life. About time too: Ed's meagre reserves had pretty much run out, and his last few bucks had gone on a deposit on a small studio to operate his physiotherapy from – well, he had to at least *look* professional. Thankfully it would, if all went to plan, only be a stopgap until the real income started. Then he'd really be set up for life. Hard work had never been Ed's favourite pastime and it was hard to make a decent living in Australia from personal training; particularly after a little weakness in the face of temptation in his youth which he'd been paying for ever since. He had a good feeling about his Vegas scheme, and his patience so far seemed to be paying off.

Ed caught his reflection in a shop window and stopped to run his hands through his thick hair. He allowed himself to feel a little smug that he'd managed to hold on to his looks, probably due to many years of fitness, fresh air and healthy food. Even this morning he'd squeezed in a few kilometres run. He found a good blast of endorphins therapeutic to start the day off. He wished he could get as much enthusiasm for training other people, but he really couldn't get interested enough in providing token therapy for overstressed arrogant city boys, nor being diplomatic to fat lazy bitches whose years of never saying 'no' to pudding had turned them into one. Massaging overpaid, spoilt footballers didn't really float his boat either. He'd rather spend the time on the field himself. At least he used to get that with the teaching. But that career possibility had been wiped out long ago.

Ed's eyes rested on a cute pink teddy bear in the window display. He suddenly thought of his daughter, and he wondered what she was doing right now. Maybe she'd received the card he'd sent? Perhaps she'd like the bear too, he wondered. He checked in his pockets but found only small change. Thank God for Paige and his new clients today; he'd be able to come back and buy the bear this afternoon. He'd be giving it to his daughter soon in person, with any luck. For someone he'd never met, he almost felt like he knew her . . . and now she'd finally be having a lot of contact with Daddy. For the first day in ages he felt there was finally a silver lining on his twenty-three-year-long cloud.

The ten-foot cinema screen began to unfurl itself noisily

as the concealed tiki bar span round slowly back into its cubby hole in the wall with all the floor lights illuminating to full brightness. A short ear-splitting burst of ZZ Top blasted out before the window blinds began to whirr down over the picture windows. Paolo frantically pressed each and every button on the huge remote. Finally everything went quiet. Paolo then spotted all the neon pool illuminations gaily flashing outside as a huge fountain was now roaring into action. All he'd wanted to do was crank up the aircon in Brandy's ridiculous mansion.

Paolo slumped into his sister's leopard-skin couch and surveyed his worldly possessions in three large holdalls in front of him. After squaring his last bill at the motel, he'd just had enough cash left for the cab ride. How had this got so out of hand? Now he was squatting in his sister's palace. If he turned himself in, he'd be charged with impersonating Brandy; add that to the past felonies on his records and it was another spell in jail. He could forget about ever working again. If he did a runner the resulting search party would alert his sister, and she would bring him to justice herself. He could forget about ever walking again. Paolo had never appreciated how much those first couple of days of playing along with a misunderstanding would escalate out of control, and he had no idea how to turn back.

He reached in his holdall for one of the miniatures he'd stashed from the Silver Slipper flight back from the Caribbean. Maybe a nip of Jack would help him along on the path to figuring out a solution. Paolo sat back in the couch and surveyed the den. If he didn't know better he would have said it had been decorated by one of Barbra Streisand's colour-blind gay poodles after getting high on catnip. The place was covered in every kind of clashing animal print, dripping in gaudy gold fittings, and accented with a vague attempt at deco, with a bizarre black and peach theme making a bid for attention. He put his feet up on what appeared to be a python-skin coffee table and tried to get his appetite going at the thought of Saltines with ketchup for lunch. Even if he had felt like mooching food off his sister, a cursory look in the refrigerator had revealed merely a slew of expensive cosmetics, enough alcohol for several parties but nothing remotely resembling calories in solid form. It was clear Brandy didn't use her kitchen much for cooking – but just maybe she'd have some Dijon in the cupboards if he fancied a walk on the wild side for a change.

'I'm so gutted I wasn't there for your big moment!' wailed Honey, as a wave of regret washed over her for missing out on her best friend's birthday weekend. Somehow this flashy birthday lunch at the Encore felt like a kiddies' tea party compared to getting engaged in the Caribbean by moonlight in front of celebrities and billionaires. In fact Honey felt the weight of a monster reality check about to engulf her as she considered how her life was careening towards some messy off-road scramble right now compared to the smooth high-speed freeway her best buddy was on.

Honey didn't feel too hungry any more, which was a bitch considering the food in this place must be clocking in at around fifty bucks per mouthful. As she pushed her food around her plate, she tried to keep in mind the modelling opportunity that had presented itself. She'd just have to make sure she turned it into something worthwhile. After all, you make your own luck in this life, she told herself.

'Oh, sweetheart, I missed you this weekend,' declared Sienna, grabbing her friend's hand from across the table. 'It was all so beautiful, so romantic, I had to keep pinching myself to check it was real. But I swear it wasn't the same without you there. In fact I've missed you so much these last few weeks, we've barely had any time together.'

'I know,' sighed Honey, 'and it's all about to change, I promise. I've decided to jack in the waitressing and concentrate on my creative stuff. What was I thinking!' She gave a little laugh, knowing full well she wasn't about to get into detail – mostly because she hadn't actually figured out the detail herself – but she had resolved she would be back on her feet and in the pages of *Elle* and *Vogue* before Sienna could shake a feather at her.

'Hooray! You're wasted on serving breakfast burritos to trailer trash who rock up with their yard-long glasses of fluorescent blue frozen margarita. That's not why you came to Vegas!' said Sienna, devouring a juicy shrimp. 'Oh, wait – how can you afford this—' She gulped.

'I have it covered,' winked Honey. 'This is your birthday treat.'

'Are you sure? I'd rather cover the bill if it leaves you short—'

'It's on me!' snapped Honey. 'I saved the money, okay?'

'Okay,' said Sienna, backing off rapidly. Honey felt awkward; she wasn't about to explain how she had earned so much cash the last couple of weeks. Sienna still believed she'd been waitressing and that was fine by her.

'Oh, I forgot these,' said Honey, changing the subject and reaching for her purse. 'Here, this card arrived after you went away, and this is a little something I got you.'

'Oh, Honey! But you've brought me here so you shouldn't have got me anything else!' Sienna scolded, ripping open the paper on the small package.

'It's tiny. It's not diamonds or anything,' she sighed, 'just something I – thought you'd like.'

Sienna opened up the box to reveal a small, perfectly formed gold brooch pin of a horse's head dressed in ornamental feathers, with a long gold tassel hanging down from the mane made from fine gold chains.

'I thought it was like your mum's rocking horse prop, and I know you've been missing her . . . ' started Honey.

'It's gorgeous!' gasped Sienna. 'I adore it!' She beamed, rising from her chair to lean over the table and plant a huge kiss on Honey's cheek. 'It'll remind me of two people I love, you and Mum,' murmured Sienna as she pinned the brooch to her sleek black Marni dress. 'There! Makes my outfit better already,' she giggled, breaking into a wide twinkling smile. Honey felt relieved she had chosen the right thing. It was hard to know what on earth to buy the girl who could have anything she asked for, but she knew Sienna appreciated the thought in things. Hell, they'd lived like impoverished students together for long enough; there was no doubt that Sienna knew the real riches in life were things no money could buy.

'Don't forget the card,' reminded Honey. 'It has a Nevada postmark; might be a secret admirer. Not that you need one!' Sienna gave a wry smile before ripping the powder-blue envelope open. She stared at the card before looking up blankly and handing it over to Honey.

'What the hell do you make of that?' she asked, raising an eyebrow.

'To a special daughter,' read Honey, opening it up. 'For my baby girl – kiss – that's it? Your mum sent you this? What's with the skipping kitten on the front?'

'That's not Mum's writing. She'd never write that neatly with her long nails. Anyway she couriered cards and flowers to Max's villa. Yeah and what's with the bloody kitten? It's for a five-year-old. Ew.' Sienna shuddered.

'It's a joke.'

'Nope, jokes are funny, Honey!'

'Ha ha. I meant it's a joker.'

'No-one knows where I live.'

'Oh, c'mon, you're Sienna Starr! You get tour buses going past your mum's house!'

'I don't care who I am, I don't advertise that I live at Mum's.'

'Just ignore it, it's a stupid prank. Forget it,' said Honey, handing the card back. 'Hey, let's order dessert. One day of carbs won't wreck your weigh-in.'

'Yeah! Now you're talking!' cheered Sienna, folding the card and disposing of it along with the torn wrapping paper as a waiter swooped past.

Once the girls had devoured Seville orange sorbet, miniature ice-cream muffins and Honey had quaffed a Brandy Alexander for the sake of irony, she ordered the bill, before excusing herself and nipping to the ladies since all the champagne, wine and digestif had taken its toll. By the time she returned to the table, Sienna was pulling on her cashmere wrap.

'Wait a sec, I just need to settle the bill,' said Honey.

'No worries, it's all done,' said Sienna cheerfully.

'What?'

'I sorted it. It was a crazy price and you can't be earning much with your temporary job so I wanted you to save your money.'

'You're not exactly on bucket loads yourself as a dancer,' bristled Honey.

'I know, but I did get a small raise for the understudy part. Don't worry, I'll just have to get Max to buy the groceries this week,' she said with a wink.

'I can't believe you just did that, you patronising, ungrateful – that was one of my presents to you!' flared up Honey.

'What?! You being here was enough,' said Sienna, startled. 'I thought it would help.'

'No! You don't know how hard I worked to earn that money and this was meant to be my present to you!'

'Wait, I—'

'No! You just wrote it off like it's just an exchange for your bloody millionaire fiancé doing the wholefoods run this week! You spoilt cow! You just get everything in your lap, don't you, the house, the car, the job, now the bloody husband, and my stupid lunch means nothing to you! Of course it doesn't, because you could probably eat here every day if you asked your mum—' Honey gasped, realising what she had just said. 'No, I didn't mean that—' Honey wanted to bite her tongue off. It was too late. Sienna had already left the table in wounded silence with her eyes to the ground.

Chapter 13

This wasn't the first time Blue's life had been hanging by a thread, in every sense. The new cast debuted in the show tonight and he was still putting some finishing stitches in Brandy's costume for her revamped opening number. If it wasn't safely completed by lunchtime he may as well chop off his own balls before Marty did. No matter how organised he was, no matter how huge his team of seamstresses, it counted for nothing if there was a dumb klutz of a dancer in the wings about to rip through her chiffon with a high heel at the last minute, or a skinny bitch who'd selfishly decided to drop a few pounds since their last fitting. Blue couldn't remember a show launch where he hadn't been sewing against the clock.

This time it was Brandy's fault. She was behaving like a Chihuahua's ass and had refused point blank to have any fittings, insisting she was the same weight. Yet when Blue had finally managed to get her to try on her swan-down coat this morning, one of the seams immediately ripped under the armpit, nearly taking the entire arm of fluffy white feathers off. She'd barked something about over-training her arms in the gym before storming from the room. Thank Christ all her other costumes were either topless or corseted, thought Blue with relief as he worked his way down the coat seam at lightning speed.

The more Blue thought back over the last few weeks, the more he realised how unsettling Brandy's behaviour had been ever since she cancelled her plastic surgery 'vacation'. The terrible beating she'd taken had obviously knocked something out of place in what was left of her prescription drug- and liquor-addled brain, and the bizarre sweet 'n' nasty act had been unnerving Blue. The calm, nice periods left Blue feeling on edge as he braced himself for an inevitable storm. And then when the flashes of temper headed over the horizon they were just a touch too low on the Richter Scale for comfort, the venomous words almost watered down into a bad sitcom script. At first Blue wondered if Brandy was on some new-fangled medication, or if her 'incident' had been a karmic wake-up call to change her poisonous ways. Maybe she would come into work a born-again Christian and decide not to do topless any more. Blue laughed out loud at the very thought. Or perhaps it was all one devious game? What had happened to the heavy partying? The potty mouth? The perma-cleavage? The arrogance? Why, Brandy had even apparently discovered the joys of camaraderie and had forged a friendship of sorts with Sienna. That display in the Caribbean three weeks ago, making snacks and serving drinks like a happy little home-maker? Irrationally jumpy at any questions? Whatever Brandy was up to this time Blue didn't trust any of it one little bit, he decided, as he powered his way round the last inches of busted seam with his needle and thread.

Excited squeals filtered through from the communal dressing area. The girls had been working so hard at their rehearsals the last few weeks, and by the sounds of it first-night jitters were setting in early out there. Blue sighed deeply. He loved the electricity in the air before an opening night. He also had his own reasons to be excited, of course: Joey the centurion would be in the audience tonight. He'd called unexpectedly earlier. Blue was definitely showing signs of getting over his last relationship with ridiculous Julian, and as he triumphantly finished his last stitch in Brandy's swan coat, Blue reckoned he could be in the mood for a date after all. How bad could it be to be rescued by a tall, dark centurion?

Honey woke up in Josh's bed to the sound of rhythmic pounding coming through the walls from the neigh-bouring apartment. She stared at the ceiling as she lay there, the fan whirring softly above, its wooden slats blur-ring before her eyes. She had to hurry up and get some modelling assignments and fast. Josh had been sleeping on his couch for two weeks now while she took his bedroom; this arrangement couldn't go on forever. After a series of rows following the disastrous lunch with Sienna, Honey knew she had to leave and sort her life out. Sienna had been distraught and begged her to stay, but Honey couldn't stay there while things were going so awry with her life. Not only was it hard to keep up the tissue of lies, but she felt like her nose was being rubbed in her failure the whole time. She had to rethink her career strategy, and come back with a bang when she was on track.

The last straw had been another blazing row when Honey had needled Sienna as to why she'd kept quiet about her upcoming first night in 'Venus in Furs'. Honey knew deep down that her friend was just trying to be sensitive by not inviting her to watch the show she'd been fired from. But Honey still felt left out ... and just a teeny bit jealous. It was all getting too messy. Honey had to get the hell out of that awkward atmosphere and sort her shit out. She had to pick herself up and give herself a reason not to feel excluded and envious any more.

She'd arrived on Josh's doorstep one lunchtime and, finding no-one at home, had waited patiently until he eventually arrived. He'd been more than a little taken aback to find her there surrounded by boxes and carrier bags full of possessions, but he'd relented after a little persuasion, agreeing she could take the sofa until she got a steady income again and could secure a rental of her own. Honey was in turn a little surprised to see that Josh lived in such modest digs; surely a successful photographer would have some kind of slick pad, no? Even so, with Josh's original words ringing in her ears that she would have no problem cracking the modelling circuit, Honey installed herself in his front room with every intention that it would be a very temporary arrangement. After just one sleepless night on the sofa, Josh had valiantly given Honey the bedroom. He didn't care about beauty sleep as much anyway.

A couple of weeks later, however, and Honey was getting impatient. Where were all these castings Josh had promised? All he seemed to want her to do was go to parties – he kept saying that's where she'd be spotted. Josh reckoned that as a new kid on the block she'd create a buzz. Honey had finally relented and they were driving across to LA this afternoon for a big fashion do in the Hills; well, at least it would take her mind off the 'Venus in Furs' show taking place tonight at the Follies. The banging through the wall that had been getting progressively faster had thankfully now stopped after a loud screaming climax. The faster Honey got back on her feet and out of this cramped beige bachelor pad the better. Roll on tonight.

An enormous gilded clamshell emerged in a haze of dry ice from the lift beneath the stage, opening as it settled in the centre position to reveal a resplendent Paolo as washes of pink light enveloped him. He had his perfect moment choreographed in his head and ready to go; this was going to be a monumental performance, flawlessly executed and timed to perfection for full dramatic impact. His head was pounding in the vice-like grip of the towering feather headdress and his feet were screaming, wedged into his four-inch heels whilst his toned body was clothed in loose dance pants and a ballet wrapover – this was the final rehearsal before the new cast debuted tonight.

As the bombastic overture segued into a swell of melo-dramatic strings, Paolo launched into his big opening routine, flanked by the pneumatic showgirls in bodysuits designed to make them look naked save for a few stra-tegically placed bursts of sparkling rhinestones. Long luxu-rious blonde wigs gave them cascading siren-like curls topped off with twinkling tiaras. The girls all separated out around Paolo in a kaleidoscope of kicking legs as he executed exquisite arabesques and sensual, elegant contortions from within his giant golden clamshell. He broke into a sweat underneath his get-up – he hadn't stretched like this since his ballet classes as a young boy. He knew Marty and Glitter had been creaming themselves at the new routines – remem-bering how mediocre Brandy used to be at dance classes in their youth, Paolo knew they were far beyond anything she could ever have done – and certainly anything she could be bothered to do. Brandy had always been much more inter-ested in the applause part rather than the actual perform-ance and the thought of breaking a sweat except between the sheets would have been beyond her.

Paolo stepped out from the clamshell and joined the showgirls in the magnificent parade as a stunning water effect filled the stage behind them in rolling waves as dolphin boys emerged from the pool, rippling torsos covered in all shades of blue crystal which sparkled and glinted as they cavorted in the swell. Paolo was actually starting to feel pig sick that he wouldn't be part of this amazing show tonight, and reminded himself why he was about to give his special swansong. Believing his own myth as Brandy and overplaying his hand could be a one-way ticket back to the Bronx. It was madness to think he could ever fool anyone in a rhinestoned bra and G-string. The yawning chasm between ambition and reality would swallow him up and Paolo knew when to pull the ripcord. It was approaching in about eight bars of music.

The clamshell began its mechanical ascent into the flies, designed to look as if doves were spiriting it away on tendrils of spun gold. Paolo took his time to get into position. All he needed was a couple of seconds' delay. *Here's your chance, Sienna,* he thought, *I'm handing this show over to you.* He took an elegant run and leapt like a gazelle, aiming for a couple of feet behind the shell for maximum impact. With an impressive-sounding crash he slammed into the prop with his shoulder as it lifted beyond his reach. Paolo fell to the stage with a piercing scream. He'd landed well. He was stunned to feel no pain as such, maybe a stinging in his shoulder, but nothing major. He clutched at his ankle and rolled around on the floor, seeing a wall of showgirls streaming towards him through his tears of feigned agony, hundreds of feet of shiny nylon tresses flying behind them as they ran.

Sienna held her head in her hands as she slumped at the fancy dining table in Brandy's dressing-room suite, her cracked wheat and cucumber salad untouched in front of her.

'You know you can do it, devotion,' said Blue through his mouthful of noodles. 'C'mon, you have to step up to the plate. Brandy and Marty didn't make you understudy for you to fall to pieces at the thought of performing. Get a grip.'

'He's right,' agreed Paolo, his shapely leg stretched out from beneath the table, his tightly bound ankle presented to Sienna and Blue like a trophy. 'This is your chance to take centre stage. It's why you auditioned, right?'

'Of course!' said Sienna. 'It's just – I didn't expect to do the press night! Pressure! Wow, if only I'd had a night to psyche myself up,' Sienna muttered. 'It's three hours away!'

'Bloody hell, it's not like Brandy planned this – for once,' chided Blue, spraying chewed noodle at Sienna.

'Oh, I know that, I'm sorry, I didn't mean to imply—'

'And what would your mum say if she heard you chickening out anyway?'

'Mum? Oh, that's something else,' exclaimed Sienna with a cynical laugh. 'You must have heard everyone whispering the last few weeks that I only got the part because of her. Why do you think I've been hanging out with Brandy so much? The girls have turned into such bloody bitches. They must think I'm deaf or something, but I hear it all. No offence, Brandy . . . ' Sienna added hastily, catching Paolo's raised eyebrow in her peripheral vision.

'Come on, like you've never heard people accuse you of

getting unfair advantages before!' retorted Blue. 'So now's your chance to prove why you earnt that part . . . did you hear that word? *Earnt* it. Fair and square.'

'He's right,' said Paolo. 'You happen to be good at what you do. Don't feel like that's a sin. And by the way, I thought we were getting on? I thought you actually liked me?' he added, pouting a little.

'Sure we do, I just meant – since all the girls have been turning against me . . . I guess I felt a bit of a loner. I thought I could turn to you since you like to keep yourself to yourself too.'

'Girls with the big "J". Tut tut, it's so unattractive, so unproductive. Ignore it, Sienna, you can't take all those politics on stage with you. Shit slinging won't make them any better as performers and in the meantime you have more important things to get on with,' said Paolo sternly.

'Yeah, like the show!' laughed Sienna. She took a deep breath and smiled. 'Brandy, I can't make your ankle better but I'm going to make sure I do you proud. I'll be the best Venus I can be, just like you've taught me. I want you to see what I can do. Imagine Max when he comes tonight – he thinks I'm just a showgirl with the chorus line! Wow, I wish Mum were here for my big debut!' Sienna visibly welled up.

'Woah, no, no, no,' muttered Blue, rubbing Sienna's back. 'No tears, devotion. Save those for when you've finished the show tonight. Jesus and Mary, you're all over the place. Calm down and just concentrate on the show, okay?'

'Got it!' smiled Sienna, holding Blue and Paolo's

hands in each of her hers and squeezing tight.

In a shadowy corner of the communal dressing room, Paige hummed as she worked away. This would be a spectacular show for everyone, she smiled to herself. It was a little fiddly to get her scissors in to all the nooks and crannies but she was a fast worker. The rest of the cast had gone to Wholefoods after the drama of the afternoon, while Sienna and Blue were in a suspicious huddle in Brandy's room, leaving Paige in peace to add her finishing touches to the show. Paige had been right behind Brandy when she'd slammed herself into that clamshell earlier, and she was pretty darn sure it wasn't Brandy's ankle that took the impact. Just when she thought her paranoia about Brandy and Sienna's new 'friendship' was out of control, Paige had realised she just wasn't being paranoid enough. She was sure it was no coincidence that her passport seemed to have 'vanished', ensuring she missed out on that cosy little Caribbean trip and the chance to show Max what he could have in place of Sienna. And to top it all, that stunt earlier stank of fish, and she reckoned Sienna must have been a part of it somehow to get her moment centre stage tonight. Well, now it was time to foil their comfy little arrangement, decided Paige. *Mummy can't get you out of this one*, she thought to herself as she unpicked every second stitch of Sienna's costume.

Honey's cheeks were sore from smiling so much and her brain ached with making mindless small talk. She didn't know much about fashion but all the PRs she had been introduced to seemed to be incredibly well connected, if surprisingly heterosexual. Maybe it was a cliché that everyone in the fashion industry was gay, thought Honey, as this lot certainly had their eyes on stalks at the flesh on display. It was certainly a lavish setting for such a glamorous crowd, a beautiful private home with an endless supply of champagne and fresh fruit platters. Honey was struck by how young some of the girls seemed. Some were intimidatingly beautiful but quite a few were surprisingly plain in the flesh. But then it was often the plain ones who photographed well, as Josh had pointed out. The one thing they all seemed to have in common was how off their faces they were. Honey guessed that the bowls of 'sugar' being served with the fruit weren't quite what they seemed. One or two of the girls were certainly going in for the Belsen look, and Honey supposed the amphetamines at least helped them with that.

Honey wasn't in the mood for a messy party, she just wanted to get down to work. She'd been making her glass of champagne last an hour; she'd drunk enough of the stuff at the Velvet Taco for the smell to vaguely remind her of vomit. It never helped her make small talk anyway, although this lot were so far unable to hold a conversation about anything other than what parties they had been to lately. So much for talking business. Honey sensed a pair of eyes boring into her and turned to see Josh staring from the other side of the room. She smiled and wandered over.

'You wanna go?' asked Honey.

'What? We only just got here. Don't you want to network?' asked Josh.

'I think I got round everyone,' Honey said, casting her eyes about the room.

'I thought you'd like to drink a bit more, relax into it,' replied Josh, grimacing.

'No, it's okay, I don't want to let loose when there are important contacts around,' smiled Honey. 'Wouldn't want them to think I'm unprofessional or anything,' she added. 'So I was thinking, when are we going to shoot my portfolio? I can't go to castings without one, surely? Seeing all the other gorgeous girls here made me realise I seriously need to look professional.'

'Be patient,' said Josh, 'all that'll come. Do a couple more of these parties and you'll be making money, I promise.'

'I just want to do a good job, that's all.'

'If you wanna do a good job then get some champagne down your neck and work the PRs properly,' snapped Josh. Honey stared back in disbelief.

'Get over it and get back out there!' yelled Blue in the dressing room, furiously flinging pieces of dismembered corsetry and swan coat into his laundry basket.

'You weren't the one having to do split leaps butt naked except for a piece of dental floss between your ass cheeks!' growled Sienna, tears of humiliation pricking her eyes as she clutched at her bare breasts. 'My bits were feeling the breeze in *public*! It was like a freakin' gynaecology exam out there! What the hell *happened*?'

'There's no time to work out what, where or why, just get into your next costume and that'll be your two big spots over for Act One. Get back out there like a pro!'

'Wait, you were the one sewing that bloody costume this morning. Was this your work?' Sienna demanded.

'Wash your mouth out!' snarled Blue. 'As if! Now get these feathers on and get your mind back on the job!'

'I can assure you there is nothing on my mind *but* the job – and how humiliating that was out there just now! Did you see that costume falling away as soon as I went into the arabesque? Did you see it?'

'More like did I hear it – the crowd nearly raised the roof! It was marvellous! What's your point?'

'Not funny! Do you know how much of a field day the press will have with this? Full nudity! They'll drag Mum into it! I know it! Oh God!' she wailed, thumping the wall in frustration.

'Sienna, you used to strip at the Monte Cristo, what's the big deal?'

'Not with inappropriate choreography! Front kicks to the audience? You go to a *peepshow* for that kind of view!'

'Sienna, the press don't have a script, they don't know that wasn't meant to happen. They just saw a great strip.'

'But this isn't a strip show, dammit!'

'No, devotion, it's a topless revue. So you just made your

mark. It's good to be unforgettable. Now will you concentrate on your next act!'

'What about Marty?'

'What do you want me to say, he loved it? No! He's spitting feathers, he's gonna fine you, but this is where you have to prove your worth. You step up and be a professional, the show goes on. You think you're the first person to have a malfunction? Your mum had them all the time. Janet Jackson stole her act! It's part of the job. That's life. It's how you deal with it that marks you out. Now for chrissake shut your mouth and get this costume on, or you'll be walking out there butt naked again and they'll close the whole darn show!'

Max dialled for his allotted casino host at the Follies. It was time to move on – it wasn't working out for him on the tables at the Wynn. Sienna would surely be expecting her white wedding within the year and right now he was unsure how he could even pay off his mounting casino markers, let alone keep his own planes in the air. Sienna would be lucky to get a ten-minute service at the carwash at this rate.

Kerry had made a dig at their last meeting about Max's inability to settle down. He said it showed a lack of commitment to any project. The fact that for the last thirty years his father had a different fuck for every change of suit was of no concern; it was about outward projection of stability and success that counted. *Success breeds success.* His father had been conspicuous by his silence since the Caribbean trip, so Max knew he must have touched a nerve with his recent activity. Kerry could hardly have missed the gossip of the grand proposal in front of the glitterati and some of his work associates on St Barth's – it had made all the diary columns as well as the *Wall Street Journal*. In fact the only thing that would have got Max more press would have been if he'd been found hanging from the Opening Bell podium in a G-string with a tangerine stuffed in his mouth. Max hoped his clients would read his engagement as a reassuring sign of stability; a kind of 'expansion' of sorts. It was high time he laid claim to Sienna anyway, before some undeserving flash prick with more money got his paws on her. Really he should be supporting her tonight, watching in the audience. But winning at blackjack was a much more important kind of support.

Sienna took her final bow to rapturous applause and cheers. As the tabs lowered for the last time, the chorus line all jumped up and down distributing hugs, kisses and high fives while Sienna fell to her knees and allowed herself a few discreet sobs into her feathers. This was supposed to be a moment of triumph. It just felt like a moment of disgrace. She knew all the girls had made a little viper's nest between them, but sabotage? Could it really be them? Who could she trust any more? If only Honey were here to give her a hug. She felt a hand at her shoulder, and looked up.

'Come on, devotion. You rocked the house. You saved it!' laughed Blue. 'Tiger would be proud of the way you handled that.' Sienna stared back, make-up running in rivers of black down her cheeks. 'There's a bottle of champagne waiting for you in the dressing room,' he smiled tentatively. 'Come on, little one.'

Sienna followed Blue wearily into the dressing room, hoping to hell Marty wouldn't be waiting for her. She prayed he'd allow her a night to lick her wounds and give his lecture in the morning. She prayed even harder she wouldn't lose her post in the show; she'd decided she would pay any fine, she didn't care about the money. Designer clothes and private jets weren't the things that made her go weak at the knees; she just didn't want to be written off by Marty, or her mum when she found out. A low murmur made her head turn and she was surprised to see the door to Brandy's private dressing room open, the rectangular frame beholding a picture of a worried-looking Brandy sprawled out on her throne, a man kneeling before her. Sienna shrank back, anxious she had interrupted a private moment; Brandy snapped her head up to show a guilty face, and Sienna was surprised to see Paige emerging from the shadows, still in her costume from the final number.

'Hi darling, there you are!' gushed Paige. 'Meet Ed, he's the physio I've been talking about for the last few weeks. You know, Mr Champagne from the Monte?' Ed turned around to shoot a smile at Sienna. 'I knew he'd be here watching me in the show tonight and I suddenly thought what a good idea it would be for him to help Brandy, since she took *such* a fall earlier,' added Paige with a sympathetic sideways glance and a pout. Blue joined Sienna at the doorway and craned his neck to see into the dressing room, as Paige sank back into the corner and chewed on a nail.

'Well, it's good news,' pronounced Ed. 'There doesn't seem to be any sign of any swelling. Are you sure it hurts?'

'Agony,' said Paolo dramatically.

'Hmm. Mystery. There's no restriction in movement, no swelling, you seem to be fine with weight on it. There's no bruising coming out, so no internal bleeding . . . I don't know what to suggest other than seeing your doctor. It's got me foxed. A bit of rheumatism, maybe?'

'But she fell earlier and was in tears of pain . . . ' Sienna said slowly.

'Yeah, that's exactly what I thought I saw too, babe,' said Paige with a smirk.

'You sure it's this one?' whispered Jesús, struggling to keep up with Tiny as he strode as fast as his fat little legs could take him across to the Follies theatre stage door.

'He told Pancho it was the biggest tit 'n' feather show on the Strip. It's this one alright,' snapped Tiny breathlessly.

'But they ain't gonna let us in just like that,' complained Jesús.

'We're jus' gonna leave a nice little message for Blue, that's all. Only fair for him to work up a sweat while we decide what to do about him. Coming on to Pancho like that, the dirty little slimeball.'

'He ain't little, Tiny.'

'Yeah but what he has in height I have in girth,' snarled Tiny. 'Besides, I have something in my pants and I ain't talkin' about my cock,' he said, patting the handgun in his pocket firmly.

Tiny swung open the door to reception and asked politely if he could leave a message for a friend. The receptionist obliged with a pen, paper and envelope before giving her attention straight back to the episode of *CSI* playing out on the tiny portable television behind the desk, cracking her gum loudly as she stared at the screen.

Hola chico guapo, Your little Latin love interest doesn't play in your sandbox. You won't want to go within 1000 miles of a bathhouse when we've finished with you.

'Poetry,' muttered Tiny proudly, slipping the note into its envelope and handing it back to the receptionist.

Sienna carefully uncaged the bottle of champagne Blue had left at her make-up station. It was perfectly clear what had been going on now. Sienna felt pure humiliation at being duped for so many weeks. She walked back to Brandy's dressing room where Brandy sat, shaking her head at Ed.

'You saw what happened to me on stage tonight, didn't

you, Brandy?' asked Sienna, shaking the bottle vigorously. 'Well, I was supposed to be celebrating my first night with this champagne, so I think it only fitting we actually use it to celebrate *your* handiwork,' she snarled, aiming the bottle squarely at Paolo's face. Sienna released the cork directly at his eye, eliciting a piercing shriek, a violent stream of cold champagne foam following the cork's wake, drenching Paolo's face and hair. His hands leapt to his face.

'That hurt, did it? Like your ankle?' yelled Sienna. 'I thought you were devious but this takes the biscuit. I knew you wanted to get rid of me for sticking up for Honey all those weeks back, and I couldn't understand why you kept me on – now I know why! This has been a big fat dish of revenge.'

'No! Aaargh!' wailed Paolo, his hand clutching at his eye.

'I knew you were a piece of work, Brandy, but I had no idea you were quite this devious. I'll hand it to you for attention to detail – swapping Paige for me – poor, poor Paige. And then I was right where you wanted me so you could embarrass me in the worst way possible, on stage, in front of the world and his dog, while I'm up there thinking I'm about to give the performance of my life! How cruel! Why couldn't you have just fired me instead of this vile punishment! To think I'd started trusting you! I thought we were friends! The weekend in the Caribbean! I confided in you! I shared my friends and my – I thought you'd changed! Changed? You've plumbed depths I didn't think even *you* were capable of.'

'No! You've got it all wrong! I'd never do something like that! I fell, I really did – I wanted you to perform tonight and be amazing! I thought you wanted it more than I needed it!'

'Bullshit!' exploded Sienna. 'You may have money and beauty and power, but you're a lowlife! I bet you did this to spite my mum too, didn't you, because she was a better showgirl than you'll ever be. I bet you thought you'd embarrass us both—'

'No!' wailed Paolo, springing up from his chair.

'Oh, you're up now. Your ankle stopped hurting, did it?' spat Sienna bitterly.

'Enough, Sienna,' said Blue, grabbing her firmly by the arms and yanking her away from the dressing room. 'Don't waste your energy, darling. I think you need to go home and sleep on this. You still have make-up running down your face, darling – you look like a madwoman. Take a breather and a moment to think things through—'

'Get off me!' snapped Sienna, wriggling free of Blue and shooting him a filthy look. 'I'll see myself out, thank you very much!' She brushed herself down dramatically before storming from the room and back to her make-up station. She checked her Blackberry. No sign of a call from Max. Where was he, dammit? thought Sienna, anxiously. Maybe he'd been so embarrassed by the performance he'd left after the first half, she fretted. As she furiously scrubbed mascara from her flushed cheeks, she looked up to see Ed staring at her from across the room.

'Can I help you?' she asked. Ed stood and stared.

'What are you looking at?' snapped Sienna, feeling as if she could barely be any more self-conscious tonight if she tried.

'Nothing, I – I just brought a gift for the leading lady. After Paige gave me a VIP invitation, I thought it was the done thing.' Ed stepped forward and held aloft a pink teddy bear. 'I thought flowers were a bit unoriginal. And they die. Hope you like it,' he smiled. Sienna checked herself and accepted the bear with an awkward smile.

'Thanks, I like the colour pink,' she said politely.

'That makes me feel so happy,' smiled Ed, staring at her with his piercing blue eyes.

Blue busied himself in the dressing room, sifting through Brandy's costumes wordlessly. He was in a bad enough mood after tonight's costume drama, let alone about the ominous note that had just been left on his sewing machine by the receptionist, leaving him with barely any fuse left to deal with Brandy, who was sitting quietly sharpening an eye pencil. Finally Paolo broke the heavy silence.

'I faked the thing with my ankle because I wanted to give Sienna a break.'

'Sure,' said Blue quietly.

'I know maybe it was wrong but my heart was in the

right place,' he mumbled. 'But I didn't do anything to that costume.'

'Sure.'

'I didn't touch it, you hear? And I don't know who did. Why would I do that?'

'To make yourself look better,' replied Blue calmly.

'How could you think that? It doesn't make any of us look good.'

'It was why you wanted Paige in the first place, because she was bad enough that she wasn't a threat to you.'

Paolo fell silent and fiddled with the eyeliner.

'You gotta admit it doesn't look too good, does it, Brandy? I mean, your track record doesn't exactly help.' Blue was feeling bold. He didn't give a fuck any more if the bitch fired him; what Sienna had said tonight added up. It was sad that Brandy was entirely capable of something that devious and protracted. Suddenly the job just didn't seem worth it any more, not for any amount of money. All the drama, the unpleasantness, the poison, the tricks, the stunts. Brandy was welcome to live in the vile well of poison of her own making, but she could do it without him. Blue leaned across with a pile of folded leotards and yanked open one of the dresser drawers. Paolo gasped and scrambled for the drawer. Blue looked down in disbelief, dropping the leotards to snatch up the Sheriff's Card that was laying on top of the bra padding. He held it inches from his nose.

'Paolo . . . Brandy, is this – but it's – you! Only . . . Paolo?'

said Blue slowly, cogs in his brain visibly whirring. Eventually he pulled his shoulders back, stood erect and folded his arms. Paolo looked up at Blue, panic-stricken. He rose from Brandy's throne, his eyes darting between Blue and the door. 'Oh no you don't,' snarled Blue. 'I think we have some explaining to do ... Paolo,' he added, locking the dressing-room door with a loud click.

Chapter 14

Sienna swept the surface of her dresser violently with the length of her arm, sending cosmetics and jewellery sailing up into the air, mingling with an ear-splitting stream of curses. Where was her engagement ring? She religiously kept it hidden in the little heart-shaped porcelain pot in her bedroom whenever she left for work – there was no way she would leave that golf ball of a diamond in the dressing rooms at the Follies. But now it was gone. She yanked the mirrored dresser-drawer from its runners and frantically emptied its contents on to the floor with a frustrated cry as she saw nothing but a flurry of peachy satin French-knicker ruffles falling to the floor. Sienna sank back onto her bed and sifted through the possibilities in her head impatiently. The only people who had been in the house recently were Max and Paige, and neither of them would have any reason to move her engagement ring. Besides, only Max actually knew where she kept it.

Sienna slumped forward and faced the mess on the floor. Pots of face cream spilled their contents pornographically next to broken scent bottles and colourful shards of costume jewellery. A mess, just like everything else in her life tonight, thought Sienna. And where was her fiancé? Sienna drew her knees up underneath her chin and buried her head in her hands, rocking back and forth anxiously on the bed. Some opening night this had been. She felt such a fool for entertaining such grand, vivid visions of her big debut on the Vegas stage, since they couldn't have been further from what had happened tonight. She couldn't even bring herself to call her mum and tell her the embarrassing news, as Tiger would be on a plane and breathing down Brandy's neck before she could say 'queen bee', which would only make the cattiness in the cast even worse. No, Sienna definitely had to fight her own battle. She wished Honey was here to talk to. But even she had jumped ship. Paige had taken her physiotherapy guy off for a drink as a 'thank you' for taking time on his night off to check out Brandy's stupid ankle, and Blue wasn't even answering his phone.

Sienna slumped back on to the bed and turned to bury her face in her fur counterpane, unable to face the full enormity of losing her own engagement ring. Why oh why hadn't she been locking it in Tiger's safe? What on earth would she say to Max? *Sorry, darling, I just misplaced that little bauble that once belonged to your mother and is worth a cool million.* He may have unlimited pots of money but a million bucks was a million bucks; there was no way Max would take this lightly. Sienna had heard him on calls barking at his business associates and snapping at casino hosts; being on the wrong side of Max Power wouldn't be pretty. What if he thought Sienna was just ungrateful, or didn't care for their engagement? Worse still that it was his own mother's, which made it irreplaceable. She realised the snivelling, choking sound in her ears was her as she cried muffled sobs into her blanket. She ached for Max, and desperately wanted just to hold him, rest her head on his sturdy shoulder, smell his neck, feel him inside her, listen to him tell her everything would be okay. Nothing felt so good as when they were close. Sienna dragged herself off the bed and fell to her knees, scrabbling among the detritus on the floor as she sobbed. Finally she found a foil tray of Ambien proffering a single last tablet of hope. Nothing but a sleeping pill would allow her to forget reality for a precious few hours, and Sienna shakily popped the pill from its packet and slung it to the back of her dry throat. She grimaced as she swallowed hard, before crawling back into her bed and drawing the covers up over her head, sobs still escaping through the fur counterpane as she lay there in the dark waiting for sleep to transport her to a few hours' respite.

Blue careened into Brandy's driveway and cut the engine.

'Okay, over to you, pretty boy. Your stage awaits you.' Blue was out of his Lamborghini Countach in a second and tapping his foot, waiting for Paolo to lead the way to the doorstep. Paolo took a deep breath. It was truth time. He still couldn't believe Blue hadn't called the cops and half wondered if he planned on doing something torturous to him once they were in Brandy's house. All he had in the way of self-defence were Brandy's eyelash curlers and a few tricks he'd learnt from the Bronx, but even a nasty left hook wouldn't be a match for Blue's bulk. Paolo tried to remind himself that Brandy hadn't exactly inspired a lot of loyalty in people, and prayed that would mean Blue would give him the opportunity to tell the truth, plain and simple.

Paolo let them both in through the huge solid oak doors and followed Blue as he made straight for the den. Blue arranged himself in a zebra-print armchair while Paolo set the chandeliers to a 'low mood lighting' setting.

'I see you've made yourself comfortable,' remarked Blue, noting Paolo's familiarity with the remote and its gadgetry.

'It took a while to get used to,' mumbled Paolo, letting an apologetic weak smile flicker across his lips before he perched himself on the leopard-skin couch that had been his bed for the last three weeks. Blue raised an eyebrow over at Paolo.

'You may as well get out of drag. I sense this may take a while,' said Blue.

'Huh?'

'The wig. The clothes. No need for disguises any more.'

'Oh . . . yeah, makes sense. Give me a minute,' said Paolo, getting up and yanking off his blonde tresses as he made for Brandy's master bathroom. Paolo peeled his eyelashes off at the huge gilt mirror and reached for a make-up wipe. Carefully he rubbed away the defined eyebrows, the glossy lips, beauty spot, the layers of careful contouring, blending and shading until the unadorned, smooth-shaven face of a beautiful young man looked back at him. His skin had become incredible, glowing and soft with all the face creams he now used. Paolo quickly changed out of Brandy's vintage Yves Saint Laurent jumpsuit into his own jeans and a faded T-shirt. One last apprehensive look in the mirror and a quick comb of his natural cropped hair with his long elegant fingers and he knew he had to face up to the potential firing squad that was Blue.

'Can I make you a coffee?' offered Paolo politely, padding through from the bathroom. 'I only have instant, though, and no milk.'

'I'm fine, thanks,' said Blue, looking intently at the floor. 'I think you have some things over here you might want to pick up, though,' he added gingerly. Paolo followed Blue's gaze to the vast roaring tiger-head rug by the couch to see a tub of Vaseline and a pink mitt.

'Oh!' he exclaimed. 'It's not what you – I don't use it for – I like to sit watching cable and I cover my face in Vaseline after all that make-up. I do my hands too. Keeps my skin really soft,' he explained hurriedly, swooping to pick up the items.

'Are you . . . ?' started Blue

'No, I like women,' blurted Paolo.

'Oh.'

'Hmm.'

'I think I'll have that coffee after all,' said Blue awkwardly.

'Great,' sighed Paolo, making for the kitchen; he realised his nails were still giving the game away, in bright shiny scarlet. Paolo opened one of the sachets of complimentary instant coffee that he brought home most nights from the Follies canteen. Old habits died hard.

'You not having one?' asked Blue suspiciously when Paolo finally brought the coffee through.

'I only have one mug here. I'm not using Brandy's stuff,' said Paolo with a courageous smile. 'This might be hard to believe but I'm not exactly thrilled about this situation. I'm not spending Brandy's money, eating her food or sleeping in her bed.'

'You're right, it's hard to believe. You didn't just happen to become Brandy by mistake – oh, this is weird,' hesitated Blue. 'I need to keep reminding myself I don't know you. God, you look like Brandy. The resemblance is jaw-dropping. The only way I can tell you two apart are by the stretchmarks round Brandy's mouth . . . ' A beat. 'Bad joke. Sorry. I don't even know what to ask first. I was actually growing to like you, dammit! I feel so – used! How did . . . why did . . . who—'

'Like I said in the dressing room, I'm Paolo, her twin.'

'No shit, Sherlock, I got that far,' said Blue. A long pause. 'This won't work if I'm asking all the questions,' he continued. 'I don't know what to ask or where to start. Remember I can just get the cops round here any time so why don't you make this easy and lead the way. I want to know when, I want to know why, I want to know how, and – fuck – where is the real Brandy?'

'I don't know!' laughed Paolo. 'I'm guessing she's on that cruise you told me about, with a brand new arse and brand new face. I haven't done anything with her if that's what you're implying.' Paolo suddenly descended into a loud peel of uncontrollable laughter. 'Oh, Blue, it's not *her* who should be scared of *me*. Ha! Oh, that's funny!'

'Granted, she didn't have a great track record,' agreed Blue, leaning back into the armchair. 'So go on then, tell me everything.'

Paolo nervously took a deep breath.

'Okay. I hadn't seen my sister for almost twenty years. My Mami – my mother – died about three months ago. I needed to find Brandy and tell her. That's how this whole mess started.'

'I'm sorry for your loss,' mumbled Blue.

'Me too,' pressed on Paolo. 'It seems Brandy wasn't too sorry when I told her, though, but I guess that shouldn't have come as a surprise. So that's it in a nutshell – I just wanted to reconnect after Mami, as Brandy is all the family I have left. Dad passed away when we were fifteen. It's just me and Luisa . . . Brandy now. Luisa was her real name. You know, I can hardly even believe we're from the same family let alone twins. These last few weeks have made me realise we may look identical but we couldn't *be* more different. It wasn't just that we grew up in our own

ways, she was always different, right from the very
start. . . anyway, I'm getting off the point. So, I had to
find Brandy, and I knew she was working this big show.
I've been keeping an interested eye on her celebrity career,
you know, kinda hard not to. She seems to pop up everywhere in the press. I came to Vegas hoping to get away
from the memories of Mami and our shithole life in the
Bronx, earn a few dollars, and I'd hoped to get the last
piece of my family back.'

'Wait, so you were broke . . . and you saw your sister
making the big time . . . and you thought maybe that . . . '

'I can see where you're going with this. I don't blame
you for assuming I'm as deceitful as she is but . . . '

'You've been impersonating her for the last six weeks
and you've installed yourself in her house so I'd say it was
a pretty fair assumption. In fact I'd call it fraud, wouldn't
you?'

Paolo fell silent, the wind taken from his sails. How
could he argue with that? A fraud. He felt so ashamed.
How could he think he was somehow above Brandy? Paolo
wandered over to the picture window and stared out over
the grounds, taking in the huge moustache-shaped pool
and neon illuminations shaped like palm trees in amongst
Grecian columns designed to look like ruins. The water-
fall feature bubbled away merrily, at one with its tacky
surroundings. Paolo sighed, suddenly struck with a numb-
ness that accompanied a lack of any sense of what was
ahead. Or was it just that he didn't care what was ahead

any more? He wasn't sure he had the energy left to press on with his story. After all, who cared about some saga from the past? Who cared what Brandy had done to him? He'd end up sounding like a child in the playground telling tales. Paolo turned back round to face Blue, who was sitting patiently awaiting an explanation. Maybe that was Paolo's problem. He'd always somehow been the one to back down or relent and take the blame; always he let someone else take centre stage, and always he seemed to allow himself to be tarred with the wrong brush. In that instant he decided he would finish his story; the truth, with dignity, then offer to call the cops himself if need be. After all, he may be a fraud, but he was no coward.

'You're wrong if you think I wanted money from my sister,' Paolo pressed on. 'I wanted nothing from her. I just hoped she might have changed; grown up, become a nice person. I hoped we might be friends somehow; we never were as kids. I hoped that I could forgive her and move on. Brandy split the family up nearly twenty years ago. I really hoped she might have changed, Blue, and I was wrong. What I've seen these few weeks, the hatred people have for her, the fear . . . I've realised she's not someone I'm proud to be related to.'

'You're not winning me over here. You've been living in her shoes dishonestly for weeks and in my book that doesn't make you any more savoury than her. You still haven't said why you did this. Or how. Let's face it, Machiavelli himself would have a job planning something like this!'

'I didn't plan it! It all happened by mistake and it just snowballed. I don't know what I was thinking; it's not as though any of this could ever lead anywhere. Brandy's gonna come back soon and then what? I guess I just couldn't face going straight back to the Bronx, back to all the memories of Mami. I thought I could put it off just for a day or two at first, that first day when you guys thought I was her. Then days turned into weeks. I guess I selfishly enjoyed the work too. I'll admit it, I began to look forward to seeing you all every day and watching the show unfold. It's always been my dream to dance in a show, although Brandy put paid to that a long time ago. If I'm really honest these past few weeks I got a kick out of undoing some of the nasty bitch-ass things my sister had done. Look, I understand that you wouldn't want to support my actions. I'm not exactly proud of myself.'

'I can't believe I was so stupid not to notice,' said Blue, quietly. 'I actually feel embarrassed! It's so obvious now. And to think I thought Brandy – you – had been beaten black and blue . . . '

'No, that was definitely real. Brandy had me beaten up by her security guys a week earlier, and she ripped my mother's necklace from my neck. Brandy said she was going on vacation and to get the hell out of Vegas by the time she came back. When I turned up at the theatre all I was trying to do was sneak back in and get Mami's crucifix back before I went back to New York. It's all I have left of her, you see. When you all thought I was my sister I couldn't quite believe it, but it seemed like a gift – the easiest way to get in and out of her dressing room without too much fuss. I guess I thought it was a joke at first. Then something took over, instinct or something, I don't know what you'd call it; I had seconds to decide what to do and all I kept thinking to myself over and over was the life Brandy stole from me. Maybe I thought in that moment that stepping into her shoes settled the balance somehow. I didn't know what I was doing. I didn't have enough time to think I'd be way in over my head. Or that it was wrong. I just kept thinking of what she'd done to us, to me, to our family. I never did find the necklace, in case you were wondering.'

Paolo looked over at Blue, realising he had been speaking with his eyes shut as he concentrated on dredging up the truth. He took a deep breath and pressed on.

'Luisa . . . Brandy was born self-absorbed. Mami used to laugh that the first word she ever spoke was her own name. It was set out from day one that she was a golden child and she was to get much more attention than anyone else somehow. I thought that was normal; we all treated her like a princess. But it never made her happy, you know. The more attention that was lavished on her the less she smiled. Dad would shower money and gifts on her as she grew up. It was never enough. She wanted dresses and toys, she got them. She wanted tap and ballet classes, she got them. Oh, you knew she was going to be famous, she'd made up her mind. It didn't matter to her how. She dragged me to every class going. You name it: tap, ballet, modern, jazz, acting, horse riding even. I was happy to accompany her to the dance classes, believe me. I just loved to dance, it felt like it was in my blood from the start, and let me tell you there weren't many boys in those classes. But at least as Brandy's sidekick I was kind of a protected species if any kids at school thought it a cause for a fight that I was learning to jeté in lunch break instead of shooting hoops. But with each class Brandy became so isolated – with self-obsession, I swear she could only see herself in a room. I'd catch her sometimes; she could be mesmerised just by the effect of her presence on people. I swear she couldn't even comprehend that anyone or anything else existed apart from to serve her, carry her bags, be her audience. She was the centre of the universe and that was that.

'Until one day I upstaged her in a dance class. I was singled out for a dance solo. I was so proud of myself but it was like a slap in the face to Brandy that for a few minutes all eyes weren't on her. It set the rot of competitiveness in her. Brandy needed to make sure I knew my place, which was to accompany her, be her minder or her butler, but not to outshine her. So after that dance class everything had a new meaning; it was all about winning or losing for her now, nothing in between. I told myself not to feel that bothered, so long as I could enjoy being able to go to classes as Brandy's 'minder' without being teased by the other kids for being a wuss. Plus Brandy's sulk had lasted a whole week, it was unbearable; she even got Dad involved when she refused to eat anything. I realised then it was going to be easier to humour her from then on and just keep a low profile. I'd have plenty of time in the future to make it to the showbiz stage, I told myself. But it didn't take long for Brandy's competitiveness to spread everywhere; it certainly wasn't reserved just for me. Where before she wouldn't notice other people, now she watched everyone suspiciously like a hawk. Worse still, she began to turn on Mami. She started to resent it if Dad spent any of his precious attention on our mother. God knows Brandy could kick up a storm, she'd be so hateful to Mami. She'd lash out, she'd tease her, mock her . . . you see, Mami wasn't from what white Americans consider to be "good stock". Our grandparents were poor Hispanic immigrants. Dad first met Mami in New York when he was on business and she was working in a bar. They had a crazy affair; she fell pregnant so they had a shotgun wedding and moved to Los Angeles. Mami was drop-dead beautiful, you see; absolutely stunning, she could silence a room with her beauty. Well, this may have kept Dad occupied in a certain way, she served as a good trophy for a bit, but Dad was – a challenging man. And he in turn needed a challenge in a woman too, someone strong. Mami just doted on him, though, she was a simple soul. And eventually that just bored Dad. Brandy was smart, of course: she noticed when Dad made his snidey putdowns to Mami. Brandy started following suit, belittling her in the same way. She made quite the bitchy team with Dad. I'd stick up for Mami but I just became "Mami's boy" – Dad hated that, he started accusing me of being "sappy" and "girlie", said he couldn't respect me. So Brandy became Daddy's proper princess; the apple of his eye. She filled his days, she was enough of a challenge for him. Meanwhile Mami hid her sadness in Valium and vodka. It was the only thing she could find to soothe the aching she had for my father's affection. We were twelve by then.

'One of the things Brandy liked to do was have me help choose outfits for her for when she would one day win Miss America. She liked to map everything out well in advance, you see. So I'd help her do her make-up sometimes or tease her hair into a bouffant. It passed the time at the weekends when Dad would be in his study working and Mami was bombed out on the sofa; she had little to stay sober for any more, and her and Dad hardly spoke. What was left to talk about when there was no respect left? Anyway, this one particular day Brandy got this idea in her head that she would make me up to look like her. It was weird. Just make-up at first, mind you. But she painted my face and then stared at me, like she was looking at herself. She started combing my hair differently and saying I should grow it to look more like her. I got angry at that point. I felt like such a prick standing there decked out like my sister. I made for the bathroom to wash everything off but Brandy did a weird thing, she started to cry. Not the temper tantrums she used to throw every five minutes with fake tears, but really sobbing. She begged me to stay and let her finish the make-up. Said she had no friends, that she was so lonely, that I was her only company. She said no-one wanted to be near her because they were so intimidated by her beauty, that everyone at school was eaten up with jealousy. I just looked at this pathetic girl and felt sorry for her. Even then at twelve I could see how deluded, how self-obsessed, how sick she was. I started to feel anger welling up at Dad that he'd been spoiling her so much and that it was so out of hand; it just hit me. Anyway Brandy was talking away and now holding a dress up against me. I remember her saying, "Please, just let me see what I'd look like as Miss America just this once. It's not the same just looking in a mirror. I'll stop going on about it after this, I promise. Don't tell anyone though," she begged. "I want it to be our secret." I relented. She was just so ridiculous. I thought if I played along this once it would be the end of it. So fast-forward ten minutes, there I was in a dress, and make-up. Suddenly Brandy's screaming, "Daddy, Daddy, Daddy!" Dad comes running for his princess and I'm standing there, the painted scapegoat in a fucking dress with Brandy screaming that she'd found me rummaging in her closet and that her underwear and make-up had been going missing for some time. Well, I got the kind of hiding no boy should ever have from anyone, let alone his own father. That was before I was thrown into the bath, my mouth stuffed with an old flannel to stop me screaming, and Brandy held me down in freezing water while Dad scrubbed at me with a boot brush until my flesh was raw, screaming that he would cure his "little faggot boy of his disease". I was locked in my room "to keep my sister safe", he said, and by the end of the next day Dad had me installed in the sanatorium. I never did get to speak to Brandy or ask her why she set me up, but she did come to the car to smile and wave me off. She winked as the car pulled away. She knew exactly what she was doing. Sick bitch. Yet there *I* was in a blue cotton pyjama suit being pumped with medication in the sanatorium for the next three years – me! Like *I* was the mad one! I was there until Dad died of a heart attack and I could be released. It turns out that at the same time I was packed off to the nuthouse, Dad also sent Mami back to New York. I know Brandy had something to do with that too. Mami never recovered from her broken heart. She got on to the strong stuff and by the time I came out of the sanatorium she was in South Bronx turning tricks to feed her crack habit. I looked after her as best I could until her liver gave out this year. As for Brandy? Well, you know what happened to her. She went on to become the superstar she always knew she would be.'

Paolo stopped. There was nothing more to say. He looked over at Blue to see him sitting still as a statue in the armchair, silent tears coursing down his cheeks.

Max counted out the last bill. Half a million bucks.

'Thanks. I owe you, Mitch.'

'Yes, you do,' replied the short, stocky Mitch as he fingered the velvet box and took one last look at Sienna's enormous sparkling engagement ring before snapping the lid shut. 'I wouldn't do this for just anyone, you know that. Still, I've got the ring and I know that's one thing you'll definitely have to come back for!'

'Er, yeah, course,' laughed Max uneasily. 'Look, I'm gonna hit the tables quickly before our poker game later,' he announced.

'Heh. Don't lose it all straightaway,' said Mitch, waving the velvet jewellery box before Max's eyes.

'See you later,' said Max before hurrying from the pokey backroom and out into the bar area. He ploughed his way straight past the pole dancers; he wasn't in the mood for tits and ass. Money was the only thing on his mind. The ring was only supposed to be a last resort, but thank God he'd thought ahead to bring it out with him; that last disastrous session of blackjack had cleared him out. Now all he needed was a cab uptown. He'd had to give his company chauffeur an unpaid 'vacation' the last couple of weeks so it was back to cabs. How the other half lived; Max shook his head at the thought. Still, it should only be a temporary cash-flow glitch, he reminded himself.

A twenty-minute ride later and Max was at the Encore, sinking a large whisky in the restaurant after the unpleasantness of grabbing a cab amongst tourists and Johns. He'd flirted with the concept of a bite to eat to get his energy up for a night of winning money, although nothing was catching his eye on the menu particularly and now he was weighing up whether he could get through the night on liquor alone. Nothing seemed to tickle his fancy any more. Thoughts of Sienna flitted through his mind and brought a wave of guilt washing over him that he still hadn't checked to see how she'd fared in her first night's performance. He shrugged it off, reminding himself that she was a fantastic performer and she would've been fine. She'd probably be celebrating with the rest of the cast, anyway; she wouldn't want to see him.

'Max?'

Max spun round in his chair. 'Paige? Nice to see you. What are you doing here?'

'I just said goodbye to my friend Ed, actually. We came here for a quick bite after the show.'

'Wow, you look amazing. I'm surprised you're not with Sienna,' remarked Max.

'Thanks! And I'm surprised *you're* not with Sienna!' laughed Paige brightly.

'I was leaving her to her inevitable celebrations with the cast,' explained Max, 'which I would have expected you to be partaking in too. How did the first night go?'

'Oh . . . you weren't there tonight?'

'Couldn't make it.'

'Ah, what a shame. So you haven't heard?'

'Heard what?'

'Oh nothing, it was all wonderful. Great show,' said Paige, pulling up a chair, deducing that Max and Sienna hadn't spoken yet. 'So, don't tell me you're here by yourself.'

'I was just on my way to the blackjack tables.'

'And no lovely lady to take care of you? It's a big bad world out there,' pouted Paige, surreptitiously rearranging the neckline of the Lanvin dress she'd 'borrowed' from Sienna earlier in the week.

'You offering?' said Max, not missing a beat.

'Thought you'd never ask,' said Paige, tapping her talons on the table and giving a sideways stare at Max.

'Oh yeah? I was just seeing if you were the type to follow through,' laughed Max. 'I don't actually expect you to find blackjack very interesting, don't worry!'

'Darlin', I always follow through and then some,' drawled Paige, not laughing, 'and who in their right mind wouldn't enjoying gambling? A little bit of risk on the menu is a turn-on, no?' She finally broke into a sly grin. Max took a moment to sling back his whisky. He wondered if Paige always laid it on this thick or if she was just feeling randy from too much champagne and surplus adrenalin from the show. He cast his mind back to the first time he spoke to her at the house when she'd dropped her towel in front of him. There was definitely something slutty about Paige that was now giving Max a twinge in his crotch. She was wide open. She was also Sienna's flatmate so had to be off limits, decided Max. That would be tacky, after all. No harm in soaking up the attention though.

'So have you ordered yet?' asked Paige, picking up the menu on the table.

'No, I didn't see anything on there that sounded appetising. You want anything?'

'I just ate here with Ed. Although I could be persuaded by dessert. You wanna skip straight to the sweet stuff? You should eat something. Big boy like you needs his energy.'

Max was definitely enjoying the trashy 'big boy' talk. Paige reminded him of new girls at strip joints; still full of enthusiasm and coming out with the corniest one-liners. He rather liked it, especially with ladles of that syrupy drawl of hers.

'C'mon, let's order something. What's the most fattening thing on here?' she murmured, running her eyes down the menu.

'Christ, but Sienna – I thought you girls were living on lettuce in that household.'

'Not me. I like to indulge, don't you?' smiled Paige.

'Well, you found the right town for that,' said Max, wondering if she might be good fun for a couple of hours of friendly company after all. 'Maybe you should come to the blackjack with me for a bit. You might bring me luck.'

'The pleasure would be all mine,' said Paige, her eyes twinkling.

Honey was feeling a little lightheaded after her fourth glass of champagne but at least it had relaxed her after

Josh's outburst earlier. He had apologised for snapping, explaining that he was just trying to give her a good shortcut into the industry via the fashion PRs and that it was best she 'relax into it' and make sure she was 'seen on the scene'; these were the guys who had all the big contacts, after all. Honey was feeling a little naughty now, though, having just escaped the party to go to the Mondrian hotel for a nightcap with the handsome Jacques, a Lebanese-French investor. One of the PRs had introduced them – Jacques was in town as a potential cash injection for a fashion label. Honey knew it might well piss off Josh again that she'd given him the slip to indulge in some personal romance instead of concentrating on the job, but what harm could a little flirtation bring? Hell, apart from the Johns at work, she hadn't had so much as a wink from a guy for months now, let alone a decent one; why shouldn't she have a few drinks with a charming gentleman like Jacques? He certainly made a change from the clientele at the Velvet Taco, although he'd been just as eager – Honey had barely even introduced herself before he was offering her a drink.

Looking at him now as Honey waited for her cocktail to arrive, she felt a tingle of excitement. He was different from any man she'd gone for before. He was older for a start. Honey put him at early forties, and very distinguished-looking in immaculate tailoring and Italian shoes. He was tall and elegant with a medium build and dark olive skin, thick curly hair cut short and deep hazel eyes. *Exotic*, she chanted to herself gleefully. She didn't see too many men as beautiful as Jacques in her home city of London, let alone in Los Angeles. Not only that but he was cultured. They'd had a good hour of chat back at the party and had covered everything from art to opera and everything in between, and all of that with his beautiful accent. She sensed he was special.

'Why don't I just have the drinks sent to my room?' asked Jacques as they sat in the Sky bar.

'Oh! I thought you might want to hang out here a little while. It's romantic in the open air,' said Honey. Blimey, he's a fast mover, she thought.

'It's a bit public, don't you think,' said Jacques, 'unless you're planning on meeting someone else, perhaps?'

'What? What a funny thing to say. No, of course not, I have no other plans!' laughed Honey. 'Okay, let's go to your room, but no funny business, okay?' Jacques roared with laughter at that. 'Funny girl. I like your humour,' he chuckled. *And I like you!*, thought Honey deliriously as she scooped up her purse and made for the elevators. As she stepped in, Honey caught the full reflection of her and Jacques standing together in the mirrored lift. No wonder she had sensed more than a few pairs of eyes staring when they had been sitting in the bar; they were a handsome couple to say the least. Honey turned to face Jacques and kissed him hard. She couldn't help herself; she was feeling the kind of butterflies in her stomach she hadn't felt for such a long time around a man. Jacques immediately pulled Honey into his arms, groaning and kissing her back with urgency. By the time the pair had reached Jacques' suite they were both ripping each other's clothes off. Jacques suddenly threw Honey onto the huge bed and stood over her as she lay there naked, his eyes wandering everywhere.

'God, you're beautiful like this,' he murmured. 'You must stay this way.'

'Huh?'

'Your face, your body . . . unspoilt. No ugly surgery. A woman's hips, curves. Natural beauty. You must stay this way,' he repeated, before reaching for a condom.

'You have to get yourself out of this mess, you have to stop the juggernaut and get out intact,' said Blue after a long silence. 'I don't know why but I believe you, and maybe I can even help you.' Paolo's story had affected him more than he was prepared to admit. It was clear that despite the lies he'd told in the major deception he'd perpetrated on the entire cast and crew, Paolo had been more of a victim of Brandy than she'd ever been of him.

'I just don't see how I can sort it out,' said Paolo. 'I guess I should turn myself in to the cops and get it over with. What you said – that I'm a fraud – you're right. I've stolen someone else's identity. What she did was wrong, but it doesn't make what I've done right. I don't know too much about the law but I'm pretty damn certain that I've broken it.'

'I suppose that's one way. But surely there's a way we can tie up loose ends and get you out safely within the week, way before Brandy gets back. Something simple, like we can say Brandy decided to take a break after all. You act like a bitch all week before you disappear and no-one will be any the wiser. Brandy's not back for another two months to give her scarring time to heal after the surgery. Give it twenty-four hours of Brandy temper once she's back in the show and everyone will have forgotten she was nice for a few weeks.'

'You mean I should go within a week?' said Paolo softly.

'Don't push it, pretty boy,' countered Blue, rising from the armchair and starting to pace.

'Sorry! I'm not being ungrateful! All I meant was – I feel like I made some real friends and I'll be so sad to go. You, Sienna—'

'You can't stay,' snapped Blue irritably from across the room. 'I feel your pain, don't worry. Your sister's a piece of work alright. I can't even imagine how you . . . never mind. But that's something you have to reconcile with her, just the two of you. I know you didn't plan this mess but you're dragging other people in if you stay, you know that.'

'I hear you,' Paolo sighed. 'Okay, one more week. Thing is, I'm going to have to resolve this thing with Sienna before I leave or it'll be a problem when Brandy comes back.'

'What thing?'

'That she thinks Brandy sabotaged her costume for her big debut after I was stupid enough to fake the ankle. How can I smooth that one out so she isn't still bitching about it when the real Brandy turns up?'

'Oh man. And I suppose I'll have to try and figure out who dicked around with that costume, too.'

'Thing is . . . I think I . . . God, this is messy . . . '

'Spit it out,' Blue sighed impatiently.

'I think I've fallen for Sienna in a big way.'

Blue groaned loudly. 'Look, Paolo, this isn't some Hollywood movie where you're going to reveal all and get the girl. She thinks you're a woman – a woman she doesn't much like at the best of times. There isn't a happy ending in sight for you two. You need to forget about Sienna and concentrate on how you're going to get out of this mess without going to jail or having Brandy come after you . . . ' Blue trailed off as he stood at the gilt mantelpiece, transfixed.

'Blue? You okay?'

'Um – there appears to be a picture of my ex-boyfriend Julian, with Brandy on his lap . . . if I'm not mistaken on that couch you were sitting on earlier,' said Blue incredulously, picking up the picture and holding it up in front of the leopard-skin couch. 'What's he been doing in Brandy's house?'

'Oh, is *that* Julian? Ah, I was wondering what the Shoe Man looked like . . . Wait, did you just say – your ex-boyfriend?'

Blue looked over at Paolo by the window and nodded sadly, his face pale.

'Oh, Blue. Put it this way, Brandy has a whole section of her closet devoted to shoes from Julian . . . if it's the same one, of course,' Blue and Paolo looked at each other before both racing up the sweeping staircase to Brandy's vast walk-in closet. Paolo took Blue straight to the cupboard in question, piled high with pristine boxes of designer shoes.

'There's a note inside each box, although you might not want to—'

It was too late. Blue had already squealed in horror upon reading one of the cards.

'The bitch! This is his handwriting alright!' he shrieked as he scrambled to open more boxes. 'Argh! This one has a picture of Julian's *cock*! For chrissake! My baby! How *could* he! How could *she*! All I did was introduce them once! Him and his bloody foot fetish! Ugh!'

'I guess since we're getting all the cards on the table – you know Brandy did it with Max too, don't you?' ventured Paolo. Blue's jaw dropped and he put his head slowly in his hands.

'I'm not even gonna ask how you know,' came Blue's voice, muffled through his fingers. 'Oh God. Poor Sienna. How could he? How could Brandy?'

'He's a prick. And she . . . well, you know what she is.'

Blue let the six-inch strappy Gucci heels that were hooked over his wrist drop to the shagpile carpet with a soft thump. He looked Paolo in the eye. 'I have to go home and get my head round this. It's all too much. You . . . Brandy . . . *Julian* . . . I feel like someone spiked my champagne earlier.'

Paolo absorbed himself in one of the love notes to get through the heavy silence that descended.

'Give me that,' snapped Blue eventually, snatching it from Paolo's hands. He stared at it for minutes before opening his mouth. 'I don't believe in God and angels but I do believe in good and evil. I think . . . I believe you're a good man who's just made some bad mistakes. I'll help you. There has to be a way out, so Brandy doesn't get her claws into you. She's spread enough hurt as it is. I'll help you get back to your life somehow. Okay?' The pair embraced tightly.

Honey padded through to the huge lounge and stretched herself out as Jacques finished up a phone call next to her. Wow, she could fall in love so easily with this guy, she thought, as she stared dreamily at his chiselled profile. The sex had been amazing; if this was what dating an older man would be like she was converted.

'I just booked you a car, so tell the driver where you need to go and I have it covered,' announced Jacques efficiently.

'Oh!' exclaimed Honey, taken aback. 'I thought . . . you don't want me to stay then? I thought we were having fun.'

'Oh darling, you were amazing. That really was great. We'll definitely do this again,' enthused Jacques warmly, reaching over to ruffle Honey's hair. She relaxed and smiled coyly, relieved the attraction was mutual. 'I don't need you to stay though,' Jacques continued. 'Thank you for thinking of me, I appreciate it, but I'll let you get on with the rest of your evening,' and he was up off the sofa and crossing the room to the bureau.

Honey sat for a moment in confused silence. Had she heard right when he said he didn't *need* her to stay? She guessed that his sentiments had got lost in translation somehow, although his English seemed pretty flawless. Ah well, Honey knew she shouldn't exactly expect a barrel load of respect for sleeping with him straight-away; it wasn't something she did normally. But she figured she'd have Jacques falling in love with her soon enough; there was plenty of time still to play hard to get. Honey rose and dressed herself quickly, already thinking ahead to what she might wear when she saw him next.

'So, do I call you direct to arrange this again?' asked Jacques.

'Er – sure!' scoffed Honey, wondering who the hell else he would need to call to make a date – her mother? Honey scribbled her number on the pad on the bureau before grabbing her purse and quickly checking her hair in the mirror. Jacques came up behind her and gently swept her tumbling curls to one side to kiss her neck. Honey reached up behind her and ran her fingers through his thick dark hair.

'This is for you, by the way,' said Jacques, pulling away and handing Honey an envelope bearing the hotel crest. Honey's heart leapt as she took it from his hand. A love note? Wow! A huge grin crept onto her face and she turned to give Jacques one last deep kiss. She knew he was special after all; for a minute back there she had worried he was dismissing her as a one-night stand. Honey said her good-byes and skipped from the hotel room, beaming from ear to ear.

'Honey?' came Jacques' voice just as she was about to pull the door shut behind her. She span round hopefully.

'You forgot these,' he chuckled, proffering her stock-ings.

'Oh! Silly me,' she laughed, before blowing a kiss and trotting off happily towards the elevator. As the bell pinged and the doors opened, Honey fingered the envelope excit-edly. She had barely stepped into the lift before she was ripping the paper open. It wasn't clear whether it was the lift descending so quickly or the contents of the envelope that brought bitter bile rising into her mouth, but as Honey counted out five crisp hundred-dollar bills she realised Jacques didn't like her in a special kind of way at all. The doors of the elevator opened at the ground floor to an awaiting bellhop and two well-dressed businessmen. Honey stood there, mouth agape, in one hand the pair of used stockings and in the other her wodge of cash. She knew exactly what it looked like, and she knew what the expressions on their faces were saying. What brought the tears to her eyes within seconds was the realisation that they were right. She'd just turned her first trick without even realising it.

Chapter 15

'Oh God, I feel sick,' groaned Sienna, clinging on to the bar for support.

'The Monte is having that effect on people at the moment,' muttered Pepper, chivvying Sienna into a seat and plonking a glass of iced water in front of her. 'Sienna, this is Detective Jack Weldon, by the way, he's been camping out here since Ma went into hospital last night,' said Pepper by way of introduction.

'I wouldn't put it like that,' said Weldon. 'Pleased to meet you, Sienna,' he added, just as she jumped up from her stool and made for the restrooms with one hand over her mouth, the other waving apologetically as she ran.

'I don't know what you think you'll find by sitting here at four in the afternoon anyway,' snapped Pepper over the bar at Detective Weldon. 'There's nothing to hear that Ma hasn't already told you guys a thousand times, and the girls don't clock on for another hour ready for the after-work drinkers so there's nothing to see yet either.'

'I just thought you could do with some company. It can't be easy for you with Ma and the cancer. She can't have long now.'

'Exactly, and I hope that your men aren't making her last few days a misery,' replied Pepper.

'Ma gave all her evidence over thirty years ago, as you keep reminding me. I just find this place interesting, that's all.'

'I bet you do. Pinkie's ghost ain't comin' back here if that's what you've been sent for.'

'No, ma'am. Just a beer, that's all I came for.' Weldon turned his head to see Sienna making her way back to her chair. 'You okay? You look a little green.'

'I think it's stress,' said Sienna, looking watery eyed. It had certainly been a crappy week – there was a strained atmosphere at the Follies after her disastrous debut, she'd hardly seen or spoken to Max since he'd been jetting around for work, and if it wasn't enough that she'd misplaced her engagement ring, she seemed to have lost quite a few other bits and pieces. Shoes she couldn't find, a couple of dresses, a Gucci blouse, even her favourite La Perla bra. The last straw had been last night when she couldn't find her stack of vintage 1950s *Paris Match* magazines, which she'd always read when she felt down and needed a quick shot of inspiration. She'd got annoyed with herself for being so disorganised and made a mental note to ask for any recommendations for a cheap housekeeper who could help in the tidiness department.

'You sure it's not a hangover making you throw up?' asked Pepper, an eyebrow raised, 'If you're anything like your mum with the champagne—'

'God no,' groaned Sienna. 'After my first night costume malfunction I've been on my best behaviour all week. It's been beauty sleep and concentration all the way. No, I just can't eat when I'm tense, that's all. Must be the nerves making me feel sick.'

'You need a break, that's what you need.'

'I had my birthday off, remember?'

'Yes dear, but that was all drama with the engagement. Don't tell me you slept a wink,' Pepper grinned.

'Um . . . '

'Why don't you nip to LA and see your mum? You always say you miss her. It's not like she's in England; it's only a forty-minute flight. The theatre's dark Tuesdays so go see her for the night, come back in time for the show Wednesday.'

'Hmm. She's always going to parties and premieres, though. She'll be busy.'

'Aw c'mon! She'll want you on her arm! Sienna, life's too short. This thing with Ma – she doesn't have family. If it wasn't for me and the girls she wouldn't even have a visitor. It's really important for you and Tiger to know you have each other.'

'But don't you need me around for a bit?'

'You'll only be gone one night! I'll be fine. Detective Weldon here seems to be propping the place up at any rate.'

'Maybe you're right,' sighed Sienna. 'I didn't get to see Mum on my birthday because she was filming . . . we do need to spend more time together. But what if she asks how work's going? She must have heard on the grapevine about the opening night disaster.'

'Oh, come on, she's proud of you whatever! Did you even get to the bottom of that costume thing anyway?' asked Pepper.

'No chance,' huffed Sienna. 'I swear it was Brandy's idea of sabotage but Blue's been trying to convince me all week that it couldn't have been. Those two seem really thick all of a sudden.'

'Paige was in here with that nice chap Ed this week. She seemed concerned for you that it might have been Brandy too. Good girl, that Paige. At least she seems to be looking out for you. Ever such a pretty girl, too.'

'I know, she's sweet, isn't she,' agreed Sienna. 'At least she's one person I can trust in the whole viper's nest.'

'Gets bitchy backstage, does it, then?' cut in Jack Weldon. 'I thought that was just a cliché.'

'So did I! Mostly there's huge support between us all,' started Sienna, looking upwards as she thought carefully, 'but these last few weeks, ever since I got the understudy part – man, forget falling on *hard* times, you find out who your friends are when you're doing *well*, that's all I'll say.'

'The higher you go up the mountain, the harder the wind blows, Ms Starr.'

'Oh. You know who I am . . . ?'

'I'm a detective,' laughed Weldon. 'Actually I was looking at that photo of Tiger a few weeks back, and Pepper told me all about you both.' He flicked his eyes across to the 'hall of fame' wall behind the bar.

'Yeah,' sighed Sienna. 'Having Tiger Starr as a mum doesn't exactly make me popular with the haters either.'

'When people find reasons to be negative it's usually a sign you're doing something right,' pointed out Detective Weldon.

'S'pose,' grunted Sienna sulkily, her eyes grazing over the framed pictures on the wall.

'Look at my beautiful friend Honey Lou,' said Sienna suddenly, pointing at a stunning shot of Honey in her twenties flapper dress, pulling a leggy pose in front of her dressing-room mirror in her Josephine Baker sequinned skullcap.

'Gorgeous,' said Weldon, sucking air over his teeth. 'Just like you if I may be so bold.'

'God, I miss her,' sighed Sienna. 'Hey! Maybe you can help me!' she exclaimed suddenly. 'You see, I've been so worried – she doesn't take my calls any more, I can't get hold of her. Can you do anything? Find her for me, just make sure she's okay?'

'I don't know about that, miss, unless you file a missing persons. If you really think she's missing then you need to take action . . . '

'No,' cut in Sienna quietly, 'she moved out a while ago, we had a few rows. I'm sure she's fine. I just wasn't sure she'd be too happy to see me, that's all.'

'I'd love to help you but I can't really just do checkups

because you've had a spat. It doesn't work like that. But if you seriously think she's at risk then let's file a report.'

'It's okay. I have an address for her downtown, hopefully she's still there. I'll have to get over my stubbornness and check up on her. When she moved out she was pretty pissed. We both said things . . . Oh, I miss her so much, I just want to know she's okay. This is the longest we've gone not speaking.'

'Oh, you girls,' said Weldon, shaking his head. 'Just go and see her, she'll be fine. But I can't launch an investigation for a girlie fight!' he laughed.

'I know,' giggled Sienna. 'I should just go round with some flowers and beg her to come back.'

'On that note, I have to go. My girlfriend's waiting at home,' said Weldon with a wink.

'Oh darn it. All the cute ones are taken,' said Pepper, hand on hip.

'Not for much longer if I keep spending so much time hanging out with beautiful women,' he laughed uneasily, before smiling and saluting Pepper. 'See you soon, ma'am. If you think of anything you'd like to tell me . . . '

'Nothing at all, Detective,' replied Pepper, keeping her grin in place until Weldon had made his way out of the club.

'He's looking for Pinkie, isn't he,' said Sienna finally. Pepper grimaced and motioned frantically at Sienna to zip her lips. Sienna cowered immediately and mouthed an apology, remembering Ma had been convinced for some time the place was bugged.

'So Weldon knows how ill Ma is,' Sienna said, changing the subject. 'How long do you reckon she has?'

'Days.'

'Can I visit?' asked Sienna.

'No, dear, she wouldn't want that, she's in such a bad way. She doesn't want any of you bright young things visiting. She wants you all to remember her the way she was in healthier days, and as the legend she lived her life as, not the poor old bag of bones she's become now.' Her voice caught on the last word. Sienna immediately reached for her hand and held tight while Pepper swallowed back her tears and composed herself. 'I'm going to the hospital again in a few hours to be by her side. I'll read to her from the *National Enquirer*, she likes to hear the gossip still.' Sienna watched sadly as a big tear made its way down Pepper's rouged cheek, plopping onto the dishtowel she held in her hand. Sienna suddenly sensed they weren't alone. Looking round, she saw Paige's friend Ed sitting at the far end of the bar, watching on quietly.

Becoming the son-in-law of a Hollywood movie star was going to be good for business, Max could tell, after the first wave of publicity for his engagement had bought him a little more stalling time with sympathetic investors, not to mention a few previously slammed doors creaking open once more for money talk. But the real eye-opener of the week had been Paige Turner. Or at least, what she'd let slip over the blackjack table when Max had asked where she was from. All this time and he'd had no idea that she was a Dallas girl with a daddy rich from oil. Why hadn't Sienna mentioned her background before? She'd always given the impression she was helping Paige out.

Max had renewed hope, and was feeling fired up and ready to revive business and morale back at his Dallas offices. As he reclined in his seat, watching fluffy clouds pass beneath as the Silver Slipper plane soared south east on its path to Texas, he had a tantalising glimpse of a reprise. All he needed was to take Paige out for dinner very soon and get a direct line of communication to her daddy. The rest would slip into place – Max Power could charm a snake when he needed to. Thank God he'd had the good sense not to screw her. That would have ruined everything. She was hungry for him, and as long as he held out, he'd get all the information and contacts he needed from her. Resisting temptation wouldn't be a problem; it was only challenges he couldn't resist. Besides there were girls like Paige Turner throwing themselves at him on a daily basis. Although admittedly not all of them with a family fortune of billions.

'Don't you think it's a bit early in the day to be coming over all Don Corleone?' complained Jesús, winding down the truck window and fanning his sweating face. Tiny had enlisted Jesús' help in staking out the stage door at the

Follies Casino Theatre to wait for Blue's arrival, and there they were now, wedged in the truck with the aircon broken and the radio needle stuck on Country Classics 104.3. Tiny had been hovering around the parking lot on a casual basis all week but hadn't seen hide nor hair of Blue, so now it was time to get professional about it and have a proper stakeout.

'Jesús, no-one makes fun of *us*. Coming on to our Pancho like a prowling . . . something that prowls,' growled Tiny. 'We'll get him today, tonight, or as long as it takes, but we ain't moving from this spot until we do. We'll flush him out one way or the other and make him pay.'

'It's weird Ed, I feel so – comfortable around you,' said Sienna. 'I can't put my finger on it.' Sienna was more than aware that she barely knew Paige's new physiotherapist friend, but he was just so easy to open up to. It seemed fortuitous that he had been at the bar today. Not that Sienna really wanted to spend the last hour talking about work, but Ed was being such a good listener, she could see why Paige got on with him so well. Sienna had ended up pouring out everything that was on her mind as they both sat there at the bar – the opening night fiasco, the bad atmosphere at work, the fact she had hardly seen Max since he'd proposed – and Ed was just so relaxed and patient, letting her talk and talk and talk. He'd been especially sympathetic when Sienna got on to the subject of Tiger, and how much it was grinding her down that people had such unfair judgements of her in light of her famous mum. Ed had seemed genuinely interested and concerned. Despite the fact that the club was filling up by the minute, it seemed that the only person Ed cared about in the whole room was Sienna.

'So you think it's a good idea to go and see Mum?' she asked finally.

'Sure, go with your heart,' said Ed gently. 'Besides, friends come and go but loyalty to family is what counts,' he added. 'It's family who take care of each other when life turns sour.'

'Funny, Pepper said exactly the same earlier,' replied Sienna. She surprised Ed by leaning over suddenly and administering a hearty hug. 'Thanks!' she exclaimed. 'I really appreciate you just being here this afternoon. I feel like I got so much off my chest, and I hardly know you! Who'da thought, Paige's "Mr Champagne" turned out to be a good guy after all. Pepper always has nice regulars, anyway. She'd have sifted you out if you were a weirdo. Oh, Ed, it's been such a stressful week. I was actually sick today, you know.'

'Wow, you need to relax!' laughed Ed softly. 'Tell you what, how about I give you a massage?'

'Oh no! You've done enough, I couldn't,' said Sienna.

'Go on! I had a VIP ticket to the show last week, you entertained me, so I'd like to give something back. Paige has had a few of my deep-tissue massages, so have some of the other girls in the show, and I've had good write-ups so far!'

'But you bought me that teddy bear on the night! That was enough of a token of appreciation!'

'Listen to you,' soothed Ed. 'You even *sound* tense. Hey, I'm not keeping the offer on the table for ever – just take it! We can go to my studio now, and you'll be walking on clouds in time for tonight's performance. Forget the bitchy bullshit in the dressing room. After one of my massages you'll feel so calm you'll be able to take on anything.'

Sienna regarded Ed thoughtfully. 'Okay. Sold. But I need to be at the theatre in good time for the first show.'

'No problem. You won't even need to warm up. By the time you get to work, you'll feel like a rubber band.' Sienna broke out in a broad smile and let Ed lead her to his car outside.

Within twenty minutes Sienna was climbing on to Ed's massage table and arranging her towel, already feeling more relaxed with the gentle sound of crashing waves being piped through to the room, accompanied by soothing wafts of incense.

'I'm ready!' she yelled, fidgeting into place face down on the table. She was really pleased she'd got to know Ed. Any reservations she'd had about him when he turned up at the Monte offering her and Paige champagne from across the bar all that time ago had dissipated, and what she now saw was a charming and helpful man. No wonder Paige seemed quite taken with him. He was certainly extremely physically attractive for someone in their forties. Sienna could only imagine what a heartbreaker he must have been in his youth. She wondered if romance might be on the cards for him and Paige.

'Okay, let's go,' said Ed as he glided back into the room and closed the door gently. She looked up lazily as she heard him turning the key in the lock. 'Just so we're not disturbed,' he smiled reassuringly. Sienna relaxed and put her head back down as Ed came to the side of the table. She felt him folding her towel down to just below the small of her back, followed by his hot, firm hands giving the first long stroke on her bare skin from her hips up to her shoulders.

'I think I've laid the groundwork for throwing Sienna off the scent of sabotage theories,' said Blue as he strolled through the parking lot with Paolo in full Brandy drag beside him.

'I wonder if we'll ever get to the bottom of who really did it,' mused Paolo, taking dainty poodle steps in his heels and swinging one of Brandy's Birkin bags from his manicured hand.

'There are so many possible green eyes in that dressing room I wouldn't like to say. Anyway, has Sienna defrosted with you at all?'

'Mm, a bit.'

'Cool. I'll sort it out once you're gone, don't worry. So what do you fancy doing for your last couple of days?'

'Have a date with Sienna?'

'Ha ha. No, really.'

'Oh, I don't know, have a last dance on the stage one lunchtime, I guess, that'll do me ... and say my good-byes in my own way.'

'I'm sure the Follies Casino will fall over themselves to comp Brandy Alexander with fine dining. How about we have a huge last supper before you go?'

'Nice! I'd be up for that. Lobster tail ... cocktails ... you'd sort that out for me?'

'Sure! I think Brandy owes us that much!'

'You can say that again!'

Blue felt his mouth watering – the Follies Michelin Star restaurant did a mean dessert, not to mention fancy cocktails made with liquid nitrogen. He loved something creative from the kitchen. At that moment Paolo let out a strangled choking noise.

'You son of a bitch!' he hissed, stopping dead in his tracks.

'Huh?'

'You! You've set me up, haven't you!' Paolo was backing away from Blue rapidly.

'What the hell?'

'My friends! Tiny and Jesús! You thought I wouldn't notice their truck there, right by the stage door, did you? You've told them about me, haven't you! How did you find them?'

'What? Who?'

'Oh, don't play the innocent! Why, you're as bad as Brandy! You told them to come here knowing I'd be in drag, you – how *could* you! After I poured my heart out! After you knew what Brandy did! Oh God! As if what she did wasn't enough humiliation!'

Blue's mind raced. Where in hell had he heard those names? So familiar, Tiny and Jesús, Tiny and Jesús, Tiny and ... Just as Blue realised exactly where he knew the names from – the night at the Monte when he'd chatted to their friend Pancho – he registered Paolo's clenched fist approaching his nose at lightning speed, a nanosecond before the lights went out.

Sienna could feel the tension uncurling and lifting from her shoulders as Ed leaned his weight into his hands, kneading and pummelling her muscles firmly. She wondered if she was slipping into a dream as she sensed his breath close to her ear.

'I knew I'd find you one day . . . you look so much like your mother. My beautiful daughter . . . '

Sienna froze. Wait. This was no dream. *My daughter?* Had Ed really said that? Sienna screamed and scrambled up from the massage table, clutching her towel to her bare skin for dear life.

'Wait!' laughed Ed. 'Not so fast. It's taken me this long to find you!'

Sienna gulped, her eyes darting around the room. Who was this freak? She turned and made a grab for the door handle, letting out another piercing scream as she realised Ed had locked the door, her hands shaking uncontrollably as she rattled the handle. Her towel slipped from her hands and Sienna dropped to the floor, scrabbling to pick it up and cover herself.

'What do you want from me, you freak!' she screamed, hoping to scare him off with volume.

'Sienna, baby—'

'I'm not your baby, you sick fuck!' she cried out with a blood-curdling squeal, before turning and rattling the door handle frantically for a second time. 'Let me out!' she wailed.

'Sienna, calm down, it's okay.'

'What are you going to do to me?' she asked, her voice wobbling.

'Nothing! Why would I hurt my own daughter?'

'Stop saying that!'

Sienna was doing her best to keep herself from crying. There was no way on God's earth she was going to drop so much as a tear in front of this stalking weirdo. That's what he wanted. To have control over her. To make her cry. Split-second memories of Tiger breaking the silence that she was Sienna's mother, not her sister, now dredged themselves up from years before, threatening to topple her steely resolve. How the hell had she got here, locked in a room half naked with only a massage table and the sound of whale song between her and some sicko pervert?

'Okay, I'll unlock the door if it means you'll trust me. I just wanted the chance to explain who I am before you ran off.'

'You're not my father. You just found out who my mum is from hanging out at the Monte and following me and my friends around, and I bet you thought you could squeeze a buck or two out of my family.'

'No! I *am* your family. I just wanted to get to know my daughter.'

'I know you're lying.'

'How?'

'Because if you really were my real father you'd never have the gall to show your face because you'd know that you're a pervert and a *rapist*.' Sienna nearly choked on the words.

'Is that what your mum told you?' said Ed, sounding incredulous.

'Oh my God, you really are ill. I know what my real father did! How do you think it makes me *feel* to know that's why I'm here?' Sienna stopped to swallow back the bile that was rising in her throat.

'We were in love,' said Ed. 'But Tiger – Poppy – was so young, it was never going to work. She lost me my job, Sienna. And I can never teach again. Now how else would I know her real name?'

Sienna squealed and put her hands over her ears. 'You're not my father! It was in all the newspapers – you could have read it anywhere! Now let me out!'

'Okay, I can see you need time,' said Ed calmly. 'Just think about it, you'll realise it's all true. It all fits into place who I am. Ed Rogers and Poppy Adams.'

'Liar! I'll go to the police!'

'Don't do that, Sienna, or I'll tell your mum what good friends we've become.'

'Let me out!'

'Okay okay, I have the key.' Ed crossed to the door and put the key in the lock.

'But before you go,' he said, turning to face Sienna earnestly, 'why don't you ask your mum something – something only she and I would know the answer to. Why don't you ask her what position she used to play in hockey? I always used to put her in centre forward. She was the best goal scorer on the team. Then you'll see I'm telling the truth.' He released the door handle and Sienna was gone.

Chapter 16

Max pulled into the driveway and took a minute to compose himself before climbing from the car. Sienna's engagement ring was long lost to yet another night of lousy luck and he'd been avoiding her calls all week. Max knew he'd have to come up with an explanation sooner or later so tonight was the night. He was missing Sienna anyway and felt guilty for giving her the silent treatment; after all, what had *she* done wrong? Guilt wasn't a sensation he entertained much in his adult years; and after the myriad of shady deals he'd presented to boardrooms full of Rottweiler investors he could scarcely believe anything less than a gun at his temple would even so much as singe his nerves. But right now he felt butterflies creeping through him, as well as the fear that Sienna would discover how sour things were turning with his business, or worse still, that she'd leave him and find some other, richer guy to be the perfect wife to. So Max had absolutely no intention of telling her the truth about the ring, of course, or she might start thinking he had some kind of gambling problem, and naturally he knew he had his favourite pastime totally under control. He'd just had an elongated spell of being dealt the wrong cards. Max had a story all mapped out about 'borrowing' the ring back so he could have a matching wedding band designed, only to lose it en route to the jewellers. He'd give her a yarn about waiting for the insurance to come through, which should give him enough time to get his cash flow back on track and replace the ring with something even more fabulous. Apparently blue diamonds were all the rage now, so with any luck Sienna would be pleased to choose something even more de rigueur. It didn't matter to him that the ring had once been his mother's. It had only been for the farcical renewal of his parents' vows after yet another of Kerry's mistresses had come out of the woodwork with a phantom paternity suit.

As Max rang Sienna's doorbell, he prepared his most convincing sheepish expression. Paige answered.

'Hey, big boy,' she giggled, looking up at his handsome face. Max's eyes darted over Paige's shoulder to check Sienna wasn't within earshot.

'Don't worry, she's not here if that's what you're worried about,' said Paige as she stepped aside and motioned for Max to come in.

'Actually, yes, I am worried, I haven't heard from her for a couple of days,' replied Max as he made his way into the coolness of the marble vestibule.

'I thought you were the one being elusive, if Sienna's to be believed,' exclaimed Paige over her shoulder as she swaggered her way slowly through the lobby with a languid swing in her hips. 'I told her maybe you were chained to the blackjack table or something.'

'You said what?' snapped Max as he trailed behind her into the kitchen. 'How dare you. I've been working, as it happens. You know, running an airline takes a bit of spare time up,' he continued sarcastically. Paige tossed a little smirk over her shoulder. Max was getting irritated now. He watched on as she took a bottle of champagne from the fridge and proceeded to uncage it.

'Lunch?' she asked, waving the bottle playfully in the air. Max stared back blankly. If Paige thought playing silly games was endearing herself to Max Power she'd be wrong. Rich bitch. Perhaps he'd take her up on the impromptu lunch offer after all and begin the process of charming some money from her family coffers. That would wipe the smile off the cocky cow's face, decided Max.

'So what time's Sienna back?' he asked.

'Oh, didn't you know?'

'Know what?'

'She's gone to her mum's.' Max fell silent. Shit. If a girl went to visit her mum without warning it usually followed a row with the boyfriend. He hoped Sienna wasn't there in LA right now deconstructing their relationship in front of Tiger Starr; who was bound to be imparting to her daughter some kind of man-eating, dick-shrivelling manifesto to bring home with her. What if Tiger was telling Sienna to get rid of him? Or worse still, setting Sienna up with some hot actor or something? He realised he should have answered Sienna's calls sooner and palmed her off with a few good excuses for his absence at least. Suddenly he missed her terribly.

Sienna watched the velvety matt black Ferrari through the gap in the topiary hedges as it purred its way slowly up to the valet. A long elegant arm laden down with a cornucopia of gold costume jewellery extended out with the car door, pushing it open dramatically, followed by a pair of slender ankles swinging down to the kerbside. Sienna's eyes travelled up from the gleaming oil-slick-black spike heels, taking in bestockinged shapely calves and a sliver of black hemline skirting the tops of the knees. Sienna realised every person looking on was holding their breath, just as she was.
  The figure that finally emerged elicited a collective sigh of appreciation and a murmur that swept round the terrace, peppered with whisperings of Sienna's name from the neighbouring dining tables. Sienna felt a stab of awe realising it was indeed her mother arriving, newly platinum blonde with a Veronica Lake-esque thick silky wave of hair falling over one feline eye, the full length of it caressing her shoulders and tumbling down her back. Her tightly tailored black lace dress accentuated every curve, and short black leather gloves and a matching clutch bag completed the ensemble. A juicy slash of vermilion lipstick was the cherry on the icing on the cake. Jessica Rabbit would have thrown in the towel had she been present.

'Darling!' exclaimed Tiger Starr as she shoo-ed the maître d' away and swept across the terrace through tables full of discreetly staring diners over to Sienna, knocking a cute waiter and his tray of Bellinis flying in her wake.

'Oh, Did I do that?' asked Tiger, looking down at the carnage with dismay.

'No ma'am,' replied the waiter politely from the floor, but giving a discreet wink up at Tiger. She wordlessly tipped him with a crisp hundred-dollar bill from her clutch purse and returned the wink, before turning her full attention upon Sienna.

'Bellissima!' she said through a deep sigh as she outstretched her arms. Sienna was on her feet and giving Tiger a tight hug within a second. Sod Hollywood protocol, this was no time for air kissing, thought Sienna. It was all she could do not to burst into tears right there on her mother's shoulder after the week she'd had. But Cecconi's was certainly not the place for those kind of displays.

'Missed you, Mum,' she managed to whisper into Tiger's creamy blonde hair.

'Look at you!' exclaimed Tiger, holding Sienna at arm's length so she could look her up and down. 'What are you, just another size zero now or something? Sit!' she insisted. 'I'm about to feed you up for lunch. Even the boys are looking sorry for themselves,' she muttered, eyeing up Sienna's breasts beneath her flimsy blouse.

'Oh, you know, weigh-ins . . . '

'Oh yes!' laughed Tiger, opening the menu. 'Only too well. Now, I'm taking you to a premiere this evening and you've got me all to yourself today as I've got no scenes to shoot. A whole day to choose how we spend it! How long are you staying? We can fit some shopping in on Rodeo Drive tomorrow and there's a fantastic place for lunch in Santa Monica if you fancy a drive one day. Lewis would love to come, I'm sure –'

'No, Mum, it's only a flying visit. I have to be back for the show tomorrow. I have a flight booked at midday.'

'Oh.' Tiger looked crestfallen. 'Are you okay, darling? Seems a bit odd for you to come just for the night. Do you need help with anything? Cash? Is the car running okay? I can come back and take care of the house after shooting finishes if you need me?'

'No!' blurted Sienna. 'I mean, I'm fine, I'm doing okay. I don't need anything. I mean – thank you for caring but really I'm doing okay, no need to fuss.'

'Just okay?'

Sienna couldn't meet Tiger's eyes with her own. She suddenly became interested in the wine list.

'Something we can talk about on the way home via Dior maybe?' asked Tiger hopefully, trying to peer into Sienna's eyes. Sienna nodded and mouthed a 'thank you' at her mother just as the waiter swooped with complimentary aperitifs. One martini was all it took to open the floodgates and for Sienna to pour her heart out to her mother about Max, the ring, the show fiasco. Tiger listened patiently and surreptitiously kept the food and drinks coming. By the time the coffee and petits fours arrived, Sienna was back on the subject of Max again.

'We just seem so close one minute and then something clouds over, like he shuts off and becomes so untouchable, out of reach – that's it, I can't seem to reach him, Mum.'

'I'm only going to say this once, darling. Max is emotionally unavailable. Mark my words. It takes one to know one, I was like that with men for years, wouldn't let them get close. Took me over ten years to let Lewis in . . . .'

Tiger fell silent and Sienna knew why. She wasn't about to revisit the abuse that had left her emotionally scarred for so long. Sienna felt her heart begin to pound as she agonised if now was the right time to bring up the freak who claimed to be her father Ed.

'Anyway, all I'm saying is you have to aim high,' continued Tiger eventually. Sienna wiped her clammy palms on her pencil skirt as she realised the moment had passed. 'And when it comes to men,' Tiger went on, 'their money means nothing when you can make your own. Concentrate on your own movie, don't be an extra in someone else's. Make your own success in life and the rest will fall in. Mum knows best. So maybe Max will grow up one day or maybe he won't. You want to waste years waiting to find out? That's all I'm saying. Now, just think of the premiere tonight and all the cute men who'll be there – ooh, Robert Pattinson doesn't have a girlfriend right now . . . Oh, actually, I don't like his hair, scrap that idea . . . ' As Tiger rambled on, getting herself excited at the prospect of matchmaking, all Sienna wanted to do was see Max's gorgeous face. At that moment a wave of nausea hit her hard. She knew she shouldn't have eaten so much just to keep her mum happy. She made a mad dash for the restrooms leaving Tiger at the table, mid flow in her list of eligible bachelors.

'Are those peonies?' asked Max, pointing at the pink flowers in a gilt vase on the kitchen table, having enjoyed a liquid lunch with Paige. She was looking amazing, Max had to admit to himself. There was something almost Sienna-like about her. Maybe it was the way she had her hair or something. In any case, try as he might he just couldn't seem to get Paige onto the subject of her family, no matter how much of Sienna's Veuve Clicquot he poured down her neck. She just kept directing the conversation back to him and Silver Slipper. Maybe she'd checked up on him through her folks in Dallas; they must have connections if her father was in oil. Maybe Max had dealt with him already. Knowing his recent run of crappy luck perhaps Paige had already discovered things were amiss with his business. Max wondered if her family were even more wealthy than she had let on. He'd have to switch to major charm offensive and throw her off the scent of any business problems.

'Yep, these are peonies alright,' replied Paige, visibly

holding down a belch from her champagne. 'You good with flowers then?' she asked with faint surprise.

'Not especially, I just know those are Sienna's favourites,' he explained. Paige shrugged dismissively and stood to clear away the afternoon's detritus from the dining table. Max felt the urge to send a message to Sienna. Maybe it wasn't too late to show how much he really cared.

I love you. Look forward to having you on my arm when you get back. Kiss. Your Max he tapped out hastily on his Blackberry, hitting the send button as Paige made her way to his side of the table.

'Dessert?' she asked with a cheeky grin that spread like sunshine across her beautiful face. Like Jekyll and Hyde, Max rose, regaining his focus, and swept the peonies off the table before lifting Paige up onto the solid oak and leaning in to her, kissing her with urgency.

'Please hear me out!' pleaded Blue as he chased Paolo round the pool.

'Fuck off, Judas!' yelled Paolo over the roar of the water features, cupping his hands to his ears as he hotfooted it into the neon palm-tree jungle.

'You're being ridiculous!' panted Blue, coming to a standstill as he wondered which tree Paolo had concealed himself behind.

'How did you get in anyway?' came a muffled voice.

'Duh, I have Brandy's keys. That's how I let you in the first time, remember . . . like a cuckoo into a nest?'

'That was below the belt!' fumed Paolo, stepping out from behind the large model plastic polar bear.

'You have to hear me out. Your friends are after *me*, not you! They don't know who Brandy is or any of that shit.'

'Why the hell would you be mixing with my Mexican friends in the first place?' ventured Paolo suspiciously.

'We need to talk. I can explain everything. I met them in a bar but if Tiny and Jesús really are your friends . . . then I think I might need your help.'

'What did you do with them?'

'Nothing! There's been a terrible mix-up . . . I'm getting threats and I'm certain it's Tiny and Jesús. Please can we just move away from this eighties neon acid trip and go into the house?'

Paolo stayed by the polar bear's side and stared at Blue blankly.

'I need you to talk to your friends for me, as the Paolo they know. There was a terrible mix-up. I'm in trouble. I can explain in the house. Please?'

Paolo finally relented and grudgingly stepped away from the polar bear to follow Blue back into Brandy's lair.

A wall of paparazzi lit up the sky with their flashes as Tiger Starr stepped on to the red carpet with Sienna.

'To your left!'

'What designer are you wearing?'

'Over here!'

'Straight ahead, ladies!'

Sienna felt her cheeks spasm as he held her smile for what seemed longer than humanly possible without looking like a ventriloquist's dummy.

'One on your own, Tiger!' yelled a paparazzi.

'I'm with my daughter,' replied Tiger before grabbing Sienna's arm and leading her up the carpet to the next pool of awaiting paps.

'I do have a name, you know,' whispered Sienna.

'Ignore them,' said Tiger through gritted teeth, 'these are just the rat paps, the good ones are inside. A few autographs for fans and then we'll go in, darling.'

Sienna kept her mouth shut. Her mum was a seasoned pro and knew what to do. She dutifully posed in the way Tiger had shown her back at the house before they left. They had both looked for something for Sienna on Rodeo Drive in a snatched hour after lunch, but Sienna's nausea and anxiety meant she couldn't be less in the mood for finding something to make her look like a goddess. Instead she had chosen something red and vintage from Tiger's fabulous wardrobe once they were home. In a funny way, wearing something of Tiger's made her feel more confident anyway. She didn't care if her mum had worn it before or if it wasn't this season; neither did she care about making it into the celebrity blogs or the diary columns with the latest 'gold dust' gown that every stylist was stabbing each other to get a hold of. Tonight of all nights she just needed to feel like she belonged, and in her mum's tried and tested archive Versace gown she felt safe. All those fashion politics were utter bullshit anyway, thought Sienna. All these actresses who had to have a minimum of fifteen possible gowns lined up for one red carpet event, stylists who carried, like, six mobile phones every eighteen-hour day they clocked in, and who would lose their job if a B-lister was then seen out in the same dress as the A-list actress the following week. Who cared? Wasn't style supposed to be about taste, personality and creativity, and wearing a dress well as opposed to politics, bribery and social climbing? Wouldn't it be nice if the press paid as much attention to the talent wearing the dress as opposed to the provenance or whether the purse was an it-bag or not, thought Sienna, before reminding herself that it wasn't necessarily talent that made someone a star. In fact most of the time blind ambition, a stellar sales technique and a massive cheek would win over talent any day, she decided with a sigh. And a well-timed sex tape, she noted to herself as she spotted Paris Hilton making her way onto the red carpet behind her.

Sienna felt Tiger's hand gripping hers and she remembered to straighten her pose. Tiger had explained that before she went to any event, she would check all angles in the mirror and figure out how to pose to show the line of the dress as well as her figure off to their best advantage. After all, if designers were to lend their dresses out, it was her duty to 'sell' them on the red carpet. It all seemed a bit too much detail for Sienna but she wanted her mum to be proud of the pictures in the papers the next day so she was making her best efforts.

'All done, darling, let's go inside,' whispered Tiger, leading Sienna into the theatre. Waiters stood attentively with trays of champagne.

'So, do you want to watch the movie or shall we slip out the back and meet them all at the party later?' asked Tiger, liberating two flutes of Dom from the waiter's tray.

'What? You mean you don't even stay to watch?' asked Sienna incredulously.

'Well, I suppose we should but not everyone does. Oh, come on, the actors have probably seen it about five hundred times already. You can't expect the poor buggers to sit through it *again*,' she groaned with a theatrical roll of her eyeballs.

'Actually I am feeling a bit sick,' admitted Sienna. 'I don't mind whichever you choose. I could happily go straight to the party rather than being cooped up in the theatre for an hour and a half.'

'On that subject,' started Tiger. 'Your dramatic dash after lunch – is there something you're not telling your mum?'

'No, I'm not bulimic, bloody hell,' guffawed Sienna. 'I just had to lose weight for the show that's all.'

'That's not what I meant,' countered Tiger with a raised eyebrow.

'What then?'

'When was your last . . . ' Tiger paused and leaned in. 'P-e-r-i-o-d?' she whispered.

'Oh, I don't know, um – oh God, you're not suggesting – Mum!'

'Just saying, that's all. I know morning sickness when I see it.'

'No! Everything's as it should be!' insisted Sienna, before knocking back her champagne. Her mum was right as usual, at least that she was late, but Sienna was sure it was down to the stress; she often skipped a period if she was under stress. She always used protection with Max anyway; it was out of the question that she was pregnant. Except for the time in the swimming pool. She'd been so upset, what with Max saying he didn't want her to meet his father. He'd swept her into his arms and made beautiful love to her. It had seemed so natural it hadn't even crossed her mind to stop for protection. They had felt so much in love . . . .

Sienna shuddered and caught Tiger giving her a sideways stare with her catlike eyes before flicking her gaze away.

'Maybe we should be seen making the effort to watch the movie. Then we'll go to the party and I'll introduce you to someone eligible and hot,' declared Tiger, allowing her champagne flute to be topped up by a passing waiter.

'Great, that's decided then,' said Sienna, relieved to move on from the subject of morning sickness. 'Just one question, Mum—' said Sienna as Tiger started to move towards the auditorium.

'Uh huh.'

'What position did you used to play in hockey?' Sienna

braced herself. It was now or never. May as well get it out of the way.

'Why?'

'Just curious. I met someone who's really into hockey . . .'

'Oh. Centre forward. I used to shoot perfect goals, ha hah!' Sienna felt her mouth go dry immediately as prickles ran up her neck.

Chapter 17

Paige minced into Sienna's bedroom and surveyed the surface of her dresser for perfume. A huge bottle of Chanel No 5 nestled next to pretty pots of fragranced body powder with swan-down powder puffs in pretty shades of pastel yellow and pink. Paige fancied something delicate and classic for waking up Max on such a fine sunny morning, and remembering being told once that perfume should be sprayed everywhere you'd like to be kissed, gave herself a liberal all-over body spritz with the Chanel. Spotting a fine chain attached to an adorable rose-gold Tiffany key dangling from the ornamental mirror, she held it up to her neck and admired her reflection, making a mental note to herself to borrow the necklace for a lunch date sometime. Sienna's life was pretty fabulous, after all, concluded Paige, padding her way back out of the bedroom. Just as she got to the doorway something pink and fluffy caught her eye by Sienna's bed. Skyscraper marabou mules? Perfect. Paige swooped and slipped them on to her dainty feet. Just the finishing touch she needed for a morning seduction.

By the time she reached her bedroom, Max was already dressed.

'Oh! Where are you off to in a hurry? I had breakfast in mind,' started Paige.

'Business,' grunted Max, not looking up from his Rolex as he fiddled with the clasp. Paige pouted to herself and furrowed her brow, certain that if he looked up for a second and checked out her gorgeous body clad only in heels and a waft of scent he'd want to stay. 'So when do we get to do this again?'

'We'll see,' concluded Max, finally looking up and straight into Paige's big brown eyes. 'When did you say you were speaking to your dad again? I'd love to meet him. Sounds like such an interesting guy.'

'Oh. Soon,' answered Paige, casually. 'Come here and give me a kiss goodbye, and I'll think about fixing up that lunch with Daddy for you.' Max dutifully walked over and administered a quick peck on the cheek.

'Just give me a call when you've fixed a date then . . . H'mm, you smell good,' he added, giving Paige a quick pat on her peachy buttocks and making for the door. He turned abruptly. 'Er – we're keeping this to ourselves, obviously?' Paige gave a tight smile of acknowledgement before flopping onto the bed and waiting for the sound of the front door as Max left. So much for a breakfast workout. She guessed that must be the flipside of setting your sights on being with a successful businessman. Free time was tight when there were so many deals to be done.

What Paige didn't know was that Max had no intention of trying to wheel and deal in futile stuffy meetings today. He was now getting threatening calls from his investors and his father's aides on an hour-by-hour basis – the last thing he wanted to do was be in a boardroom with them. Instead, Max was taking the other definition of a high-risk approach and was heading straight for the blackjack tables again for another furtive attempt to claw some of his fortune back.

Sienna checked the flight information board and, checking her watch, calculated she had just about enough time to take the pregnancy test she'd bought this morning. This was all she needed, especially after the shock of finding out that Ed wasn't a faker, at least not entirely. He'd certainly demonstrated that he knew her mother as a girl; it may just be possible he could be her biological father. But it was also possible he could just be a clever stalker. He still hadn't proved he was actually Ed Rogers. Sienna couldn't devote any thoughts to that sleazebag right now while she had to focus on the pregnancy test. She hated the thought of finding out something so crucial in an airport restroom of all places, but her increasing anxiety was demanding she put her mind to rest one way or the other. At least it was one question in her life today she could get an almost instant answer to. Sienna scoured her surroundings for a restroom sign, just as she felt her phone vibrate from within her purse. It was possibly the first time ever she'd hoped it *wasn't* Max as she scrabbled to retrieve the phone.

She did a double-take as she read *Monte Cristo* flashing up on the display. Pepper never called people for chit-chat.

'Well?' asked Blue the second Paolo answered the front door. This was quickly followed by a step backwards as Blue took in Paolo's appearance in jeans and a sweatshirt, with mussed-up hair and a stubbled jaw. 'You do look kinda different with a bit of regrowth,' he remarked, barging past and straight into Brandy's lobby. Paolo turned and let the door click shut.

'That's a nice hello,' he remarked, eyeing up Blue, who was now wringing his hands apprehensively as he stood under the garishly stuffed, rhinestoned and gilded-horned rhino head mounted on the wall.

'Sorry, didn't mean to be rude. Well?'

'Tiny and Jesús? You could say they were surprised to see me,' started Paolo, 'considering I "disappeared" a couple of months ago. They thought I'd gone back to New York. Looked like they'd seen a ghost when I turned up on their doorstep.'

'Yeah yeah, but did you talk to them? Do they know it was all a misunderstanding now? That I wasn't flirting with Pancho?' pressed Blue impatiently.

'Well . . . yes, but it wasn't easy. I had to cover up for myself too. I made up some elaborate story about being a janitor at the theatre to explain how I knew you. I also had to make up a hot new girlfriend to explain why I hadn't been around for a while. Took a while for them to believe me but I think I smoothed it out.'

'Whaddya mean you *think*? Are they still going to come after me or is the coast clear?'

'You're fine. I had to stick up for you, mind. They were pretty pissed.'

'*They* were pretty pissed, huh!' muttered Blue under his breath. '*I* should be pretty pissed that homophobia is alive and kicking in Vegas of all places.'

'They just thought you were an old creep trying to bait their young, cute and very straight buddy.'

'Me? Old?!'

'Okay, old*er*. Anyway, think of me! I was just the messenger and let's say things got a little . . . heated,' said Paolo with a grimace, clenching his fists to illustrate his point.

'Oh man. I'm sorry.'

'Yeah. Anyway you're all free now. I sorted it out.'

'You didn't get—'

'No. And if I got a crack on the chin it would have been nothing compared to what my own sister dished up. And their prejudice is nothing to what my father was like. At least they don't seem to know any better . . . '

'You would have taken a hit for me?'

'Hey, I didn't go expecting them to be all best pals about it. Sure, I thought I might have to give or take a punch, especially with Tiny's temper. Anyway, everyone calmed down and it's all fine. Job done.' Paolo walked through into the den soberly. Blue followed after a minute and stood watching as Paolo packed the last of his things into his holdall.

'I know I owe you,' said Blue, piercing the heavy silence.

'S'okay. You're letting me go without blowing the whistle. I appreciate that,' said Paolo quietly. Blue perched on the edge of one of Brandy's chairs and looked over at Paolo sadly. He would miss him in a strange way. It had become fun having him around, especially towards the end.

'There must be one thing you can think of that you'd like before you go, surely?' ventured Blue. 'You know, my way of saying thanks for smoothing out a messy misunderstanding with gun-toting Mexicans. I feel I owe it to you.'

'Apart from international fame, a million bucks and a roof over my head?' laughed Paolo. 'No, don't worry, Blue, there's so much I need help with I wouldn't know where to start.'

Blue looked at him thoughtfully. 'You haven't been in a Vegas show yet though, have you?'

'What are you talking about? Where have you been for eight weeks?'

'Ah, but you've never actually performed in the show. With the audience. Curtain up, lights, orchestra! Come on, rehearsals hardly compare!'

'I know. But in case you hadn't noticed, the package in my sequinned G-string and my flat chest might raise an alarm bell.'

'I can fix that! I can run up some new costume pieces, it's amazing what frills can hide. To be honest, I'd adore the challenge of it! You don't have to do topless if you don't want either; it'll only be for one night. Let's face it, your butt is perfect – not that I've been looking – nice dainty ankles too . . . no-one need notice a thing once I've finished with you! What do you say? Just stay one more week. That's all I need to get the costume pieces adapted, and you'll get your moment in the spotlight before you leave!' Paolo regarded Blue warily. 'I know it's always been your ambition . . . ' insisted Blue. 'It would make me feel better for what you just did for me.' He sat on the chair, waiting with bated breath. 'You'd get to be near Sienna Starr for another week, too . . . ' he added, before squealing and clapping his hands as he watched a broad grin creep across Paolo's face, a twinkle appearing in his eyes that Blue had never seen before. 'It's showtime!' hooted Blue.

Sienna boarded the plane, wondering if there really was truth in the yin and yang of the universe that saw one life expire and another created. Even though everyone had been prepared for Ma to bow out gracefully, it didn't diminish the sadness of losing her. Pepper had been audibly shaken on the phone. Neither did the news create the finest state of mind for Sienna's discovery that she was expecting Max's baby. It had been a genuine shock for her, perhaps because deep down she'd been in denial;

after all, the physical symptoms were obvious enough in retrospect.

A very camp air steward motioned Sienna to her business-class seat and gave a broad smile that seemed to last a second too long. Sienna wondered if it was a knowing expression or if she was being paranoid. Could he tell she was with child? Tiger had suspected immediately yesterday too, so perhaps Sienna looked different already? Weren't pregnant women supposed to 'glow' or something? Sienna hadn't felt very radiant of late, that was for sure, and she sure as hell didn't feel full of joy right now either. Sienna eased herself into her seat with a subconscious awareness that she needed to be taking care of herself. When she had seen the little blue line appearing earlier, she had just stared in disbelief, thinking somehow it was a mistake. A frantic flick of her eyes over the '99.7% accurate' strapline on the box made her snap back to the reality of the situation. She suddenly felt grateful for the short flight ahead. At least she'd have an hour of solitude to begin to gather her thoughts and figure out her next step. How did an unplanned pregnancy fit in with her career path, her plans, her ambitions? Never mind that the only contact she'd had from the father of her unborn child was one text in the last week!

The air steward was back proffering a tray of champagne. Sienna reached out for a glass in an act of defiance, fully aware a pregnant woman should not be drinking. As she brought the champagne towards her lips, she wondered if the little flip she just felt in her stomach was nerves or the baby growing. What was she thinking! Sienna felt a stab of shame as she reminded herself *she* hadn't exactly been planned – let alone what her own mother had to sacrifice to have her. Why, Tiger's childhood had been shattered, her family had disowned her, and she'd had to give up the right to call herself a mother so that she could keep some contact with her own child by posing as her sister. A wave of guilt and unbearable sadness enveloped Sienna, and she motioned for the air steward to take her champagne away, before clutching at her stomach protectively. She reminded herself that Tiger even had to live with the knowledge that her rapist had walked away unpunished. And now he was apparently back, waiting in Vegas for his daughter. Sienna took a deep breath, relieved she had this hour to herself to think, before she had to face the music in Las Vegas.

Honey rose majestically from the hot tub and dried herself off, keeping the show going to the bitter end. Within five minutes she had dressed and was on her way home with her cash tucked away in her purse. Freddie had been a generous client, booking her for the whole night, and she hadn't even had to do anything too intimate; he couldn't last too long so just liked the pleasure of watching a good floor-show mainly. If only they could all be like him, even if it would mean losing the rest of the day to sleep after such a long night's work, Honey thought sadly as the cab pulled up to her rental. She'd moved out from Josh's apartment immediately after that LA party. The humiliation that he'd groomed her for that whole party scene and that she'd been mug enough to fall for it had proven too much. If this was what she was reduced to then she'd do it under her own steam. Besides, she'd found the Swallow Club, a small lap-dance joint that had recently opened where she could 'hostess' and meet clientele under one roof before leaving for assignments. The club just charged her a hundred bucks per night 'floor charge' and it was busy enough for her to do her business without having to interact with the other girls too much. She didn't feel in a social mood at all these days, strangely.

Honey stepped into her small apartment and chucked the keys onto the hallway table with a clatter, which echoed through the sparsely furnished space. She didn't see the point in splashing out on rugs and fancy furniture yet, particularly when she had no idea how much money she would be making so early into her new line of work. At least the apartment was clean and refreshingly neutral in palette. It was an oasis of beige and cream. So what if it could have fitted easily into one of the closets in Tiger Starr's house – at least it was somewhere where she could hide. Hell, she wasn't sure she could even stick it out in Vegas much longer. She kicked off her shoes and climbed wearily onto her bed, shutting the scene of her spartan bedroom from her vision immediately. Although what was left to go home to back in England if she left Vegas she had no idea. The city built on vice had pretty much chewed her up and was about to spit her out.

Chapter 18

Paolo ran his tongue along his gleaming white teeth in the mirror and nodded at the dentist. It was dedicated work, maintaining a Hollywood smile fit for a star of the stage, he had discovered. It had been anything but comfortable sitting in the dentist's chair for forty-five minutes in fetching goggles with his mouth clamped open and searing peroxide smeared all over his teeth. This beauty lark was definitely a whole other world of pain. He was still red and sore from this morning's back, sack and crack waxing session, and he was still wrinkling his nose up at the pungent aroma of fake tan. Blue had generously arranged for Paolo to be comped at the gay beauty centre Stitch 'n' Bitch, as Blue had accrued so many loyalty points over the years, having his pencil moustache waxed and his hands manicured. All that remained to be done now were the Botox shots. Blue had suggested some fillers to give his cheeks a youthful pertness, and maybe a thread lift at the temples, but Paolo had drawn the line there. Prettiness was something he definitely didn't need any more of. If Paolo had thought it had been tough passing as a woman before, he hadn't realised the new levels of pain he was letting himself in for in order to make himself 'stage-ready'. As Blue was fond of pointing out, there was a huge difference between Paolo being Brandy in off-stage glamour mode, and passing as his sister on stage wearing only the brightest of spotlights and under the scrutiny of a huge live audience, not to mention the front row of press with their pesky telephoto lenses.

As he waited patiently for the doctor to summon him for his Botox shots, Paolo occupied himself looking in the mirror. He admired his jaw line, more to remind himself of his manliness than out of vanity. Being surrounded by so much oestrogen for the last couple of months was enough to make any man start to miss the odd baseball game and six-pack of beer. Still, he'd had a stay of execution now he had a whole extra week at the Follies, extra time with Sienna, and the prospect of finally fulfilling his big childhood dream. A day being put to the limits of his pain threshold at Stitch 'n' Bitch was a small price to pay for looking his very best in his hour of glory on the Vegas stage in front of two thousand people. He was determined to enjoy every single second of this last week. After all, with the future looking anything but rosy, at least he would have some fond memories now to replace the nightmares. Seeing the doctor popping his head round the door and nodding, Paolo dutifully moved on through to the next beauty treatment room for the last stage of the artwork to be completed.

'Why are you doing this to yourself, Pepper?' pleaded Sienna, looking around at the punters having a grand old time watching the early shift at the Monte. Sienna hadn't been able to raise Max since she'd touched down in Vegas and was desperate to find him. He needed to know he was going to be a father. But right now, Pepper had to take priority. Her soul mate had gone to the great rhine-stoned gates in the sky and Sienna was going to make damn sure she knew she had support and friends she could lean on.

'Ma wanted everything to carry on as normal, she said so,' explained Pepper, 'and this place is mine now. Ma chose to pass it down to me so I'm going to make sure I repay her by running it exactly as she would have wanted. You know she never skipped a day except for the annual anniversary of Pinkie's disappearance.'

'But it seems so – wrong!' lamented Sienna. 'And the fact you're having to carry on like normal when you must be distraught!'

'It makes me happy to know Ma would have wanted this. Anyway, who said anything about carrying on as normal?' countered Pepper. 'Look at the stage and tell me that's a normal Monte Cristo stage show.'

Sienna looked to the stage to see the chorus line in matching black lace mourning veils completely covering their faces and black fringe leotards with Candy and Shandy swinging above them suspended from jet-black glass chandeliers, as they executed a camp routine to Donna Summer's 'Last Dance'.

'I got veils for the whole cast and we'll all be in

black until the funeral has passed,' explained Pepper.

'Even Griselda?'

'Especially Griselda. Gives us all a break from his ugly face. I can thank Ma for that at least.' Pepper made the sign of the cross and gave a quick glance to the heavens. 'At least the Feds have gone. The place has been crawling with them all morning, going through every nook and cranny, all the bedrooms, every cupboard . . . so undignified.' Pepper's voice cracked.

'Oh darling!' wailed Sienna. 'I wasn't even here to support you!'

'Don't be silly, you were in LA!' scoffed Pepper. 'I'm just glad you saw your mum. I spoke to her once you were on the plane. She'll fly in for the funeral.'

'Oh, that's great,' said Sienna gingerly, realising she'd have to decide by then how she would break the news to her mother she was pregnant. She couldn't see how a funeral could ever be a good time, but Tiger would be sure to ask, she never missed a trick. She would also know immediately if Sienna was telling a porky.

'So when is the funeral?'

'Saturday. No doubt the Feds will turn up for that.'

'At Ma's funeral?' tutted Sienna in disbelief.

'They're especially keen to be there – they're expecting a special guest, of course. They think Pinkie's going to show after all this time. At least when they realise there's nothing to see it should be the end of this case once and for all, God help us.' Pepper looked to the heavens once more, before raising an eyebrow over towards the bar. 'At least this one here seems like a nice enough guy.'

Sienna followed Pepper's glance to see Detective Jack Weldon at the bar, chatting to a punter who sat with his back to them. Weldon looked up to see the ladies standing there and waved a hand up at them. Sienna wandered over to be polite.

'Ms Starr. Sorry to be seeing you under such sad circumstances,'

'Yes, it's a sad day.'

'You know Ed here, don't you?' continued Weldon. The gentleman Weldon had been making small talk at the bar with turned round in his stool.

'Hi Sienna, fancy seeing you here again,' winked Ed Rogers. 'Do join us.' Sienna froze.

Max discreetly threw up in the casino's VIP restroom. Must be an ulcer, he concluded, not considering that a day of whisky on an empty stomach was more likely to be the cause. He stood before the mirror, wavering slightly on the spot before deciding his eyes were giving the sobriety façade away. He splashed his face with cold water and selected some Acqua di Parma aftershave from the silver platter laid out by the washbasin. A quick spritz and he'd be refreshed and ready to take his mind off his troubles. He was a few thousand bucks up today, nothing that would help any debts immediately but enough small change to cover a good night out. Paige had just arrived with a bag of Meow Meow and was in the mood to pick up where they'd left off that morning, before she had to leave for the late-night show at the Follies. With any luck she'd have news that she'd arranged that lunch with her rich daddy and then Max would be back on track any time soon. It was the only real reason he was continuing to bother with her, after all. The brief thrill had most definitely gone now that he'd fucked her and sampled the goods, but if her father could get him out of hot water then she was worth his attention. At least she could administer an outstanding blowjob. And tonight was definitely a night to take his mind off his troubles, starting with another bottle of Macallan and a penthouse suite.

'Are you blackmailing me?' snarled Sienna, wondering how in hell this scumbag had persuaded her to come out to the parking lot for a private chat. She wished Detective Weldon was still inside, but she'd seen him leave already.

'Blackmail is such a strong word,' laughed Ed. 'How could you think I would do that to my own flesh and blood! I'm just saying your old dad could do with a bit of help with the rent. The cost of living is so expensive these days. Especially in Vegas. But I need to be close to my little girl.'

'I'm not your "girl", and I don't want you anywhere near me,' snapped Sienna. 'I don't even know for real that you're Ed Rogers. You could just have spent a lot of time researching on the internet.'

'Oh! Don't you think you have my eyes, sweetie?'

'No, I do *not*!' snarled Sienna. 'I look like my *mother*.'

'Hm. Trying to be tricky with me, eh? Okay. This mean anything?' Ed held up his driver's licence. Sienna went pale as she read the name, clear as clear could be: *Ed Rogers*. 'Like I said, I can go straight to Tiger and tell her how close we've become. I know she'll be at the funeral, Pepper was telling me all about that. I'm sure your mum would feel so uplifted to know how much of a bond we've developed, how you invited your dear dad to be there especially to support your debut performance . . . and how you let me drive the Ferrari your mum bought you . . . '

'What? Enough!' spat Sienna. 'You go near Mum with those lies and I'll—'

'You'll do what?' Sienna's mouth gaped and she regarded Ed incredulously.

'W-what do you want?' she stuttered eventually.

'Ten thousand bucks a month should do it.'

'Are you *crazy*?'

'I know that's pocket money for you. Tiger probably gives you that for shoes alone.' Sienna raised her hand to slap Ed but he caught her wrist and held it tight.

'I take nothing from my mother, I earn my *own* money,' growled Sienna. 'Now let me go!'

'You're living in her mansion, poor little rich girl!' laughed Ed.

'I pay my way!'

'I hear Tiger pays your way actually . . . into shows and things . . . '

'How dare you! She does nothing of the sort! Who the hell told you that?'

'Just something Paige . . . a few people have told me.' Ed shrugged casually. Sienna squealed and wrestled to free her wrist. 'That *bitch* Paige!'

'Shush now,' soothed Ed, grabbing Sienna's other wrist and pulling her close so she could feel his breath on her cheek. 'Wouldn't want anyone to hear you being nasty about a co-star – doesn't make you sound too good.'

'Wait, you probably made that bit up about Paige, didn't you! Like you lie about everything! I know what you did to Mum. You can lie to me but you can't lie to yourself. I don't know how you can *live* with yourself – you're scum! You're not my father, you're not even a man. You're just the evil coward who raped my mother!'

Sienna struggled against Ed's iron grip, which became even tighter the harder she resisted. She yelped in pain before relenting. As she looked into Ed's eyes a shiver ran down her spine at the expression of pure evil looking back at her. If there had ever been any doubt in her mind that her mum had told the truth about the abuse she suffered at his hands, Sienna knew in an instant she believed every single word of it.

'Let go of me,' she whispered, trying not to shake with fear. 'I have a show tonight and you're giving me bruises. You want me to tell everyone how they got there? Let go!'

'Do we have a deal?'

'What do you mean?'

'The money.'

'I don't have that sort of money. I – I don't earn much as a dancer yet.'

'You can get it. Or like I said I can go to Tiger . . . Or maybe I should just go direct to the press. I bet the super-market rags would pay handsomely for my side of the story even now. Especially now that Tiger seems to be making it real big as a movie star . . . who'd have thought it of sweet little Poppy Adams? A wanton, calculating Lolita, then a desperate stripper, and now finally clawing her way onto the silver screen as an actress . . . wonder whose casting couch she's been draping herself over this time, huh?'

'No! That's a pack of disgusting lies! She worked her way up the hard way and you know it! Leave her alone! I don't want you anywhere near my mum. You almost destroyed her once, not again. If you hurt her . . . '

'So, do we have a deal?'

Sienna wondered where in hell she could lay her hands on ten thousand bucks at short notice. She didn't even have an engagement ring any more to pawn. Maybe she'd sell the car. Although with it being in Tiger's name that would be tricky. Max. Of course. He had millions. She'd never asked for anything from him before, so he could help her just this once, until she could figure a way out of this mess . . . If only she could get hold of him.

'When do you want it?' asked Sienna.

'I'll be generous and give you until the funeral.'

'What? But that's only three days—'

'Come up with the cash by then and I'll make sure I have something else to do that day so I don't accidentally bump into Tiger. Same day of every month after that should be easy enough for you to remember.'

'Done,' said Sienna after a beat.

'Good girl,' smiled Ed, relaxing his grip on Sienna's wrists a little. He leaned in to plant a tender kiss on the top of Sienna's head before letting go.

'See you soon,' he chirped. Sienna ran behind the nearest car and vomited bile.

Paige staggered towards the bed giggling, nearly tripping herself on an empty bottle of Veuve discarded on the deep pile carpet.

'Let's go dancing!' she squealed over the loud music pumping through the speakers concealed in the wall, before flinging herself onto the emperor-sized bed and straddling Max coquettishly.

'Okay, I'll call my driver,' slurred Max, too high to remember he didn't have one any more. 'Wait – aren't you going to be late for work?'

'No, plenty of time!' hooted Paige, rolling on to her back and checking out her glorious body in the mirror-panelled ceiling. 'Come on, baby, let's carry on the party!'

'I think you're too wobbly on your feet for any kind of dancing,' laughed Max.

'Rubbish! I'm even better with a drink inside me. Besides, I could be crawling on my knees and I'd still be a better dancer than Sss—' Paige caught herself, not about to remind Max he technically still had a girlfriend. 'I'd still be a better dancer than Brandy Alexander,' she declared. A flash of inspiration suddenly came over Paige. It would be so easy to claim Max as hers right now in such a way he could never go back to Sienna. He was obviously besotted with Paige anyway; she could tell by the way he had fucked her like an animal tonight. Max was ravenous for her. She didn't feel bad about Sienna. It wasn't as though a spoilt brat like her needed Max's money when she had Mummy's riches on tap. It didn't seem fair she should have *everything*, so why not orchestrate a little redistribution of resources? Paige sprang into action and swung her shapely legs down from the bed. She racked up a huge line of Meow and returned to Max with a rolled fifty. She climbed on top of him and wafted the line under his nose. Max hoovered it up, sighing deeply with the hit.

'Let's get married,' giggled Paige into his ear.

'Good idea,' burbled Max, his eyes rolling to the back of his skull for a second.

It proved a little difficult for Paige to manoeuvre Max's six-foot three-inch bulk back into his suit and tip him into a limo which she ordered from the concierge, but at least that meant he was nice and pliant for Paige's scheme. After the drive to the wedding chapel via the licence office across the street, Max had at least sobered up enough to walk and talk again. Obviously not quite enough to make an informed decision about tying the knot to a two-night stand, but at least the breath of fresh air had loosened his tongue enough to slur a few words. Ten minutes was all it took to exchange *I dos*. Not the most romantic experience ever, thought Paige, but as she walked out of the twee little chapel arm in arm with Max, or rather, him hanging off her arm as he concentrated on putting one foot in front of the other, she took a split second to bask under the stars with elation at what she'd just achieved. She could barely contain herself, in fact. Trailer-park princess Paige Turner had only bagged the most eligible bachelor – *in the world* – and not a pre-nup in sight! If only miss Krispy Syrup Queen Velveeta Weinstein could see her now! Paige had fast-tracked herself to the big time and hit the jackpot!

Safely back in the limo, Paige realised she'd completely missed curtain-up at the Follies. Oops! Well, they probably wouldn't miss her in the chorus. She had a much bigger role to play now anyway – Mrs Maximilian Power. She cackled with laughter, realising she didn't even need to worry about working ever again; tonight was the start of a whole new lifestyle for Paige. Now all she had to do was make sure the marriage was consummated just in case her new husband or his family got any silly ideas about

annulment. Looking affectionately at Max lolling all over
the black leather, she realised she'd have to sober him up
a little more for any of that kind of action. She reckoned
some more amphetamines back at the hotel before a cele-
bratory hot tub ought to do the trick and seal the deal.

A little later Max managed to lift his eyelids to be greeted
with the sight of a towering pyramid of multi-coloured
cupcakes decorated with candles as music blared out. He
realised he was slumped at the table of a huge hotel suite,
still in his suit. Had he fallen asleep? God, he felt like
crap. Where was he? Who was he here with? He whipped
his head around to see a magnificent bare ass bent over
the hot tub. Sienna? The woman straightened herself and
turned.

'Baby!' Paige? What the hell was *she* doing here? Max
tried to piece together how he came to be partying in a
hotel. He remembered hitting the liquor hard after his
luck changed for the better on the blackjack tables this
afternoon. He vaguely remembered unanswered calls from
Sienna . . . but the tower of cake?

'Hey,' answered Max groggily. 'So, what's the deal, is it
– is it someone's birthday or something? Are we at a party?'

'No, baby, it's our wedding! You like the cake? Isn't it
amazing what you can get on room service? ' yelled Paige
over the music. Max blinked in disbelief. Had he been
asleep for, like, a year or something? When did this happen?
He was sure Sienna was his fiancée last time he checked.

'So now we need to celebrate, just you and me,' purred Paige, appearing at Max's side and reaching for his crotch. Hazy recollections came filtering through, of Sienna fleeing to Los Angeles yesterday, and him and Paige having a little fun after she promised she would arrange a meeting with – hang on a minute – if Max was thinking correctly, he was now the son-in-law to an oil billionaire.

'So you're my wife now?' ventured Max, suddenly sitting upright.

'Oh wow! That's the first time you've said that word . . . my darling husband,' sighed Paige, draping herself round Max's shoulders and kissing him tenderly on the forehead. Out of nowhere Max found the energy to scoop Paige up, carrying her squealing over to the hot tub. Thanks to his new daddy-in-law, Max could see a light at the end of the tunnel finally, and for once it wasn't an oncoming train.

Chapter 19

Sienna sat in the Follies dressing room with her carton of salad, taking a breather, having finally managed to fend off the last showgirl who had descended on her asking if she'd seen Paige since her sensational no-show last night. No cast member in their right mind ever missed a performance unless they were on their death bed – there was always another dancer to step in your place in a second if it appeared that you didn't want the part enough. Sienna had shrugged off any drama, saying Paige was fine but she had no idea when she'd be back. Right now she had enough on her plate with desperately needing to find Max, raise the cash to pay off Ed, and figure out what on earth she was going to do about her own career now that she was pregnant. Truth was, Sienna hadn't seen Paige back at home since she'd returned from LA yesterday afternoon. The only contact she'd had was a short, cryptic text asking if she would pass the message on to Marty that Paige wouldn't be coming back to work as she'd decided to quit dancing. It sounded so ridiculous and out of the blue that Sienna guessed it was probably just a premenstrual bid for attention, but dutifully passed on the message nonetheless. Although if Paige had been bitching about her to Ed then she was the last person Sienna wanted to help out.

Sienna turned her thoughts to Max. She couldn't believe she hadn't seen him in two weeks. He didn't even know she'd lost her engagement ring, let alone that she was expecting his child. It wasn't the kind of news she could deliver in a text or a voicemail message. She had made the decision she was keeping her baby and Max needed to know. After Tiger's sacrifices to keep her own daughter, it would be an insult if Sienna didn't take her responsibilities seriously and bring her baby into the world. Work and plans would have to wait. Besides, this baby had been conceived out of so much love, Sienna had already begun to feel a bond with the life growing inside her. But how to go about telling Max such huge news when all she'd had by way of response to her recent calls was a single, mildly mollifying *I love you* message from him in LA? Tied up with business he might be, but just one measly text was pretty lame. On the one hand Sienna was damned if she would turn into the kind of clingy bitch who gave other women a bad name, the kind who would be needy, or put their life on hold while they waited for phone calls and affirmations, like a puppy waiting for food scraps from the table. On the other hand, even she was feeling insecure with the resounding silence. Whilst she was stubbornly ignoring Tiger's advice to ditch him, she still wondered what the hell she was supposed to do. March round to Max's house? How could that help? She couldn't *force* him to be thinking about her. Sure, they'd had weeks apart before when Max had been snowed under with work, and Sienna had enjoyed having that bit of time to herself as she always had plenty of things to do and people to see. Cramming an oversized lettuce leaf undaintily into her mouth, she started to wonder if Max was running into problems with his father. From what Sienna had seen so far, it was the one time when Max would clam up and push away the people who loved him most.

'Sienna?' She jolted, nearly dropping her salad, and span round to see Brandy standing ten feet away. They were alone now that the rest of the cast had disappeared off to the canteen.

'Sorry, I didn't mean to make you jump.'

'That's okay, I was just daydreaming,' said Sienna awkwardly, placing her evening snack on the dresser. 'Wow, you look . . . great . . . different. Have you been tanning?'

'Er, yeah, something like that.'

'Hmm. You look really well,' conceded Sienna. An uncomfortable silence hung in the air.

'I know we've never had a chance to really talk since . . . your opening night and I just wanted to say one more time that despite what you think, I didn't do it,' garbled Paolo finally.

'Let's just move on,' said Sienna quietly, manufacturing a polite smile.

'If you like,' replied Paolo, fiddling with a false nail

uneasily. He took a deep breath. 'There's something you ought to know – I'm leaving at the end of the week. That vacation I was supposed to take – well, I've decided I'll go after all. And now my ankle is better I'd just like to do one performance before I take my break. You know . . . just to check I've still got it . . . '

'Oh! Oh, I see, yes, of course.'

'So that's why I wanted to be sure you completely trust that I didn't sabotage your costume that night, because I'll be gone next week . . . and I guess I didn't want us to part on bad terms.'

'I see. But you'll be back in a couple of months though?'

'Maybe, yes. I might be – feeling a little different by then,' said Paolo, a little recklessly. 'Look, I have some rather good gin in my dressing room, would you like to share a martini just between friends? I know you've had a bad week after the news about your old boss at the Monte Cristo.'

'Oh.'

'Blue told me. I'm sorry for your loss. A martini won't change anything but it might help the show pass a little quicker, just for tonight? You seem so subdued. A little friendly support never did anyone any harm.'

Sienna looked at Brandy for a moment before nodding.

'Why not . . . although could I have something non-alcoholic? I don't drink before a show.'

'You're kidding,' laughed Paolo. 'I see you girls knocking back the champagne all the time!'

'I'm just er . . . trying to cut down. Thanks.'

'No problem,' smiled Paolo, stepping back and motioning Sienna into Brandy's palatial dressing room.

Within twenty minutes Sienna had defrosted and the pair were chatting away about costumes over their chilled orange juice like they'd been friends for years. Sienna was admiring Brandy's collection of rhinestoned corsets in every colour imaginable. Brandy was right, thought Sienna, a little friendship went a long way in depressing times.

'Look, I have to get ready for curtain-up,' started Sienna with trepidation, 'but there's a favour I'd like to ask.'

'Of course! Anything!' gushed Paolo, hopefully.

'Um, I know you're done with your own rehearsals for the day but could you stay until after the show for a chat? I have a little problem that I think you may be able to help me with, but I need time to explain it properly, you see. It's not something I can really tell you right before the show. I wouldn't ask normally but . . . you're the only person who may be able to help.'

'Of course! Just say the word! I'll be here waiting.'

'You don't know what I'm going to ask yet!' laughed Sienna uneasily, still unsure of whether it was a brainwave or sheer madness to ask Brandy for the ten thousand dollars of cash she needed by Saturday, but feeling that she had no alternative but to believe in the sincerity of Brandy's olive branch. There was no way Sienna could risk Ed carrying out his threats of either going to the papers or even lying to Tiger that she had formed some kind of bond with her 'father'. Both would destroy her. It might be early in her own pregnancy, but now that she was expecting her own child, she'd started to think more about all Tiger had had to go through for her. Protecting her mum now was the least she could do by way of acknowledgement of the sacrifices she had made for her. But with Max nowhere to be found, and suspecting Blue would blow the whistle immediately, Sienna had no other resources for that kind of instant cash.

'It's okay,' reassured Paolo earnestly, 'I'll be here waiting. I'm just pleased you know you can trust me.' *I don't though*, thought Sienna to herself, *I just have nowhere left to turn*.

'We'll take a bottle of Cristal, please,' murmured Honey to the waiter. She turned back to the gentleman sat next to her in the gloomy booth. She usually chose the older ones to approach as they tended to have more money, although this guy seemed appealing as he looked fairly reserved. The last few nights had proffered boisterous men with crazy demands, and Honey was praying for a quiet, uncomplicated night. He also happened to be cute, which made a change, and at least gave Honey something nice to look at while she was making small talk.

'So perhaps we can go for a drink elsewhere later?' she asked, testing the water immediately. If he wanted extras she'd make an effort with the chitchat. If he just wanted a lap dance she'd knock back the champagne, collect a tip and move on.

'I don't know, you seem a little tall for me, not my usual type,' smiled the guy apologetically.

'I could bend over,' deadpanned Honey.

'Erm, we'll see. Where did you have in mind for a drink?'

'The Golden Nugget – a couple of blocks over?'

'Oh. Why not stay here?'

Honey sighed, unable to decide whether this one might be worth working on or whether she should cut her losses and move on. Either way, she had a sense it was going to be a long night after all.

'Of course I'll help you!' said Paolo, wondering how long he could keep his eyes off Sienna's breasts with her diamanté nipple covers. If only the girls would cover up a bit more in the dressing rooms before and after shows, he agonised guiltily. They jiggled around naked with each other, chatting and horsing around as though pasties and G-strings made them fully dressed; he bet they wouldn't be so free in the wind if they knew he was looking at them through the eyes of a red-blooded male.

'Amazing, I don't know how to thank you!' said Sienna, a wave of relief washing over her face. 'Could you deliver the cash to Ed's massage salon for me too? I don't think I could face that creep again. He makes my skin crawl.'

'Of course! You haven't told me how much though,' asked Paolo, pretty sure he could borrow a couple of hundred bucks from Tiny at short notice; his wily

Mexican buddy always had a secret stash in his sock drawer.

'Ten thousand.' Paolo's face froze as he suppressed a gulp. 'I know it's just a couple of Donna Karan dresses for someone like you,' continued Sienna, 'but on my wages . . . I just feel so embarrassed asking,' she admitted, her eyes downcast as she blushed. Paolo smiled weakly. Holy crap, how could he ever help with this one?

'No problem,' he squeaked.

'It's so ridiculous,' continued Sienna. 'If people only knew the shit money we're on here – half the girls in the chorus are holding down casual jobs elsewhere to keep themselves going. Thandie just got herself a part-time bank clerk position for a few afternoons a week and Tashonya works Spearmint Rhino on Thursdays, Fridays and Saturdays too! Imagine that straight after a show! Some kind of glamour, huh. All the tens of thousands of dollars of costume that I wear every night and yet I'm barely worth a cent,' she complained, throwing her hands up in exasperation. 'All so I might get the lead one day and people will think I'm brilliant and successful.'

'Oh, come on!' countered Paolo, instinctively reaching out to embrace Sienna. 'You *are* brilliant and successful! I thought you were living your dream? If this job makes you happy, who cares about the money? So you'd rather be a ratbag attorney chasing ambulances for a living because it earns more cash?'

'No! I guess . . . I just wonder what's it all for

sometimes. I look at Max. He earns so much but he's always so stressed – like, when does he get to actually enjoy his money?' Paolo bit his tongue and squeezed Sienna hard. 'And then I think how hard I work at this job,' added Sienna, 'and I sacrifice things like money and a social life just so that I can experience that feeling on stage every night.'

'Hey, money isn't the barometer of achievement, you know. There's plenty of things it can't buy, anyway.'

'I guess. All I want to do is to make my mark on the world so Mum can be proud. But sometimes I feel like I'm so busy trying to be what other people will think is successful that I haven't even asked myself what it is I'm doing or even why. And I may have to stop performing soon anyway . . . God, I'm just going to be a nobody, a nothing.'

'Christ! Listen to yourself, Sienna. Nobody is a nobody. Success isn't what other people think of you, it isn't what other people see, they aren't living your life for you! Besides, however fabulous you are to the outside world, it means nothing – because other people can only ever see you through their own baggage anyway. Isn't success about *you* being happy? Why do you need other people to tell you at what point you're allowed to feel pleased with yourself? When was the last time *you* felt happy?'

Sienna looked up at Paolo through glassy eyes and bit her lip.

'I can't believe you just said something smart, Brandy.'

'I don't know if that was an insult or a compliment,' replied Paolo.

'Sorry,' said Sienna softly. Paolo just wanted to make everything better for Sienna. There was so much he wanted to say to her but couldn't, so much he could tell her about what was important in life. Sienna had her face buried in his shoulder and he could feel her eyelashes against his skin, dampened by tears. He tipped her chin up towards his face and bent his lips to hers, slowly, his eyes closing.

'Euurrrgh! What are you *doing*!' shrieked Sienna, recoiling. Paolo snapped his eyes open. Shit. The mask had slipped.

'Ow! That went right in my ass cheek!' growled Paolo an hour later.

'Well, stop fidgeting,' lisped Blue through a mouthful of dressmaking pins as he readjusted the fabric on the frilly panties. 'I have a date later and I don't want to be late just because you can't keep still. And why are you in such a pissy mood anyway? I'm trying to help you here!'

'I've had the evening from hell, that's all. And it's not being helped by being so uncomfortable here. This tucking thing is outrageous,' grumbled Paolo. 'There must be another way of concealing the pouch, Blue. I can't dance properly with my balls nearly up in my throat.'

'Get used to it. You want to go on stage Saturday night, don't you?'

'You know I do!'

'So trust me. It's important you look flawless. Even Brandy would think she's looking in the mirror by the time I've finished with you. Now just stay still for half a minute, for chrissake.'

'I'm sorry, I know you're trying,' mumbled Paolo. Blue worked his way round the costume, snipping fabric and pinning until the shape fit Paolo's form like a glove, giving him a nipped-in waist where he needed one and padding his butt subtly. With filigree lace heavily rhinestoned and laid over skin-coloured bust forms, it was impossible to tell that the breasts were fake too. Blue had created a beautiful work of artful illusion. Paolo actually felt a little freaked out when he finally looked in the full-length mirror in Brandy's chintzy bedroom, and a little shiver ran up his spine.

'Yes, you're certainly not a natural tranny, darling, but you'll have everyone fooled, if I say so myself,' concluded Blue as he stood back to survey the work. He saw Paolo's expression. 'Oh, don't tell me you're having second thoughts now I've done all this work?'

'No, not at all,' sighed Paolo. 'Although looking like I have the body of a hot chick *is* fucking with my head, to be honest, in more ways than you'd think. Actually, the real problem is Sienna . . . '

'Oh God,' groaned Blue. 'What now? You want to marry her?'

'Not exactly. God, where do I start? She – asked me something tonight after the show. She didn't want to ask you because she couldn't risk her mum knowing, so I need to know that you can keep this to yourself.'

'I don't know yet until I know the secret . . . '

'I can't tell you until you promise.'

'Paolo, this is silly.'

'Promise?'

'That's unfair. Oh, alright then. My lips are sealed.' Blue huffed dramatically and put his pins down.

'Sienna's father is blackmailing her. She needs cash. A lot. Ten Gs a month.'

Blue narrowed his eyes up at Paolo and stroked his pencil moustache slowly. 'Is this a sick joke?' he asked finally.

'No, I just don't have that kind of money. I don't even have ten bucks let alone ten thousand. She thinks I'm Brandy and that I spend that in a shopping spree every lunchtime. Can you help?'

'I meant, is this a sick joke about her father? He can't be in town. Don't you know the story?'

'No,' replied Paolo forlornly.

'Woah, where do I start,' sighed Blue, shaking his head. 'Right, get the costume off and your balls back down. I need to tell you everything, and you need to tell *me* everything Sienna said about Ed.'

An hour later Paolo's mouth was still open in shock.

'So now you know about Sienna and Tiger,' said Blue, finally.

'Such a sad story,' murmured Paolo. It just went to show

that you should never judge a book by its cover. Most people would assume that successful stars like Tiger led charmed lives, that somehow fairytales really happened and that fairies waved magic wands and turned people into superstars overnight like winning the lottery. But the truth was, it was often a long road to glitz and glamour and sometimes it started from a place that held a whole lot of pain. For Sienna, too. Now her earlier anxiety made so much more sense. But Paolo knew from his own experiences just how much his tragic childhood had shaped him and made him stronger, or at least more able to laugh at the shit that life slung at him on a daily basis. Clearly with Tiger and Sienna their drive for success hid a simple quest for an antidote to their painful past . . . or perhaps just a nice, neat 'fuck you' to everyone who'd screwed them over. Paolo admired them for bouncing back like that, over and over. He'd not even been able to turn his own life around let alone his Mami's after what Brandy did. Staying alive and sane was quite an achievement in itself given his past. Blue's voice jolted him out of his thoughts.

'So how do we deal with this bastard Ed? I don't have the spare cash either after I just cleared my Amex bill having bought my ass-hat of an ex that Ferrari for his birthday! What a waste! The timing couldn't be worse,' moaned Blue, raising his hands theatrically to the heavens. 'Look at us, living the life of princesses without two cents to rub together between us. I feel so pathetic. Come on, all our friends are loaded, who can we ask without raising suspicion?' The two men sat in silence with furrowed brows as a minute ticked by.

'We're not going to give Sienna any cash,' announced Paolo suddenly, springing up and pacing.

'Why not? We need to help her!'

'Letting Sienna give him the cash doesn't solve anything. How long can she keep that up for? Years? No, I'm going to get him. I want to do that for Sienna.'

'A punch won't solve anything,' snorted Blue. 'Ed'll just have you arrested for assault.'

'I'm smarter than that,' said Paolo with a grin as he stood before Blue. 'I know where his salon is, and I know leopards don't change their spots too. Besides, my sister taught me a thing or two about the art of the set-up, remember.'

'This sounds ominous.'

'Yeah, best not to ask questions . . . ' The mischievous look in Paolo's eyes suddenly turned to panic. 'Although there's something I haven't told you yet about tonight with Sienna,' he added, sitting down again and putting his head in his hands.

'Go on . . . '

'Um, I kissed her.'

'You did *what*? Paolo, you idiot! What were you thinking?!'

'That I'm a red-blooded male?'

'Noooo! You're *Brandy* when you're at the Follies!'

'You think I don't know that? I just . . . forgot myself.

I got caught up in the moment, she seemed so . . . I just wanted to . . . It's too late now. Sienna thinks I'm a sneaky lesbian with an agenda. Just when I'd convinced her I was a true friend! What a fool . . . '

'Yes, and you knew when I came over for the fitting that I had a date tonight, and you just thought you'd keep that little bombshell quiet right up until the last minute? Thanks!'

'I didn't want to make you late, honest,' protested Paolo. 'I was scared to bring it up, that's all. I can't believe I was such a jerk.'

'Good, because you're going to have to stew in your own juices on this one tonight, I'm afraid,' snapped Blue. 'My centurion is waiting for me at the Monte Cristo and after what your sister did with my last boyfriend, I think I deserve a nice new partner. So I'm going to leave you to figure out how to undo the mess you've caused with your one-track mind.' Blue rose from the couch and tossed a look over at Paolo, who was perched forlornly in the armchair with his head hanging. 'Dick for brains,' he muttered under his breath, before flouncing from the room.

Jack Weldon decanted his second glass of champagne discreetly under the table. He knew Honey was concentrating so much on doing the same that she wouldn't notice him. He was usually so good with faces but it had taken him a full ten minutes to realise that 'Kandy with a "K" was in fact Sienna's friend Honey, whose photograph he'd seen behind the bar at the Monte Cristo. She looked so different now, sitting by his side in this dive. Tired and hollow cheeked. Nothing like the picture of vivaciousness in the photograph. Weldon had been assigned this new case only this morning. Money laundering amongst other things. From Honey's conversation it was clear the girls knew exactly what they could and couldn't say or do so as not to be found to be technically soliciting on the premises. Weldon just wanted to keep Honey in front of him as long as possible so he could glean what kind of state she was in and how she was living. From the way the waiting staff were eyeing him up, it was clear they were suspicious of him. He may as well settle in and act like a convincing John for at least another half hour. He waved twenty bucks at Honey and asked for a lap dance.

'What's Cleopatra doing behind the bar?' asked Joey the centurion.

'Huh?' grunted Blue, topping up Joey's champagne flute with ice-cold Dom and waving at Jeffrey to bring another bottle. He'd brought Joey to Pepper's as it was always his home away from home and he sensed he'd get a kick out of basking in some of Vegas's history.

'Cleo!' Joey laughed, pointing a tanned hand at Pepper's wall of fame.

'Paige?'

'Oh yeah, that was her name, Paige ... Turner. Ha! Well, I never,' crowed Joey, blue eyes sparkling.

'Uh, you're losing me . . . '

'Paige used to work with me at Caesars. She graduated from toga girl waitressing by the pool to being a Cleopatra in the casino area, mainly around Cleopatra's barge. She also used to have to stand by the golden gate and pose for pictures with the guests. She seemed alright at first, she kind of bamboozled people with her stunning looks. But when you got to know her she could get bitchy, and you realised the quiet act was just her way of being sly, keeping an eye on things, watching and observing things all the time. Anyway, she put a few of the girls' backs up at Caesars. Things went missing from the locker room regularly. Eventually all the girls pointed the finger at Paige but they had no proof. One day she took off without warning and defected to New York, New York as the Statue of Liberty. Caesars management were hot on her heels for not returning her Cleo costume but had no idea where she'd gone. Until word got round the hotels that the Statue of Liberty had just got the sack for, well, let's call it fraternising with guests in the elevators. In costume no less.'

'No way!'

'Yes way. Apparently she was found out after an elderly guest walked in on her flashing in full regalia; gave the poor guest some heart complications. Anyway New York, New York swooped on her gear in their restrooms and found her Cleo stuff too. Check her Sheriff's Card, she's been blacklisted from working the casino floor in any hotel.

Paige Turner's a legend in this town, I can assure you!' howled Joey.

'I'm stunned! She seemed so sweet! So that's . . . hang on . . . Joey, do you know anything else about her? Where she came from?'

'The trailer-trash princess? Ooh, which story has she told you, I wonder? There are a few to choose from.' Joey winked.

'Ah. Another drink, darling?' grinned Blue at his handsome date. 'This could get interesting.'

Chapter 20

Ed Rogers hummed as he prepared his massage table for his next client. He had a nice busy morning booked: a lady wanting a lymphatic drainage massage followed by two sports massages. Ironic that things were really starting to pick up just as he was expecting his cash to start flowing in from Sienna. The funeral was tomorrow, so if he was lucky she'd bring the payment in today to be on the safe side. She seemed like she'd probably be a sensible girl like that. At least once the income from her was regular he could kick back and take a break from any real work. Real estate was cheap in Vegas after the recession; he could get himself a decent pad, live the lifestyle, and keep an eye on his nest egg. Maybe he could even squeeze a car out of Sienna too. She must be rolling in her mother's cash.

A loud knocking prompted Ed to cross the studio and open the door.

'Hey. You Mr Rogers? I'm here for the massage. Jenny,' said the pretty young thing who was looking up at him through her huge dark shades and smiling broadly as she chewed gum noisily. Ed noticed through the open door that two men were settling in the waiting area. He nodded

Jenny through before craning his neck back towards the guys.

'Are you here for appointments?' he asked.

'Yeah. Sports massage? Bit early, I know. Okay if we wait here?'

'Sure,' said Ed warmly. 'That's what it's for. Help yourself to coffee. Magazines are on the table.'

Ed clicked the door shut and pointed at a small curtained-off area.

'You can undress down to your underwear behind the screen,' he explained. 'You may find it more comfortable to take your bra off as well. There are warm clean towels stacked on the shelf for you to cover up with.'

'Sure,' chirped Jenny, obediently moving behind the curtains. Ed could hear her cheap gold jangling noisily as she disrobed. Ed had already switched on his whale-song music at a low volume and warmed his aromatherapy oils, and he was now rubbing his hands idly, waiting for Jenny. She seemed to be taking an age. Ed picked up a plastic surgery magazine and lazily flicked through to the breast augmentation advice column. Suddenly a shrill scream rang out and Ed heard the ripping of fabric.

'Are – are you okay in there?' asked Ed, putting the magazine down and taking a step forward. Another howl and something smashing.

'Jenny, do you need help?' asked Ed, urgently.

'Get off me, you animal!' shrieked Jenny.

'Oh – are you on the phone back there?' asked Ed, a

confused smile flickering across his face. Another scream and the curtain came crashing down. Jenny careened through in only a towel and flung herself against the wall, yelping, before swiping her arm across the table of oils, sending them crashing to the floor. Ed saw she had a bloodied scratch over one eyebrow and what appeared to be a huge red mark at her other eye, as she picked up shards of glass and held them in her hands, letting out another deafening scream.

'Wha – what are you—' stuttered Ed, wondering who this madwoman was smashing up his studio. Was she high on PCP or something? Within seconds the two guys from outside had piled into the room.

'Thank God,' said Ed. 'This woman is crazy, she—'

'He just attacked me!' screamed Jenny, now smeared with blood. She let her towel drop to the floor and Ed saw that she had red marks all over her.

'Are you mad?' yelled Ed incredulously.

'*Hijo di puta!*' growled one of the men at Ed in Spanish.

'Wait! You don't actually believe her, do you? She's nuts, I tell you. I didn't touch her!'

'We just heard everything from outside!'

'We call the police!' said the guys in unison.

'Police? What for?' said Ed, panicking. He couldn't get in trouble with the police, especially not for assault on a woman. They'd check his records and then – Ed began to shake. 'No! Don't do that! This woman, she's a nut bag! I didn't do anything,' he yelled over the noise of Jenny wailing loudly like a baby as she buried her face in one of the guy's shoulders.

'Look at her! She's shaking, you bastard!'

'No, I swear, I haven't touched her! She must have had those bruises already when she came in!'

'They look fresh to us! We saw her when she was knocking on your door an' she had nothing on her face.' The two guys nodded at each other in agreement. 'We call the police!'

'No! Wait, we can sort this out somehow between us,' Ed muttered, still trying to figure out what the hell just happened.

Paolo waited in the parking lot in Tiny's truck and checked his watch. Jesús and Tiny should be coming out with Ed right about . . . now. Paolo burst with pride at the camaraderie they were displaying. He knew they'd help him out especially after he'd thoroughly shamed them for being such fag haters towards Blue. Besides, if there was once thing they were united in, it was their contempt for a man who could violate a women. Paolo hadn't had to go into too much detail about Ed to make his pals realise they'd be contributing to a worthy cause. As if on cue, Paolo saw Ed being pushed calmly from the fire-escape door out into the bright daylight. Paolo knew Ed was keeping calm right now because he had Tiny's gun in the small of his back. But he wouldn't be getting off that easily. Now it was Paolo's turn. He pulled his baseball cap down and checked his shades were secure. The kicking he was about to give Ed wasn't just for what he did to Tiger and Sienna, but for every guy who'd ever touched his Mami, for the trucker who killed Ramone, for his dead father who'd thrashed him and sent him to the institute, for every cop who'd kicked him and spat on him, for the goons who'd kicked the shit out of him when he got to Vegas, and for every man who'd ever abused a woman. This was Paolo's revenge. Tiny's sister Jenny climbed into the truck, panting.

'You okay?' asked Paolo. She nodded, catching her breath.

'Great make-up, pretty boy,' she giggled. 'He totally went for it, thought they were real. Got a few scratches for real when I got carried away smashing the place up though. I was imagining bustin' my ex-boyfriend's ass after I found him in bed with that tramp Maritza. It was fun lettin' off steam like that. Anyway, main thing is Ed thinks he's being brought to rights for assault.'

'He is, just not this one. Now to make sure he gets out of town and never comes back,' said Paolo, taking a deep breath and cracking his knuckles.

Chapter 21

The stage was set: chorus-line girls swimming in black chiffon framed the picture of an eclectic cast, Griselda rearing up at the back like a large black sequinned mother-octopus sporting a mass of oily black bouffant, with a cornucopia of rouged, powdered drag queens and feathered showgirls before him, flanked by midgets dressed as the cast of *The Godfather* and a huddle of leathery old men in pinstripes and trench coats. Tiger Starr stood statuesque at the helm, poured into an immaculate tight black Prada dress, virginal white hair tumbling over one eye, and Chantilly lace mantilla draped over a towering Spanish peineta, holding gloved hands with two quivering elderly ladies stooped under the weight of their ancient fox furs and diamonds. Sienna and Blue in their matching midnight-coloured velvet dwarfed the diminutive Pepper as they all stood beside the jet rhinestoned coffin, transfixed as it was lowered into the earth to the accompaniment of a live rendition of 'My Way' by an old torch singer friend of Ma's, backed by a soaring string arrangement. The co-ordinated cluster of musicians wore funereal Victoriana which sent pungent wafts of mothballs into the air

with every draw of bow against string. As the song reached
its rousing climax and the first handful of earth was thrown
down onto the casket, squeals rang out from the older
ladies as one of the pythons escaped from a snake charmer
somewhere to the left of the midgets. Trees and hedges
twitched as a dense gathering of FBI monitored the
outbreak of drama from as close as they dare.

'Oh Jesus and Mary,' murmured Blue, making the sign
of the cross and raising his eyes to the sky as the crowd
disbanded rapidly about them with people frantically trying
to recover the python. Sienna's eyes darted about anxiously
through her tears, watching the pandemonium escalating.
Still no sign of Ed, thank God. At least Tiger thought
Sienna's jumpiness was down to grief. Despite Brandy's
stilted call last night to say she'd handled Ed's demands,
Sienna could barely keep the paranoia at bay that he might
show his face. Particularly as Sienna didn't know if she
could believe a word that came out of Brandy's mouth any
more. She couldn't believe the crazy bitch had tried to kiss
her! What a piece of work! It seemed every single thing
she did turned out to be in the name of self-interest. And
yet had she really paid Ed off? Perhaps even that was just
to curry favour rather than out of any sense of friendship
or compassion. Sienna just couldn't figure her out but she
was determined to repay the money to Brandy as soon as
possible. There was no way she wanted to be beholden to
a fruit loop like that. Who knew what Brandy would try
next?

To add to Sienna's anxiety there was no sign of Honey today. She had harboured a glimmer of hope that her friend might have heard the news somehow and attended the funeral. Sienna had tried calling but she'd got no answer. Honey obviously had a new number now. To cap it all Blue had given Sienna some cryptic message that he needed to talk to her urgently about Paige but that the day of Ma's funeral wasn't the right time. So with all that on her plate, an ambitious snake making a bid for greener pastures was the least of Sienna's concerns on this day of utter blackness, she thought irritably, as she surveyed the chaos it was causing around her.

Paolo peeled cool, wafer-thin cucumber slices from his eyes and blinked up through the steamy air at glossy black granite ceiling tiles with inlaid twinkling rhinestone stars. A glance back down at his hands revealed slender finger-tips pruning under the hot bathwater. He languidly stretched out a smooth, bronzed and toned leg and saw that the fresh rose-petal bath oil had left his skin silken smooth. *If I was gay I'd fuck me*, he thought to himself, before rising from the deep vintage ceramic tub and grabbing one of Brandy's pink leopard-skin fluffy towels from the heated towel rail. Stepping out onto cool fish-scale-shaped floor tiles, he patted himself dry before using the same towel to expertly wrap his damp hair up in a turban.

Liza Minnelli always used to focus the entire day of a performance solely around the show; at least so he'd been told by Blue. Similarly, all that mattered today was Paolo's one big moment on stage in front of his audience. He'd spent his life preparing for this, and now Blue had given him a chance to live the dream for one night. He was going to savour every second. First he would do his stretches for the day while he was nice and warm from the bath. Then a few chin-ups and press-ups out by the pool under the sun to expel some of the butterflies that were already forming in the pit of his stomach. A last good healthy meal of chicken salad and fruit juice out on the terrace would see him prepared and relaxed; he may as well make the most of the lavish, spacious, if horrifically tacky setting before he had to return to real life on the East Coast.

Paolo reminded himself he had support tonight – once Blue had paid his respects to Ma Barker at the funeral he would be making his way to the Follies show to make sure Paolo was ready for his close-up and looked as flawless as a supermodel. He snorted to himself at the absurdity that just twenty-four hours ago he had been putting the finishing touches to the crippling of Ed Rogers' blackmail scheme with his own bare knuckles, and here he was now surrounded by pink marabou and powder puffs, perfecting his transformation into showgirl extraordinaire; ready to dance his way into the hearts of thousands on one of Vegas's biggest stages. His father would be spinning in his grave if he could see him now, thought Paolo, roaring out loud with a bitter cackle. He silenced himself

immediately with the thought that he may have successfully dispatched that louse Ed, but beautiful sweet Sienna
now thought he was a scheming bitch after that hopeless attempt at a kiss. What had he been thinking? With
a lonely sigh, Paolo was beginning to come to the conclusion that the forces of nature were stacked up against any
kind of relationship, friendship or otherwise with that
amazing creature. Yet another reminder that when something's just not meant to be, you can't force it. At least
Paolo had this one moment of glory on stage tonight to
look forward to . . . although he knew he'd give it up in
a heartbeat for just the glimmer of a chance to be with
Sienna.

A magnificent spread was awaiting the guests back at the
Monte Cristo, and since Ma had given strict instructions
to Pepper that her wake would be a celebration of her life,
an eight-piece band was playing back-to-back Rat Pack
songs, and Pepper had given the entire cast a paid evening
off to eat, drink and dance in Ma's memory. Sienna now
sat with Pepper, adding a little salt to her celery juice as
a big fat tear plopped into the glass in front of her.

'Why didn't Max come today?' asked Pepper.

'Get straight to the point, why don't you?' snapped
Sienna before melting immediately and wiping away a
tear. 'I'm sorry, Pepper, I know this is a difficult day for
everyone. I didn't mean to snap.'

'It's okay, darling. I can see it's a sore point.'

'Don't mention it in front of Mum,' pleaded Sienna, turning to see Tiger engaged in a slow-dance with a midget dressed as Don Corleone to 'Smoke Gets In Your Eyes'.

'Why not?'

Sienna paused to look into Pepper's eyes. She was no fool, she knew what was going on and this was no time for flannel. 'Okay, Mum thinks that I should dump Max. So I can't tell her I'm hung up on him; she'll give me a hard time. She reckons he's too much of a child. He's thirty-four! And with a multi-million-pound global business!'

'And with no time for his fiancée . . . '

'Oh God, I've been in hell these last two weeks. Do you know how it makes me feel that the man I'm supposed to be marrying can't even pick up the phone? One measly text! That's all I've had in two weeks! I've given up calling. I really don't want to make a fool out of myself and look like I'm some nagging needy girlfriend!'

'But you need to tell him something, right?' said Pepper, a glint in her eye.

'Yeah. I lost the engagement ring. It must be an omen.'

'No, not that.'

'What then?'

'He has a right to know . . . '

'What? What do you mean? How did—'

'Come on, Sienna. I'm eighty-five. I'm a woman who's been round the block a few times. I know a pregnant woman when I see one.'

'You mean . . . Did Mum say something? Is she the one who told you?' gasped Sienna.

'Yeah, she might have whispered something to me. Just out of concern. She told me when I rang to break the news about Ma. Said you'd avoided the subject when she confronted you in LA but she suspects alright, the minute you started throwing up. Don't worry, it's only us two who know the secret.'

'Oh God,' said Sienna, burying her head in her hands at the bar. 'I really love him, Pepper. I miss him! I'm numb without him so I've just been keeping myself busy, anything to take my mind off him, and just hoping he'll see me in his own time. We didn't argue or anything, he just – closed off, shut down. Maybe after he'd put a ring on my finger he thought he didn't need to try any more. I don't even understand why he proposed now. I figured he needed space at first, that work must be getting to him. He didn't even come to my opening night! What am I going to do?'

'Find him! He's your man, right? Well, forget about being all nonchalant "new woman", go and stake your claim! And if your mother doesn't like him – well, the right man was staring her in the face for over ten years yet she managed to go for all the douches. I wouldn't necessarily trust *her* intuition. You have to figure things out for yourself, and if it feels natural for you to be with Max right now, then that's what you must do.'

'He obviously doesn't want me,' snivelled Sienna.

'Oh, get a grip. Stop pining and go and find him. I

remember what he was like when he used to come in here every week hoping for just a glimpse of you. He could have had anyone, but no, he'd singled *you* out, you were the one for him. He did everything he could to get to you, and he persevered until he got his prize. And now you're giving up at the first sign that his mind's on something else? Be a man, Sienna, and go get him.'

Sienna looked up at Pepper, shocked, before bursting into laughter. 'When you put it like that . . . !'

'Exactly. Life's too short. And on that note, I say we drink a toast to Ma.'

'Of course! To Ma,' agreed Sienna, raising her glass and flicking her eyes up to heaven.

'Don't want to interrupt, ladies,' came a deep voice.

'Detective Weldon,' sighed Pepper.

'Looks like this may be the last time you'll be seeing me,' he smiled.

'I don't know what to say to that,' said Pepper. 'I can't exactly say "that's wonderful" without offending you, but I'm not sad to see you all going. I kept telling you there would be nothing here for you. I could have saved you all a lot of time.'

'Do I look like the kind of guy to be offended by anything?'

'I'm thrilled you're closing the case anyway,' said Pepper. 'It's been long enough.'

'I didn't say that. Nothing is official.'

'Come on, I know what you meant.' Pepper winked and Weldon winked back with a soft laugh.

'Thank you, Pepper, you've been most cooperative. It's been a pleasure meeting you.'

'You too. I'd invite you to stay for a drink but . . . I wouldn't want to be inappropriate, and knowing you have a girlfriend at home too.'

'Oh no, um – she had enough. My unsociable hours are bad enough for me, but when the lady wants taking out of an evening, the extra hours spent on a case become a bit of a problem. But what can I do?'

'I'm sorry,' said Pepper, flicking a sympathetic look his way.

'Don't be. My problem,' shrugged Weldon, a flash of regret registering in his face. 'Anyway, I must get back to the office. Paperwork. The usual. Good evening.'

He turned to Sienna and leaned in. 'Just thought you'd like to know I met a girl who looked just like the girl in that picture.' He pointed over at the image of Honey behind the bar on the wall of fame. 'You might want to go and see her dancing at the Swallow Club downtown,' he said sombrely.

'The what? *That* crusty dive. But all the girls there are – oh God, she's not doing *that* kind of dancing, is she? You sure it was Honey?'

'She said her name was Kandy. I don't know who she is, but she looked like *that picture*. She also looked like the kind of girl who could use a friend near her right now.'

And with that Weldon left before Sienna could even thank him for the information. Sienna looked at Pepper.

'Tell Mum I've left. This can't wait. There are two people I have to find tonight.'

'Co-ee,' called out Blue as he let himself into Brandy's dressing room. Blue stopped dead in his tracks and sucked air over his teeth at the sight of Paolo, Amazonian and resplendent in his first costume of the show. A perfect hourglass, padded and cinched in all the right places, the full-length gown of rhinestoned gorgeousness enveloping and skimming every synthetic shimmering curve.

'How's the corset underneath?' asked Blue suspiciously.

'Great!'

'You pulled your own strings?'

'What do you think these muscles are for,' smiled Paolo, flexing a lean, ripped bicep.

'Tucked?'

'Of course. Can't you tell my voice is higher?'

'Ha-ha. Just gotta check everything. Detail, Paolo, it can make or break us tonight.'

'Yeah,' sighed Paolo, narrowing his eyes. 'Can you imagine if Brandy could see me now?' Blue paused before breaking out into a dirty cackle. 'God, if we pull this off . . . ' whispered Paolo, half to himself.

'We have to,' reminded Blue sternly. 'I don't want to incur the wrath of your sister, thanks. I won't escape with my life. That's if I don't rot in jail first. Ugh.'

'Brandy Alexander and Scene One chorus line, this is your ten-minute call,' crackled a voice over the tannoy. Blue and Paolo looked at each other. Paolo thumped Blue on the back heartily.

'Thanks, bro,' he said gruffly. Blue shot him a filthy look. 'I mean, thank you, darling.' Paolo simpered with his best Brandy impression, bevelling his ankle and holding out a limp wrist. Blue winked. 'Break a nail,' he whispered, letting in a wave of squeals and squawks from the chorus line as he opened the dressing-room door for Paolo to make his way to his waiting stage.

Sienna roared along the freeway in her Ferrari, stereo cranked up to the kind of volume that was making surrounding cars vibrate. She felt fantastically clear-headed. She was on her way to claim her beloved Max, give him the amazing news he was about to become a father, and then they would find Honey and bring her home where she belonged. She was going to sort everything out. Now that she had her mind made up, everything had clicked into place in Sienna's head. She was going to be a mum! Maybe she could get her head around having a break from the stage, after all, especially since the Follies hadn't been the friendliest place to be working the last few weeks. Somehow it had all left a bad taste in Sienna's mouth. She was glad she was missing the show tonight to reclaim her life. Brandy was welcome to her part and it was unlikely Sienna would be there much longer anyway with her bump about to show anytime soon. Perhaps this baby was happening now for a reason, and the universe was looking after her. Sienna reached for her tummy instinctively. Perhaps success wasn't just fame, money and column inches after all – or at least perhaps that wasn't *everyone's* measure of success. She realised that out of everything she had achieved, this might just be the one thing that would make Tiger proudest of her. Once she told her officially, that is. She felt a little lump at her throat, and chastised herself for getting emotional. All these hormones raging in her bloodstream, no wonder she'd been all over the place recently, and getting all worked up over Max. Well, things were about to fall into place, she thought happily as she pulled off the road and towards Max's estate, feeling a tingle of excitement that she was going to see her sweetheart.

She craned her neck as she pulled up the driveway. None of Max's cars were visible. Surely he couldn't have taken them *all* out? How was that possible? She knew he'd rather sell his beloved cars before he'd let anyone else behind the wheel either. Sienna pulled her purring car round to the back of the mansion and cut the engine, deciding to take a quick peek inside for signs of life. She still had a key, although one of Max's staff was bound to be at home pottering in the kitchen, preparing his evening meal. Sienna found the door locked. She let herself in, and quickly punched the alarm code into the panel by the door upon hearing the high-pitched beeps. Obviously no-one home then. Where were his staff? He always had at least *someone* at his pad, guarding the empire. Sienna wandered through the granite and steel kitchen into the spacious fawn and white Eames-era lounge, smelling a familiar, reassuring hint of Max's aftershave in the air. She idly clip-clopped her way across the expanse of reclaimed vintage floorboards, wondering what to do now. Curl up in one of his vintage leather couches and surprise him or try his mobile once more? However, Sienna's mind was soon taken off her quandary as her eyes flicked over what appeared to be her favourite patterned skyscraper Prada shoes, tossed idly by the foot of the huge open staircase. She'd been looking for them for weeks! She didn't remember leaving them behind at Max's. What were they doing by his stairs?

Sienna suddenly realised something was not quite right with the room. Nothing out of place – Max was a neat-freak at the best of times – but just small details that jarred. Like the vase of lilies over on the kidney-bean shaped coffee table. Sienna hated lilies, they made her sneeze. Max would never normally have lilies in the house on her account, let alone flowers that he didn't like. He would never buy anything that didn't fit with his décor style. And what was with the vanity cases by the door? Was his maid trying out for a show on the Strip or something? Sienna bent down to examine the cases. Hello Kitty? Who had Hello Kitty luggage . . . ? Sienna straightened herself and ran her fingers through her hair agitatedly, looking about the room again. Her heart skipped with relief as she heard the familiar distinctive sound of Max's Lamborghini growling its way into the driveway. Thank God, she could fall into his arms and let him reassure her everything was fine. There was nothing like seeing someone face to face for killing off silly paranoias, thought Sienna. She hurriedly smoothed her black velvet dress down and reached out to twitch the blinds, hoping for a quick, heart-fluttering peek at his handsome face before he opened the door.

Sienna froze. Paige? What in God's name was Paige doing climbing out of Max's car with groceries? Was this some crazy joke? Sienna stood transfixed as she watched Max now emerging from the car with a face like thunder. Sienna shrank back from the door, her heart racing. Max and Paige? Since when! Was she dreaming or something? Sienna didn't know whether to run back the way she came or wait by the door and confront the situation. Her eyes darted as she heard the jangling of keys at the keyhole.

The door swung open and Honey dragged herself inside before collapsing in a crumpled heap on the vinyl floor of her apartment, tears pouring down her already mascara-stained cheeks. How in hell had she slipped up back there in the club? She had been so careful with all her propositions up to now, making sure everything was coded language. Turns out the place had been swarming with Feds all week. No wonder barely any of the guys she was working on were hiring her, they were simply casing the joint. How on earth had she not spotted they were cops? All the other girls seemed to have sussed them out; how nice of them to warn Honey. Now it was on her files that she'd been booked for soliciting. Soliciting! The humiliation of having her mugshots taken, her fingers printed. This wasn't what she came to Vegas for. She thought back to the first time she'd arrived in town by private jet in a blaze of glamour with Tiger Starr and her entourage of Starrlets to dance in a promo for Tiger's smash show. That was just five years ago. From being fresh-faced, talented and beautiful, and full of energy, hope and ambition, now Honey Lou Parker was reduced to crying on the floor of her empty apartment, broke, alone and with a police record to her name. How had she got onto such a slippery slope? Surely it couldn't be so difficult just to be a humble dancer in the land of entertainment – clearly she was so inept she couldn't even manage that simple task. She'd alienated the family she left behind to come to Vegas, and she'd lost her friends in this town too. Who could she talk to now? And what were her friends doing now? Being successful in a fabulous show, living in a beautiful house, finding their Prince Charmings, making fabulous lives for themselves, that's what, said Honey to herself despairingly. So much for her big dream. She felt so stupid. Stupid for being so sure that she could come to Vegas and succeed, when in fact she was just a pathetic failure. Honey could see nowhere to turn, no way to move forward. Lying on the floor, she felt the walls rearing up and closing in on her. Would anyone miss her if she was gone? No-one would even know, she realised. Her mind turned to the bottle of cleaning bleach she had in the bathroom cupboard. Perhaps there was a way out after all . . .

The dream was destroyed. Smashed to fragments like the vase she had just flung to the floor, spewing its lilies and stagnant water onto the varnished wood. Clearly this was what Blue had been itching to tell her. Sienna couldn't believe he had known that Paige and Max had been sleeping together. Why was he waiting to tell her the bad news? How could he? Had she no friends left in the world? She'd thought Blue was one person she could trust her own life with. How could she keep getting people so wrong?

'Sienna, calm down,' urged Max, taking a step towards her.

'Don't you dare go near her, she's just being a drama queen!' snapped Paige, grabbing Max's elbow roughly.

'How could you, Max? With one of my so-called friends, too! It's just so trashy!' Sienna knew she should just turn around and walk out – try to salvage some dignity from the situation – and if it had been just her she would have done it without a doubt. However, she had to think about what was best for her baby as well as herself and surely it was better for it to have a father even if he was obviously a cheating rat?

'It's not you, it's me—'

'Oh God! I can't believe you said that!' gasped Sienna. 'Of all the rotten stinking clichés!'

'I meant to say, it means nothing,' bargained Max. 'It was just sex—'

'What?' squealed Paige.

'Argh! Stop with the clichés, I can't stand it!' hollered Sienna, tears of humiliation running down her face. 'Okay, Max. It's obvious what's been going on here but we can get over it. I . . . I can try to forgive you. People often have affairs when they feel . . . under pressure. You haven't been yourself lately, I can see that . . . Let's not go over what's happened, let's try and move forward,' she whispered hoarsely through her tears. 'It's not too late . . . I can forgive you, baby,' she sobbed, her shoulders shuddering. Even as she said it, she wondered if it was true. Would she be able to get over such a horrendous betrayal? For the sake of their child, she had to believe she could.

'What the hell—' started Paige.

'Shut it, bitch!' snarled Sienna, firing Paige a death-ray glare before turning back to Max and looking straight into his beautiful brown eyes. 'We can put this . . . all this mess behind us, darling. I know you've been working so hard, you haven't been thinking straight. Max, there's something you need to know. The reason I came here – I'm pregnant.' Max's jaw fell open.

'Oh great, that's all the world needs, not one but two spoilt Sienna Starrs,' sneered Paige. 'How does he even know it's his . . . ?'

'I said shut it, *bitch,* or I'll ram those Pradas you stole so far up your backside you'll be able to taste shoe leather!' Sienna countered coolly. 'Max,' she whispered, turning her tear-stained face immediately back to him. 'Come back, baby. It's true, you're going to be a daddy. Isn't that amazing?' A glimmer of hope flickered across her face as Max stood silent. 'I know it won't be easy to get over this but we can still be together. You and me . . . and our baby. Ours.'

'This is all I fucking need,' grumbled Paige under her breath, bending to start picking up the groceries she had dropped in shock when she had walked through the front door.

'NO!' roared Max, suddenly. 'Sienna, what are you thinking! You stupid . . . STUPID! I could *never* be a father!' he raged. Sienna drew back. 'Do you know what my father is like? What he did to me? How much he bullied me, how cruel – Sienna, you have no idea, do you! Everything in your life is one big rhinestoned rosebed. How could you ever know what it feels like to have people trying to stab you in the back and trip you up because they think you've got everything on a plate, yet they don't know the *abuse* you've had to suffer? My father is an evil man. I could *never* have my own child. I don't want to be a father! Do you understand that?' Sienna shook with tears. Not just for Max's pain but with her own frustration and painful memories too. How could she even begin to tell Max about her own father, here, like this, in front of that vile backstabbing cuckoo Paige Turner? Sienna hadn't even told him that she had thought her own mother was her sister for nineteen years. She wasn't even sure if he'd heard the story or not. Max wasn't one for reading gossip magazines and if he knew about the skeletons in her closet he'd never let on and they'd certainly never talked about it. She'd hoped she wouldn't have reason to, that she could finally put the past behind her and move forward as a normal daughter. She hadn't wanted her past to be the thing that defined her present. How could she reach out to Max now and explain she understood him more than he could ever imagine?

'No, Sienna, I could never bring some baby into the world that'll depend on me,' continued Max. 'I can never give it what it needs! I'll hate it! I know I will! All I'll see in front of me is the same snivelling, pathetic little kid that I was – and that my father despised. I won't do it, Sienna, I won't!' Max fell to his knees, trembling.

'You were just a child . . . ' whispered Sienna through her choking breaths as she knelt down before Max, her face contorting with sobs. 'It's not normal for a father to despise his child. I'm so sorry, Max, I'm sorry for what you went through. This wasn't planned but I want this baby and you can be different. You're not your dad. This can be your chance to move forward, to change the outcome. We can love our baby together. I'm here, and I love you, Max. You're not pathetic or wretched, you're my Max and I love you,' she snivelled, shaking uncontrollably as she clutched at her tummy.

'Stop it!' screamed Paige, launching a bottle of ketchup from the groceries at Sienna. 'He's married *to me* now! He's *mine!*' The bottle smashed against the coffee table in an explosion of gaudy red stickiness, making Sienna jump in shock. Married?! Sienna stared at Max in disbelief, completely unaware of Paige lunging forward. She pushed Sienna violently to the floor, eliciting a deafening yelp as Sienna's head connected with wood.

'Leave him alone! You don't need him, he's better off with me!' screeched Paige like a banshee. 'Besides, you're too late. Hell could freeze over before I divorce him!'

As Paige's words finally sunk in, Sienna tried to get up but Paige was now pinning her to the ground, hitting her in the stomach repeatedly.

'Nooo!' howled Sienna, trying to crawl away from the blows, shards of broken vase sticking in her hands as she pawed desperately at the floor. Paige continued with a rain of frenzied kicks and punches as Max knelt on the ground like a child, his hands covering his face as he shook his head and whimpered to himself. A ghastly guttural primal scream came from Sienna's mouth as she contorted in appalling pain. But her haunting wails continued to fall on deaf ears, as she realised that it wasn't just Max she was losing . . .

Chapter 22

Paolo opened one eye, realising the banging wasn't in his dreams. It sounded like someone was practically kicking the front door down. He sat bolt upright and took a split second to reorientate himself. Brandy's house. Show last night. Best night of his life! Standing ovation. No incident. Holdalls packed. Leaving town today. So who the hell was at the door? The banging continued. Paolo grabbed one of Brandy's gaudy three-foot porcelain roaring leopards – which, if smashed over an unwanted visitor's head could gain him a few seconds if necessary – before treading quietly through to the front door. Peering through the spy hole he sighed and put the leopard down. What was Blue doing here so early? What had he done wrong now?

'Relax, I'm leaving today,' groaned Paolo as he opened the door to Blue's anxious face and a flood of Vegas morning sun.

'Oh thank God, devotion, I thought you'd gone already. I've been banging away for ten minutes. Lost my bloody key and couldn't let myself in.'

'I was hoping for a lie-in before I go – it was a busy

night after all,' said Paolo, drawing back as Blue pushed past forcefully and minced into the lounge.

'You're not going,' he said over his shoulder.

'Of course I am. It's okay, everything's packed and I'll be out of your life, don't worry. Just give me a chance to wake up, jeez,' said Paolo through a cavernous yawn, shutting out the blazing beam of sunshine as he slammed the door shut.

'No, you don't understand, you can't go now,' announced Blue, turning to face Paolo.

'What? I have to, like we agreed, right? Don't worry. I keep my word, I'm no con artist. Well, in a manner of speaking.'

'No, you don't understand. You have to stay. Look at this.' Blue threw a *Vegas Times* down onto the coffee table. There on the front cover was a picture of Paolo from the show last night with the headline 'Alexander the Great'.

'What's this?'

'You made front pages with rave reviews of last night. Just check out the pictures, you look astonishing. Brandy hasn't been seen on stage for two months, remember. She hasn't even been doing the party circuit. So the minute you pop up on stage the whole of Vegas has ground to a halt. Not only that but you were sensational, the press are comparing your footwork to the likes of Cyd Charisse, for chrissake. Marty's been on the phone this morning, says he's been ringing the house but no answer.'

'Oh ... I have the phone unplugged. All these guys

kept leaving answerphone messages for my sister, some of it was kind of gross so I just disconnected everything. She obviously likes her men. A lot.'

'Well, you can't go now. Marty wants you to do a big gala performance with Lady Gaga in a week. This is major. If you go now, Marty will try and track you down and he's bound to stumble across the real Brandy if that happens. This is a disaster. Why did you have to be so good?'

'Thanks,' grunted Paolo, slumping down on to the couch and putting his head in his hands. 'I just want to get off the ride now, for chrissake.'

'We can do it. You just do the next week, do the gala, and then say you're taking a vacation. Your sister then comes back a month after, no-one knows any different. Even if the whole of Vegas is still talking about it then and hasn't moved on to the next celeb drama, she's ditzy and egotistical enough to just accept the praise. By then I think I'll have jumped ship too, I can't stand the pace any more, devotion. It's bad for my roots. I actually found a grey hair yesterday. A grey hair!'

'Be grateful it was on your head,' said Paolo.

'It's no laughing matter,' grumbled Blue. 'So, you're going to stay, aren't you?'

'I just don't know,' sighed Paolo after a long pause. 'I've psyched myself up to go back now. I feel like I'd be outstaying my welcome . . . not that I was ever welcome in the first place, you know?'

'Hey, after the vile treatment Brandy gave everyone, you

were a breath of fresh air, I can tell you,' said Blue. 'But seriously, you have to stay and finish this off. Come on! It's just one more measly week,' he pleaded.

'Something in my gut is telling me to get the hell out, Blue. I can't keep up the drag thing much longer. Really. I want to be able to sit with my legs spread. My balls need to feel air. I want to use the men's restrooms. I want to talk and walk normally. I'm fed up of checking if my bum looks big in something. I'm fed up of spending three hours trowelling on creams and make-up and another hour scraping it off every day. I'm fed up of the agony of waxing. The stink of fake tan. It's exhausting being a chick. Besides, I'm a red-blooded male and I'm starting to make dumb mistakes. I forgot myself and tried to kiss Sienna the other day, remember? Nightmare. If she didn't already hate me I bet she does now!'

'She didn't mention it at the funeral, and I haven't seen her since I left everyone at the Monte yesterday evening. Please, Paolo, you need to finish what you started.'

'I'm . . . I'm just not feeling it.'

'Stop being a diva!'

Paolo fixed his green-eyed gaze on Blue. 'A week, you say?'

'That's all. Then we're home and dry.'

'You're sure?'

'Promise.'

'Jeez, another week of heels, I don't know if my ankles can take the strain,' muttered Paolo.

'Was that a "yes"?'

'That was a "don't suppose I have much choice",' said Paolo with a scowl.

'Great! I'll treat you to a facial at Stitch 'n' Bitch.'

'God, not more poking and prodding,' sighed Paolo.

'Then a beer and a bucket of fried chicken in front of some sweaty sports event?'

'Now you're talking.'

'Done.'

Brandy Alexander turned her nose up at the myriad break-fast trays, deciding there was nothing much she fancied. She was so bored of international cuisine, all these silly exotic fruits she'd never heard the names of. She had no idea how many calories were in any of it and had just been grazing at egg-white omelettes and steamed asparagus with hot lemon-water chasers for two months. What she really fancied right now after weeks of abstinence was to gorge on a juicy Burger King . . . and a hot man. But since they were at least four days from the next port she guessed she'd have to wait. She idly flicked on the TV. She had been trying to enjoy the isolation of the yacht as she recov-ered from her endless list of surgical procedures. She'd brought a meditation guru with her for the trip but found her thoughts wandering to sex all too often for the medi-tation classes to work. Instead Brandy found herself blissed out on painkillers and sleeping pills most of the time. Not watching TV or reading any newspapers had been the only surprisingly pleasant aspect of her recovery. In fact Brandy hadn't realised how much stress she gave herself by keeping too close an eye on what all the other showbiz bitches were up to; it had been rather relaxing not monitoring the competition for a while. No-one realised the nervous strain Brandy was under whenever there was some jammy actress stealing valuable column inches by bagging a hotter lover, or a better gig. Still, there was no harm in watching the shopping channels, was there? She could do with giving her credit card a little spank since she hadn't bought any trinkets for weeks.

Nothing much took Brandy's fancy as she flicked over to QVC, and she'd already bought up the whole Joan Rivers range anyway. She cautiously flicked back to the entertainment news, which was now chattering on about some music awards ceremony and dissecting the red-carpet gown parade. Brandy realised as she longingly watched the media circus unfolding on the TV screen that she could hardly wait for her bruising to be healed so she could get back into the drama of the social circuit again and back in everyone's consciousness. Everyone must be missing her thoroughly by now anyway. Wincing with pain, she manoeuvred herself off the enormous bed and shuffled over to the mirror.

Every day she examined her temporarily grotesque face carefully, looking for the minute signs of healing, bruising changing colour, puffiness reducing. She had been in a world of pain after having ten procedures in one session.

She'd had a constant splitting headache since the surgery, and her face was permanently throbbing. At least she had a legitimate reason for not bothering to smile now. Her legs and ass were looking in supreme shape now that she'd also had a general resculpt, although the pain of the lipo was still excruciating – just brushing past someone accidentally could bring her to her knees. All for shaving off a millimetre here and there . . . but it would be worth it, she thought smugly. As for the breasts, they were pure perfection – rock hard, smooth and pointing skywards. After this overhaul she'd easily added another few decades to her earning potential.

She reached for her vitamin E oil, wondering which part of her bruised skin to massage first. At least it had improved immeasurably the last couple of weeks, with just a few last splotches left now. Flicking her eyes up at the plasma screen she saw a rather beautiful picture of her old self, smiling, unusually. Brandy set about applying her oil and kept one ear on the story, wondering what the feature was about – perhaps her beauty or her riches, or even her impeccable style . . . there was always so much to talk about with her. It's what set her apart from other less beautiful or gifted people.

'Miss Alexander brought down the house last night in Vegas with an incredible comeback after two months of absence from the stage . . . ' The bottle of oil fell from Brandy's hand as she froze in horror, the story unfolding in front of her. She screwed her eyes up at the screen.

That was definitely her up there. Had she taken too much Xanax last night? Was this some weird nightmare she was trapped in? How could she have been dancing in her own show last night? Perhaps this was a terrible dream in which the world continued without her? The horror! Surely there was no-one in the world beautiful enough to even think of being her imposter? No, that was definitely her up there, looking amazing, beautifully polished and toned. Was she seeing properly? Brandy felt shooting pain as she pulled a face. Yelping as her hands flew up to cradle her throbbing jaw, she realised she was very much awake. Who the hell was this fake? She needed to get back to Vegas immediately and get to the bottom of this nightmare, even if it meant jumping off this damn boat and swimming to the next port herself. But how could she let anyone see her like this? She wasn't perfect enough to be unveiled in public yet! She sprang up from her dressing table and cried out in pain as she hobbled her way to the telephone. This was turning into a disaster. Heads were going to roll when she got back in town, she raged, picking up the receiver. Now, who could she scream at first?

Sienna could hear voices outside her room. Hopefully that was the preamble to her being discharged. She'd been monitored overnight, and the worst of her pain had passed now. She just wanted to get back to her own bed and come to terms with the loss of her baby and her relationship with Max alone. She wished she could have had Blue by her side as hospitals were scary at the best of times, but she wasn't sure how much she should trust him now. He must have known about Paige and Max. How could he have kept it from her like that? She'd never felt so alone. She was too ashamed even to call her mum, who'd been right about Max all along and had warned her daughter in no uncertain terms that she was inviting a world of heartache into her life if she stuck with him. Besides, she could hardly tell her mum she'd lost the baby when she'd denied even being pregnant to her. She couldn't help but feel that she'd let Tiger down in so many ways – by ignoring her advice, and not trusting her to have her daughter's interests at heart. There was a soft rap at the door.

'Come in,' said Sienna, pulling herself up into a sitting position. The nurse stuck her head round the door.

'I have a visitor for you, a Detective Jack Weldon? He'd like to talk to you.'

'Oh!' exclaimed Sienna, her heart beating immediately, worrying what the problem could be. How did he know she was even here? She hadn't called or notified anyone. 'Sure, I can talk,' said Sienna anxiously, quickly smoothing out her hair and hoping she didn't look too bedraggled. Weldon shuffled through, thanked the nurse and shut the door softly behind him. He pulled up a chair and perched at Sienna's side. Sienna managed a little smile. Weldon managed an awkward grin.

'So. This isn't strictly professional, more of a personal visit. I was here last night on another case and – to my horror saw you being wheeled through A&E. I know we don't really know each other but I've spent enough time at the Monte to know how much Pepper thinks of you, and well . . . I was worried, I suppose. Just wanted to check up that you were doing okay?'

'Oh. Right. I don't know what I'm supposed to say. Thank you?'

'Is there anything I can do for you? Anything you need?'

'No. I'm hoping to get out today.'

'Oh good. I don't mean to intrude but it looked serious when I saw you last night. I saw you had the cops in earlier too.'

'It's kind of personal but I'm going to be fine. Physically anyway. I'm not sure how well I'm doing on the other stuff, Detective Weldon.'

'Jack. Call me Jack. Look, the cops – anything I should know about? You in trouble? Do you need me to call anyone or . . .'

'No. Definitely, no. I'm not the one they were after. It's . . . kind of personal, like I said. I won't be pressing charges right now, anyway. I can't dredge up what happened so soon after. Maybe when I've healed I'll think about it. Sorry, I just don't feel like speaking to anyone. I'm fed up of explaining or excusing myself, to be honest. I'll be fine.'

'If you're sure . . . ?'

'There's no-one I really want to talk to right now.'

Jack Weldon was usually a master at persuading someone to open up, but now his conscience told him not to probe; that Sienna deserved to have her way. He'd done due diligence and made sure her physical health was stable, he reassured himself. Although a nagging feeling made him want to stay . . . it wasn't a feeling he was used to . . . Ah, concern. Weldon was usually so detached from his work. To get emotionally involved was professional suicide. But sitting with Sienna now, he truly cared to know she was going to be okay.

'You know how it is, Sienna, Vegas is peculiar. You can be surrounded by people and bright lights all the time and yet feel more alone than anywhere else in the world.'

Sienna regarded Weldon thoughtfully.

'Maybe. And sometimes . . . ' she said expressionlessly, 'sometimes I wonder where's the normality? I'm not sure where my *roots* are any more, I guess. Does that make sense?'

'This town is built on vice. It does things to people after prolonged exposure,' said Weldon with a hollow laugh. 'You have good people around you, though. Want me to call Pepper?'

'No. Really, this is a private thing.'

'Want me to go? I feel like I'm intruding a little?'

'It's okay, in a weird way I know I can trust you! I guess in that way it's good that we don't know each other. It's nice to talk to someone who I don't feel is judging me or harbouring an ulterior motive for once . . . ' Sienna trailed off as her lip wobbled and a tear ran down her cheek. Weldon shifted in his seat uncomfortably before placing his hand gingerly on Sienna's arm. He reminded himself he hadn't meant to delve, and felt immediately guilty for upsetting her.

'I can go, it's okay. You need your privacy.'

'Please stay,' whispered Sienna, more tears pouring down her face. 'I've had a rough couple of days, I guess, and I'm wondering where did it all go so wrong?' she asked, half to herself, half to Weldon. She tried to smile through her tears. 'Maybe you can help me stop feeling so sorry for myself?'

'I'm not so sure about that but I can try. You can trust me, you know.'

'I've just been really badly let down by a few people I thought I could trust. I had this dream, you know, and it's all got screwed up. And I guess I'm wondering why some people want to try to destroy others they see doing well? How does that make them feel better about themselves? It doesn't make sense.' Sienna let out a small strangled sob as Paige's face, contorted with anger and bitterness, flashed before her eyes. 'I never did anything wrong, I just tried my best. And that seems to make other people so angry.' Sienna broke down into sobs and clutched at Weldon's arm. Minutes passed and he just sat in silence and let her cry.

'Some people,' he murmured eventually, 'they can't face the reality that only they are responsible for their happiness. They need to find someone else to blame if things aren't going right. And if you've got what they want, that makes you the easy target.'

'It's just sad,' snivelled Sienna, reaching for her tenth tissue from her bedside table.

'Erm . . . You know sometimes people harm themselves too. They turn the destructiveness inwards,' said Weldon, thinking now was as good a time as any to reveal to Sienna why he had been at the hospital in the first place.

'I guess that too.'

'Which leads me on to something kind of . . . difficult.'

'Go on,' said Sienna warily.

'The reason I was here last night,' started Weldon, reaching into his inside pocket for his notepad, 'I found a young lady who had tried to harm herself at her home. She drank bleach. She's here in this hospital. I'm afraid it's your friend – Honey Lou Parker.' He read the name from his scribbles.

'Oh God,' gasped Sienna.

'The doctors say she's stable.'

'I want to see her,' said Sienna, flinging her bedclothes off and trying to manoeuvre herself off the bed whilst screwing up her face in pain.

'Let me get a nurse,' said Weldon.

'Just take me to her,' begged Sienna.

'Relax, she's going to be okay.'

'What happened? What made her do such a stupid thing?'

'I'll have to let her tell you that herself, Sienna.'

Weldon wasn't about to disclose that one of his colleagues had booked Honey for soliciting at the Swallow Club last night. Weldon had hit the roof, insisting she was only small fry compared to the more pressing case of the money laundering and narcotics involvement. Apart from his obvious personal reason to be exasperated that she of all the girls had been booked, charging a hostess only alerted the club to the fact they were under surveillance. Weldon had been outraged at the stupidity of his deputy for falling into the trap of going for trivial, premature and utterly counterproductive results, just so he would have a charge on the rap sheet to his name. Weldon had decided to go above the call of duty and visit Honey's apartment. He just had a gut instinct that he should check she was okay, after he had seen the desperation in her eyes when he had encountered her at the club for himself. Thank God he had. He had no doubt if no-one had called round, she would have got the results she was aiming for − to bring her life to an undignified end.

Now, as Weldon led Sienna across the corridor to Honey's room, he squeezed her arm gently.

'I'll check she's okay to see you,' he whispered.

'Of course she's fucking okay to see me! Let me in there!' snapped Sienna, snatching her arm back and barging in to the room.

'Honey?' whispered Sienna, barely able to believe the emaciated, exhausted face on the pillow before her belonged to her once healthy, young, beautiful friend Honey.

'Sienna? Is that really you?' ventured Honey. 'What are you doing here? You look terrible, are you okay?' Without another word, Sienna ran to Honey's arms and the two girls cradled each other, sobbing into each other's shoulders. Weldon softly closed the door behind them, knowing they needed time alone to tell their stories.

Chapter 23

Four days had passed and Brandy had finally worked out that her brother Paolo was at the bottom of the mystery. So, the ambitious little twinkle toes had finally found a way to upstage her? Curiously, Brandy hadn't gone nuclear about it, as the thought of getting even was much more of a mouth-watering prospect. Much better to bide her time until she could deal with the matter in person than unleashing a mouthful over the phone, giving Paolo advance warning to skip town and run away to hide in his stinking little rat hole on the East Coast. Besides she could almost feel a tiny bit flattered that he had gone to so much trouble to emulate her beauty. Although how he dare ever think he had the level of looks and talent that had been Brandy's fortune was blatant cheek. She was about to shine the kind of black light into his life that would make him wish their father had just beaten him to death there and then instead of giving him a cushy reprise in the form of the mental home.

Today the yacht was finally reaching Australia. Brandy was glad she'd been forced to take the time to think through her plans carefully instead of jumping the gun. It had given her the time to weigh up what would be the most fitting punishment. Now all that stood between her and Vegas was a twenty-hour flight – enough time to rest and relax, and prepare herself for Operation Vengeance. She'd seen all the advertising for the gala performance that was taking place tomorrow, and she'd be back in the nick of time. She'd also already placed a call with the goons who had done such a good job on Paolo last time. Everything was lined up nicely for a humiliating showdown for her ridiculous, insignificant, good-for-nothing little brother.

Blue was still recovering from the last hour of revelations from Sienna. Unable to reach her after the day of the funeral and with everyone worried by her silence, Blue had decided to employ the key Tiger had left him with for emergency access to the Starr family mansion. There he had found Sienna, holed up in her bedroom and wrapped up in her satin pyjamas with several days' worth of tear-stained tissues littering the floor. She hadn't heard Blue entering over the sound of her jagged snivels which mingled with the strains of 1950s ballads of broken hearts and unrequited love emanating softly from her battered old-style record player, so when he entered the room she'd jumped nearly a foot in the air.

Once opening hostilities had been exchanged and Blue had threatened to get Tiger on the phone there and then if Sienna didn't tell him what was going on, Sienna had opened the floodgates, not before venting her spleen at

Blue for apparently keeping quiet about Max and Paige's ludicrous marriage. Blue nearly passed out on the spot, not just with incredulity at the news, but that Sienna thought even for a second that he could betray her like that. He made it clear all he knew were the stories Joey the centurion had relayed about Paige's trailer-park upbringing culminating in taking the crown as the most ridiculous and destructive fantasist since Walter Mitty. He thought Sienna deserved to know that truth about her friend – he even thought it might amuse her. He was devastated to learn what had been happening to Sienna in the meantime. So Sienna had only finally revealed how she came to be in hospital the night of the funeral once she had made Blue swear on the sacred memory of Liberace that he wouldn't tell any of it to her mother.

Blue had sat there feeling like a helpless, useless fool as Sienna poured out her story. How could he possibly help? What could he ever do to reach out and fix things? He was a guy; how could he ever understand what it had felt like for Sienna this week? Never mind that she'd gone through it alone, thinking she had no support from those who loved her. Blue felt as useless as when Tiger's past had brought her life crashing down around her five years ago. Moreover, he'd felt faintly ridiculous that Sienna had started to comfort him when a tear found its way onto his cheek. Shouldn't *he* be the one offering the comfort? But what could he possibly say or do apart from going to Max's new marital bed with a freshly severed horse's head?

At least the pair had eventually managed ten minutes of hilarity inventing punishments they could mete out upon Max and Paige. Between them they totally exorcised any remaining rose tint through which Sienna might have been viewing her relationship with Max. But Blue was still frustrated that Sienna wasn't about to press charges against Paige yet for the assault. She said she was still so raw she just didn't feel ready to relive her experiences to a cop. Of course, Blue had no idea about Sienna's shock reconciliation with Honey, or how hard it had hit Sienna on top of everything, her friend's suicide attempt magnifying her own painfully tangled frame of mind. Neither was he to know that Sienna intended to shield her dear friend's secret from everyone to allow her the time to heal herself before facing the world. So it came as a mild surprise that she was singularly disinterested in any more drama, least of all the good news that she was to be blackmailed no longer, now that Ed had 'disappeared'.

Blue explained carefully that Brandy had removed him from Sienna's life for good, not giving away how exactly, but driving home the selflessness of the act nonetheless. Sienna's response? 'I appreciate what she's done, but I can't return Brandy's affections in *that* way.' Blue had cursed inwardly as he reminded himself of Paolo's moment of utter idiocy in kissing Sienna. Blue had brought their conversation to a close, insisting Sienna should have a change of scenery and convincing her to meet him at the Artisan Hotel for a breath of air. Now, as he sped along the freeway to his next stop in his Lamborghini, he knew that what he was about to do was the right thing.

'What's this?' asked Paolo, looking blankly at the expensive-looking suit Blue had laid out on Brandy's couch after barging his way through the front door moments earlier.

'Armani,' said Blue, casually.

'What's it for?'

'It's for you to wear.'

'What for?'

'Truth Day.'

'Huh?'

'It's time for the truth. Now's the time you stand before Sienna as Paolo . . . and tell her the truth.'

'What? But she hates me! I destroyed her trust in me already as it is. She'll flip if I do this.'

'She doesn't hate *you*. She just thinks you're Brandy. This will clarify in her mind why the weird behaviour moments were justified. You've been lumbered with your sister's legacy of shit and I'd say you've done your best to put some of her actions right, no? That legacy also means it's never exactly been a level playing field as far as popularity's concerned. Now listen, Sienna's just had the week from hell, to put it mildly. I can't say any more, but I don't want you asking her questions about it. All you need to know is everything she thought she knew about the people around her has been shattered. So that means it's time for her to see all the cards out on the table, so she realises who the good guys really are.'

'Are you kidding? If she's having a tough time surely this is the last thing she needs right now. *Hey, all this time you thought I was Badass Bitch with tits on a stick, I'm actually Mr Good Guy packing a pouch* . . . Yet another blow to her perception of reality, the icing on the cake. She's just gonna throw a punch at me or something.'

'I disagree. I think it means she's able to see things in a new light. She's a smart girl when it comes to a math problem, but in life she's so busy trying to please everyone she turns a blind eye to things that stare her in the face half the time. She began with Max on a tight leash, but in the end let him walk all over her because her good nature got in the way. And how on earth she didn't spot Paige – mind, even I didn't see that bull coming into the china shop. But make no mistake, if you tell her the truth about how you came to be Brandy, she'll get it. Stupid she's not. Now I saw how you protected her from her father. You didn't have to do that. I think you deserve the chance to explain yourself. It's time for Sienna to know who you really are, Paolo. You've stuck your neck out for her, now give her the gift of knowing you did what you did to Ed out of genuine concern and support for her. Don't you think this is when you should be stepping out from the mask? I dunno, seems to me like there's something more . . . honourable in you standing before her and telling the truth.'

'What if she blows the whistle and tells everyone?'

'I guess it's a risk you have to take. But remember what

I said, Sienna's smart deep down, no matter how ditzy she might come across. Also remember that Brandy was just dreadful to everyone. Anyone in their right mind would be positively relieved you're not Brandy. Think about it. Be the man you are. Take the risk.'

'Sure.' Paolo sat and stared at the pattern of the rug for a minute. 'I hear what you're saying. I guess I just don't like hearing that I've been such a coward. It's true, I know . . . but when it's said out loud . . . well, no-one wants to listen to that being said about themselves.'

'I didn't say anything about being a coward.'

'You didn't need to, it was all there.'

'I wouldn't say a coward takes a beating from a pack of heavies and bounces back. I wouldn't say a coward takes the rap day after day in silence for all the shit your sister slung at others. Or saves my bacon from gun-wielding Mexicans. Or risks jail getting rid of a blackmailing parasite like Ed. Or makes huge sacrifices for his mother—'

'Who wouldn't, though? No, I'm a coward. I can admit it – a coward who has always let his sister do disgusting things, let her plot and connive and get away with it.'

'You were a child! You were innocent – and didn't know any better. And you wanted a quiet life!'

'But I don't have that excuse now. What kind of grown man doesn't stand up to a Gucci-bag full of wind and shit like that? I feel like a total prick.'

Blue watched as Paolo rocked back and forth on the

sofa agitatedly, holding his clamped fists up at his mouth, his brow furrowed. 'Get the suit on,' said Blue quietly. 'I'll be outside in the car ready to take you to Sienna.'

Sienna answered the front door to Honey, Detective Weldon and two large suitcases.

'Thank you so much, Detective,' said Sienna, rushing forward to give Honey a cuddle.

'Jack, call me Jack. This was just a personal errand. Like I said, I just wanted to make sure Honey got to you safely.'

'Would you like to come in for a coffee?' asked Sienna, immediately wheeling Honey's cases over the threshold into the lobby.

'Thank you, but I'm fine, I should be going now.' Weldon nodded his head and patted Honey on the shoulder. 'You take care, Miss Parker.'

'Thank you,' said Honey coyly, 'thanks for . . . everything.' Weldon paused and reached for his notepad. He scribbled out a number and handed it to Sienna.

'Here's my cell just in case you – either of you – need anything.'

'Thank you . . . Jack,' smiled Sienna, watching as he made his way back to his car, before closing the door softly.

'How you feeling?' asked Sienna.

'Not too bad today,' replied Honey awkwardly.

'I'm so glad you're back,' whispered Sienna, throwing her arms around her friend and embracing her tightly. 'English breakfast tea with toast and Marmite?'

'You have Marmite?' asked Honey, pulling back, her eyes lighting up.

'Sure. Come on, let's make a mess in the kitchen. This is your home again.'

After raiding the cupboards for every snack they could lay their hands on, the girls were lolling in the kitchen, stuffed and relaxed. Sienna checked her watch and gasped.

'Hell, I was supposed to meet Blue five minutes ago, I forgot. Jeez. Let me call and cancel.'

'No! I'm okay on my own. I'd quite like to unpack, soak in a hot bubble bath . . . '

Sienna stared back at Honey, eyebrows raised.

'Oh, don't insult me like that, you of all people,' protested Honey. 'What do you think I'm gonna do, drown myself in your house?'

'I didn't think . . . no, not exactly. I just don't want you to think I'm leaving you, that's all.'

'I'm twenty-five. I think I can cope for a few hours on my own. Go on, go see Blue. We have plenty of time for catching up. I'm not about to do anything silly. Not when I know I've got you on my side.'

'Always. Well, if you're sure?'

'Go. You could be there in half an hour. You need to get out of the house at least for an hour or two. Now you're free of that ass Max, you have a new life ahead of you.' Sienna nodded uncomfortably. 'Go!' urged Honey, pointing at the car keys on the kitchen table.

*   *   *

Paige sighed as Max flicked through the cable channels. He was really getting under her feet. Why was he hanging around during the day anyway? And why wasn't he taking his calls any more? There were hundreds of messages from his father on the answerphone. He obviously needed Max urgently for something.

'Why don't you meet up with your dad?' ventured Paige. 'Sounds like he wants to see you.'

'What would you know about that?' snapped Max.

'I just thought . . . well, maybe I could meet him. We are married now, after all.'

'Yeah, maybe I could meet *your* dad too in that case?' asked Max pointedly.

'Why?'

'We work in the same business.'

'Huh? How do you figure that out?'

'Oil, Paige. Aeroplanes? Fuel? Oil?'

'Oh, that.'

'Look, I wouldn't mind seeing if we have a few contacts in common. Come on, you said you'd set up a lunch ages ago, before we got married, for chrissake. Stop pissing around.' Paige drew back, affronted. How dare he speak to her in that tone! If provocation was what he was after she'd see what she could rustle up. Starting with a dollop of truth.

'Right,' she said slowly, 'when I said he was in oil, what I meant was . . . he's a garage pump attendant.'

'Yeah ha-ha.'

'No, really. It was just a joke. Didn't think you'd take it so seriously.' She shrugged, a touch of a smirk at the corners of her mouth. Max fixed a gaze on Paige of pure steaming hatred.

Paolo had been staring at the wall clock for thirty-three minutes. Sienna wasn't coming, he had a gut feeling. She wasn't the type to be over half an hour late for anyone. Blue was camped out at the Cheesecake Factory on the next block in case something like this happened. Paolo had one swig of whisky left; now he had a choice to make. Hang in there and have one last drink or cut his losses and get back to Blue.

'Another Macallan, sir?' asked the waiter. Two girls at the other side of the bar were nudging each other and smiling flirtatiously over at Paolo. 'I'm all set, thanks,' he replied to the waiter with a sigh. If Sienna wasn't here by now, she wasn't coming, he reasoned. He tossed twenty bucks down and made for the lobby. He could grab a quick bite with Blue and be back at home ready for his daily buffing and waxing session within the hour. Thank God the rigorous beauty regime would be history once he left Vegas. As he approached the door it swung open violently, knocking him in the shoulder.

'Excuse me, sir!' panted Sienna, glancing at Paolo as she scampered by in a cloud of hair and perfume. Paolo watched as she came to a standstill and span round to look at him. He tried to smile but his nerves wouldn't let him. Sienna squinted her eyes quizzically before turning back slowly and walking on towards the bar. After a few paces she paused again and turned to Paolo once more. He ran his hand anxiously through his short blond hair and swallowed hard. The pair stared at each other.

Chapter 24

Brandy checked herself in the rear-view mirror of her Porsche 911, which was now parked up at the Follies Casino stage door. The reflection staring back was the result of a few hours' careful dressing and strategic grooming that afternoon before she'd disembarked her private jet. A Pucci headscarf to hide the tiny scars at her hairline and over her ears, huge Prada shades to hide the last of the discolouration around her eyes, and a thick, even covering of foundation over her angular cheekbones to even out her skin tone and any last smudges of bruising. Thankfully her lips were still nice and plumped up from the fillers; at least they were looking fantastic. Certainly the whole look was one of her more dramatic and mysterious, but it was the only choice given that she wasn't quite camera ready yet after the surgery, and wasn't about to scare people by looking like the bride of Wildenstein on her first public outing.

Brandy looked across at the passenger seat and sneered at Paolo's holdalls sitting there on the leather upholstery, ready to be dumped in the nearest trash skip. The very thought of his stuff tainting her beautiful home made her retch. When she'd arrived back at the mansion an hour ago she hadn't been overly surprised to see that her free-loading sibling had evidently been enjoying the comfort of her couch. At least he hadn't been sleeping in her bed and there was no initial evidence of any major theft. Also Paolo seemed at first glance to have kept the place clean. Nonetheless Brandy intended to have her staff disinfect and de-louse the whole place first thing tomorrow, just as soon as she got this little errand done and dusted and she could get her full attention back to her fabulous life. She'd never make the mistake of leaving a job unfinished again, she thought grimly, putting her mobile to her ear.

'Voislav? Brandy Alexander . . . yes, I'm at the Follies as discussed. I expect your guys here in thirty minutes on the dot . . . Yes, tell them to come straight to my dressing room. All the bitches will have their bony asses out getting ready for the show so make sure the boys are focused solely on finding me and my cocksucking little brother. You got the brief earlier? Good . . . two main things for them to remember: break his legs, he must never dance again. And get his face good – acid, carving knife, whatever, I don't care, those pretty-boy looks have to go. Oh and one more thing. I'd like to think they'll take their time over it and leave him nicely at that tipping point between agony and unconsciousness. Can't have him unable to taste every second of his just desert. Oh and Voislav? Leave him alive. I don't want any of that mess out in the desert. It'll find its way back to me somehow, and besides I don't want him getting off lightly like that anyway . . . No, he's going to endure the consequences of his actions and he'll just have to finish himself off with a rusty flick-knife in a gutter somewhere once he can't bear looking in the mirror every day and seeing the Elephant Man staring back any longer. All set your end? Great. Call me when you have good news for me. I'll tip you very . . . *very* handsomely on top of our agreement. You know I always take care of my crew . . . *Ciao*.' Brandy tossed her phone back in her Chanel tote and took a deep breath. Now all she had to do was wait to savour every moment of Paolo's downfall.

Paige peeled her face off the pillow and sat up in the bed. She was sure she'd heard banging at the door. What had happened to all Max's staff anyway? She knew he used to have people waiting on him hand and foot to do boring things like opening doors to visitors. She sincerely hoped he wasn't expecting Mrs Paige Power to start doing things like that in their place. She looked over at the bristly, snoring lump next to her and wrinkled her nose up at the smell of stale alcohol and sweat. Was this really the prize she'd snagged? And why was he sleeping in bed all day like a slob after he'd been out all night? He'd not said a word to her since yesterday when she'd told him she had been joking about her dad. Jeez, surely he hadn't taken her seriously about having a rich daddy. Why would she be shacking up with a spoilt bitch like Sienna if she had access to a rich family? She'd only said it so Max wouldn't suspect she was gold-digging. Speaking of which, didn't Max have important work to be getting on with in the meantime? Surely all these millions didn't just make themselves – since when did he swap flying around between high-powered meetings and barking down the phone all day for lounging around and knocking back whisky?

Paige guessed the honeymoon was over a lot more quickly than she'd thought: there was no question she'd have to get to work quicker than she'd anticipated and figure out how to start siphoning Max's money off. Married to a multi-millionaire and she hadn't even had so much as a pair of Louboutins out of him yet, for chrissake! She'd got more out of Sienna and her mommy. Paige knew the first stage would be setting herself up in her own plush pad that Max could buy for her. She'd start house-hunting this week and get that underway before negotiating a good meaty housekeeping allowance and some store cards. Furnishing the new apartment would be a fun project to do to fill her time. More banging downstairs. Paige groaned, realising her head was still tender from the bottle of Jack she'd knocked back out of boredom in Max's absence last night. Max rolled over in the bed and farted loudly. Paige slumped back into the pillow and ground her teeth together as the incessant banging downstairs mingled with the throbbing in her head.

Paolo ignored the banging at the dressing-room door as he gave his magnificent head of hair a last spritz of Elnett.

It was probably only a chorus-line girl wanting a bob pin. He needed to concentrate on channelling the butterflies that were forming in his stomach. This was it, the performance of his life in Vegas, sharing the stage with Lady Gaga. He hoped to God Sienna had forgiven him after yesterday. It hadn't exactly been welcome news that he wasn't who she thought he was. Blue had to abandon his cheesecake feast from across the block and come to the rescue to mediate and talk everything through, especially after Sienna had held her head in her hands wailing, *No, not again, not again*. Everyone in the bar had been shooting daggers at Paolo as Sienna howled – it looked for all the world like he was a two-timing boyfriend. Over and above the embarrassment it had suddenly hit Paolo that maybe Sienna saw his honesty as purely selfish rather than selfless: offloading his own guilt and upsetting her rather than leaving her in peace. Paolo persevered with Blue's help and Sienna stayed patiently at the table as he told her everything. He never did disclose exactly what he did to Ed, despite her asking several times. Suffice to say she just seemed progressively more shell-shocked with Paolo's story, and finally excused herself after three hours of huddling in the corner booth of the bar, saying she needed to go home and get her head around things. Paolo hoped to God he had done the right thing. He'd rushed out after her to the parking lot in a last moment of panic.

'I'm sorry, Sienna, I'm so sorry for the deception.'

'So you said.'

'All this drama . . . caused by a nobody. I'm so sorry. I hope you can forgive me.'

Sienna had stood there a while in silence. Eventually she smiled a little sadly and said, 'Remember what you said to me in the dressing room last week? Nobody is a nobody.'

'Wish I could take my own advice,' Paolo had mumbled.

'I thought a lot about what you said, you know. I realised things were more simple than I thought.'

'Oh?'

'Yeah. All this scratching and clawing to get places and you have no idea why you want it or where it all ends. It's like that pot of gold at the end of the rainbow – it keeps moving when you think you're close.'

'I wouldn't know. I never had the balls to have much ambition.'

'Ha! Ambitions! I had all these big plans. But this week I realised all these goals I'd set, all these targets I had to reach, it was all about one thing.'

'Which is . . . ?'

'All my life I've been superstar Tiger Starr's little sister, and then superstar Tiger Starr's daughter. I just wanted to have a name. I want to be known as Sienna, not an appendage to someone else. I want recognition as me, Sienna Starr. And then I got to thinking after our chat – that's all about what other people think of me. What other people call me, right? So my worth is all wrapped up in other people's opinions? Something so intangible and irrelevant can drive the direction of my entire life? How about I do something because I enjoy it or value it myself? Because I want to better *myself*? Isn't that more honest?'

Paolo had stood awkwardly scuffing the floor with his shoe. There wasn't much he could contribute to the topic of honesty. 'Just be yourself, Sienna. You're too smart to get bothered by labels. That's all I would ever ask of someone,' Paolo had continued quietly. 'And after tomorrow I'll have a lifetime of being myself again. I'm kinda looking forward to it after these last three months.'

Sienna had sighed and wordlessly headed back to her car. Perhaps Paolo would never see her again. There could be no recalls for Brandy this time.

Paolo now ignored the incessant rapping at the door as he pulled back and checked himself in the mirror. Flawless. By the wall clock he was early – he'd evidently become lightning quick at his make-up now. He took a perch on Brandy's throne and tried to savour every second of being at the Follies, knowing this was truly his last night. He wondered if perhaps he would employ the 'Press for Champagne' button, after all; at least once before he left for good.

'Hello, darling,' came a familiar voice at the door. Paolo span round. Who the hell was this all bundled up with scarves and shades at night?

'Didn't want to open the door to your sister?'

Paolo stared at the bizarre-looking creature in front of him. Wait – Brandy? 'How did you get—'

'Never mind how, darling, all that matters is that

Cinderella has come to get rid of the ugly sister from her throne,' said Brandy through clenched teeth. 'Or should that be ugly brother . . . '

Sienna held on to Tiger's hand as they made their way to their VIP box escorted by a hostess.

'This feels so weird,' whispered Sienna tearfully as she settled into a velvet seat. 'I should be on that stage, not here in the audience. I've thrown everything away, haven't I?'

'Go easy on yourself, darling,' said Tiger, jangling her gold as she put a comforting arm about Sienna's shoulder. 'After everything that's happened, give yourself a break. You're doing the right thing just coming, okay? It's the right thing to support Paolo.'

'You think so?'

'I know so. He deserves a medal for what he's had to put up with from that bitch of a sister. But most of all I thank God you told me everything. Don't ever suffer on your own again. That's what mothers are for, to be here when you need us.'

'I thought you'd be so angry. I thought you'd never speak to me.'

'How could you think that! I'm just furious you didn't tell me earlier. You miscarried in a miserable hospital cubicle on your own? You should have called me, I should have been there for you! And Max? Ed? Why, I'd have come over and taken care of them with my own bare hands—'

'That's what I was afraid of. I didn't want to involve you. And I was so scared about what Ed might do ... The lies he might tell.'

'Sienna, wash your mouth out. He can't touch us, you hear? Nothing comes between us ever again. Anyway, I'd have been the least of your worries. If Ma had still been alive to know about it, Max and Ed would be full of bullets and pushing up cacti in the Nevada desert by now.'

'Huh?'

'Oh, come on, darling. You knew the real story, didn't you?'

'I don't understand.'

'Didn't Pepper tell you? About Pinkie?' Sienna looked blank. Tiger sighed and leaned in. 'He was running a numbers racket,' she murmured, 'but the police were taking backhanders from him. One corrupt little weasel, Detective Schwebel, decided Pinkie was doing too well. He wanted to increase the payments. It was a harmless racket, just a few numbers getting swapped round. No-one got hurt, no drugs involved, nothing nasty went down ... just money. But the police had to get greedy. Things got nasty in the backroom one day and Schwebel drew a gun on Pinkie. Ma walked into the room, right in the middle of it all. She hid behind Pinkie like a frightened rabbit. Only she was no rabbit, she was just taking his gun from his belt ... she got Schwebel before he could pull his own trigger.'

'Ma? She killed—'

'Pinkie took the gun from her and left immediately. Left his life – he could never come back. All to protect Ma. But, you see, she'd saved him in the first place. That's why the funeral was crawling with Feds, nothing to do with money laundering like the rumours that were flying while Ma was ill. No, they thought Pinkie would come back to pay his respects and they could pin the murder of a cop in cold blood on him finally.'

'So Pinkie had already passed away then?'

'I didn't say that.'

'So Ma *did* know where he was?'

Tiger turned to Sienna and winked. 'All I'm saying is, it's not always the nice guy who's the good guy. And sometimes, impossible situations present themselves, where there is no choice. Come on, darling. You think I wanted to grow up as your sister? I did what I had to. And I got my reward after all that time. I got my daughter back. You're doing the right thing to support Paolo now. He's had your back, like your real friends have. He protected you from that thing that calls himself your father and got rid of him. He isn't a poisonous snake like his sister, and let's face it, you can't punish him for his family; you know that more than anyone. Now it's your turn to be a friend. Let him leave in peace tomorrow, and you keep his secret.'

'I hear you,' said Sienna quietly.

'Hey. I'll get Max for you, don't worry.'

'*Mum*,' Sienna scolded.

'I will. When he least expects it.'

'You'd have to hold me back from getting there first,' smirked Sienna. Tiger laughed loudly. 'Darling, something tells me he'll dig his own grave, mark my words. Now let's enjoy the show, okay?'

'Yeah,' sighed Sienna. 'Now that Marty's chucked me off the show after I disappeared for a week, I don't suppose Pepper will take me back at the Monte for a bit, would she?'

'I'm sure she'd love to have the princess bestow her royalty upon the Monte any time. Although something tells me you'll find another show soon enough, sweetheart. You can do anything you put your mind to, but you've just got to do it for *you*,' grinned Tiger, squeezing Sienna's hand and settling back into her velvet seat ready for the performance.

'If you want to get out of this alive, this is what you're going to do: I'm going to watch with pleasure as you walk on stage in front of all those people,' purred Brandy, 'all those celebrities and all the press who've come to see the big gala performance, and I'll be watching you "out" yourself in front of them, dear brother. I'll watch as you pull off the wig and explain who you really are. I'll be waiting in the wings with my guys, watching every humiliating second. You've got a few minutes to go before your big reveal. Wanna touch up your lipstick, darling? An extra slick of gloss over that lovely red? My boys will be here any second. I'm sure they'd love it if you look nice for them.'

'Yeah? Bring 'em on,' sneered Paolo. 'Same goons as last time?'

'Yep. Although they'll be doing a better job of it tonight, but that's the dessert after your little performance,' promised Brandy. Paolo kept a poker face as he felt the weight of dread in the pit of his stomach. The champagne button. Could he use it to summon someone who knew his secret? Blue? No, he was merrily out there chatting up the press. Besides Blue shouldn't be involved in this mess any more than he was already. Perhaps Paolo could climb out of the window in the restroom? They'd probably catch him in the parking lot. He faced the reality that the time had come. He had to take it like a man. If he was humiliated on stage, who cared? The people who mattered knew the truth. After being humiliated all his life, this would be a walk in the park. In any case, this was unfinished business between him and Brandy. What was bothering him more was what she had planned for after his stage appearance.

'Ladies of the chorus and Brandy Alexander, this is your ten-minute call,' crackled the intercom.

'T minus ten,' cackled Brandy. Paolo braced himself for his showbiz execution.

'Nooo!' screamed Paige as masked men barged past into the lounge and set upon the furniture with baseball bats, sending shards of mirror, glass and ceramic flying through the air all around her. Paige cowered as she yelled for Max. Within seconds he was staggering down the stairs in his boxer shorts. Seeing the men, he turned on his heel and ran back up the stairs.

'Wait – Max! What are you – where are you going!' screamed Paige, horrified that he was leaving her with these Neanderthals. More men piled into the house and began dousing the furniture with petrol.

'You can't do this!' squealed Paige as one of the men grabbed her hands and held them behind her back.

'We're taking back what he owes us,' growled the man in her ear. 'One way or another. We've had the business, the cars, now it's house time.'

'What?' trembled Paige. 'What are you talking about, you asshole! He has money!'

'That's what he told you?'

'He's a millionaire!'

'He lost all that a long time ago.'

'But we're – married!' wailed Paige.

'Oh boys, looks like the little lady's been in the dark about Max's games!' sneered the man. 'Careful, or we'll take you as part payment too,' he snarled.

'Max!' screeched Paige. 'Maaaax!'

'Whassamatter? Casanova not coming back for you? Don't worry, he won't get very far, we'll find him,' laughed the man. A deafening explosion outside rocked the house.

'Nice. That'll be the last of the cars,' said the man. 'The ones that aren't worth selling.' Paige screamed.

Paolo and Brandy jumped as the dressing-room door crashed open. Paolo immediately recognised the two men at the front from his last assault. The first standing six feet tall, broad shouldered and with a buffed, smooth shaven head, the second with the distinctive square jaw line and impassive stare of Russian descent. They stepped inside the door followed by two others, and closed it with a little more elegance than the way they'd opened it.

'This could get interesting,' said Paolo in his most syrupy voice, holding out a perfectly manicured hand. 'Four men at once, must be my lucky day,' he simpered. If the bitch Brandy wanted a show, that's what he'd give, thought Paolo defiantly. Without a word, the men stepped forward and grabbed his sister's wrists.

'What are you doing?' she laughed. 'Very funny, guys, but I'm not in the mood for joking around. *I'm* Brandy, dickwad.' Paolo saw a sliver of opportunity opening up right before his eyes and took the gamble unquestioningly.

'Really,' he gushed. 'He doesn't even look like me. Look at his face, for chrissake, boys! Look at all that make-up! He's caked in the stuff!'

'What are you doing? Stop that stupid voice, Paolo, I don't sound like that!' screeched out Brandy.

'He doesn't even have my nose,' persevered Paolo, flouncing his hips and flicking his mane emphatically. 'Just look at it! And that terrible attempt at collagen. You'll never be a woman no matter how hard you try, Paolo.'

'Are you off your head?' spluttered Brandy, struggling against the men's iron grip on her hands. 'Ow, you're hurting me!'

'I say get rid of him now, boys,' said Paolo dismissively, with a flick of red talons.

'Bastard!' hissed Brandy. 'Stop this charade! *I'm* Brandy! And that's *my* car outside! Everyone knows I'm Brandy!'

'Nice try, lady-boy, but you don't even look like her – your face is totally different,' sniggered the Russian, before clamping his big hairy paw over her mouth to muffle her protestations. 'And I remember that poncey necklace you were wearing from last time, anyway – got an eye for detail,' he added gruffly into Brandy's ear. Paolo did a double take and realised Brandy was wearing Mami's crucifix she had ripped from his throat the night she had him set upon. So she *had* kept it after all. He was sure it was for twisted reasons – presumably Brandy had guessed how much the necklace meant to him. But her attempt to rub salt in the wound had backfired. She had been well and truly hoist by her own petard.

Sienna watched as the red curtains parted to a rousing fanfare and legions of showgirls paraded onto the stage. A series of pyros exploded in quick succession sending sparkling stars into the air. Paolo emerged through the billowing puff of smoke as all four spotlights trained on him to rapturous applause. Sienna gasped at the beauty of the apparition; he looked like the most stunning Boticelli painting, statuesque, slim and exquisitely sculpted into sleek curves, tightly encased in floor-sweeping filigree shimmering ivory lace, a vast coat of swan down billowing out into a twenty-foot train behind him. Sienna squinted her eyes, scrutinising the vision for seams and padding, but could barely fault the artwork before her. Paolo swept straight into an exquisite presentation flanked by all sixty of the glorious showgirls in full feathered regalia. Sienna gulped at the splendour of it all, wishing she could be up there with him.

'Is that what I look like when I'm up there?' she whispered to her mum. Tiger gave her a quizzical look and tutted. 'You really have no idea, do you, Sienna Starr?'

'See, this is my car!' shrieked Brandy as she struggled against the Russian's iron grip out in the parking lot.

'Sure you're gonna say that,' he grunted back.

'I have the keys – wait! Oh damn, my purse, it's still in the dressing room, you fools!'

'No problem, I'll open it for you,' replied the Russian, punching his fist straight through the window and setting off the ear-splitting alarm. 'Oh look, some of your things. Let's take a look, boys.'

'No! Not that stuff, that's not mine!' Brandy shrilled, struggling to free her hands. 'Let go!' Her words fell on deaf ears as the men unzipped Paolo's holdall on the front seat.

'Speedstick, boxer shorts, socks, men's trainers. Way to go, Paolo, you're really convincing us here,' snarled the Russian. 'Chuck him in the truck, boys. Let's get out of here.'

'You're making a big mistake! Put me on to Voislav! I'll have you sacked in a New York minute!' shrieked Brandy.

'Wait! I can prove to you that I'm a woman – let me show you.'

'Cut it out, you freak! Nobody wants to see what you keep down there!' The Russian held her whilst his buffed-headed accomplice landed a punch squarely in the middle of her face. Blood appeared at her nose immediately.

'My new nose!' Brandy wailed.

'That's just an amuse-bouche,' snarled the Russian. 'We haven't even started yet.'

Paolo was overcome as he saw the audience begin to stand, one at a time at first, and before long whole rows standing to applaud until the whole theatre was on their feet and cheering. He knew the time had come to put an end to Brandy Alexander. He had redeemed her in the eyes of the public, and he'd fulfilled his dream on stage, but now he had to stop the roller coaster and get off. He reached for his wig and discreetly began to pull the bobby pins from the back, ready to reveal that Brandy had been a man all along. His hands shook as he fiddled. Faces in the audience swam before his eyes. Something felt wrong. Sure it would be fun to kill off the character of Brandy by saying she had been a man all along . . . but didn't that mean she just lived on as Paolo? And that all those years of her vile behaviour would always be attributed to Paolo? Did he really want to step in and take over the reins of her vacuous life, albeit as a man? The red curtains swung in and the chorus line rearranged themselves for the encore.

There was no time left, there had to be a better solution. The crowd screamed as the curtains parted once more. The first beaming face Paolo saw as they swung open was Sienna's, up ahead in the VIP box, the distinctive face of Tiger beside her. His heart leapt. He stepped forward and held his hand up to silence the audience.

'Ladies and gentlemen. I love you all, and thank you for your undying support. But Brandy will not be returning to the stage after tonight.' The audience gasped. 'After much thought I have realised I want to leave on a high. I am retiring from the business. Please make way for the new queen of "Venus in Furs" who will now take my crown. She's here tonight in the audience – Sienna Starr!' The audience erupted into cheers as the spotlights found their way onto Sienna up in the box, looking shocked and with tears at her eyes. As the crowd applauded and turned to celebrate her, no-one noticed that Paolo had already slipped away from the stage, his wig already ripped from his head. Brandy Alexander had left the building.

'Where are you taking me?' asked Brandy with a trembling voice from the back of the van. Her wrists were raw from struggling against the rope that tied her. Two of the men sat sentry in the back with her. The Russian turned from his position in the front seat and looked through the wire partition into the back.

'We're going for a trip to the desert, mister. We have

some lovely things lined up for you. Brandy gave us a detailed menu.'

'You've got the wrong person, I swear,' gulped Brandy, remembering in terrible detail the orders she had given to Voislav. The Russian pointed a gun straight between Brandy's eyes. 'I've kinda had enough of your whining. You certainly *sound* like that bitch-ass sister of yours, that's for sure. So – you wanna shut up or shall I shut you up? She told me not to kill you but I have a short fuse so . . . who knows. The desert's a big, lonely place. Plenty of room for one more body . . . '

Twelve months later

It was the wedding of the year. The whole of Vegas turned out to see Blue get hitched to his handsome centurion, Joey. Showgirls hung from the rafters of the wedding chapel, and of course there at the front with them as bridesmaid of honour was Sienna Starr, complete with the ultimate showbiz diva accessory, a miniature Yorkshire Terrier, borrowed for the day from her mother – well, she had to look the part for the wedding of Vegas royalty, Tiger had insisted. Sienna snatched a glance behind her at the sea of incredible-looking guests, but it wasn't the feathers and rhinestones that had caught her eye: Jack Weldon's rugged face looked straight back at her from the fourth row. He winked, before blowing a discreet kiss, a delicious smile on his face that reached his velvety black eyes. Sienna couldn't keep the grin from her face as she turned back to hear the vows unfolding before her.

It was early days in the relationship, but Jack had managed to completely sweep Sienna off her feet, even though she'd been so busy turning the Monte Cristo into Vegas's hottest property since Liberace. After a fantastically received three-month run as the star of 'Venus in Furs', Sienna had made the tough decision to leave, feeling that it held too many bad memories. Since then she had taken over the Monte's artistic reins from Pepper, revamping it, devising amazing new shows, and, with Paolo by her side as her chief choreographer, turning it into the hottest ticket in town. It was a veritable goldmine. Sienna was thoroughly enjoying working hard behind the scenes, but now and again gave herself a solo spot, just to feel that fabulous warmth from bathing naked in a spotlight. But the real moment in the sun was heading her way in the form of a *Vanity Fair* cover, as the bright new showbiz impresario to be reckoned with. Jack Weldon was so proud of his new girlfriend. And even though they both worked so hard, especially now he had been promoted to running the FBI's Vegas office, at least the hours they kept suited each other perfectly.

Paolo had, of course, taken a little time to recover from his unrequited love for Sienna, but was faring well under the expert care of Kittie de Winter, a rather hot young actress from LA who had been introduced to him by Tiger. They made quite the handsome couple and were certainly causing a stir on the showbiz scene. Paolo was hoping to spend even more time with her now that he was negotiating a juicy contract to choreograph a Hollywood blockbuster, having been touted as the new Fosse after his work at the Monte. As he now stood proudly at Blue's right as his best man, he couldn't help but stifle a giggle as he watched Tiger's dog, Gravy, casually try to cock his leg on Joey's Italian brogues.

Sitting in the pews next to Jack Weldon, enjoying the circus of the wedding ceremony, was Honey, looking resplendent in top-to-toe Dior. She was on top of the world since her memoir, *Diary of a Vegas Call-Girl*, had stormed straight into number one in the book charts, but an even bigger pay cheque was right around the corner as a huge TV network had just snapped up the rights to turn it into a series.

Paige probably wouldn't be reading Honey's book any time soon – it was unlikely she'd be able to find a copy in jail. Max had successfully – with a lot of help from his father, given Max's descent into an alcoholic, drug-hazed stupor these days – managed to pin much of his fraudulent activity on a naïve Paige and extricate himself from some very shady dealings he'd had to do to get out of his financial mess. Although it looked as though with a little luck and a fair wind, Paige might get her sentence reduced from twelve to ten years. Meanwhile, Max continued to look over his shoulder, knowing his father always sought retribution with weak links that caused him trouble. He'd certainly caused Kerry a fair amount of expense and embarrassment over the last twelve months, to say the least. Tonight, however, Max had no idea that the escort he had ordered was arriving with a little present from his father in the shape of a lethal cocktail of drugs to be slipped into his champagne. Overdoses happened all the time in Vegas and it looked as though Max was next on the list.

No-one saw or heard of Brandy Alexander ever again. Who knows if a lone figure had ever emerged staggering from the Nevada desert. But the next time you're at a Coney Island freak show, and you see The World's Ugliest Woman, take a good look at her grotesquely disfigured face and wonder maybe, just maybe . . .

TEASE
Immodesty Blaize

The bigger the star, the further they have to fall...

On the surface, Tiger Starr has it all. As Britain's number one showgirl, her life is a whirlwind of glamour, celebrity parties and more than her fair share of suitors.

But as she prepares for the most important show of her life, it seems somebody is intent on exposing the dark secrets of her carefully guarded past.

Unfortunately, there's more than one likely suspect. Is it one of Tiger's discarded lovers? A jealous rival? Or obsessive fan? As her world starts to unravel, Tiger will have to fight for survival, by delivering the performance of her life...

'Packed full of glamour, revenge and oodles of sex...' *Heat*
'Roll over Jackie Collins!' *Evening Standard*
'Irresistible' *The Times*
'Sensational!' *Time Out*

STEP SISTERS
Rupert James

First they were strangers...

Elizabeth Miller is a recent graduate, planning the perfect wedding to her charming fiancé. As far as she's concerned Rachel Barnes is a complete stranger. Only the fact that Elizabeth's father has just married Rachel's flighty mother, Anna, makes them related.

Then they were family...

Elizabeth doesn't want to like her new stepsister but, annoyingly both she and her brother, Chris, find the pretty teenager charming. If she has to have a baby sister then at least Rachel is sweet, bright and talented.

Now they're enemies...

Years later and the two women are no longer sisters, no longer speaking after a devastating betrayal ripped their new family apart.

Now an actress, Rachel is dating a rock star and one role away from making it big in Hollywood. Elizabeth is a tabloid journalist, one who knows one too many secrets about Rachel's past. And both women are about to discover that hell hath no fury like a stepsister scorned...

'Sexy, funny, compelling' Tilly Bagshawe

'Taking on the gossipy tone of the very best Jilly Cooper novels and giving it a modern twist, this is a 21st century bonkbuster with attitude' *Elle Magazine*